THE DEVENSHIRE CHRONICLES

BOOK TWO

PREDATOR AND PREY

TOM SECHRIST

COPYRIGHT © 2012 Tom E. Sechrist, Jr.
The Devenshire Chronicles, Predator and Prey
By Tom Sechrist
ISBN-13: 978-0615985299 (Tom\Sechrist)
ISBN-10: 0615985297
All rights reserved.

www.tomsechrist.com

Editing and Formatting Services provided by
Literary Editor Rogena Mitchell-Jones
Rogena Mitchell-Jones Manuscript Service
www.rogenamitchell.com

For Renee...
My fantasy that became my reality!

CONTENTS

PROLOGUE

Caleb inched along the narrow ledge, feeling his breath shallow up in his throat. He felt sure that his heart would beat itself out of his chest as well. Each sliding step dislodged more pebbles and dirt from the ledge that was barely wide enough to accommodate one of his feet. The debris plummeted down the sheer jagged rock face to disappear into the woods far below.

"Perhaps now would be a good time to re-think this plan," Josiah whispered from his place next to Caleb. They both watched the last of the dislodged debris vanish from sight. Caleb swallowed hard and squeezed his eyes shut against the sudden bout of vertigo. He could not argue Josiah's point at this juncture. Swallowing again against the hard dry lump in his throat, he forced his eyes open and quickly shook his head. "Nonsense. We have come this far. We might as well finish the trek. Besides," he paused to try to settle the sudden wave of nausea that swept through his stomach, "we are almost there."

Josiah looked up into the brilliantly blue sky. It was a maneuver to try to calm his terrified nerves, and to some small degree, it worked. A sparrow fluttered past mere feet above him, and a cool breeze tossed his sandy brown hair about. It appeared as though the sparrow was pausing to study the humans who were foolish enough to be this high up the face of Mt. Kil'tafore. "This is suicide!" Josiah muttered hoarsely, his breath hanging heavily in his throat.

Caleb tightened his fingertip grip on the jagged face of the mountain and forced his breath out slowly, fighting against his panic. He tilted his head back to force himself not to look at the dizzying drop off, roughly four hundred feet to the forest below. "The scrolls say that Devenshire once came through here. The cave he occupied is just ahead," Caleb said, taking a moment to steady his nerves.

"The scrolls!" Talmond scoffed from his position to Josiah's right. "Those cursed scrolls have led us to the brink of our deaths!" His anxious gaze also locked tightly to the sheer drop off below.

"No!" Caleb replied sternly. The echo bounded off the rock face to reverberate across the scenic valley below. After taking a moment to recover from the tremble of terror that had rippled through him, he swallowed hard and continued. "The scrolls have given us much insight into the earlier days of Devenshire's life! They have given us the exceedingly few artifacts of his life that still exist."

"Artifacts?" Talmond asked incredulously. "Those artifacts are pieces of junk that could have belonged to anyone at anytime. Now we follow them to our deaths!"

Caleb snapped his head around to glare at Talmond. "Then be gone! Depart, and allow the rest of us to complete our quest unmolested by your negativity!" Talmond had been increasingly negative about the quest and the possibility of ever finding anything substantial of Devenshire. Between the harrowing journey to this mountain range, and the terrifying climb toward a cave that may or may not exist, he was growing very weary of Talmond's pessimism.

Talmond paused to look down the drop off and then back at the trail they had traversed to this point. For a handful of seconds, he seriously considered abandoning the insane quest. While the 'artifacts' they had uncovered *might* have belonged to Devenshire, there was no solid proof that they had.

"Well?" Caleb demanded hotly.

Talmond exchanged glances with Josiah, and then with each of the other four men strung behind him along the thin ledge. While he saw the gut wrenching fear in each of their eyes, he also saw the hardened determination to see this quest out to its conclusion. A part of his mind acknowledged the insanity of even having this conversation in his position. What would he do — try to maneuver his way down the ledge, around the other men? With a hard, dry swallow, he shook his head. "I will see it through."

Shoring up his determination, Caleb continued his agonizingly slow progress across the ledge. It angled slowly upwards as it wound its way toward the summit. In some places, the ledge was wide enough that they could almost walk normally. In others, it was so narrow that they clung to tiny outcroppings of rock by their fingertips. He could not fault Talmond for his skepticism about the scrolls, which had been acquired under the most dubious of circumstances. He had purchased them off a drunk in a small tavern in a city south of here. The city had been built on the ruins of another city from Devenshire's time. It was a city that was said to have been a din of evil, a lair of the truly wicked. Caleb dredged his mind for the name of the long forgotten city, more as a means to take his mind off his perilous predicament than from any historical fascination for accuracy.

Lurp? Slurp? Lyre? Lira? Caleb paused to catch his breath and to readjust his fingertip grip on the rocks that jutted out for handholds. What was the name of that city?

Lirpa?

Yes! That was it! Lirpa! He smiled to himself with the accuracy of his memory. Legends spoke of Lirpa as a hub of wickedness cast out into the wilderness. It had been a din of evil masked by a thin veneer of civilization. By the reckoning of the scholars, the time of Lirpa's existence was over a century ago. Lirpa had existed in Devenshire's time. Had Devenshire ever visited the city? What a fascinating possibility that he had walked the same ground trod upon by Devenshire.

"Why would Devenshire take such a perilous journey as the one we take now? What would be gained from it?" Josiah asked in a shallow, breathless voice as they slowly inched along the sheer cliff face.

Caleb sorely wished to reach for his water pouch to flood his dry throat with gallons of water. He licked his parched lips before shaking his head to answer. "In Devenshire's time, the Mt. Kil'tafore range was twice the size it is now," he said as he slowly slid his hand along the wall in front of him to find another substantial hold. His hands bore the ravages of the intense climb up the mountain face. His fingers were cut from the jagged rocks and starting to swell. Moving with deliberate slowness, he slid his left foot along the ledge, making sure he had solid footing, and then slid his right foot to meet his left. Each move was slow and deliberate. "All of this would have probably been fairly level ground, or at the very least, more than just a ledge. A hundred years ago, we could have probably been able to traverse this distance as easily as walking across a street."

"What happened?" Josiah asked more to take his mind off their predicament than any historical curiosity.

"Legends speak of a terrible shaking of the ground that destroyed a great deal and altered the landscape as we now know it. It is said that almost half of the Mt. Kil'tafore mountain range heaved, and then fell away," Talmond answered in shallow tones.

"What caused such a thing?" Josiah asked.

Caleb paused again to catch his breath and steady his faltering nerves. He opened his mouth to answer as he lifted his gaze to the trail ahead. What he saw made the words hang in his throat, "Dear Lord..."

"What is it?" Josiah asked.

Caleb blinked rapidly to clear the stinging droplets of sweat and beaming rays of sunshine from his eyes, so that he could be sure that he had seen what he thought he saw. Yes. It was there. Just as the scrolls had said it would be. "The cave. We have found the cave," he whispered.

For several moments, all six of the men simply squinted up through the bright sunshine at the black hole in the side of the rock face. It was definitely a cave, and whether or not it was the cave they sought, it would definitely be a respite from this perilous climb. With renewed vigor, they resumed their climb, now burdened with the need to balance their desire to reach the cave quickly with the need not to make a misstep that would send them plummeting down the mountain.

By the time they had reached the entrance of the cave, they had all but forgotten their terror and fatigue at the treacherous journey. They stood in the opening of a cave that most likely no one had stood in for over a century. Caleb simply stood in the darkened silence and soaked in the possibilities. If Devenshire had ever visited this cave, he could very well have been the last one. Could he have stood in this very spot? It comforted him to think so.

"So what are we supposed to find here?" Talmond asked as he bent over, trying to ease his heavy breathing.

Caleb squinted into the gloom, not knowing what he was searching for, but knowing he would know it when he found it. "I'm not sure. The scrolls simply say he spent some time here. Perhaps we will find another clue as to where the chronicles are."

Josiah sniffed as he was finally able to gain control of his breathing. He retrieved his water pouch and wasted little time in uncorking it. As he raised it to his lips, he looked at Caleb, and asked, "Do you honestly think it'll be that easy?"

Caleb smiled tightly as he shook his head and peered into the gloom further into the cave. "No. But it's nice to consider."

Talmond stood upright and swung his water pouch off his shoulder. "We should rest before exploring… I am in no hurry to begin the trip back down."

There came mumbled agreements from the rest of the group as they, too, began retrieving their water pouches. Caleb slowly took his water pouch and began to drink deeply from it, his eyes continuing to scan the darkened interior of the cave. He knew he should rest, but his soul could not wait to delve into the mysteries before him. He lowered his pack to the stone floor and quickly set about trying to pull out the lantern he'd packed away. The lamp had been wrapped tightly in linen to protect it from the hard climb. He unwrapped it and set it aside, as he reached back into his pack to pull out a leather pouch which contained the lantern oil. After filling the lamp, he retrieved a flint rock from his pack. He mulled about in the gloom, but could find nothing to use to build a fire. He finally settled on a piece of the linen that had been used to wrap the lamp. Soaking it in oil, he laid it on the floor, retrieved a dagger, and began hitting the blade with glancing blows of the flint, creating sparks.

Finally, a spark caught on the rag and it began to smolder. Caleb carefully cupped his hands around the smoldering rag and gently blew on it. After a few gentle breaths on the rag, it ignited. Caleb used the tip of his dagger to pick up the burning cloth and touched it to the spout of the lamp, igniting the oil within. Dropping the cloth to the stone floor, he stood up and held the lamp high, casting a pale yellow light into the darkness. Already his eyes were growing wide in breathless anticipation of what he would find.

He vaguely acknowledged that the others were more content with stretching out on the stone floor, easing their cramped muscles, and recovering from the terrifying trip up the mountain. He moved slowly toward the back of the cave, holding the lamp high to illuminate as much of the interior as possible. There was nothing of consequence that he could see. As he moved further into the darkness, he realized the cave wasn't very large. He could already make out the irregular curve of the back wall. Disappointment tried to intrude upon his thoughts as he saw nothing that presented itself as the evidence he had climbed up here to find.

Calm yourself, he told himself. *It won't be as easy as simply walking in here and tripping over whatever it is you are to find here,* his thoughts whispered through his mind. He paused before the back wall and studied the floor around the back of the cave intently, searching for the slightest thing, the tiniest marginal evidence that Devenshire had been here.

"They begin to lose faith."

Caleb spun quickly in a start, his breath seizing in his throat. The flickering lantern light showed him Josiah's face made eerie by the pale light. "Damn! You startled me!" Caleb snapped in reply.

"My apologies, but I sought a moment alone, out of earshot of the others." He paused to look back over his shoulder at the group still resting at the cave entrance.

Caleb watched them, also. "They are tired. The journey has been hard. They will recover their faith."

Josiah slowly swung his head back around to lock an intense look with Caleb. "This is far more than fatigue or nerves. We have been pursuing Devenshire for a year and a half, and we keep coming up short. We find a promising piece of new evidence and it leads nowhere. They are beginning to believe that Devenshire truly is a man of the myths."

Caleb could see the hard truth in Josiah's eyes. A deeply buried part of him had to admit the harsh truth of his friend's words. The pursuit of the legend of Devenshire had taken them far and wide, and always led them to a dead end. It was as if the spirit of Devenshire were torturing them, taunting them with hinted whispers of his legend, and then laughing in sadistic glee when they rounded the next bend in their trek and found a solid wall, a blocked path, a handful of empty, meaningless promises. Caleb looked down at the cave floor and pondered what was to come. What if there was nothing here? What if this was yet another dead end? Could he rally his friends back to the quest? His brow furrowed as the next thought slipped unbidden into his mind. Could he rally himself back to the quest? He shook his head sharply, dispelling the doubts. He had to continue. He had lost too much to stop now. He had to find Devenshire or, at the very least, his chronicles. No other option was acceptable. He raised his once again defiant gaze to Josiah. "Then let them leave the quest. I cannot make them continue. I must continue."

Josiah's expression shifted into an uncomfortable one. "Caleb. Please know that I have faith in you, and I believe in the legend of Devenshire as you do..."

"But?" Caleb asked, knowing there was more to come and feeling sure that he would not like it.

"But you have to at least acknowledge the possibility that simply too much time has passed and Devenshire's life is lost to us."

"No!" Caleb replied even before Josiah had uttered the last word, "He existed. He lived and I will find him! If it is the last thing I do, I will find him! You claim to believe in one breath and doubt in the next? Perhaps you have lost the most faith of all."

Josiah's expression tightened under the assault and the truth in the accusation. "I simply meant that we should take a break from the quest and re-evaluate our next action."

Caleb's eyes narrowed. "No. You wish to coax me into doubting. You try to make me give up something that is dearer to me than anything else. Do not poison me with your doubts!"

"I have no doubt that the legend of Devenshire is that important to you. Cassandra is proof of that," Josiah snapped in reply.

Caleb's eyes flew wide at the accusation, as though Josiah had just slapped him in the face. Just as quickly as they widened, they narrowed in suddenly released anger. "Mind your tongue, Josiah! You go too far!" The sharp edge of dangerous anger honed the dagger of his words.

"Do I? Perhaps I am the only voice of reason left within your skull. My Lords, man! Look at what this quest has cost you! Your craft, your wife, your life as you knew it? Is any shadowy myth worth what you have cast aside for it?"

Caleb felt his body tremble in the icy grip of an anger that was growing beyond his ability to control. Josiah's words hit their mark with a sharp, ripping truth that rent his heart and pierced his soul. Cassandra's angelic face floated into his mind, and for a moment, the intense sadness of losing her squeezed his chest. He quickly called on the anger to help ward off the sentimental attack. The anger had been his best friend, his staunchest supporter in the days following the loss of his precious Cassandra. He called on their bond again to help him through this muddling sentimental attack. The anger responded, wiping her face from his mind and hacked at the sadness, driving it back into the deeper recesses of his heart. His hard stare locked deep into Josiah's, and when he spoke, his voice was deep, low, and dripped venom. "If you no longer believe, then depart now! Leave my sight and never enter it again! If you believe, then stay and help me, but do one or the other now! I will complete this quest. Period! There is no other option. There is no other discussion to be had on the matter. Do you understand?"

Josiah's face twisted in deep regret as he finally realized that there would be no talking his friend out of this insane quest. The madness of the man of the myths had claimed his mind completely. "Caleb, please listen to reason…"

"Choose! Now! Or so help me, I will throw you out through the cave entrance!"

Josiah looked deep into Caleb's eyes and saw nothing but rage and the hard, if not insane, truth of the situation. He knew that Caleb would pursue this to its conclusion or his death, whichever came first. For a long moment, the two friends stared at each other—one in anger, the other in growing pity. Finally, Josiah nodded. "Very well. I will stay with the quest. I will rest now." Without waiting for a response, he turned and began walking back to the others.

Caleb watched him go, feeling the edge of his anger begin to dull as the intense emotions were subdued. He knew that later, he would regret the harsh way he had spoken to his friend. At this moment, however, there was no regret, no sympathy. Only the drive to find his life's dream. He turned back to face the cave wall to continue his search. He slowly scanned the cave wall, his eyes locked intently to every detail in the rock. It would help, he mused, if he knew what it was he was looking for. All the scrolls had revealed to him was that Devenshire had led what could best be described as an army through this region, and had used this cave as shelter. Glancing around at the small cave, he wondered how an army could have rested here.

A thorough visual search revealed nothing. There were shards of broken glass scattered about the back wall, a small circle of stones with charred ancient ashes in the center, and some small animal bones strewn about, but nothing of any consequence. The air was stale and musty, and it was obvious no one had been there for a very long time. Caleb stood at the back wall, his eyes taking in the debris around him, feeling the old familiar stirrings of disappointment, his constant companion of late, began to settle around him. He had failed again. Devenshire had eluded him again. Maybe Josiah had been right. Maybe too much time had lapsed from Devenshire's time to now, and he was lost to the ages. Perhaps the Devenshire Chronicles were a pile of dust in some long lost or buried chamber somewhere in the world. What if they never existed in the first place? He felt a sharp chill spread through him as another thought surfaced: what if Devenshire had never existed? His mind fought back valiantly, using every weapon at its disposal to drive the chilled thoughts of doubt back, to banish them from his mind, but the doubt had gained a strong foothold in his consciousness. He turned slowly to look at the others lounging in the cave entrance... *what if?* He shuttered to think of the folly of his actions if Devenshire had never existed.

"No..." he whispered softly into the musty air of the cave. It was so soft that no one else heard it, but it really didn't matter if the others had heard him... he had heard himself. He suddenly felt very tired, very defeated. Had it all been for nothing? Had he truly been chasing a ghost? A specter of his own shortcomings that he could never reconcile? He turned back to the jagged wall of the cave and let his eyes sweep across the area, seeing even less now than when he had first come upon it. He had failed again, and this time it was not just that he had failed in his quest to find the man of the myths, but he had failed in his entire life. Everything was gone now. His brows furrowed and his hollow eyes continued to look around the ancient campsite, he had lost it all, and for what? What did he have to show for his staunch beliefs?

Absolutely nothing.

It was time to admit the truth in Josiah's words. He simply could not accept another failure, another piece of evidence that he, in every sense of the word, was a failure. His soul was weary, his heart heavy, and his resolution tattered and worn. Perhaps it was time to admit defeat, to acknowledge that his desire to find something of Devenshire was stronger than the harsh reality of the situation. With a heavy sigh, he was about to turn around, to face his friends as well as the brutal truth of the situation, when something in the back wall caught his attention. It was a flickering glimpse of something that didn't belong. He turned back and raised the lantern high, peering hard into the area, he thought he saw something, but yet saw nothing. His brow furrowed as he willed whatever it had been to appear. For several moments, he continued to search the area, certain he had seen something, but again, finding nothing.

His shoulders slumped, and he sighed in weary frustration. He was sure he had seen something. He started to turn again and, once again, something beckoned for his attention. He spun back around only to find the blank back wall again. He was positive he had seen something that time. The first time he might have considered a trick of the flickering light from the lantern, but the second? No. He had definitely seen something, and yet an in depth study still revealed nothing. What in the seven levels of hell was going on here? Perhaps the lantern light was playing tricks on his vision. Then it hit him: the flickering lantern light. Perhaps what he had seen wasn't a trick of the lantern light, after all. Maybe it was what he *wasn't* seeing.

He lowered the lantern to shoulder level in his left hand and then extended it straight out from his body. As though it were a working of magic, a definite crevice appeared with a flash of white tucked neatly inside of it. The jagged edge of the lip of the crevice was so closely matched to the shape of the back wall that full on lantern light hid the crevice as though it were not there at all.

However, holding the light at an angle from the crevice and it appeared. He smiled in silent celebration as he knelt and peered into the crevice and at the flash of white that had caught his attention. Holding the lantern closer he found what appeared to be a rolled up piece of parchment. His heart began to thump hard in his chest and his hands began to tremble. His imagination ran rampant with the possibilities of what this parchment could be. He gently touched the roll and heard the distinct crack of extremely old and dry parchment. The document or whatever it was, had been exposed to the elements for a long time, and was extraordinarily fragile. It would have to be handled with extreme care.

Gingerly, he took a hold of the parchment and carefully began drawing it out of the crevice. He grimaced at each crack of the ancient paper as he slowly pulled on it. After what seemed like an eternity, the end of the long tube of rolled parchment appeared from the deep crevice.

"What have you found?" Josiah called from the entrance.

"I'm not sure, perhaps a map of some sort," Caleb replied absently as he continued to focus all of his concentration on retrieving the artifact.

"Are you sure?" Talmond asked.

Caleb pursed his lips in annoyance. "Not until I open it."

He heard the group collectively rise to their feet and hurry over. He knew that most of them had not truly expected to find anything. The fact that they had was like a blast of cold wind on their sleepy interest in the quest.

"I need more light!" Caleb called as he gently moved the roll to a more open area and laid it lightly on the floor. Other members of the team hurriedly retrieved lamps from their packs and set about filling and lighting them.

Josiah and Talmond remained with Caleb. "What do you suppose it is?" Josiah asked.

Caleb kept his gaze locked tightly on the rolled up parchment, trying to see through the rolls to what lie within. He shook his head. "I would have to say a map of some sort."

"It is very old," Talmond observed. "I seriously doubt we will be able to unroll it without destroying it."

"I agree. We should return to Tanezia and let the scholars examine it," Josiah added.

Caleb never took his eyes off the roll as he shook his head. "Not in a thousand lifetimes! Those brigands will steal it away and claim whatever lies within as their discovery. If this is a clue to Devenshire or his chronicles, it is the first tangible proof we have found, and I will be damned to the fires of hell before I surrender it to anyone!"

"But what if you destroy it while trying to unroll it?" Talmond asked.

Caleb could not argue with the logic of that argument, but he could not bring himself to surrender his prize to anyone, especially in this warm light of having been proven right in his belief of the quest. He would not give up his prize, least of all to the so-called scholars back in Tanezia. "A chance I am willing to take," he muttered and winched at how hollow his words sounded to his own ears.

Finally, the others arrived with lanterns burning brightly. The added light made it very easy to see. It also threw the incredible age of the rolled up parchment into disturbingly sharp relief. Caleb had to acknowledge that it would be a small miracle if the document survived the attempt to open it. Yet he had no choice. He had to know. Exhaling a deep breath, Caleb set his lamp to one side and wiped his hands on his shirt to dry the sweat from them. As he reached for the roll, his hands trembled.

"Caleb. Please do not make the attempt," one of the others said.

"Yes. Do not destroy this piece of history. Regardless of whether or not it pertains to Devenshire, it is a historical artifact and should be preserved," another chimed in.

"Be silent or be gone!" Caleb snapped in reply. He clenched his fists for a moment and forced himself to calm down, to approach the task calmly. He knew, with a sickening growth of clarity, that he could very well destroy the parchment and any information it contained if he proceeded too hastily. If it proved to be a scroll with information pertaining to Devenshire and he destroyed it, he was relatively sure he would dive out the cave entrance without a moment's hesitation. The group huddled around him, but remained silent as he gently reached forward again. This time his hands were rock steady, his gaze intense as he tried to force his will onto the parchment and command it to hold together, to reveal its secrets to them.

He gently drew down one corner of one edge of the parchment. It cracked in protest of being moved but held together. Once he had the corner on the stone floor, he used a rock to hold it in place.

He moved to the next corner and quickly broke off the corner as he tried to pry it way from the roll. Wincing in imagined pain, Caleb was more careful with his next attempt and was finally able to coax the corner down and under the firm weight of another rock. As added stability, he placed another rock between the first two.

"Well done," Josiah whispered as he, like the others, realized that he had been holding his breath while Caleb anchored the edges of the parchment.

Caleb paused to wipe the sweat from his brow. "Do not congratulate me yet. That was the easy part." He again took a moment to wipe the perspiration from his fingers and then flex them in an attempt to loosen them up. "Here we go," he whispered as he reached for the roll. With all the tenderness he could muster into his hands and fingers, he began to deftly unroll the parchment. It creaked, cracked, and made other horrible destructive sounds that made each man wince. Caleb lovingly coaxed the parchment through another unroll before having to pause to gather himself. It was already clear in the small part that he had opened that this was indeed a map. Of what, and of how it pertained to Devenshire, was still locked tightly in the dry protesting rolls left to be revealed. It took a considerable amount of time, but Caleb was able to completely unroll the map with only minor damage to its overall condition. It was an impressive feat, and the assembled group was impressed to no small degree.

"It is a map, but of what?" Josiah asked as he bent lower to examine it closer.

Caleb gently set more rocks on the edges of the map in order to hold it down and free him to study it more intently. "I am not sure," Caleb replied as he screwed his eyes into the faded drawings on the ancient paper.

"This looks like what used to be known as Prothtow Province," Talmond said as he pointed to a section of the map with a stick he had found. He was careful not to actually touch the map with it.

"Yes. I believe you're right," Josiah commented tilting his head to study that section of the map.

Caleb nodded in agreement. "That's all part of the Nadal region, to the south of here."

"Well, if that's Prothtow, then that must be Kahla," another member pointed out.

"And this," another man said pointing to another section of the map, "must have been where Lirpa had been."

Caleb nodded, vaguely recognizing the ancient landmarks. "Then this," he said pointing to a spot north of where Lirpa had once been, "must be where the Mt. Kil'tafore mountain range used to start. So that would put this cave right about here," he said pointing to a spot on the map that was barely legible.

"Ok. We've found our present location on a very old map. Now what?" Talmond asked with growing sarcasm.

"Wait!" Caleb said as he leaned further over the map. He squinted, trying to force the faded ink to reveal what he thought he saw.

"What?" Josiah asked leaning further forward.

"There's a dotted line… a route," Caleb announced.

"Are you sure?" Talmond asked hoisting a lamp and bringing it over the map, shedding more light on it.

"Be careful!" Caleb scolded. "This map will burn to ash in the span of a single breath!"

Talmond said nothing, but his irritated glance said what his voice refused to proclaim.

"I think you're right," Josiah said studying the faded map. "It looks like someone drew a course on the map."

Caleb used a trembling index finger to trace the very faint dotted line north from where they deducted the cave was. It extended to almost the top edge of the map.

"Where was he going?" another member of the party asked. Caleb suppressed a smile. The man had asked the question as though, in his mind, he knew the map had belonged to Devenshire. The more rational parts of Caleb's mind knew there was no way to know whom this ancient map had belonged to, but it helped to believe it had been Devenshire's.

"I don't know," Caleb replied. "What lies in that direction?"

For several moments, the collective group studied the faded map, each trying to ascertain what the destination had been. Discussions began as each member identified landmarks on the map. Others began drawing out their more current maps and unrolled them, checking them against the old one. For the better part of an hour, debates continued over landmarks and possible destinations of the hand drawn route.

Josiah had lapsed into silence as he studied a map in his hands and compared what he saw with the old map on the floor. A thought had occurred to him, and he had withdrawn from the debates to consider it. Finally, he glanced from one map to the other and back again. "It looks like he was heading for the Wastelands. It's the only thing that far north of here."

Caleb had been arguing the location of a landmark that appeared on the old map, but not on any of the maps that they carried. At Josiah's comment, he stopped. He then began to follow his friend's logic comparing the old map versus the one in his hands. After several back and forth glances, he nodded slowly as he looked up at the man. "Indeed. If we are right about this map and the landmarks it represents, then this could very well be a trail to the Wastelands."

"It could also lead to a thousand other destinations not included on the map," Talmond said with disbelief.

"Where do you think the trail leads?" Josiah asked with a hard edge to his voice. Talmond was the pessimist of the group. Every discovery was met with his customary cynicism.

"I don't know and that's the point. None of us knows. It is pure speculation on our parts," Talmond replied with obvious tones of boredom.

Josiah chuckled tiredly. "Talmond? This entire quest has been one giant speculation. Why should this instance be any different?" Other members of the group mumbled in agreement.

Talmond frowned. "Even if you are all correct, who in their right mind would go there? It's madness!"

"I don't know," Caleb answered as he looked back down at the map, feeling sheer thrilling excitement course through his veins. "But whoever held this map was planning a trip to the Wastelands, and I'm willing to wager it was Devenshire."

"Now just a moment!" Talmond exclaimed. "That's quite a leap of deduction! We don't know who owned this map, or what the purpose of this trail means."

Caleb looked up at him. "Then explain why a scroll we bought led us to this map? Coincidence?"

Talmond shrugged. "Perhaps, but this is just too much of a coincidence to me."

"I have to admit, Caleb. That is quite a leap," Josiah chimed in.

"Then you explain what this could mean," Caleb challenged.

"It could mean anything. This could be a map of a trader plotting out his next route!" Talmond argued.

"To where? What else lies that far north besides the Wastelands? What trader would plot a route there?" Caleb snipped in reply.

"That was one possibility," Talmond argued. "Perhaps it was a trapper seeking to find unique pelts."

Caleb nodded in exaggerated consideration. "Hmmm... perhaps. Since absolutely nothing lives in the Wastelands, I can see the value of any pelts he might find there."

"Stop this! You can no more prove that this map belonged to Devenshire than I can prove it did not!" Talmond retorted.

Caleb shook his head. "I don't have to prove it belonged to him. I *know* it did."

"How can you possibly know that?" Talmond asked.

"You fail to remember that this entire quest has been based on faith, blind faith, in a man that there is virtually no proof that he ever existed. Yet we keep finding whispered hints that he did. We keep losing his trail and yet keep finding it again." Caleb paused to motion toward the old map. "It is pure assumption to say that this map belonged to Devenshire, a true leap of faith that I'm willing to take. Do you know why?"

"Why?" Talmond asked, his expression saying he wasn't ready to risk a trip to the Wastelands based solely on a very old map that could have belonged to anyone, and knowing the faded hand drawn trail could lead anywhere.

Caleb smiled. It was a warm and inviting sight, and one filled with pure emotion. "Because I believe. I have faith. Sometimes that's all you have. Sometimes, it's all you need."

The assembled group glanced at each other and then finally at Caleb. The myriad of thoughts and opinions surrounding the map, its owner, and the possible meaning of the route to the north were lost in the purity of Caleb's belief. It was so strong, so entrenched in his being, that it was nearly tangible in the musty air. It was also quite infectious, and they were all swept up in it as well.

Talmond was the last to falter from his stance of questioning the map. He looked down at it and the washed out dotted line that disappeared off the edge of the old parchment. He glanced up at the others and found, by their expressions, that they had been caught up in Caleb's faith yet again. He sighed in weary exasperation, as he stood upright, his face taking on a deep expression of dread. "We're going to the Wastelands, aren't we?"

His hopelessness was so complete that it was amusing. First Josiah chuckled and then another man. Soon the cave echoed in merry laughter until even Talmond smiled and then broke into laughter.

"Wake up!"

Caleb stopped laughing to look at his comrades to see who had told him to wake up. They all continued to share a hearty laugh.

"Wake up!" the cracking voice echoed off the interior of the cave again.

"Who said that?" he asked, but none of his friends gave any indication that they had heard him.

"Wake up, or I will drag you out into the snow!"

There was something hauntingly familiar about the voice. It was an old man's voice, and for some reason, he recognized it. Yet he couldn't place when or where he had heard it before.

Suddenly something rapped his ribcage. He flinched and reached for the assaulted area. "Who did that?" he demanded, but again his companions gave no indication that they had heard him.

"This is not funny!" he shouted.

"I will show you something even less amusing if you do not wake up this instant!"

"Who said that? Who is here?" Caleb demanded.

You may call me sir.

In a wash of white light and intense cold, his companions winked out of existence. He felt as though he were falling through a blindingly white vortex. His body began to ache. His fingers and toes throbbed with a burning pain he couldn't have imagined existed.

Sir.

The Wastelands.

The blizzard.

The old man in the cave.

It all came slamming into his mind as though a large and very sharp icicle had been driven through the top of his skull and deep into his brain. All of it came back with sickening clarity, the loss of each one of those men in the cave so long ago. The sheer thrill of discovering Devenshire's map had turned to horror as one man after another died on the bitter trail.

Caleb moaned as he opened his eyes to the same muddy pool of incoherence he had first encountered when he awoke in the cave with his cantankerous savior. He blinked several times and was finally able to bring his faltering sight into focus. The first thing he saw was the old man's craggy face looming over him, looking as though he had just bitten into the most sour, most bitter fruit ever produced.

"You may have enough time left in your life to sleep it away, but I do not! It is past time to wake!" the old man snarled, rapping Caleb in the ribs with his cane again.

"I was dreaming," Caleb rasped out. It seemed as though all the recovery he had made the previous day was gone now.

"I know! A waste of perfectly good sleeping time! Now get up! The fire needs tending!" The old man snapped as he turned and walked toward his chair, using the cane to steady himself.

"You have a cane? I don't remember you having a cane yesterday," Caleb observed.

The old man paused and turned back to face him, his eyes snapping in irritation. "Impressive. You deduced with nothing but a single glance that some days I require the use of a cane and other days I do not!" He paused for an exaggerated nod of faux approval. Then his face twisted into irritation. "Now why do you not use some of those impressive mental faculties to get your lazy ass up and stoke the fire?"

Caleb tried to rise and found every inch of his body screamed in painful protest at being moved. He groaned as he rolled to his stomach. "Gods! I feel like I could die!"

"You may very well die if you do not get the fire stoked!" the old man snapped. "Get the fire going, and I will brew more tea. It will help you, but I cannot brew it without fire. You do remember *fire*? The yellow flickering stuff in the fireplace?"

Caleb only groaned as he shored up his determination and tried to rise again. Every muscle ached, every joint burned, and every bone felt as though it would break if he exerted too much force on it. After a long battle with his own body, Caleb was able to rise and limp over to the fireplace. All that remained of the load of wood he had placed on the fire the night before were small, blackened chunks and a rapidly dying bed of coals. He took a handful of kindling from the wood box and laid them on the coals. He bent low to blow across the embers. His lungs stabbed with intense pain each time he took in a deep breath, but he was soon rewarded by faint flickering tongues of flame that tasted the tiny sticks of wood, liked what they tasted, and began consuming them.

As the fire took hold of the kindling, Caleb began adding small sticks of wood, and once those caught, he graduated up to larger logs. In what seemed like the passage of a painful millennium, the fire was once again roaring within the fireplace. With his torturous task completed, Caleb crawled back to his furs and collapsed upon them, ready to die if that were to be his fate for surely death would be far less torturous an existence than this.

He was dimly aware of the old man shuffling around the cave as he set about brewing more tea. The foul stuff was horrible, but Caleb found himself looking forward to it if it provided just a fraction of the relief it had delivered yesterday. After another tortured millennium passed, he felt the end of the cane poke him in the small of the back. "Get up! Your tea is ready!"

Caleb rolled over and battled against his own rebellious body until he was sitting upright, and gratefully accepting the hot tin mug. Without saying anything, the old man ambled back to his chair and set about packing himself a pipe for a morning smoke.

Caleb took a deep gulp of the hot tea and quickly swallowed, wanting to usher in the relief as quickly as possible. He winced against the bitter taste and scalding heat of the brew, but welcomed the warmth that instantly swelled outward from his belly.

"Drink it slowly, you glutton! Gulping it down will do you no good!" the old man snapped. "All you will accomplish is to scald your mouth and stomach."

Caleb only nodded as he closed his eyes, embracing the marginal relief the foul tea provided. He sipped the tea, keeping his eyes closed, and savoring the gradual relief that rippled through his tortured body. Whatever was in the tea, regardless of how foul the brew was, served as his salvation.

"How were you so sure that map belonged to Devenshire?" the old man asked as he puffed the pipe to life.

Caleb's eyes snapped open as he looked up at the old man. "How did you know about that?"

The old man harrumphed and snarled. "You talk in your sleep. Answer the question."

The feeling that the old man had the ability to look into his mind and learn anything he wished returned. He had felt this the day before when he had first awoken in this cave, and the old man spoke of his resolution to die as though Caleb had told him of it. Just like the day before, the sensation caused him trepidation. "I just knew," he whispered.

"That is it? You just knew?" the old man asked incredulously.

"I can't explain it. I looked at the map and something within me just knew that the map had belonged to Devenshire."

The old man studied him intently as he puffed on his pipe. His only response was a slow nod of his head. "I see."

"Why do you ask?" Caleb inquired, unsure of why the old man was so curious about his intuition.

The contemplative stare in the old man's eyes snapped into anger. "Because this is my home, and I can bloody well ask any question I wish to ask!"

Caleb, despite feeling as though he were in the clutches of death, could not help the weary chuckle that rattled from his raw throat. He continued to sip the tea and marveled how each sip eased his suffering. "So what happened to them once they escaped Lirpa?" he asked, surprised at how normal his voice sounded. It only had a hint of the rasp it had held only moments ago. He glanced down into the nearly empty mug and considered asking the old man what was in the tea. His benefactor's grumpy disposition dissuaded him.

"They rode their horses through the night and into the next day and then they stopped. Much as my story will stop if you do not stop asking such stupid questions and start waiting for the story to unfold as it should!" The old man sighed and shook his head. "You young people! I swear by the Fates! You should learn how a well told story could stir the soul and refresh the spirit. You young people want to race ahead to the destination and fail to understand that the journey can be every bit as pleasurable as said destination!"

Caleb smiled faintly and nodded. "Point well made and well taken."

"Are you finished with your breakfast?" the old man asked.

Caleb looked at his benefactor and then down into his tin. "That was breakfast?"

"Indeed," he replied expelling a plume of grey smoke with just the tiniest hint of satisfaction lingering at the edges of his eyes.

"What did you have?" Caleb asked feeling his stomach rumble in protest at the bitter and very unsubstantial meal.

"Oh, my meal was quite tasty. I had eggs and porridge with a nice slice of ham on the side. I also had a nice hot cup of tea, as well." The old man smiled warmly and it looked completely alien to Caleb. He was relatively sure the old man was incapable of such an expression.

"I am to have only tea?"

The warm, pleasant expression melted from the old man's face as he fixed Caleb with a hard look. "You could have had the same breakfast as I, but you decided to sleep through it."

"You could have awoken me," Caleb replied, looking back down into the nearly empty tin, feeling quite disappointed.

"I could have, but I was too busy preparing breakfast," the old man replied as he packed the smoldering tobacco deeper into the bowl of the pipe. He took a moment to examine the contents of the bowl before lifting his grey eyes back to Caleb. "Now, are we to debate the tragic loss of your breakfast or are we to get back to Devenshire's story? You do remember the story that you just had to have?"

"But I'm hungry," Caleb said, feeling his stomach rumble even harder in the grip of what was growing into considerable hunger. A part of him knew his protest was wasted, but he had to try.

"Then perhaps that will be another lesson you can learn while you are here."

"What lesson is that?" Caleb asked, feeling quite despondent at his lost breakfast. "That I should not sleep so late in the day? I was lost in a blizzard and nearly died. I think my sleeping so late is quite understandable."

The old man's look grew even harder as he glared at the younger man. "I am not running an inn here! I am not your personal servant, and I will not jump to and fro on your whining whims! That is the lesson to be learned here!" The old man paused to take a careful wheezing breath before continuing. "So you were in a blizzard and nearly died. So what? That is the problem with this realm. People have become weak and have lost their wills. I can promise you that had our situations been reversed, I would not have missed breakfast! In my time, men understood that their survival was up to them! When I was your age, there is no way in hell that I would have sat on the floor of an old man's cave and whined because I had slept too late and missed breakfast! I would have been up and made sure my host had breakfast waiting for him when he rose as a way to show my gratitude for his hospitality! I can see that such manners are far too trivial to be considered in this day and age!"

Caleb sighed heavily. Not only had he lost the debate and breakfast, he had triggered a sermon from his cantankerous host on the shortcomings of the current age. With a deep sigh, he nodded. "I understand, and I apologize for my apparent lack of gratitude for not only saving me from the storm, but nursing me back to health and for giving me Devenshire's story. I fear I am not myself, and I forget my upbringing." Perhaps he would get a chance at lunch later. For now, he would have to make do with the tea.

A tiny fragment of the hardness left the old man's eyes as he returned the pipe stem to his mouth and puffed. "At least you possess enough humility to recognize your rudeness and apologize for it."

Caleb nodded again, looking up at the old man. "Thank you for forgiving my rudeness."

"Who said I forgave you?" The old man bolted upright in the chair, the harsh edge returning to his eyes and voice. "I did no such thing! All you did was utter words, not much more than noises!" The old man raised his left hand and made a motion mimicking a talking mouth. "Bah! Meaningless! Actions speak to me much louder and with more sincerity than empty, meaningless words! Time will show me your regret for your rudeness, and then, perhaps, I will forgive you!" The man took a breath to continue his tongue-lashing, and this spawned a coughing fit. The harsh coughs racked the frail body with white-hot lances of pain, and the old man doubled over under the onslaught. The fluids deep inside the old man's lungs swished and gurgled with each horrendous contraction of his ribs and stomach. When one spell of coughs would subside, the old man would instinctually try to suck in more air in a loud, ghastly wheezing sound, which only fueled the coughing fit. The man slipped from the heavily padded chair to fall on his knees, the pipe clattering to the floor as he wrapped one skinny arm around his midsection and used the other to support his weight.

"Sir?" Caleb asked setting the tin cup down, unsure of what to do to help the frail man. "Is there anything I can do?"

The old man slowly lowered himself to his side, drawing his knees up to him and wrapping both arms about his pain wracked torso. The coughs were much harder than they had been the day before. Suddenly, one extremely hard cough slammed through the old man and blood exploded from his lips to splash across the hearth of the fireplace.

Caleb forced himself to his knees and crawled toward the old man, unsure of what he could do, but determined to do something. He reached the violently contracting body of the man and placed a trembling hand on his quaking shoulder. "Sir! What can I do?"

"My... my goblet..." he wheezed out between harsh coughs and bubbling blood. His right arm uncurled from his body, and a boney, trembling finger pointed toward the side table next to his chair.

Caleb turned his head and spotted the large golden goblet. It was the same one he had seen there yesterday. He leaned over and lifted it from the table, careful not to drop it or spill its contents. He slipped his left arm under the old man's neck and began trying to lift him up while bringing the goblet around toward his mouth. The thick red liquid inside had an odd aroma to it. The man continued to be wracked by one bone-jarring cough after another and Caleb wondered how the old man was going to be able to get a breath of air, let alone take a drink from the goblet.

"Here," Caleb said, wincing from the protests of his body in trying to support the old man's weight. Even though he was very old, and weighed next to nothing, Caleb's frostbitten limbs protested the additional strain. After several more moments, the old man was able to gain enough control over the fit to take a deep swallow from the goblet. A few more coughs wracked his body, but they were nowhere near as hard as their predecessors. For several moments, the old man simply slumped against Caleb's arm, his chest heaving under the load of trying to get enough oxygen back into the diseased lungs.

After a few more moments, the old man lifted his head, and Caleb brought the goblet back to his blood stained lips. This time the man took a deep draught from the cup, swallowing the soothing liquid greedily. Finally, the depleted lungs demanded that he stop drinking to allow them access to air. Dropping his head back into the crook of Caleb's arm, the old man simply relaxed and closed his eyes. For several long moments, he simply laid there, his breathing easing up a little bit with each moment. Caleb studied the craggy features and wondered just how much longer he would live. The disease that ravaged his lungs must surely be advanced.

"What is wrong with you?" Caleb asked softly.

"Old age," came the harsh, hoarse reply.

"Can nothing be done?"

The old head shook slowly. "No. As I said yesterday, all will be as it should be in the fullness of time," he shrugged weakly. "Very soon it will simply be my time."

"Is there anything I can do?" Caleb asked, honestly wanting to alleviate the old man's suffering.

"You can stop asking me questions while I am trying to catch my breath!" came the hard reply. "Only an imbecile would ask a man starved for air to answer so many questions!"

Caleb wrestled with feelings of anger on one hand and fond amusement on the other. While he knew the old man meant every word, there was something very endearing about his cranky disposition. "May I...," he started and stopped himself from asking another question. With a slight smile, he shifted the question into a statement. "I will help you to your chair when you're ready." The old man simply nodded in reply.

Eventually, the old man's breathing returned to normal and he opened his eyes. He nodded, indicating that he was ready to get up. With a great deal of effort, Caleb was finally able to help the old man into his chair. He handed the goblet back to him, and he wasted no time in taking another deep drink. Caleb turned and started to walk back to his pallet of furs when the old man stopped him. "My pipe."

Caleb turned and looked down at the pipe near the hearth. "Do you really think you should be smoking with your condition?" Almost instantly, as soon as he saw the hard look return to the man's eyes, he knew he had just incurred his wrath again.

"So you are a healer now? A healer and a noble explorer? I had no idea that you were a man of so many talents," he hissed with thick sarcasm.

"I simply meant that perhaps you could ease your suffering by not smoking," Caleb defended.

"I am dying! There is no force or might within this realm to stop that! If I am to be forced out of this existence, I will go out doing what I damn well please! I am doomed regardless of whether I smoke or not. I choose to at least enjoy the fleeting amount of time I have left. Now mind your own business and hand me my pipe!"

Caleb resisted the urge to wince under the withering gaze and words of his host. He bent over, retrieved the pipe and handed it back to the old man carefully, fearful that he would lash out at him. He moved over to the small table that held the writing materials and the finished pages from yesterday.

"A moment," the old man said as he eased back into the thick padding of the chair. "Allow me a moment to collect myself, and I will prepare you another tin of tea."

"I can pour it. You should rest," Caleb answered as he lifted the tin from the floor and stood up carefully.

"Only I can prepare the tea. You do not know how to make it to where it will ease your pain. Bring me your tin and then prepare for today's story."

Caleb took the tin to the old man and then returned to his small table. As the old man rose to make another tin of tea, Caleb prepared for today's writing. After the tea was prepared, and Caleb had taken a few sips, he situated himself and uncapped the ink well before taking up a quill. Again, he marveled at how the bitter brew almost instantaneously began easing his suffering. He wanted to ask the old man what was in the tea, but he had asked far too many questions already. He glanced up to find the old man lighting another pipe full of fresh tobacco. With a sigh of disapproval, he turned back to his table. After dipping the end of it in the ink, he poised the quill over the blank page.

"So they had made good their escape from Lirpa," Caleb said by way of prompting the old man to pick up the story.

With a mischievous glint in his gray eyes, the old man pulled the pipe from his lips, examined the smoldering bowl of tobacco for a moment, and then looked back up at Caleb.

"Who said they had made good their escape?"

CHAPTER ONE

Devenshire crouched low, straining his senses for the location of whoever was trailing him. A full moon overhead, filtered by the canopy of branches, made it possible to navigate the forest with care, but it also provided deep shadows that any manner of predator could hide. He was far from the campsite they had made earlier in the evening and, therefore, on his own. He had an arrow nocked in his bow, and the tension of the bowstring provided some marginal comfort. Twisting his head around, he searched the shadows and patches of bright moonlight for any indication of where his stalker might be. He found it ironic that in the span of a heartbeat he had gone from predator to prey. Absently he acknowledged that he wasn't a huge fan of irony.

Their escape from Lirpa had been harrowing, leaving a great many unanswered questions in its wake. To better increase their lead over Captain Armand and the Royal Guard, they had pushed on through the next day and well into the evening before stopping to rest. Brianna's arm needed tending to, the mounts needed to rest, and they all could use a moment to take a breath that wasn't being listened for by a guard or sheriff. While camp was being made, he had taken his bow from his pack and set off on a hunt for mountain hares. They were camped at the base of the Mt. Kil'tafore range and the large hares were plentiful in this region. He didn't particularly like the bow, but it was the only weapon he had to take the wild animals at a distance. He was, by no stretch of anyone's imagination, an archer, but he possessed enough skill to hunt with the weapon, which was all he ever used it for.

He had been well into the hunt before he became acutely aware of being watched. He softened his breathing and willed himself to remain calm as he continued to search his surroundings while straining his senses for any indication where the stalker might be. He could hear the faint breeze rustling branches and bushes, mixed with the constant chirping of crickets. Occasionally, an owl would call out, and in the distance, a wolf would cry out in its solitude, all normal sounds of the night. His eyes strained into the darkness, but showed him nothing but shadowy images and insubstantial masses that could be anything. He gently took a deep breath and then released it softly, calming his nerves and readying himself to summon his powers. His mortal senses were useless. Half closing his eyes, he released his powers and reached out, searching. He detected the presence of several rodents, insects, several meat serpents on hunts of their own, and even some of the mountain hares he had come to hunt, but no trace of anything that shouldn't be there.

Closing his eyes completely, he applied more power to his search and expanded the perimeter of his spell. All he found was more of the same, nothing that shouldn't be there and nothing with any malevolent intent; at least not toward him. He was about to pull the spell back when the outer edge of it touched something, something that did not belong. He focused the spell, pulling the power from a wide circular search to a fine line that surrounded the object that had caught his attention. It was a person, but that was all he could glean from the spell at this distance. Whoever it was, they were at the outer most limits of the reach of his powers, which made discerning details difficult at best. Maintaining a tight mystical lock on the person, he opened his eyes and turned in the direction the person lie in. He rose slowly and quietly to a standing position and began moving slowly toward the person, using great care to keep his steps light. His hope was to bring them further within the range of his spell and, thereby, learn more about who they were.

The familiar tingle of his natural sense of the Arts began running up and down his spine. Whoever the person was, they were now using magic to keep a mystical lock on him. He paused to kneel, laying the bow on the ground. He quickly, but quietly, slid the quiver of bows from his shoulder and laid them next to the bow. Standing upright again, he gently drew his sword, feeling more confident in his abilities with it over that of the bow. Moving with all the stealth he could muster, he continued toward his invisible target. It was going to be a difficult hunt because he would need his physical senses to navigate the darkened forest and using them would detract from his mystical senses. The person began to solidify in his mind, he could make out a cloaked figure crouched low in the brush. He could not make out any weapons, but that did not mean they didn't have any. As he moved around a tree and stooped low under a branch, he focused on the figure's face. It was a grey, featureless blob at the moment, but he knew that as he drew closer, he would be able to make out more detail. Devenshire paused to concentrate on his vision spell, abandoning his physical senses in favor of his mystical ones. As he did, more details began to coalesce in his mind. The figure was just below average height. The heavy cloak they wore made details of their physical build hard to make out, so he focused his attention on their head. Slowly, the grey mass shifted into a face-shaped oval. Indentions for eyes and a mouth began to sink inward as a bulb in the middle of the face began to grow outward to form the nose. He resisted the urge to hurry the image to form. Working the Mystical

Arts was meticulous and time consuming, and impatience was one of the quickest ways to ruin a spell. More features formed and soon he would be able to discern if the person was man or woman, and once he had their face locked in his mind, he would be able to search the Mystical Tides for their identity. He closed his eyes and forced more concentration into make the face solidify. Just as the eyes began to come into focus, the figure shifted and was gone.

Devenshire's eyes snapped open, instantly locking in the direction the figure had been. They had moved, as if they had known he was about to learn their identity. By having so much of his energies focused on the figures' face, all they had to do was move and they would be outside the reach of his focused spell. He quickly expanded his focus outward and just barely picked up the impression of the figure retreating into the woods at a brisk walk. Mumbling a curse, Devenshire set off after the fleeting figure. Again, he was forced to divide his attention between keeping a mystical lock on the person while using his physical sense to navigate the perilous path in the dark. It was a taxing bit of work, and he could already feel the beginning barbs of a headache begin working its sharp tentacles into his brain. The person knew he was on the move for they quickened their pace to stay just on the edges of his ability to sense them. This troubled him as much as if someone were stalking him. Was the fact that they were at the outermost limits of his powers because of a limitation on their part, or were they luring him into some form of trap? His opponent increased their pace, and Devenshire had to quicken his pace even further to keep up. The added task of using his physical body and senses took away from his mystical ability to find out who the person was. At this point, all he could do with his powers was to keep a fleeting lock on their position. His mystical gifts were being taxed to their limits with trying to keep up with them, and the path they were following was physically demanding as well. It was almost as if they were testing him, trying to see just how much concentration he could spare for the spell while navigating a treacherous path through the dark. Several times, he stumbled or caught a grazing slap of a branch as he bounded through the dark. His breath heaved in his lungs, and it took all of his concentration to keep the duel demands on his focus under control.

Suddenly, whoever it was stopped and turned back to face him. Devenshire instantly slid to a stop and crouched into a defensive posture. For whomever it was to be so intent on escape, and then suddenly stop and turn back, meant that they were either making a stand or were ready to spring their trap. The maneuver had been sudden and had taken him by surprise. Devenshire tightened his grip on the sword and released some of his hold on the mystical energies, opting to concentrate more, now, on his physical senses. So far, all he heard was the steady song of the night and his taxed breathing. Nothing else was registering on his mystical senses save for the mysterious person just ahead. What they were waiting for, he had no idea. The element of surprise for a trap was lost, but that did not mean one was not waiting for him.

An immeasurable amount of time passed with Devenshire and his opponent squared off against each other across a distance far outside either of their fields of vision. Devenshire studied his options, weighing his next course of action. This was a dangerous game and not one he intended to lose. He decided to increase the power of his spell and make another attempt to find out whom this person was. He grimaced as he realized that using more power on the spell would increase the strength of the already pounding headache.

Then, they were gone.

Devenshire blinked even though the action would have no bearing on his spell. The person had not turned and moved out of range of his spell, but rather they had simply vanished, as if into thin air. He felt himself tense, preparing for the attack. Surely, it would come now, as the person would use the distraction of an attack to cover their escape. Time passed and nothing happened. Devenshire's joints began to ache from holding the defensive posture and waiting. It became obvious that whoever it was who had been following and watching him, was gone now. He straightened up and turned a slow circle, searching with all of his senses, and found nothing that wasn't supposed to be there. With more than a little irritation, he noted that most of the mountain hares had scattered with his driving run through the forest. It would now take longer to track them down, and with his throbbing headache, it promised to be a very unpleasant hunt.

Moving off through the woods with stealth, he moved back toward the bow and arrows, so he could resume the hunt. He was unaware of the cloaked figure that stepped from the shadows to occupy the spot he had just left. They watched him move through the darkness as a tight smile graced their lips.

"Very good," they whispered softly before turning and melting into the night.

CHAPTER TWO

Consciousness came slowly and very painfully for Gregory Armand. The first coherent thought his mind could form was a question of just how deeply into hell had he been cast? Surely, this must be hell, for no living being could endure this magnitude of pain, and still be counted among the living. His head pounded as though someone of incredible size and strength were using a giant mallet to beat his skull into a fine powder. Every single joint felt as though red-hot daggers were being plunged deep into them, twisted in an irregular circle, ripped out, only to be driven in again. Nausea twisted and flipped his stomach while every inch of his skin felt as though a wasp or hornet were driving their barbed stingers, dipped in acid, deep, and injecting poison. He moaned softly and rolled his head to one side only to be rewarded with what felt like the vertebrae in his neck shattering, the fragmented bones grinding against each other while shards of bone sliced through muscle, sinew, and nerves... nerves that were most definitely still alive and performing their tasks with sickening and agonizing accuracy.

"Captain?" a voice called. It took him a moment to understand that what he had heard was a voice and not the incessant buzz that threatened to deafen him. It took him another moment to correlate the word in his mind and make the connection that it pertained to him. Even then, he simply did not have the strength to answer while warding off the onslaught of what had to be his transition from life to death. "Captain Armand? Can you hear me?" the annoying voice called out again. Why wouldn't they leave him be? Couldn't they see he was trying to die? Why postpone the hellish event by trying to talk to him? An odd thought popped into the twisted, globed, congealed sludge that, at one time, had been his brain. What had brought him to the threshold between life and death?

Even though the act increased the size of the mallet being used to reduce his head to a bloody soup, he dug deep into his discombobulated memory for what had brought him here. The images were slow to come and were fuzzy, distant memories at first. Something had happened in Lirpa. Murder, mutilation of bodies, and horrendous acts that even he, as a seasoned veteran of the Royal Guard, had never seen. There had been a conversation with someone, someone of incredible size. The image of the large, heavily muscled man hovered just outside the reach of his soupy mind. There was mention of two wanted men... rogue vagabonds on the loose for far too long. What were their names? They were right on the tip of what felt like his slowly decaying tongue. With growing frustration, he couldn't get the remnants of his mind to cooperate. He knew the names as well as he knew his own, but could not conjure them to the surface. There had been another conversation, a conversation with a man of great honor and pursuing a path of holy justice against the dark servants of hell. That conversation stood out sharply in the foggy essence of his mind. It had been that conversation that had set on him the path of a vampire, a true demon who had claimed the lives of a local whore and someone close to him. Just like the names of the vagabonds, the name of that person also escaped him.

"Captain Armand? You must wake. Master Lordalise draws near," the voice called out again. This time, though, the voice didn't irritate him. The voice had said the name of Lordalise and, like turning a key, the stubborn locks of his mind turned loose, and the memories came flooding out of the misty vault.

Lordalise.

It had been the vampire hunter who had told him who was responsible for the horrendous mutilations at the inn. It had been a vampire who had mutilated the men at the inn, had killed the whore named Lorinda, and who had taken the life of his dear friend, Constable Liston.

Devenshire, the bastard child of Satan himself!

Memories of the intense pursuit began to come into sharp focus within his slowly stabilizing consciousness. They had arrested Zandorth Krahl and Brianna Standish followed by what appeared to be the easy arrest of Daimion Devenshire, one of the two vagabonds he had been having trouble remembering. As his mind continued to fight its way back to a fully conscious level, he realized that the arrest had been far too easy for the type of creature Devenshire was. In hindsight, he realized he should have known it wouldn't have been that easy. So much had happened in such a short span of time. The death of the local whore, which now, was obviously a diversion to lure Lordalise and he away from the jail to give Devenshire ample time and opportunity to kill Constable Liston. The wrenching memories of what he had to do to Liston's body to ensure he would be forever free from Devenshire's hellish reach.

Then the blurred mad dash through the streets of Lirpa in pursuit of the criminals which had seen acts that would be debated for seasons on how crafty or how utterly insane they had been. The chase had ended in a clearing outside Lirpa with all four of the criminals surrounded. Armand remembered how he had watched the ensuing battle, and for a brief time, feared the criminals would actually best his guards and make good their escape even though his guards outnumbered them three to one. Finally, Brianna Standish had been wounded and captured, followed by the disgraced warrior, Krahl, and a younger woman who had just joined the group during their escape attempt. With no small amount of shame, he recalled how he had used Standish's capture to secure Devenshire's surrender. The images were growing clearer and clearer as he recalled them, and he could clearly see himself standing over Devenshire's bound form upon his knees. He had struck the demon and had been amazed to see blood trickle from a split lip. This thought troubled him. Vampires were dead. Their hearts did not beat and yet blood had oozed from Devenshire's lip.

How was such a thing possible?

Then the horrifying memory of how his men began falling asleep came, one by one until he, alone, was left. Panic had ripped through him, terrifying him at the thought of having to deal with the vampire on his own. Then he had seen Standish and recalled how Devenshire had seemed protective of her. Perhaps he could regain the advantage by threatening her again. It had turned out to be an enormous mistake, and it had unlocked the final question in his slowly awakening mind, on how he had come to the pain riddled entrance to the afterlife. He had pulled a dagger and was making his way toward Standish. Devenshire had freed himself as he rose to his feet, calling on his hellish power to summon a blue, glowing orb of light that crackled with mystical energies. Devenshire's eyes had taken on the same blue glow of light, and the sight had chilled him to the core. At that moment, Devenshire appeared truly evil. His words surfaced within his mind, and they were driven home with the pounding of the mallet into his skull. *"Take another step toward her, and you will most definitely live to regret it!"*

In a last ditch act of desperation, he had tried to hurl the dagger into the woman's throat. It was to be his final act of vengeance against the demon, and it had failed. The horribly painful orb of light had taken his mind and body, twisted them in upon themselves, and snuffed out his consciousness as though it were a candle caught in a maelstrom.

"Captain? Are you well?" the voice asked, and it was all Armand could do not to laugh. It was the most ludicrous question he had ever heard.

"A moment," he whispered out through his incredibly dry throat. He cracked his eyes open and was rewarded by the blurred vision of the gray dawning sky through the treetops. He closed his eyes and then opened them a little wider. This time the treetops began to spin in a sickening kaleidoscope that went straight to the nausea, flipping his stomach over and over and over again. He felt his stomach contract violently and knew he only had a moment. With a sudden, jerking movement that made his already tortured body scream in agony, he rolled to his side just in time to vomit violently.

"…you will most definitely live to regret it!" At least on this point, Armand reflected as he continued to be tortured by his own body, Devenshire had been a demon of his word.

It took a considerable amount of time for Armand to finally gain enough control of his ravaged body to sit upright and accept a few sips of tepid water from someone's pouch. He tried to recall if there had ever been a time in his life where he had felt this horrible and none came to mind. Just as the symptoms of Devenshire's hellish spell would start to fade, he would breathe or blink, and they would return in full force. He began to wonder if the symptoms would ever fade. Armand was finally able to stand, albeit unsteadily. He refused offers from some of his men to assist him. He was in command and he dared not show weakness, especially in light of how he had allowed the criminals to escape.

He took stock of his men. Several were injured and would need to be tended to by a healer, but none had been killed. This, too, struck an odd chord in his mind. Why had the criminals injured but not killed? Surely, they would know that leaving any member of the Royal Guard alive to pursue them again would be folly. Yet not one single man had been killed. What of Devenshire? Would the demon not have had a feast on the unconscious men? Why had he left Armand alive? The questions nagged at his throbbing brain unmercifully. Just as the blood that had trickled from Devenshire's split lip, these things simply did not make sense. A crackling of brush heralded the arrival of Lordalise and his men. With a deep sigh, Armand knew the Hunter would not be happy about the turn of events.

As the vampire hunter entered the clearing, he had taken a long slow sweeping survey of the clearing. The disappointment and disapproval were clear on his features as he failed to see the criminals. His hazel eyes came to rest on Armand and the captain could see the disappointment triple. Taking a deep breath and mentally screaming at the man inside his skull with the mallet beating on the bones behind his eyes to stop, Armand placed his hat on his head, squared his shoulders, and prepared himself for what was to come.

"Captain," Lordalise said coolly.

"Master Lordalise," Armand replied evenly.

"What happened?"

Armand took a deep breath and launched into a recap of what had transpired, including the eerie way his men had fallen asleep and ending with the blast of magic that had rendered him unconscious. With each detail revealed, Lordalise's features grew tighter and grimmer.

"How many men did you lose?" Lordalise asked after Armand

finished.

"None."

Lordalise's face twisted into a confused expression. "None? Not one man? All of your men are accounted for?"

"They are all present and accounted for. I have several injured, but none were lost."

"Odd," Lordalise mumbled as he looked about the clearing.

"That Devenshire did not feast on a single man. Even the wounded." Armand completed the silent thought that had been haunting him. Everything he had learned about vampires, and from what he had seen from the night before, he had honestly expected to never awaken again, much less to awaken and find every one of his men present and alive.

"You all should be dead now... drained," Lordalise commented without concern of how it almost sounded as though he were disappointed in the outcome of the battle.

Armand resisted the urge to promise the vampire hunter, with thick sarcasm, that they would try harder to be butchered next time. "It does not follow what I have learned to expect from a vampire," he replied instead.

Lordalise continued to study the clearing intently, his eyes narrowing with intense concentration. Devenshire's behavior had both surprised and confused him. While he had originally accused Devenshire of being a vampire just to gain the assistance of Captain Armand, he now found himself wondering if, perhaps, Devenshire really was a vampire. "What game is he playing?" Lordalise asked no one in particular. He felt off balance, out of his element. Vampires, in many respects, were tediously predictable. They came out at night, and they fed on as much blood as they could get. Never, in his long association with the Hunters, had a vampire ever passed up the smorgasbord of blood that had been presented to Devenshire just a few short hours ago. He seriously doubted a vampire *could* pass up such a feast. Again, the doubts that Devenshire was the vampire he sought crept into his mind and threatened to loosen his convictions. He took a moment to consider his steps to this point. While he had yet to test Devenshire to verify his suspicions, there was ample proof that Devenshire was, indeed, the vampire. Such as his escape from the jail, the deaths of the whore and the constable in the manner of the vampire, all were conclusive proof that Devenshire was a vampire.

Wait! It was all conclusive proof that there was *a* vampire lose within Lirpa... not necessarily that Devenshire was a vampire. His mind wrestled with the horrifying prospect that he had been wrong and that they had been pursuing an innocent group of people. His narrow mindedness had allowed the true demon to escape, to find a dark place to hole up for the day, only to unleash its terror upon Lirpa at the setting sun. Doubt and self-recrimination began to form within him, shaking his confidence in his own abilities. How could he have been wrong? How could he have made such a blatant error in judgment?

Rotella. His mind whispered to him.

Lordalise pulled up short as the image of his man draped backwards across a tree limb flashed through his mind. His men had attacked Devenshire and his party to rob them and had met with an embarrassing defeat. While surveying the battle scene, they had discovered Rotella's body dangling high in a tree, his throat bearing the jagged puncture marks of the vampire. The two vampire-related deaths in Lirpa had not occurred until after Devenshire and his party had entered town. With a sharp shake of his head, Lordalise banished the doubts. It may remain to be seen if Devenshire is actually the vampire or not, but there was no doubt that a vampire was within the group he traveled with.

"A trick," Lordalise finally said with conviction.

"Sir?" Armand asked, removing his hat to wipe at the sheen of sweat on his forehead. The splitting pain of his head, the nausea wrecking havoc with his stomach, and his body caught in what had to be what rigor mortis felt like was causing him considerable problems.

"Devenshire's not feeding on the lot of you. It is a trick. A ruse of some sort to make us do exactly what we have spent our time doing: wasting these past few precious moments doubting ourselves."

"If a vampire is capable of everything I have heard they are capable of, why would he even need to use such tactics? From what I have seen, he can take whatever he wants," Armand replied tiredly.

Lordalise only partially heard Armand's question as his mind continued to try to race ahead of Devenshire's, to try to figure out what the demon's next move would be. "No one can know what hellish thoughts the demon is following. We can only move forward and try to be ready for the next confrontation." He finally settled his eyes on the ill captain and took in his state. "Are you well enough to continue?"

Armand drew up to his full height. "I will be fine. Do not concern yourself with it."

Lordalise didn't believe it for a moment, but let it stand. "We should set after them immediately. We have already lost precious time."

"I must have my wounded carried back to Lirpa to be seen by a healer. I need reinforcements and a tracker," Armand replied.

Lordalise shook his head. "Surely you can dispatch a man to fetch assistance from Lirpa for your wounded, and can none of your men track? We are falling further behind with each moment!"

Armand stifled the irritation before it could raise high enough to lose control. While he shared Lordalise's desire to destroy Devenshire before the bastard could kill again, he knew that plunging headlong into pursuit was foolhardy and dangerous. The repeated splitting of his skull in time with his heartbeat served as ample proof. He looked up and shook his head. "You wish for me to leave wounded men behind? To leave them alone in this clearing while someone else goes for help? I think not, Master Lordalise. I understand the need for expediency in our pursuit of Devenshire, but I have obligations to these men, and I shall not shirk them. Besides, it is practically dawn now. Devenshire will have to find a place to hide from the light of day. It would seem to me we have ample time to pick up his trail."

Lordalise sighed heavily as he fought down his irritation. Spoken like someone who had no idea how to hunt vampires. Taking a deep breath to calm his frustrations, he forced his voice into a neutral tone as he replied, "You are correct. Devenshire, as we speak, is holed up in some dark space somewhere. His companions, however, are not. They do not need to hide from the light of day. They are moving forward, no doubt scouting out a place for Devenshire to hide the next day. You are also correct that we do not have to worry about Devenshire striking again until nightfall. What you are not considering, however, is that we could ride within a hands space of Devenshire's hiding place and not knowing it. We could ride right past him and give him the opportunity to strike us from behind or return to Lirpa for another night of hellish deaths. If we catch up to his minions, we could extract the location of his hiding place and dispatch him before any more souls are lost!"

Armand nodded slowly, reluctantly admitting that once again his lack of experience in dealing with vampires was proving to be a hindrance. His mind switched gears, bringing the soldier within him to the forefront. "You are right, of course, Master Lordalise." He stood in silence for a moment before looking out over his assembled men. The wounded were being tended to with the limited knowledge his men held of the healing arts. His eyes shifted painfully toward the approaching dawn. He felt pulled in two directions by his dual responsibilities. He knew his duty demanded that he capture all of the criminals and aid in the destruction of the demon-spawned bastard known as Devenshire. Yet he also had wounded men that needed assistance. Their lives were his responsibility. Again, the soldier snapped to the forefront, and he made his decision. "Lieutenant!" he barked out. Almost instantly, a man jogged up to him and snapped his body into a rigid stance of attention.

"Sir!" he replied.

"Pick three men to remain with the wounded. Make sure they have plenty of water and supplies for an extended wait. Pick another man to ride back to our garrison for assistance in getting the wounded men back to Lirpa and to a healer as quickly as possible. Also, have this man round up reinforcements and our best tracker. Master Lordalise, the balance of our regiment, and myself, will begin our pursuit of these criminals. Have our reinforcements and tracker catch up to us without haste. Am I clear?"

"Yes, sir! Very clear!" the lieutenant answered.

"Carry out my orders," Armand commanded. The lieutenant saluted and moved off to carry out the orders. Armand looked up at Lordalise. "All of my men possess tracking skills. We will set off in pursuit of the criminals. Reinforcements and a skilled tracker should catch up to us by mid-day."

Lordalise nodded. "Very good. We should begin immediately."

Armand nodded slowly again. He was in no condition to set out immediately, but he was not about to be the reason, again, why the capture of Devenshire and his companions eluded them. He directed his men to mount up and picked his strongest tracker from his ranks.

CHAPTER THREE

Zebadiah Constance sat on his mount, staring intently at the Lirpa skyline in the fading afternoon light. He was vaguely aware of the balance of the Honor Guard behind him, awaiting his next orders.

"They definitely came this way. I can still make out their tracks." One of his men said as he knelt over the hoof prints in the loose soil.

Constance nodded absently as his angry gaze continued to study Lirpa. He could still feel the rage coursing through his veins. His mind traveled back to the previous morning when one of Brianna's chambermaids had summoned him with the news that Brianna was not in her chambers.

Despite breeching several protocols, he had entered Brianna's room. Her bed had not been slept in, and the doors leading out to her balcony had been left slightly ajar. Ignoring the chambermaid's protests to his entrance to Brianna's room, he continued to study the room intently with the trained eyes of a soldier for any sign of what had become of the Lord of Prothtow.

He had instantly spied the folded parchment on her desk and wasted no time in crossing the room to retrieve it. Just before reaching the desk, he had looked up at the nude portrait of Brianna laying on her bed and felt his cheeks flush from both embarrassment and rage. The portrait was completely inappropriate for a lady, to say nothing of the governing lord of the province. He silently added it to the list of topics he intended to discuss with Brianna once he found her.

He had wasted no time in taking up the parchment that had his named scrolled across the folded page just below Brianna's seal. He opened the missive and let his eyes scan across the elegant flow of her handwriting:

My dearest Zeb,

No doubt, you will be exceedingly furious with me once you learn what I have done, and in your position, I can safely say my rage would surpass yours. I can only hope that you will understand the gravity of the situation and that I did what I felt that I must for the preservation of my province and my people.

The annihilation of Shantira's village was not the random act of bandits, but rather the cold and calculated massacre of innocent people by a raving madman. His name is Xavier and he attacked Nelton in order to secure The Stones of Andarus. I have it on good authority that these stones, in the hands of Xavier, spell nothing but certain doom for our country, if not our entire realm. I have left with a group of people with the intentions of stopping whatever sinister plans Xavier has for the Stones. We are heading to Lirpa, and then north toward a place called the Duvall Retreat.

I wish I had more information for you as you certainly deserve it. However, I have told you the bulk of my knowledge on the subject, and that time is a precious commodity that we have a vanishingly short supply of. Immediate action was required, and I could do no less than what I would have asked of you and your men.

I realize my actions could very well lead to my being expelled from the Lordship and my being stripped of my title and lands. If these are to be my final instructions to you, then please see to the safety of the people. Protect them as fiercely as you have protected me. Immediately dispatch a courier with this information to His Majesty so that preparations can be made for whatever is to come.

You have become a valued confidant, a true friend, and the closest thing to a father that I have known since the passing of mine. May the Fates favor you as they have favored me with your guidance and protection.

With my undying love and gratitude,

Bri.

He had read the note three more times, just to make sure he understood its contents. Then he had slowly lowered his arm to his side, his fist curling slowly into a trembling fist, crumpling the parchment into a tight ball. For an uncounted amount of time, he had stood rigidly at the desk, his posture stiff, almost statue-like.

"Captain?" the chambermaid asked tentatively, not sure if she truly wanted to roust Constance from what appeared to be a rage induced catatonic state. She had come to wake Lady Standish since it was getting late into the morning. She had found her chambers empty and quickly searched the room, finding no sign of her mistress. That was when she alerted Captain Constance who wasted no time in coming to Brianna's room, though such a thing was not generally permitted.

"Undisciplined, spoiled little bitch!" Constance hissed as he finally turned away from the desk. "She is going to do nothing but get herself killed!" The anger was clear on his weathered features, but deep in his gray eyes was the torment of worry.

The chambermaid gasped as her hand shot to cover her mouth. "Captain! You must not speak of M'Lady Standish in such a way!" Not only had Constance violated several protocols by even entering Brianna's room, but now he had insulted her as well. The chambermaid was relatively sure she would be forced to watch him flogged within an inch of his life.

"I will speak of her little whimsical, undisciplined, spoiled arse in any way I wish! She should be turned over a knee and thrashed!" he snapped in reply as he began a slow pace about the room, Brianna's note still clutched tightly in his right fist. "Of all the insolent gall!"

"What has happened, sir?" the chambermaid asked, unsure of how to react to such blatant actions and words.

"Your mistress has taken it upon herself to run off and play heroine to the entire realm with a group of people that I know nothing about! I am thankful that Lord Trenton is not alive to see this! He would surely go after her, drag her back here, and then make sure she could not sit down for at least a season!" he snapped in reply as he continued to pace, his voice trailing off as he began talking more to himself than to the chambermaid. "All she had to do was explain the situation to me... let me help... do my duty. But no... she is Brianna Standish, and she is immortal, invincible!"

"Sir?" the chambermaid asked, not sure whom he was talking to.

He spun on her, his frustration, anger, and concern reaching a nearly unbearable level. "Nothing! Summon Lieutenant Travers! Have him muster the entire honor guard. I want them at attention and ready for instructions within the quarter hour!"

Startled by the sudden venom in his voice, the chambermaid nodded quickly before gathering the folds of her skirt and turning to leave the room. Constance quickly crossed the room and took her by the arm. The grip was so hard that she gasped in shocked pain as she looked from her arm in his fist, and then to his angry stare locked deep into her eyes.

"Say nothing of this to anyone, and I mean no one. None must know that Lady Standish is not here," he said in low menacing tones.

"Sir?" she asked, not entirely sure what he meant.

"You and I are the only ones who know that Lady Standish is not within her keep. It must remain such. If word leaked out that the Lord of the province was missing, can you imagine the panic and ensuing anarchy that would reign?"

The chambermaid took a moment to play the scenario through her mind, instantly realizing the wisdom in the captain's command. She nodded her understanding and silent promise of compliance. Constance answered with a short quick nod of his own before releasing her arm allowing her to quickly make a hasty departure from the room. Constance continued to wrestle with his rage and concern. He wanted to run out, chase her down and to whip her, as her father would have, while another part wanted nothing more than to make sure she was safe within the protective walls of the keep.

Constance had never married, had never had children of his own, but he could imagine the sheer rage and terror ripping through him at this moment was what it felt like to be a father. He shook his head sharply. How had Lord Trenton Standish endured it? He forced his emotions back under the stifling yolk of his control and started to leave the room. He paused a moment and fixed Brianna's portrait of office with a hard stare comprised of intense anger and soul-rending concern.

"You had better hope I catch up to you before you get yourself into some real trouble, trouble your little playmates will not be able to protect you from! This is not finished, young lady, not by a sight!"

The memory faded from the forefront of his mind as the image of Lirpa again assumed the center of his focus. He had pressed his men hard and had made up a lot of ground, but they still had not caught up to Brianna and her rag-tag group before they reached the city. The anger was as fresh as it had been at its onset, but the more time that passed, the deep-rooted concern for her grew and caused him a trepidation and anxiety he had not thought possible within one person.

"Let us move," he muttered as he gathered the reins to his mount and urged his horse forward.

~*~

Xavier dozed as his coach rumbled past another tedious mile. The rough ride made deep sleep impossible, but the light napping allowed him to occupy his mind with thoughts of how best to tap into the Stones. It was not going to be a simple matter of going into them and unleashing the power within. History was replete with mages and sorcerers who had tried and who had been destroyed. There was some kind of mystical barrier around the Stones that made direct contact with what lie within exceedingly dangerous, supposedly impossible. Was the barrier a side effect of the creation of the Stones? Was it interference from the Fates to protect what had been taken from them? After studying the Stones intently for two days, he could not honestly say what the barrier was or how to negate it. The only solid answer he knew was that he had to find a way to circumvent the barrier, or all of his grand schemes for the Stones and the realm were nothing but fluffy dreams.

Fluffy dreams.

As his mind wandered the border of the land of dreams, he found his attention leaving the Stones and drifting aimlessly among his memories. Fluffy dreams... very much like fluffy clouds one would find on a beautiful clear day. Images came, unbidden, into his mind of a time when he was laying on his back on a green rolling field, his youthful eyes taking in the myriad shapes that the clouds would take on.

"A dragon," a man's voice echoed from his memory, and he instantly recognized it as belonging to his father. When he had been a small boy, he and his father would take long hikes through their massive tracks of land. They would fish or hunt game, chop firewood, gather roots and herbs from the ever-growing list his mother would always seem to need every time they would set out. On occasion, they would come across a wide-open plain and decide to do, as his father called it, scout the sky. They would lie upon their backs and see how many different cloud shapes they could identify.

"It is not a very large dragon," he heard his child-like voice answer as they studied the cloud in question.

"It has been my experience that a little dragon goes a long way," his father answered with a chuckle. The answer had caused the boy to laugh, and as the memory played within his mind, his physical lips turned upward in a smile.

"Have you ever faced a dragon, Father?" young Xavier asked, his eyes searching the sky for other cloud shapes he could recognize, but his eyes kept drifting back to the dragon shaped cloud.

"No. Most of the dragons have left human lands and now live far away. A dragon has not been seen in these lands in many seasons," his father answered.

Young Xavier fixed his gaze on the dragon shaped cloud and tried to conjure up what a real dragon would look like. A soft breeze rolled across the field, rustling his black hair and carrying an array of aromas such as flowers and grass. He closed his eyes and breathed in deeply, savoring the smells and basking in the warmth of the sun and his father's love. As his eyes opened again, he saw that the dragon cloud appeared to be growing in size and seemed more substantial than before. A tiny sliver of fear pricked the back of his mind, and he contemplated the stories he had heard of dragons. "Is it true they ate children?" he asked, trying to make the question sound matter-of-fact.

His father chuckled softly as he folded one arm up under his head. "A dragon eats anything it wishes. Generally, though, a child is too small a meal for the effort required to capture it. Dragons usually resigned themselves to cattle or other large game."

"That is good," young Xavier proclaimed, feeling the sliver of fear dissipate in the echoes of his father's melodious voice. "I would not be worth the effort to eat."

Xavier's father laughed and patted his son's head. "No, my son. You are far too small for a dragon to bother with."

The warm memories spread through him with surprising swiftness. It seemed so very long ago, but he remembered how he had been the center of his father's world. There was little that the man did that he did not include his son in…

In his memory, he was still on the grassy field watching the dragon shaped cloud. The cloud began to change. Instead of dissipating and loosing the shape of the dragon, it shifted and began looking more like a real dragon. A strange duality took shape in his perceptions. In one scene, the dragon cloud was indeed dissipating and losing its dragon shape. In the other, the dragon continued to solidify and take on more and more characteristics of the real article.

His father loved his son deeply, without exception, without hesitation.

TOM SECHRIST | 39

His life had been the stuff of fairy tales…

The white cloud began to turn gray, and in some areas, green. The edges of the cloud began to take on hard lines and the sliver of fear returned twice the size as before. "Father?" his voice asked with just a touch of a tremble to it.

It had been as though his father had been a king, his mother a queen, and he, their son, had been their prince…

In his memory, the small boy he had been watched transfixed as the dragon shaped cloud no longer looked like a cloud. There was the definite long tail with the spade on the end of it. Scales in incredible detail began forming on the body. A part of his young mind began to fear that the cloud was trying to turn itself into a real dragon. "Father?" he asked again, more fear encroaching upon his voice.

"What is wrong, Xavier?" his father had asked as though he were not seeing the transformation taking place in the sky over them.

"The cloud looks more like a real dragon," he replied trying valiantly to keep the fear at bay.

"That is because it is a real dragon," his father replied. "It has come to cleanse the land of a terrible blight."

Panic spiked within him and he tried to sit up. That was when he realized that his father held him to the ground with surprising force. "Father? The dragon!" he exclaimed as he tried to wrestle free of his father's grip.

His father had suddenly gone from being laid out next to him to sitting straddle of him, holding him to the ground. The warm and loving expression on his face shifted into one of dark malevolence, "Yes… the dragon… all hail the power of the dragon!" his father had hissed in evil malevolence. His fear instantly tripled, and he struggled to free himself from the vice-like grip his father held him in. His young mind struggled to understand what was happening.

"Father? Help me! Let me go!" young Xavier pleaded.

"I am helping you, Xavier! I am showing you why you must die! Why you must not be allowed to continue to be a blight upon our lives!" his father hissed, the crazed look in his eyes frightening him more than the dragon. His shifted his terrified eyes to the sky to see that the cloud had completed its transition into a real dragon. Leathery wings beat the sky as it circled the clearing high above them. At some point, the clouds had turned to dark colors and had grown to obscure the sky, blotting out the brilliant sunshine that had been there only a moment ago. The warm air had chilled as the wind took on a harsh, biting force. Lightening split the sky while horrendous claps of thunder reverberated across the land. The dragon screamed in reply to the approaching storm, and the sound rattled the fear deep within him. The dragon looked down, seeming to see them on the grass. It shifted its flight and began a sharp dive toward them, its mouth opening to reveal rows of sharp, pointed teeth.

"I do not want to die, Father! Please help me! I will be good, I promise!" he begged as his struggles increased. His small mind could not comprehend what was happening while his adult mind understood all too well, and it stoked the deep, long burning fury within him. His father's insane glare locked to his young eyes, and for a moment, the soft and gentle expression his father normally wore returned. His eyes softened with sadness as the dragon swooped down on them. Just as the beast reached them, a single tear shone in his father's eye as he shook his head slowly,

"No... you will not."

Xavier shouted as he bolted upright in his carriage seat. For a moment, he was not entirely sure what he had just experienced had been real or a dream. He was breathing hard, and a thin sheen of sweat covered his body. His eyes took in the interior of his coach, and he began searching himself for any indication that he had been harmed. There were no injuries. The dragon had been a dream, a very real, very terrifying, dream. He closed his eyes and took a moment to compose himself. While the dragon attack had been a dream, the scene of he and his father making shapes out of the clouds had actually happened. The memories also fueled his fury, and his hard eyes snapped open, driving the memories and the fear down that had been stoked by the dream. He reached for the bottle of liquor, uncorked it, and took several deep draws from it.

The warm memories were of a time in his life that no longer existed and he could never return. He had seen to that personally. It served as a reminder as to why he had searched out the darkness over the light. Sunshine, grassy fields, making silly shapes out of clouds and the entire sappy emotionalism that accompanied them were disease! Things used to trick children into obedience to parents who were vile beings. Beings that sucked the life and will out of you, and left you crippled before the realm, the dragon, to be eaten alive slowly. He had freed himself from the dragon. He had proved too cunning for the vile beings and had escaped their treachery... their betrayal. He pulled back one of the drapes covering his carriage window and watched in disgust as the surrounding landscape was bathed in nauseating sunshine. He took a few more deep breaths to calm his nerves before taking another deep drink from the bottle.

Along the tree line, he spied a rabbit. The small furry creature was hopping along, searching out food. The site angered him. It reminded him of the weak, pathetic fool he had been as a child who would have delighted at such a vision. Disgusting creatures designed by the Fates to lure children into the false world of happiness and contentment. There was no contentment, there was no happiness save for what you carved out for yourself. He fixed his hard gaze on the rabbit and slowly curled his right hand into a fist. His eyes began to shimmer in red light as a red aura began to glow around his trembling fist. A hard, cruel smile creased his lips as his mind conjured up the vision of himself, standing before the now empty Stones of Andarus, glowing with the unfathomable power that was now his. He would remake this realm. He would reshape it. He would ensure that children would be free from the lies and deceit of their parents. He would lead them from their poisonous prisons into the darkness of the new order of the realm!

A ball of red light shot from his carriage and engulfed the rabbit. It squealed in intense pain as it flopped about, trying to escape the sudden agony it found itself in. Suddenly, a small fireball flashed, leaving nothing but charred bones and singed tatters of fur in its wake.

Inside the carriage, Xavier laughed as he corked the bottle and returned it to the pouch it had been riding in. As he laid his head back and closed his eyes, he smiled.

Soon. Very soon.

CHAPTER FOUR

Devenshire stepped out of the forest and paused at the edge of the clearing, his eyes focusing on the small campfire directly ahead. He could make out the silhouettes of Brianna and Shantira seated by the fire, warming themselves against the growing chill of the night. Darkseed had left right after they had made camp, saying he had an errand to run and would return soon. His eyes darted around the area lit by the fire, but could not find Zandorth. It was odd that the warrior would have left the women alone. While they were perfectly capable of defending themselves, Zandorth's 'warrior code would not have permitted him to leave them unprotected. Suddenly, he tensed as he simultaneously heard a faint rustle of brush and felt the definite point of a sword being pressed into his back.

"You take dangerous chances," came the deep timber of Zandorth's voice from behind him.

Devenshire relaxed and smiled. "It warms me to know that you are covering my back," he said.

"You very nearly had my sword in your back. It is unwise to sneak up on someone's camp unannounced," Zandorth replied gruffly.

"I was not sneaking. Besides, I heard your approach. Not your usual level of skill at stealth," Devenshire replied. It had been a very tense few days, and he felt that some of his antagonistic banter with Zandorth might ease the tension.

Zandorth stepped around in front of Devenshire as he sheathed his massive broadsword. He leveled a hard look into Devenshire's eyes, but there was the tiniest glint of mischief in their gray depths. "You heard what I wanted you to hear. I have been tracking you since your last kill." Only the faintest traces of a grin tugged at the corners of his lips as he took in Devenshire's uncomfortable response.

"I see," Devenshire replied uneasily as he realized that nearly half an hour had passed since he had killed the last hare. Could he have been so focused on the hunt that he had missed Zandorth's presence? Or could the incident earlier in the hunt with the mysterious stalker have had his attention preoccupied? Then again, he reflected, Warriors of the Ancient Class were renowned for their stealth.

Zandorth looked down at the four mountain hare carcasses in Devenshire's hand, and nodded slowly. "Impressive. I did not think you had the heart of a hunter."

Devenshire arched one eyebrow and smiled with a tired chuckle.

"Hunger can inspire great feats of skill."

Zandorth nodded again. "True."

The two men began walking toward the fire. As they walked, Devenshire looked up at the rim of the crater and tried to gauge if the glow from the small campfire could be easily seen from the trail below. Following their harrowing escape from Lirpa, they had ridden through the next day and into the evening, trying to put as much distance between them and the city as possible. As the sun had started to set, he had begun looking for landmarks he remembered from earlier treks into this area. They were riding into the Kil'tafore Mountain range, which was a mixed blessing. The rugged terrain meant Captain Armand would have a difficult time making up lost ground, and it would provide ample hiding places should the need arise. It would also slow their progress in their pursuit of Xavier. Ever since they had left Lirpa, Zandorth had tried to locate the Follower's trail, but could not find it. That meant that Xavier had skirted Lirpa and was bearing due north, the shortest route back to the Duval retreat. Devenshire knew that he would have to consult his maps very soon and try to pick the quickest path to intercept him.

As they grew closer to the fire, his eyes came to rest on Shantira, who was seated close to Brianna. Concern flared within him again over what had happened to the young woman. Her behavior since arriving in Lirpa had been strange, to say the least. Brianna had told him how she had forsaken Zandorth's and her own safety to secure Brianna's security at the hands of the Royal Guards. While he knew little about her, what he did know did not lend itself to Shantira being given to bouts of panic. He recalled his first encounter with her when the bandits had her cornered in the woods outside her village. She had been outnumbered and wounded, and had still managed to kill one of the bandits before being captured. The fight with the sheriffs and Royal Guards last night showed her rigid control over her emotions as she had fought with the fervor to rival most men. So what was it about Brianna that made her panic at the softest whisper of danger to her? His unease was heightened by her repeated requests over the past day that they stop to tend to Brianna's wound. At first, they were pleasant, but as she issued each one, they became more and more demanding. He had tried to explain to her that Brianna was fine and that they needed to make as much ground on Armand as possible, but she seemed to only focus on Brianna's needs and safety. Finally, he had to bring Shantira and Brianna together so that Brianna could reassure her that she was fine and could wait until they made camp. At that moment, the insistence ceased, and Shantira returned to her normal behavior. It was odd, to say the least, and would definitely bear keeping an eye on.

He watched in satisfaction as both women looked up at them long before they entered the circle of light from the fire. He also noted that both women had their hands on the hilts of their swords. It would be pure folly, indeed, to make the mistake of trying to sneak up on these two. Brianna regarded the four large hares, and nodded. "I am impressed, Daimion. I did not know that hunting was among your many talents."

Devenshire arched one brow, and smiled seductively at her. "It depends entirely upon what I am hunting." They locked eyes as that silent understanding passed between them. Brianna's lips twisted into a smile, and her eyes sparkled lightly as she knew full well what he had meant.

"Oh by the Fates!" Zandorth exclaimed as he took the carcasses from Devenshire. "Do you two ever stop?"

"Indeed," Shantira agreed. She shifted her gaze to Brianna and Devenshire and felt the now familiar twinge of jealousy flare within her chest. She, like Brianna, had known exactly what Devenshire had meant by his response, and the thought of their intimacy annoyed her more with each passing occurrence. She pointed toward the hares in Zandorth's hand. "I could help you with those." She sorely wanted to make up for her behavior the night before.

Zandorth leveled a hard glare at her. "I can manage." He didn't wait for an answer as he moved off to begin cleaning the hares.

Shantira's face fell in disappointment as she realized that getting back into the Warrior's good graces was going to be more difficult than she had imagined. Brianna reached over with her right hand and patted Shantira on the arm. "Give it time."

Devenshire chuckled tiredly as he laid his bow and quiver of arrows on the ground before lowering himself to an upended log near the fire. "A lot of time."

Shantira pulled her emotions back under control and shifted her gaze to the shadowed area where Zandorth had begun dressing the hares. She put her right elbow on her knee and propped her chin in the palm of her hand. "How long?"

Devenshire shrugged. "It depends. He is a hard man with hard ways. Trust is not something that comes easily with him, and once it is violated, it is twice as difficult to earn back."

Shantira only nodded as she swiveled her eyes back to the shadowed image of the warrior. She remembered every event as clearly as if they had just happened, and at the same time, there was a haze surrounding the memories that was nearly impossible to define. It was as though she had been outside her body watching the events unfold as though she were a spectator and not a participant. Her brow furrowed deeply as she tried to piece together the fragmented ends of her reasoning and make a connection between her actions and why she had performed them.

She suddenly realized that Zandorth was far enough away from the fire to be practically working in the dark. "How is he dressing the hares in the dark?"

Devenshire looked back over his shoulder at Zandorth's silhouette. "Warriors of the Ancient Class are often required to work under less than ideal conditions. That includes performing tasks in near total darkness." He chuckled as he shifted his attention back forward. "I would wager that he will do a much better job dressing out the hares in the dark than any of us could do in full sunlight."

Devenshire leaned forward, resting his elbows on his knees and clasping his hands together in front of him. He lowered his head and closed his eyes, taking a moment to rest and to try to sort through the conglomeration of thoughts running rampant through his mind. How far ahead of Armand were they? How far behind Xavier were they? Who had been stalking him during the hunt? Who was Lordalise, and why was he going to so much effort to make it appear that he was a vampire? Was there a vampire in the area? Who had summoned the demon at the inn? Who was Rachelle Tambrey? Why had she followed them to Lirpa? Why had she gone to the trouble of saving him and healing his wounds only to dismiss him as though he were distasteful to her? Why could he not get her completely out of his mind? Could Xavier tap into the Stones of Andarus? If he could, would he be able to control the uncontrollable? His temples began to throb as he tried to sort through each of the questions that would spin off into other questions. He sighed heavily. He needed to eat and get some rest before trying to sort through the homogenous mess in his mind.

He raised his head and looked across the fire to Brianna. She was tired, nearing exhaustion. Her features were pale and dark crescents hung under her bloodshot eyes. He was used to seeing a bright sparkling light in them, not the dull sheen he saw now. Her clothes were torn and tattered, her hair was splayed out in every direction, and the thick bandage on her left bicep served to remind him of just how hard the last day had been on her. The sword strike had been deep, reaching nearly to the bone. Devenshire had been able to perform a minor healing on the deeper parts of the wound, and Shantira had bound it tightly to help staunch the bleeding, but neither of those things did anything for the pain and loss of blood. While they all bore the ravages of their flight from Lirpa, Brianna had taken the hardest share.

"How are you feeling?" he asked softly.

Brianna smiled tiredly and shook her head. "That is the twelfth time today you have asked me that question."

"Fourteenth, but who is counting?" Devenshire replied with a warm smile.

Brianna chuckled softly. "I am fine."

"You will forgive me if I doubt the sincerity of your answer," Devenshire replied with only a hint of mischief in his voice. "With all due respect, M'Lady, you look like hell."

Brianna sighed heavily as she leaned forward, resting her right elbow on her knee, careful to keep her left arm at her side and still. "I would remind you of what a bastard you are, but I am too tired."

Devenshire chuckled and nodded. "I know, and you would have me no other way."

Brianna smiled wearily as she gazed deep into the heart of the fire. She was mesmerized by the intricate colors and shades of red and yellow as they consumed the logs. The flickering flames danced about the wood, taking pieces of it with each nearly sensual lick. Her mind, through a combination of exhaustion and relaxation, began wandering through the dark, twisted forest of her thoughts. All the questions formed the trees while the mystery of the answers created the gloom, darkness, and chilling apprehension. Who was Lordalise? Why was he going to such great lengths to convince Armand, and anyone else who would listen, that Devenshire was a vampire? How far would the captain of the Royal Guard pursue them? What was behind Shantira's bizarre behavior? Was it the unreleased grief from the destruction of her village or was it something else? This was to say nothing of the purpose of their quest, Xavier and the Stones of Andarus. She knew little to nothing about the Stones, just a few folklore legends really. Were they as powerful as rumor described? Devenshire and Darkseed's reaction to them would indicate that they were. While she knew little about the Stones, she knew absolutely nothing about Xavier. She had heard the tales of him and had tallied the stories up to exaggerated rumors of who was probably nothing more than a common criminal. Again, judging from Devenshire and Darkseed's reactions to him, the rumors were far truer than any tale.

Darkseed presented another mystery and a source of concern for her. He had been so adamant about not helping them beyond their escape from the jail, and yet he had appeared at the most dire moment of their escape. He had made it possible for Devenshire to free himself and unleash a powerful spell that had saved her life. She squeezed her eyes shut to block the malevolent image of Devenshire right before he threw the glowing blue orb of his powers into Armand. She quickly forced her thoughts back to her growing concern over Darkseed. She lifted her weary gaze from the fire to Devenshire who she saw was lost in his own mesmerized gaze into the depths of the fire.

"How long have you known Darkseed?" she asked, trying to make her question seem like idle conversation.

Devenshire's features never shifted nor did his eyes leave the fire. "Most of my life. We grew up together." his lips curled into a mischievous smile and a fond glint ignited within his eyes. "We have been through much."

Brianna nodded as she absently bit her bottom lip, trying to find a way to express her concerns over Darkseed without offending Devenshire. "Do you trust him?"

Devenshire's eyes lifted from the fire and locked deep into hers. He didn't blink, didn't waiver, as he answered. "With my life."

Brianna accepted Devenshire's comment, but it did not alter her own reservations about the man. "How did you meet?" Brianna was not fond of mysteries. They were the one thing that would irritate her like an itch she could not reach to scratch, and in Devenshire, there were more than enough itches that she dearly wanted to scratch. Perhaps, she reasoned, if she learned more about Darkseed, she might learn more about Devenshire.

"We lived in the same village and were drawn toward each other. I cannot honestly remember the exact details surrounding our initial meeting, but we soon formed a fast friendship," he answered with apparent ease as his eyes drifted back to the fire, his mind already making the journey back over time and space to the two dirty, poverty stricken young boys who fought with all their might just to survive one more day. "It was discovered that he and I had the latent abilities of the Mystical Arts. We were sent to a nearby retreat where our abilities could be studied, nurtured, and developed to their fullest potential."

"I have never understood much about the Mystical Arts. Are they something anyone can learn to manipulate?" Shantira asked with genuine curiosity.

Devenshire shook his head. "No, only certain individuals possess the ability. It is something you are born with, something that allows you to harness mystical energies and bend them to your will. Within those that are born with this ability, there are varying levels of skill. Darkseed was discovered to possess a great deal of latent ability, and his skills grew at a very rapid rate, nearly an alarming rate. There were some who feared Darkseed was amassing power without the level of discipline to control it."

"I do not understand. How could he possess the power, and yet not be able to control it?" Shantira asked.

Devenshire glanced up at her. "It takes a great deal of discipline to manipulate mystical energies. It is very similar to handing a sword to a child. They know what a sword is, they know what it can do, but they do not possess the skill to use it properly. A sword, in the hands of a novice, can be a very dangerous thing, even for the person holding it. You see, it is not just a matter of waving your hands and making things happen. There is a balance that must be maintained at all times."

"A balance?" Brianna asked, genuinely interested in the topic now, more so than learning further of Devenshire's mysteries.

He nodded. "Our realm is a magical place. It is held together by, and operates through, an intricate balance of light and dark mystical energies. On one side, you have the light, the Mystical Arts. On the other are the Dark Arts. Light and dark, or good and evil if you will, it takes both. For one to win dominance over the other will spell the end of our realm as we know it."

Shantira's face twisted into a confused expression as she grappled with the concept. "How can it be a bad thing if good wins out over evil?" The gruesome destruction of her village, and all who lived within it, while never far from her mind, shot to the surface with surprising swiftness, tearing open the massive wound of grief within her soul.

Devenshire gazed intently at her. "What is good without evil?"

"It's the domination of evil, it is the eradication of darkness, it is the ultimate victory over the lowly scum that stalk the shadows of our realm and destroy all that is good and pure!" she snapped in reply, struggling against the fresh stab of grief.

"Yes, but without evil, what is good?" he reiterated.

"I do not understand," she replied.

"What happens if evil is eradicated?" Devenshire asked.

"Then only good remains, and there is no longer any need to fear, no longer any need to grieve over losses that should have never occurred in the first place," she replied.

Devenshire nodded. "True, and there is also no longer any struggle, and without struggle, what becomes of us?"

"We would lead very peaceful lives, very safe and secure lives. It would be paradise," she replied with conviction.

"That sounds very nice. No struggle, no strife, and no challenge," Devenshire responded. "Very soon, we simply just exist in our perfect paradise with no challenges to strengthen us. No strife, no confrontations with evil to show us our true natures, no fires of challenge to harden us into the metal of what we are as human beings. No measure of good or evil to warrant who and what we are." He paused to cock his head as he stared at her. "Tell me something, Shantira. What would happen if there were no night?"

Shantira blinked in confusion. "What?"

"What would happen if there were never another sunset?" he repeated, his gaze locked fast to hers, and his expression waiting, expectant.

Shantira had to pause a moment to form an answer. "There would only be day."

He nodded. "Exactly. There are many bad creatures that inhabit the night. Many deeds of evil are executed under the cover of darkness. So doing away with night should prove as beneficial as eliminating evil, correct?"

Shantira stared at him for a moment, wondering where he was going with this train of thought. Reluctantly she finally nodded. "Correct."

"Then, without night, how would you separate one day from the next? How would you know or measure the passing of the seasons? That is to say nothing of the nocturnal creatures, the ones who feed only at night. What is to become of them?"

Shantira's eyes drifted downward as she contemplated his question. "I suppose they would all die away or adapt and learn to hunt during the day," she replied haltingly, unsure of where he was taking her.

"True, some creatures would adapt, but many more would not, could not. Their very design demands they hunt at night. So when these predators die, what becomes of their prey?" he asked.

His train of thought began to dawn within her mind, and she slowly began to understand. "Their numbers would grow, and with no natural predators to control them, they would soon dominate the land," she replied slowly.

Again, he nodded. "Say all serpents vanished. The rat population would quickly grow beyond our ability to control, and they would overrun us, spreading disease and famine in their wake. They would continue to breed, their numbers growing until nothing would remain."

"I think that is a bit over simplified, Daimion," Brianna injected, a touch of reproach in her voice.

"Is it?" he asked earnestly. "True, it is a basic example of the need for balance, but very similar to the need for good and evil. Serpents are considered evil, and they have the reputation of being Satan's pets. Some serpents are venomous, and their bite has killed uncounted people. Yet, for all their evil reputation, they are a vital part of the system that keeps our realm in check. Without them, we would be overrun by all manner of vermin. The same holds true of the mystical energies of this realm. One can never, ever gain dominance over the other, for to do so, would unleash," glancing back at Brianna, "in simpler terms, a wave of rats and vermin that we could never hope to control. Without evil, without the need to struggle against it and try to dominate it, we become soft, meaningless shells that simply eek out an existence from meaningless day to meaningless day." He paused to glance into the fire for a moment, collecting his thoughts. He suddenly smiled as a thought came to mind, and he looked up at both women. "In even simpler terms, if it never rained, what would be so special about a sunny day?"

The camp was silent for several moments save for the crackling of the fire and the music of the night. Shantira and Brianna took the time to consider what Devenshire had said. Neither of them wanted to admit that they would actually need evil, but through Devenshire's explanation, they were forced to do that very thing. It was unsettling, to say the least. Finally, it was Shantira who forged the conversation ahead, wanting to shift away from the disturbing reality she had just been forced to accept. "So you were saying that Darkseed's powers were growing rapidly?"

Devenshire nodded. "He was very skilled. His natural ability within the Arts was unheard of. Many feared that Darkseed's skill would grow faster than his discipline, and that would lead him down the path toward darkness." He knew they would question him, so he forged ahead with the explanation. "Without the discipline to understand how the mystical energies work, and how to keep them aligned, the thirst for more and greater power can lead a practitioner of the arts down the path to dark magic. It is a very thin and treacherous path to navigate, and many have been consumed by the Dark Arts because they lacked the discipline to master their powers instead of allowing their powers to master them. Fortunately, Darkseed possessed an even greater discipline than he did any natural command of the Arts."

"So the Dark Arts are easier to master than the Mystical Arts?" Shantira asked.

Devenshire shook his head. "Not easier exactly. A Dark Mystic can unlock levels of power equal to, or surpassing, the Mystical Arts with a little less discipline than what would be required of the Mystical Arts; however, the cost is their soul. They lose the ability to choose for themselves how and when to manipulate their powers. They become a part of the collective of Dark Magic and have very little free will in what actions they pursue. Their powers drive and dictate them, whereas a practitioner of the Mystical Arts chooses when and where and how to use their powers."

Brianna nodded, absorbing what he had said, realizing that there was much she still needed to learn about the Mystical Arts. She understood the basics, but the deeper meaning of the balance of power eluded her. She decided to switch the subject back to her original path of finding out more about Devenshire. "So what level did you reach?"

Devenshire chuckled and settled his gaze back into the fire. "I achieved only the most rudimentary levels of spell work. I can perform only some basic spells."

Brianna gazed intently at him as he stared into the fire. What she had seen the night before was far more than just an elementary command of the Arts. "Why only the most rudimentary levels?"

Devenshire paused for several moments before answering, as

though he were picking his words carefully. "I lacked discipline. The hours of long study and meditation were tedious to me. I found myself growing restless and impatient. I left the retreat before the completion of my first season of study," he replied with what appeared to be sincere honesty, but Brianna didn't buy it. Not for a second. While there were a great many mysteries surrounding him, and he possessed his share of faults, she knew his core personality and traits. For all of his faults, she knew a lack of discipline was not among them. She had seen, first hand, just how disciplined he could be. Be it in his pursuit of her, or his contest with Krahl or in combat, or dealing with the heart wrenching destruction of Shantira's village, Daimion Devenshire was probably the most disciplined person she knew. No one who kept as tight a yolk of control on his emotions as Devenshire did lacked discipline. She bit her bottom lip again as she studied his flickering features in the firelight. There was another reason behind the abandonment of his studies and, despite his claim of mastering only the most rudimentary levels of power, what she had seen last night spoke of a level of power far beyond rudimentary.

As if feeling her eyes on him, Devenshire raised his head and looked into her eyes. She had the distinct impression he knew what she was thinking and was happy to leave her with that mystery. Of course, she mused, he would.

"What level is Darkseed?" Shantira asked with genuine curiosity.

Devenshire shook his head, shifting his gaze to her. "I am not sure. Had he stayed with the retreat, I am sure he would be an Adept by now."

"What is an Adept?" Shantira asked.

"An Adept is the highest level you can achieve in the Mystical Arts. To find someone with the level of skill and mastery to reach Adept status is exceedingly rare. There are only a small handful of Adept practitioners within the realm. Just when Darkseed seemed destined to be ordained as an Adept, he left the retreat and ventured out on his own."

"Why did he leave the retreat? Why would he not stay and achieve that which he had worked so hard to obtain?" Shantira asked with confusion. It was beyond her why someone would dedicate so much time and energy into obtaining a goal, and then to abandon it when it was so close to being achieved.

Devenshire shrugged with a fond, tight smile creasing his face. "Raven can be a very unpredictable man when he wants to be. I would venture a guess that he wishes to maintain an absolute mastery over his powers instead of letting them master him. He continually seeks out challenges that force him to resolve them without the use of his powers." He smiled warmly. "He told me once that he masters the Arts, not the reverse."

Zandorth strode back into the camp with the four dressed out carcasses and one of them on a spit. Without comment, he began positioning one of the hares over the fire while Shantira retrieved her pack and began digging through her supplies for a few seasonings she had brought.

"Darkseed lacked the courage to face his destiny," Zandorth commented as he worked on fashioning a spit for the next carcass.

Devenshire chuckled. "Of all the things that I can think of to fault Darkseed for, a lack of courage is not one of them."

"The Fates have fashioned a destiny for each of us. A path we are to follow to reach a true understanding of who we are. To shy away from that path is cowardice! It means you lack the courage to face your potential and ultimately yourself," the warrior replied. "You and Darkseed turned away from your paths because you are afraid of what you could become. It was easier to be what you are now which is a hollow shell of what the Fates intended for you."

Devenshire studied Zandorth as he worked. "Who is to say we are not following the path the Fates intended for us? Who is to say that Darkseed and I are not exactly where we are supposed to be, doing what we are supposed to be doing?"

Zandorth shook his head. "Only you can answer those questions, Devenshire. You left your studies because they were too difficult. That is cowardice. Darkseed worked to achieve the ultimate goal and quit before reaching it. He was afraid of claiming that which he sought, he was afraid of the ultimate responsibility that comes with that kind of power. By definition, that is cowardice!" There was no sense of judgment or condemnation from Krahl, simply a statement of the facts, as he perceived them.

Devenshire narrowed his eyes as he studied the Warrior. It was not anger that claimed his thoughts, but a sincere curiosity of a perception that he had thought Krahl incapable of having. While he did not agree with his assessment, Devenshire had to admit that there was more to the warrior than thick muscle and hardened battle skills. Also, judging from the fact that he had heard his conversation with Brianna and Shantira meant he had acuteness to his hearing that was nothing short of amazing.

"That is not fair, Zandorth! Daimion is not a coward. You, yourself, have seen him in combat," Brianna replied tersely.

"There are many forms of cowardice. A man can be a brave and noble warrior and still shy away from his destiny, which is cowardice. There is far more to bravery than fighting with swords. There is a conviction to face your life and take from it all that is granted you by the Fates. Upon your entrance into this realm, you are given nothing. You are naked and helpless, and it is up to you to forge out your destiny, it will not be handed to you," he replied as he began spitting the second hare while Shantira seasoned the first.

"Interesting," Devenshire replied thoughtfully. "I did not realize you were also a philosopher, Zandorth." There was only the smallest hint of humor in his voice.

"Bah! It is not philosophy! It is the cold, hard facts of our existence!" Zandorth scoffed in reply.

Devenshire smiled and nodded. "But you profess a dislike of the Mystical Arts, and yet you are saying that Darkseed and I should have stayed with our studies?"

Again, the warrior commented without ceasing his work. "We each have our destinies, Devenshire. There are those who are destined to be mighty warriors. There are those who are destined to be paltry practitioners of the devil's magic. As you said before, there must be a balance."

Devenshire smiled wider as he recognized Zandorth's baiting carelessly hidden within his words. "I believe it was a paltry practitioner of the devil's magic who saved your stubborn hide last night, was it not?"

Zandorth shifted his gaze to Devenshire and, for a tiny fragment of a second, a thin smile played within his eyes before it was whisked away by the warrior's control and a shrug.

"Such was his destiny."

~*~

"We have been duped," the tracker said as he squatted low and examined the ground.

The sun was passing its high point of the day. Armand, still feeling the heavy effects of whatever damnable magic Devenshire had unleashed upon him, leaned back in the saddle and removed his hat to wipe at the sheen of sweat on his forehead. "What do you mean?"

The tracker and reinforcements from the garrison had made good time and had caught up to Armand's party quickly. The tracker immediately began following the trail. Now his eyes were locked on the ground. He moved about the trail ahead of them, stopping occasionally to kneel down and brush his fingertips lightly through the dirt. He then moved to the rear of the group of Royal Guards and Lordalise's men and began studying the path intently.

"What do you mean, we have been duped?" Armand asked again with more of an edge to his voice. His body ached, his head pounded with a tremendous headache, and his stomach constantly threatened to void its contents violently. His mood was foul and his patience short.

"We have been following a ghost trail," the tracker said as he finally stood upright, abandoning his search.

"What are you saying?" Armand asked hotly.

The tracker moved up through the group to stand beside

Armand's mount. "Somehow they created a false trail to lure us away from their true path. The trail stops here, and there is no trace of it behind us where I saw it earlier."

Armand looked over at Lordalise and could see the tightening lines form on his face. He knew the answer as surely as Armand. "The bastard used his dark powers to conjure a false trail. Damn!"

The tracker locked eyes with Armand and simply looked at him. Magic was outside his realm of expertise. He was a tracker, not a sorcerer. "What are we to do now?" he asked.

"The only thing we can do. We return to the clearing where we started and try to pick up their true trail," Lordalise answered. He shook his head in frustration. "This will put us even further behind them!"

"A moment, Lordalise," Armand said as he took a moment to consider his thoughts. He had been so preoccupied with the after-effects of Devenshire's spell and the emotions running rampant through him at the death of Constable Liston that he had not been thinking like a soldier. Something the Lady Standish had said the night before suddenly rang out in his mind. He had told Krahl and Brianna that they would need to wait in the jail with the other guests of the inn. Krahl had appeared to resist, and Armand had feared he would have to use more stringent means in order to secure their cooperation. Then Standish had stepped up beside the warrior, saying, *"Very well. We will go. Please do not detain us long. We have urgent business to the north and cannot be delayed for long."*

"North," Armand whispered.

"What?" Lordalise asked.

"They were heading north. The clearing where we lost them was north of the city, and the false trail is leading us to the southeast," Armand mumbled as he began forcing the pieces of the answer together through the wrecked ruins of what he felt was his brain. "Of course!"

"What are you talking about?" Lordalise asked.

"You have to think like them! They were heading north. They used a spell to lure us in almost the opposite direction. Damn! If I had not been so preoccupied with other matters, I would have seen this ruse from the beginning! Very clever!"

Lordalise nodded as his mind locked on to the same train of thought Armand's had. "Of course. They are heading north. They would almost have to be heading into the Kil'tafore Mountains. There would be ample places for Devenshire to hide from the light of day. So obvious, and we missed it!"

Armand placed his hat back on his head and shifted his eyes to the tracker. "Find us the most direct route north toward the Kil'tafore Mountain range. I suspect we will pick up their trail there."

The tracker nodded as he moved toward his mount.

Armand looked at Lordalise. "The bastard is resourceful, I will give him that."

Lordalise nodded as he gathered his reins. "He has had many more seasons upon this realm than us. He has had much more time to hone his wits. We will have to proceed very carefully and very diligently. Mistakes such as this one could be costly and very deadly."

CHAPTER FIVE

The man struggled violently, valiantly trying to save himself from a fate that was set the moment his throat had been punctured. Hot blood pulsed from the dual puncture wounds and down Darius' throat. It was hot and rich and the man's fear only added to the intoxicating effects of drawing it deep into his being. A strangled gasp rattled up from the man's throat as his struggles began to subside. Even now, in the fleeting moments of consciousness, he tried to understand what was happening to him, even though he was fully aware that he was dying. The fear clouded his mind, made his perceptions alter into a more primitive state. It was very much like the panicked struggles of a deer in the powerful jaws of a lion. It knew on a basic level that it was pointless to struggle, that it was already dead, but it continued to struggle, to fight to live.

As the man's blood filled his cheeks, Thiberian swallowed and felt the sharp jolt to his perceptions. His limbs, which were nearly numb, suddenly tingled with wave after wave of sensations. It was painful, much like a limb waking after having fallen asleep, but the pain was welcomed as it filled the void left by the numbness. His mind swirled in a myriad of colors, which were in sharp contrast to the constant monotone perceptions of black and white that made up his existence. The most pleasant aspect to feeding came as the eternal chill that surrounded him was displaced momentarily. It called to him of a time when he walked in the sunshine and the warmth that cascaded around him. Along with the rich, deep colors that suddenly flooded his mind, there was a dizzying remoteness to his perceptions, as though he were drunk. Unlike the pitiful state that mortals called intoxication, this was much, much more. It was far deeper, far more enriching, far more meaningful, and far more fulfilling than any simple drunken state. This was the wine of the Fates, and damn them, he was going to drink his fill!

He could feel the man's heartbeat begin to slow and he knew he would have to release him soon. At the moment he had sank his fangs deep into the man's throat, he had become connected to his victim. He could feel his rapid heartbeat as clearly as if it were his own long dead heart. He could feel the man's fear, could touch his memories, and knew all that the man knew. It was very erotic, more so than any pitiful, clumsy joining of a man and woman. Sex among mortals was a clumsy, almost humorous slapping of bodies in comparison to the erogenous act of feeding. There was no climax known to mortals as fulfilling as what he felt at this moment, at the threshold between life and death.

The man's grip on his shoulders loosened and then released as he lost consciousness. Thiberian continued to draw the last of his victim's lifeblood deep into his throat. The man's heartbeat slowed and then began to flutter. Death was here! It was at this moment that all the sensations swelled up to sweep him away in a torrent of rich color, deep warmth, an intoxicating heightening of his perceptions, and a sexual experience that no mortal could ever hope to understand, let alone experience.

As the man's heart twitched its last beat, he violently threw his head back. His eyes were closed, his bloody mouth agape in a long, slow growling sigh of deep satisfaction on countless levels. He let the dead weight of the corpse drop from his grip as he continued to bask in the swirling, drunken, erogenous afterglow. He did not move, did not think. He just existed in this delicious moment that was going to leave him all too soon. He cracked his ice blue eyes open and took in the swollen orb of the full moon far overhead. He was one with the moon, with the night, with the hell-spawned powers that made his existence possible. He felt no guilt or remorse for the death of the man at his feet; in fact, the man was now nothing more than something that would need to be stepped over to prevent himself from tripping. At the moment the man had died, he had ceased to be anything more than just another piece of his surroundings. The power was coursing through him with heated intensity. His body felt alive, his mind thought in color again, the realm seemed to realign itself to his whim. Even after the long span of time since accepting the Dark Gift, he still could not articulate what it was like to feed, and he was amazed by the act each time. He simply stood bathed in the pale glow of moonlight and breathed heavily, his lungs drawing in air that he did not need. The act of breathing heavily in the wake of such an intense experience was a remnant of his time as a mortal.

Slowly, the rush of sensations began to fade and he lowered his head, closing his eyes again as he sought to savor every last moment of the feelings. The rich colors within his mind muted to grayish hues of black and white. The deep intoxication slid from his mind, and his limbs began to grow numb again. The warmth, which seemed to permeate every fiber of his being, began to bleed away, drawn from him by the chill of the night, the realm of his existence. As the last sensation flittered from him, he sighed slowly, almost sadly. He opened his eyes as he reached up to wipe the blood from his chin. He began a slow pace around the chilling corpse as he licked the blood from his fingers.

While the pleasurable sensations of feeding had faded, he could feel his powers begin to swell. The one long lingering by-product of feeding was the boost to his powers. He felt strong, powerful, and far more aware than he had ever been as a mortal. In a remote part of his mind, he actually felt a tiny stab of pity for the mortals. Their consciousness, their level of awareness was so far below his. They could not even begin to fathom the power he possessed, the clarity of his thoughts and emotions, the purest form of connection with the realm. They scurried around their short, pointless, meaningless lives, and then, in an instant, they were gone, whisked away to be nothing more than a fading memory in another mortal's limited mind. They never knew the level of awareness he enjoyed. They never knew what it was like to be as connected to the realm as he was, especially in this moment after feeding. He wasn't just a being in the night... he was a part of the night. It flowed through him as easily as he flowed through it. They were one and the same, forever connected at a level very few beings ever understood.

He paused as he looked down at the body. Normally, he would have called upon the other creatures of the night to devour the body, to hide all traces of his having fed. On this night, however, he wanted his feeding to be known. With a dark grin, he knew that when the body was found, the blame for the man's death would be laid at the feet of another. It was as though he had been given free rein to feed to his dead heart's content.

As enjoyable as it was that another would be held responsible for what the mortals perceived as his crimes, he knew he would have to take care for the man who would be blamed was traveling with her, and no harm must come to her in their attempts to capture the mortal. A dark chuckle rattled his throat as he savored the irony of the situation. He could not have devised a better scenario than the one the Hunter had provided him. The Hunter had convinced the Royal Guard that the one known as Devenshire was a vampire. The incident with Devenshire in the inn with the demon was connected to the dark magic that had first brought him to the ruins of the village the night before. The Hunter was angered over the death of one of his men. The fool who had dared lay hands on Sienna, or Brianna, as they knew her, and swiftly paid for his insolence! The Hunter, in his thirst for vengeance, had locked onto the easiest target, and thereby handed him with a night of consequence free feeding. The blood from the whore and the Constable had been enriching and quite enjoyable, especially the Constable's. His secrets were the darkest, and therefore, the most delicious.

There was still one more victim for the sheriff's of Lirpa to discover and to blame Devenshire. Once he had fed off the Constable, he had made his way to the Constable's dwelling and found the young village girl he had purchased bound and naked in the cellar.

He had tormented her until her fear was palpable, nearly a physical thing in the air. He had taken her and her fear-laden blood had been quite intoxicating. He had fed more in the past two nights than he had in the last several months. He would have to be careful to not allow himself to grow dependent on such frequent feedings. Such dependence would force him into making a mistake that would bring the Hunters down upon him. It was not that he feared the Hunters, but he simply had better things to do with his time than search for ways to avoid them. They could destroy him, and in that measure, he would give them a wide berth, but in the end, they were mortals.

As he began walking toward the area he knew Sienna was in, he began pondering other problems, situations that posed a definite threat to his plans. For starters, there was another vampire nearby. He had felt their presence that night upon the trail when the bandits had attacked, and he had felt their presence again last night. He had sought to find the other one and gauge the level of threat they would be to him. It had been this search that had prevented him from being there when the soldiers had captured Sienna's group and wounded her in the process. He cursed himself for not being there when she needed him, but he had to know what the other vampire's purpose was.

Through his link with the village girl, he had seen how Devenshire had saved Sienna and then tended her wound. It was hard to discern the facts through the horribly muddled, nearly primitive thought processes of the girl. The grief at the destruction of her village, as well as her dawning feelings for Devenshire, made her mind a convoluted quagmire of racing random thoughts and conflicting emotions. She cared deeply for Sienna, or Brianna, which made the suggestions he had planted deep into her mind easy for him to manipulate. It was far easier to control someone when what he wanted them to do was something they were prone to do in the first place. There were certain thoughts within her mind that angered him. There was something between Sienna and Devenshire. Something linked to matters of the heart or something along those lines. It was hard to discern the truth of the situation through the unorganized thoughts within the girl's mind. If Devenshire were romantically linked with Brianna, it would prove detrimental to him. While he was grateful to Devenshire for saving Sienna's life, any emotional involvement with her secured him a terrifyingly painful death.

It was still awkward calling her Brianna. He knew her as Sienna, the name she had carried when she had been his. Through the enormous span of time since his acceptance of the Dark Gift, she had drifted into and out of his existence many times, each time as a different woman with a different name, but at her core, she was still Sienna.

Another thought came to him. The dark energies that had first caught his attention were directly tied with the quest that Sienna and her group were involved. He knew that the mortals with her were not capable of standing against this dark, evil force. Though it was galling to him, he had to admit that he wasn't sure he could stand against such power. While his sole focus was on Sienna, he had to be constantly conscious of the entity they were following. He could not gauge if this entity was something he should welcome or be prepared to destroy, and he knew he dared not act out of impulse... in either dealing with reclaiming Sienna or with this entity. He would have to learn more.

He walked easily through the darkness, letting his senses guide him through the pitch-blackness of the forest. He sought out the link with the village girl through the tides of dark power. He found her and subtly probed for information. During the daylight hours, he could not manipulate her thoughts with any degree of accuracy, but once night fell, and his powers returned, he could know what the girl knew and guide her thoughts. He was immediately surprised by how far ahead of him they were. They had made respectable distance since the night before, and he would be hard pressed to catch up to them by sunrise. He knew he would have to take to the air to make up the distance. He was just beginning to draw his powers about him to alter his form when he felt the presence of the other one like him. It was a fleeting, whispery impression at the edges of his perceptions, but it was there... they were there.

He considered going after them, but he had lost nearly half of the night before in the chase. It was a trait of the vampire, to know when kindred were near. It served as welcome and warning. Whoever they were, they had eluded him easily while staying just outside his mental reach. He could not tell if they were male or female, how long they had possessed the Dark Gift, or their level of power. The fact that they could easily evade him spoke of a considerable skill... or luck. He paused for a moment, gathering his mental energies to cast his thoughts upon the dark tides.

Who are you?

There was no response, not that he had expected one. If they had responded, he would have been better able to find them. He knew he had broadcast his position by sending out the thought, and he hoped that they would come for him. He paused to study the teasing, ghostly impression their essence left on the very edge of his perceptions, hoping they would strengthen as they approached. To his frustration, they vanished from his awareness, stepping beyond his ability to detect. He scowled as he began calling on the power to alter his form. He did not like being treated as a plaything, and this other kindred was toying with him very much like a cat with a mouse. As he took to the night air, he swore that the cat would learn a very deadly lesson on how foolish it was to underestimate the mouse.

CHAPTER SIX

The aroma of cooking meat filled the small crater campsite and soon stomachs began to rumble as the smell rousted latent, long ignored hunger. The first hare vanished quickly as they ate with the urgency born of a hunger none of them realized they possessed. It was the first meal any of them had had in almost two days. As the first hare was being consumed, the third was spitted next to the second one and seasoned with the herbs and spices Shantira had the forethought to bring. Devenshire had rounded up their water pouches and filled them with fresh water while the first hare had been cooking. He had filled tins with water and passed them around the group, but Brianna had trumped his fresh water with a bottle of whiskey from the stores of her keep. The tins of water were quickly emptied in favor of the liquor. With food and drink at hand, the group lapsed into the silence that hunger driven feasting often spawns.

Well into the second hare, Zandorth looked up from his meal to address Devenshire, his lips and fingers glistening in the light of the campfire from the grease of his meal. "We should be alert for scavengers. They will be coming soon."

Devenshire nodded in agreement, as he chewed a mouthful of meat. He shifted the mouthful to one side so that he could answer. "If we leave the innards, hides, and bones far enough outside the campsite, perhaps that will discourage them from coming any closer."

Zandorth swallowed a mouthful of meat before adding, "That would depend upon the scavenger."

"What kind of scavengers?" Shantira asked carefully.

Devenshire shrugged as he took a sip from his tin. "Rodents mainly, but there are also meat snakes and the wild dogs of the lower mountain ranges."

"Meat snakes?" she asked with the subtle revulsion most people feel toward snakes.

Devenshire nodded as he nonchalantly took another bite from his hunk of roasted meat. The bite was small enough to allow him to answer her as he chewed. "Yes, large reptiles capable of swallowing a full grown mountain hare whole."

"Poisonous?" she asked.

"Very much so," Zandorth injected. "A bite from a meat snake can kill in seconds."

Shantira suddenly lost the look of comfort that had come over her as she had begun to eat and take in the apparent peacefulness of the night. Despite her best efforts, she began studying the ground around her.

Devenshire's eyes began to gleam as he secretly winked at Zandorth. "But I would not worry too much about the snakes. The mud beetles would probably finish you off before the meat snakes could even get close enough to bite you."

"Mud... mud beetles?" Shantira asked, forcing a front of indifference to the surface.

"They travel in groups of thousands, and I have seen them fell and consume a large cow in a matter of minutes. They burrow under the ground with amazing speed, and it is said they can smell a potential meal from many feet underground. Very efficient hunters," Zandorth injected, his lips twitching under the hidden smile.

"Efficient and intelligent. I have heard tell that they will swarm their prey and bite it just enough to kill it or paralyze it, then withdraw and wait for another scavenger to approach only to attack the scavenger and enjoy two meals," Devenshire added.

Shantira was nearly to the point of standing up upon the log on which she sat. The mental images racing through her mind were scaring her to the edge of panic.

"But they only hunt down and eat bastards!" Brianna finally said, casting a disapproving look at Devenshire and Zandorth. "Stop scaring her!"

Shantira looked up at the two men only to realize, by their poorly hidden smiles, that she had, unknowingly, supplied them with the evening's entertainment.

"The meat snake?" she asked Brianna.

"They are poisonous and, like most snakes, are more afraid of you than you are of it. It will not come close to humans and will not attack unless cornered. They do not slither into human camps and attack sleeping victims," she answered fixing the men with a stern look.

With a dawning realization just how blindly she had fallen for their baiting, Shantira shot stern glares at both men before rising and stalking away from the fire.

"Do not forget about the dogs!" Devenshire called out, finally falling into a hearty laugh. Zandorth chuckled and shook his head as he resumed his meal, careful to avoid the harsh look on Brianna's face.

"Be silent, Daimion!" she hissed. Only after Shantira was far enough away did Brianna smile and shake her head at Devenshire. "You are such a bastard!" she said only loud enough for him to hear.

"I was not alone in the jest," he replied looking over at Zandorth. The warrior simply shook his head and continued to eat.

Brianna sighed in irritation. "Men!" she spat as she sat her plate aside and rose to go comfort Shantira. After she had gone, Devenshire looked at Zandorth who had been watching Brianna walk away. He turned his gaze to Devenshire's and both men shrugged in unison before looking down at their food, hiding smiles that would no doubt enrage the women only more.

After a while, the women returned to the fire and the meal. Shantira was more than obviously angry at having been the brunt of the men's sense of humor. Brianna glared at them, daring them with her expression to even think of saying anything else to the younger woman.

Finally, Devenshire cleared his throat and eased forward. "I apologize, Shantira. We meant no harm. Just releasing a little of the tension from last night."

"There is no need to apologize. I knew very quickly what the two of you were doing," she lied, her voice still tight and her tones clipped in anger.

"I see," he replied as he smiled and eased back to lean against the log he was sitting against. "Just the same, I wished for you to know that we were not attempting to make fun of you."

"I know," she almost snapped in reply. "Let us speak no more of it!"

Devenshire hid his smile, and nodded. "As you wish."

Silence reined over the meal once more as they resumed eating. Soon, the second hare was nothing but a pile of clean picked bones, and the fourth carcass was spitted and set over the fire.

Suddenly, Devenshire bolted upright, his eyes alert and looking off into the darkness. He quickly set his plate aside and climbed to his feet as his right hand slowly drifted toward his sword. Almost as suddenly, Zandorth leapt to his feet as well. The women looked up in startled surprise at the sudden movement, and their eyes looked from one man to the other and finally off into the darkness.

"What is it?" Brianna asked, her hand reaching up toward the hilt of her sword.

Devenshire was frozen, his body rigid, and his gaze delving deep into the darkness. For a moment, his eyes drooped, as though they were about to close and then they opened fully again. He smiled, nodded once, and seemed to relax. "It is Darkseed. He has returned and is accompanied by four others."

"Four?" Zandorth asked. His tone was one of a warrior confirming the number of opponents facing him.

"Relax, Zandorth. They are with Darkseed, I doubt they have evil intentions," Devenshire replied.

Zandorth snorted. "I will be the judge of their intentions!" He sat his plate down, wiping his hand on his breaches before letting it drift near his sword. Brianna and Shantira rose as well.

Devenshire ignored their unease as five shadows appeared and gradually solidified into human forms as they drew near the camp. Darkseed was in the lead as they stepped further into the light of the fire. The four individuals behind him were in dark cloaks with the hoods drawn, casting their features into darkness. Even though the cloaks were drawn completely around them, Devenshire could see that they were small of stature.

"It is customary to announce yourself before entering someone's camp," Devenshire said with a broad smile across his face.

"Why announce my approach when you knew of it in advance?" Darkseed asked as his eyes found the meat roasting over the fire. "The meal smells delicious, my compliments to the cook."

"The smell is almost all that you had to enjoy!" Zandorth grumbled.

Darkseed regarded the Warrior with an arched eyebrow before turning to Devenshire. "Is he always this much fun?"

Devenshire chuckled. "Most of the time."

"Who are they?" Zandorth asked in a stern voice, jerking his chin toward the cloaked figures behind Darkseed.

"Ah. Allow me to introduce the newest members of our little expedition," Darkseed replied as he turned halfway around and raised his arm to invite one of the figures to step forward. Although Devenshire was sure the figure could not see the gesture through the hood of its cloak, it stepped forward and raised its hands up to draw the hood back. "This is Arness," Darkseed introduced.

The man was much shorter than Darkseed and his face was delicate in appearance save for the sky blue of his eyes, which spoke of a wisdom, and clarity of perception, that should not be underestimated. The thick mane of blond hair was pulled back and tied at the nape of the neck, revealing his ears that instantly identified his race and the explanation for his small build and almost feminine features. The ears swept elegantly upward to a point. Arness was an elf.

"Elven." Devenshire stated.

Arness turned his intent gaze to Devenshire and something akin to subdued mock amazement flashed through his eyes as he slowly nodded. "Very observant," he said in light tones.

Devenshire arched an eyebrow at Arness' sarcasm, but let it pass for the moment. He nodded by way of greeting. "I meant no offense. I was not aware that there were any elves still in this region. I had heard that you had all left for the higher mountain ranges across the great ocean."

"There was no offense taken. My presence here obviously proves that there are, indeed, still elves in this region," Arness answered with another layer of sarcasm in his voice.

"Allow me to introduce the others," Darkseed injected, wishing to cut off Devenshire's building retort. The second figure stepped forward and drew his hood back revealing jet-black hair and deeper blue eyes. As with Arness, the hair was very long, and pulled back and tied.

"This is Petera."

"I am also Elven," he said as he looked up at Devenshire, a faint smile shadowed at the corners of his lips. There was sarcasm in his bearing, but it spoke of good-natured sarcasm and a deep sense of humor, a stark contrast to the rigid sense of superiority in Arness.

"This is Stant," Darkseed said as the third figure stepped forward and withdrew his hood. Stant was older than Arness and Petera for his black hair was streaked with gray, and the lines around his eyes and mouth were deeper. There was a sense of strength and wisdom in his hazel eyes, of having a far deeper well of experience to draw from than his companions had. He could very easily have been the leader of this small band of elves, but he was one that chose not to lead, but follow and use the freedom of following to observe and learn all that he could. As his eyes looked Devenshire over from head to foot, he could almost feel the man's eyes soak in and memorize every detail. Devenshire could not shake the feeling that the older eyes saw far more than just his outward appearance.

"My pleasure," Stant said in rich mellow tones, smiling warmly at the group.

"And this is Kendra," Darkseed finished, and the fourth figure stepped up and drew back the hood. Devenshire was instantly taken with the beauty of the Elven female. Her hair was a rich golden blonde and shone with a luster that caught even the faintest light and reflected it back with brilliance. Her blue eyes flickered from person to person around the group before coming to rest on Devenshire. With a slow blink, she studied him intently, and he could not miss the mixture of seductive amusement in their depths.

She nodded slowly with an obvious appreciation of his form layered thickly in her expression. "My pleasure, I am sure."

She moved with a grace that rivaled the most graceful of women, and her build was proportioned to add both strength and sensuality to her form. She was lithe and sensual while also being strong and sturdy. The startling contrasts in just her form and appearance piqued Devenshire's curiosity on many levels. As if sensing his appraisal of her, Kendra smiled a crooked knowing smile and cocked her head to one side.

"I am Daimion Devenshire," he said, tearing his attention from Kendra and forcing it to introducing the others. "This is Zandorth Krahl."

"A Warrior of the Ancient Class. I am impressed," Arness commented as he bowed low. There was no trace of sarcasm in his words as there had been in his brief exchange with Devenshire.

"Why?" Zandorth asked cautiously.

"Warriors of the Ancient Class are known for their honor. For you to be a part of this expedition speaks not only of its urgent nature but of its value in pursuit," Arness answered. "I have had the honor of entering battle with other Warriors of the Ancient Class and they were the most honorable of men I have ever met."

Zandorth gave no visible reaction to Arness' praise. Then again, Devenshire reflected, he would not. Warriors took praise in the same vein as criticism. They were words only, and words were all but meaningless to a Warrior.

"This is Shantira Dubris," Devenshire continued, and the elves greeted her with the same bow of greeting that was customary of their race. There was no sense of submission in their bows, only the ancient ritual movements of their ancestors.

"And this is The Lady Brianna Standish," Devenshire completed the introductions.

Brianna smiled her most charming of smiles and returned the elves bow with the same elegance as they had bowed to her. Devenshire was surprised to see the bow executed with such grace. Then again, he reflected, the diplomatic demands of her office would require no less.

"You are the daughter of Lord Trenton Standish of Prothtow Province?" Stant asked.

"Yes," she replied pleasantly.

A very fond smile graced his features. "I had the privilege of serving with General Standish during The Goblin Wars. He was a fierce warrior, a good man, and a true comrade."

"Father rarely spoke of the War, but when he did, he spoke very highly of the elves he had served with," Brianna replied pleasantly before glancing down at the fire. Devenshire caught the subtle shift of her gaze and shifted his attention to her. Brianna was not the type of woman to avert her eyes from anyone for any reason. It was a tiny peculiarity, but one that was glaring to someone who knew her as well as he did. He silently acknowledged that her father was not an entirely pleasant topic for her. A new layer of her had just been revealed.

"How is Lord Standish? I have not seen nor heard from him in many seasons," Stant asked, his face beaming with fond memories.

Brianna's face became unreadable as she paused for only a moment before answering. "Father died four seasons ago."

Stant's expression shifted into remorse as he slowly nodded. "My deepest condolences, M'Lady. The realm has lost a true hero with his passing."

She smiled tightly and nodded, accepting Stant's remorse. Devenshire studied her even more closely, the sense of reluctant dread he had previously sensed in her seeming to double in intensity. Was it her father's passing that disturbed her or her father in general? Interesting, to say the least. It dawned on him that he had never heard her speak of her father, or her mother for that matter. It was an element to her that he had never considered before, and her subdued reactions to the reference to her father spoke of another aspect of her he knew nothing about.

"Be welcomed," Devenshire said in conclusion to the introductions.

"Raven tells us that you are facing a great battle and are in need of skilled warriors," Arness said as he moved into the circle of logs around the fire and sat down. The others followed him and seated themselves, as well.

"Yes. We are in pursuit of an evil man with even more evil intentions," Devenshire replied as he sat down across from Arness, and he could not help but notice, next to Kendra. He had not planned to position himself next to her, but he did not find the prospect displeasing.

Stant chuckled. "All men are evil to one extent or another and the evilness of their intentions is directly related to their own level of evilness."

"Granted," Devenshire acknowledged. "But this man is possessed of the deepest levels of evil, and therefore, so are his intentions."

"Who is this man?" Arness asked.

"Xavier," Devenshire answered as a matter of fact.

He did not miss the veiled look that passed among the elves as dark recognition clouded each of their eyes.

"THE Xavier? Founder of the Followers?" Petera asked.

"The same," Devenshire answered.

"I was not aware that his sphere of evil influence had expanded this far south of his realm," Kendra said.

"It has," Shantira answered bitterly. "Three nights ago he attacked my village and destroyed it along with all who lived there. Men, women and children were hacked down and mutilated in a fashion not even the most vicious of predators would be guilty of."

"For what purpose?" Arness asked, stunned by the venom in her voice.

"To satisfy his twisted blood lust! His sick desire to kill for the sheer pleasure of killing and looting. What he sought to take would have been given to him without a single drop of blood being spilled!" Shantira spat

"What did he take? What was worth such a needless slaughter?" Petera asked, taken aback at the horrible brutality that had left its imprint on the young woman.

"The Stones of Andarus," Devenshire answered, hoping to spare

Shantira any further description of the horrors that would haunt her until her last day upon the realm.

The four elves looked up at Devenshire with blank looks that clearly said they had no idea what he was talking about. "What are they?" Kendra asked.

"I have to admit, Daimion, I have heard of them, but I do not know anything of the legend surrounding them," Brianna added.

Devenshire looked at Darkseed, seeking his friend's counsel in exactly what to tell them. Darkseed held his gaze for a moment before he finally shrugged. "They should know what we face," he said.

Devenshire nodded in agreement, as he took a moment to collect his thoughts and relay the story of the Stones. He bent over and picked up his tin cup, draining the last of the whiskey from it before cupping it between his hands. He leaned forward, resting his knees on his elbows, gazing deeply into the fire as if drawing strength to tell a tale that he would sooner not repeat. "Nearly four hundred seasons ago, there was a great Sorcerer named Andarus. It was said that there had never been a practitioner of the Mystical Arts with Andarus' level of skill before or since. It is said that Andarus did more to advance the study of the Mystical Arts than any practitioner in history. All that changed, however, when his wife and child were smitten with a strange ailment. Once it became clear to him that whatever ailed them was beyond his abilities to cure, he had summoned healers from far and wide, but none of them could do anything to cure them or even put a name to their sickness. Andarus searched through every mystic scroll and tome, searching frantically for a cure, but could find none. He traveled through both the physical and mystical realms in search of information and a cure, but again, he could find nothing. After his wife and child died from their illness, it is said that Andarus went insane with grief. He was consumed with finding a way to return them to him, to bring them back from the Afterlife."

"Such a thing is not possible. It is blasphemy against the Fates to even think of such a thing, let alone try it," Kendra injected.

Devenshire nodded. "Such concerns were lost to Andarus. Nothing else mattered save for the resurrection of his family. He made many attempts to bring them back to the living. He researched spell after spell, incantation after incantation, and each attempt failed. He studied every tome and scroll he could find on the subject. Each one would leave him drunk with the promise of success and each failure only sunk him further into the grip of grief and madness. During one attempt, it is said that he was able to tap into the mystical energies of the Great Beyond, the home of the Fates. It is said that the very power that formed our world and spawned the first life came from there. It is said that no human can handle exposure to the pure, raw mystical energies of the Great Beyond, and any who tries will quickly be absorbed back into where life first began, leaving a crumbling empty shell behind. Indeed, that first contact with the Great Beyond nearly killed Andarus. He was discovered in his chambers, nearly dead, and he had aged many seasons in mere moments.

"It took over a season for Andarus to recover enough to leave his bed. It was said that although he recovered most of his physical strength and mystical powers, his mind was never the same again. His focus became harnessing just some of the power he had encountered within the Great Beyond. He abandoned all other pursuits in favor of ongoing study and mediation on how to safely breach the Great Beyond. He was literally trying to find a way to harness the power of creation." Devenshire paused and fixed each person with a look that he hoped drove to their cores just what Andarus had been attempting.

Each person was silent as each contemplated just what Andarus had been trying to accomplish. Finally, it was Stant who found his voice. "He was beyond mad."

Darkseed nodded. "That is what the legends say. That he had somehow managed to survive contact with the Great Beyond, and what he saw and felt in that brief touch left him changed in more ways than just physical appearance. At the time of his first contact with the powers, he had been in his thirtieth season, mere moments later he had the appearance of a man in his sixtieth season. Many other sorcerers and wizards tried to reverse the effects, but the touch of the powers of the Great Beyond could not be negated nor reversed."

"By the Fates…" Kendra whispered, not believing, or wanting to believe, that someone would dare think one could ever hope to accomplish such a thing. "Was he truly trying to capture the power of creation?" Kendra asked softly, not believing, or not wanting to believe, that someone would dare to think that one could even hope to accomplish such a thing.

Devenshire nodded as he rose from his log and crossed to where Brianna sat with the bottle of whiskey. He continued his story as he set about uncorking the bottle and pouring a healthy amount into his tin. "Yes. Legend says that during his study of a very ancient scroll of spells, he happened across one that was said to hold the power to eradicate all forms of illness. It is unclear if the ancient spell was one that allowed access to the Great Beyond, or if some error in Andarus' casting of it lead to his encounter. But what he found there spoke of the promise of the ability to not only destroy the illness but to return life to the dead bodies of his wife and child. Not the mindless re-animation of a corpse, but a return of the true life force that had originally inhabited their forms." Devenshire re-corked the bottle and handed it back to Brianna with a brief smile and a quick nod. He took a sip from the tin before returning to his story.

"If Andarus had gone mad, he had not lost his mental capacity for some rational thought for he knew he could not survive another direct encounter with the massive expanse of unlimited power within the Great Beyond. So he turned his efforts to finding some way to harness just a small fraction of that power, containing it so that he could deal with the power on a smaller, more easily manageable scale.

"Many seasons passed, and with the passing of each one, more and more of Andarus' reason passed with them. Each experimental harnessing spell met with utter failure, and each failure maddened him even further. He withdrew further and further into himself and his studies. His circle of friends dwindled, his appearances outside his tower shrank in number, and it was soon that many people thought he had died since he had not been seen in many months. Some say that Andarus died the day he first touched the power of the Great Beyond and that some evil spirit inhabited his body within the heartbeats' span of time between life and death. Others say that the Fates were outraged at his attempt and cursed him with a madness that no power of this realm could reverse," he concluded as he slowly walked back to the log he had been sitting on.

Solemnly, Darkseed added, "There are even legends that say that Andarus was a man evil of heart, and he had always walked the dark path, seeking to use the Mystical Arts as a means to his ends."

"Tis true. There are many different tales concerning just what kind of man Andarus was. His true bearing and demeanor are forever lost in the mists of time," Devenshire amended as he settled back down on his seat.

"So what became of him?" Brianna asked.

Again, Devenshire and Darkseed exchanged dark glances of a knowledge that weighed heavily upon them and revulsion at having to impart such dark knowledge upon others.

Finally, it was Devenshire who continued the tale. "Andarus grew desperate for the flow of the river of life was sweeping him toward his own end, an event hastened by his advanced aging from that initial contact with the Great Beyond. With each passing season, more and more of his great power faded, his spells dwindled in strength, and each spell took longer for him to recover. He knew his time was fading rapidly, and soon he would lack the power to breach into the Great Beyond and the pure mystical power that taunted him in his fevered slumber... on the rare occasion that he was said to have slept.

"From this point, the legends branch off into nearly countless directions. There are so many different variations on what happened next that the true tale might never be known. What I tell now is the most common and most widely believed version of what transpired on a dark night nearly four hundred seasons ago." Devenshire paused and took a deep breath as his eyes glazed over and looked deep into the campfire once again, as if he could span the distance of time and see the truth of what had happened next.

"Andarus had learned of a form of crystal that was rumored to contain great mystical properties. It was said that these crystals could absorb and hold great amounts of mystical energy, to act as a depository of magical powers. Of course, it has never been proven that these crystals truly existed then or now, but it is said that Andarus had found their location. He had traveled to a very distant land on a quest to find them, and he was gone for nearly two seasons. Most people believed he had succumbed to his advanced age, others believed he had become lost in a distant land and lived out his life still searching for the answer to the question that had driven him mad. However, he returned, looking even older, yet his eyes burning with the fire of victory. Legend also speaks of how his eyes no longer bore any trace of sane thought within his mind or soul, that the madness had finally claimed him completely.

"He returned with a canvas bag containing three beautiful pieces of crystal. Very few saw them, but those who did say that the crystals beauty was beyond description, that they seemed to draw in light and reflected back the beautiful colors of a rainbow that no rain filled sky could ever hope to duplicate. It was said that simply looking deep into the crystals left one feeling as if they had touched an essence of such purity that left them feeling unworthy of existence.

"Andarus retreated back into his tower and sealed himself inside. What he did in those final days is unknown, but several nights after his return a terrible storm tore across the land. Hard driving rain, fierce winds, and blinding bolts of lightning that seemed to tear the very fabric of the sky, were accompanied by growling, rumbling thunder that shook the earth to its core. The ground shook with furry, to the point that buildings and mountains alike collapsed. Massive wind devils twisted from the sky to tear swaths across the lands that remain to this day. There had never been a storm like it before, nor has there been one like it since. Legend says that the crystals had been the property of the Fates, and once they had discovered their theft, they unleashed their fury in the form of the storm. The wind devils were said to be sentinels of the Fates, scouring the land in search of the stolen crystals.

"The legends speak of the storm seeming to stop and form itself around Andarus' tower. Lightning bolts struck the stone and mortar, blasting out chunks of it that landed miles away. The tower was said to sway under the sheer force of the wind, and several wind devils circled the tower, as though they sought a way inside to strike out at Andarus for insolence. Some say that Andarus appeared, briefly, on the top of his tower, his arms spread wide above his head while he screamed in malevolent defiance of the storm and the Fates themselves.

"As the storm seemed to reach its pinnacle, there was a truly deafening roar of wind, a thunderous crash of thunder and a blinding flash of lightening, and the storm was gone. It did not fade as storms normally do, but rather ceased as suddenly as it had started. None dared to leave their shelter for the remainder of the night, which was said to have lasted three days. During this long night, it was said strange flashes of light came from the direction of Andarus' tower and that terrible screams echoed across the land, screams that sounded almost human, and yet unlike any human sound any had ever heard.

"In the months and seasons that followed, tales of that long night told of ghostly apparitions seen floating down the lanes of town toward the Tower of Andarus. Demons of pure hellish origins tore through the town, killing many, devouring their flesh after having devoured their souls. It was said that the souls were to be taken back to Satan himself in the fires of hell, while the flesh was the demons reward for stealing the soul. It is even rumored that one of these demons defied the Dark Master and remained in our realm in the form of a human, finding that it could thrive on the blood of humans, and thus the first vampire was born. Much of our mythology can find its origins from that long night. Many of the beasts that roam our land now are said to have come from that unholy unleashing of demons that night.

"When the sun finally found the courage to rise again, people began to come out and survey the results of not only the storm, but of the parade of ghosts and demons that had swept through their land as freely as humans had. The butchered remains of the demons' victims were found twisted in the debris. Other bodies were found untouched. No mark or tear of flesh could be found upon them, and it was said that these people had been touched by the ghosts and that their spirits had been drawn from them in the ghosts attempts to return to the land of the living.

"Then those first people found the remains of the Tower of Andarus. It lay in ruins with the top section of the tower having been blasted away. There were massive holes torn in the sides of what remained of the tower, and the smaller buildings surrounding it lay in charred, twisted ruin. It took many days before any gathered enough nerve to enter the tower to see what had become of Andarus.

"At the very top of what was left of the tower was Andarus' study where he was said to have spent all of his time pouring over ancient spells and ancient scrolls of knowledge. The room had been ravaged by fire; no book or scroll remained. Not one piece of furniture could be found. Only the walls, floor, and a heavy dusting of ash remained. The only other thing in the room was three large, egg shaped stones with blood red runes burned into their surface. They were found in the very center of the room... the Stones of Andarus.

"Legend has it that the crystals had been reformed by the power of the Fates and the incredible spells Andarus had cast during that long night. There are countless accounts of what had transformed the crystals, but the most popular is that Andarus had cast off his own life force, channeling it into the three crystals. When a human life ends, it is said that a tendril of power from the Great Beyond sweeps forth to reclaim that fading life force and take it back where it originated. When that tendril of power sought Andarus' life force within the crystals, it was absorbed into them, trapped by a powerful spell he had created. The sheer power of that tiny tendril was said to have turned the crystals to stone. I am sure that Andarus had planned to return his life force to his body once the power from the Great Beyond was inside the crystals, but the transformation of the crystals to stone trapped his essence, his soul, within the stones. True or fantasy, Andarus was never seen again and his body was never found.

"In the seasons that followed, many powerful mages, sorcerers, and wizards attempted to tap into the Stones, to learn what lay within them. Only tiny piles of sand were found following each attempt. It was said that the stones contained a fragment of power from the Great Beyond mixed with the dark twisted essence of Andarus. Any practitioner of the Mystic Arts that dared to tap into the stones were instantly absorbed into the stones because of the mutated nature of the power. Many believed it was Andarus' attempt to gain enough power to free himself from his tri-sectional eternal prison. The Stones were locked away in a vault for nearly two hundred seasons until a powerful mage named Nortromus came. He believed he held enough power to tap into the Stones and learn their true origins and what manner of power resided within them. Despite the warnings of other mages, and the legends surrounding the Stones, Nortromus entered the vault and made his attempt.

"Three days later, a very old and frail man emerged from the vault where a strapping young man had entered. The old man wore the robes of Nortromus, and it was all he had to identify himself as the young mage who had dared to enter the vault. Almost instantly, the old man collapsed into a deep slumber that no magic could break, no spell could cast aside. The body and soul of Nortromus remained intact, but none could reach his essence, and many tried.

"Just before Nortromus died, he woke from his mysterious slumber, and in a fevered, near panicked warning spoke of the very power of creation residing within the Stones, but that the purity of power had been tainted by the darkness of Andarus' soul, and what now lie within the Stones should never be touched or released for to do so would bring about the unleashing of powers that would bring our world, as we know it, to an end."

THE DEVENSHIRE CHRONICLES

Devenshire finally pulled his gaze back from the fire and looked from one person to another as he finished. "Nortromus' final words were: *'Beware the triad: Heaven, earth, and hell! They must remain separate; to join them is to destroy them!'*"

CHAPTER SEVEN

As Devenshire's words faded into the darkness, no other sounds came. Even the crackling of the fire and the sounds of the night seemed muted in their wake. While the blackness of the night seemed to deepen, each person sat in stunned silence as each contemplated the legends and what such power in the hands of a madman like Xavier could mean. Devenshire and Darkseed watched each person wrestle with the story, and even though they knew it by heart, had studied it in depth, they too felt the chill drift forth from the darkness.

"But..." Shantira started and paused as she tried to force her mind to form the words to express her thoughts. Finally, her terrified expression found Devenshire's, and the terror gave way to pleading, "But it is only legend."

"All legends have their origins in fact," Darkseed replied softly. "The true facts of how the Stones came into being may be shrouded in fantasy and exaggerated tales, but the fact that they exist, and the power they contain, cannot be dismissed by claiming they are simply legend."

Devenshire nodded slowly. "Darkseed and I have both studied the scrolls of the Stones. We have followed the legends, have seen the preserved remains of Nortromus, and have read his scrolls. The Stones are real. Their true power may not be known, but there is a sinister power within them, and the risk is simply too high to ignore."

"But all who have attempted to reach into the Stones have failed and been destroyed. Will not the same happen to Xavier?" Arness asked, the sarcastic edge of his bearing having been dulled by the sheer force of the legend.

Darkseed shrugged as he pulled a cigar from his vest pocket. "That cannot be known. Xavier was a very powerful Adept before he joined with the Dark Mystics. With his natural skill in the Mystic Arts combined with the power of the Dark Mystics... who can know?" He leaned forward to pick a burning piece of bark from the fire in order to light the cigar.

"Xavier will try to not only tap into the Stones to unleash their power, but attempt to control it as well. If Xavier succeeds in unleashing the power of the Stones, it is doubtful that even he will be able to control it. Such power released, unchecked, is just as chilling as the thought of such power under Xavier's control," Devenshire said.

Again, silence reigned as they absorbed the news and the very real dangerous possibilities that lie ahead. What would happen? What manner of power would be unleashed upon the realm, and what form would that power assume? Once it was released, could it be contained? Could any mystic force in this realm possibly return the tainted power of creation back into the Stones of Andarus?

"Can you stop him?" Kendra's simple but desperate question was directed at both Devenshire and Darkseed.

They looked at one another, each trying to search their own soul for the most honest answer. Finally, they shrugged, and Devenshire sighed heavily. "Alone?" he asked before shaking his head. "Neither of us can possibly stand up to Xavier's power." He paused as he gazed into the fire once again. "I do not know if our powers combined could fare any better." He then looked up into Kendra's frightened blue eyes. "But we have to try," he amended as he took a healthy swallow from the tin.

"If we can reach Xavier before he attempts to unleash the power of the Stones, then we have a chance of victory," Darkseed added. "If we reach him after he unleashes the power, then there is no chance. No power of this realm will be able to stop him then."

"Then there is the threat of the Followers," Zandorth injected, seeming to finally find his voice. They all turned to regard him as he swept his gaze around the campsite. "Xavier has a massive following of not only humans, but warriors and mystics, as well."

"How many?" Stant asked, his voice sounding small in the ominous cloud that hung over them all.

Zandorth regarded the elf for a moment before answering. "Enough to be considered an army."

Silence once again took control of the group as each considered the very ominous and formidable task before them. Finally, it was Arness who found not only his voice, but his sarcasm as well. "Allow me to set this into its proper perspective. We are two mages, four elves, a Warrior of the Ancient Class, and two women... against an army?" he paused to level a hard look at each person. "Is it just me, or is there something horribly amiss in the balance of power here?"

"Arness," Stant said reproachfully.

"What?" Arness snapped in reply. "Am I to be condemned for taking what appears to be the first honest evaluation of the odds against us?" The elf then turned his angry gaze to Darkseed. "You deceived us! You said nothing about facing the twisted powers of creation in the hands of a madman when you enlisted us to join this quest!"

Darkseed calmly drew a puff from the cigar and exhaled it through his nostrils before answering in a tone of voice that was eerily calm. "I did not deceive you, Arness. I simply did not tell you the entire tale."

"I admire the way you can alter your perceptions to ease your conscience, if you truly have one!" Arness snapped back.

The corners of Darkseed's mouth curled upwards in a grin that held only dark humor in it. "If you feel that you are unequalled to the task before us, then depart!" Arness shot to his feet and glared at Darkseed. "You dare question my bravery? My skill?"

"I question nothing. It is you who obviously have doubts about your bravery and skill," Darkseed replied with a dangerous grin mixed with a hard glare in his eyes. "It is you, after all, who mentioned them, not I."

Arness' fair complexion darkened to deep red as his anger flashed through him. "You bastard! I should kill you where you sit!"

Darkseed's eyes narrowed as he spread his hands before him in invitation. "You are free to make the attempt."

Devenshire rose to his feet and stepped between the two combatants. "Stop this! This will gain us nothing and weaken us even more than we already are!"

"I do not believe anyone asked for your intervention, mage!" Arness hissed as his hard glare cut into Devenshire. After a moment, his heated glower shifted back to Darkseed who simply sat against the log and stared hard back at Arness.

"Arness! Stop this at once!" Stant barked as he rose to his feet as well.

"No one is making you accompany us," Devenshire said. "If you do not believe in our cause or our chances of success, then feel free to depart."

"We are all very much aware of what we face," Darkseed added. "I felt the same as you do and I refused to go along at first. However, the danger is too great to leave to the flimsy chance that Xavier will fail. We may very well fail. We all may die long before we even reach Xavier, but I wish to go to my death knowing I tried to stop him. I am sure that dying in the attempt is far preferable than what awaits us should he succeed."

Arness glared at Darkseed, then at Devenshire. "You are both mad! There is no reason within either of you! I do not fear death, but I will be damned if I go to my death following madmen! This madness is yours and yours alone!" He turned to the other elves. "Let us leave them to their madness!" Arness strode from the fire. Anger drove each of his steps and soon he was fading into the darkness. He paused and turned back, genuinely surprised to find himself alone. "Let us depart! This is none of our affair!" he said to the other elves who kept their place, a look of sorrowful dread spreading across their features. Arness's features went slack as he realized they would not accompany him. His wide eyes looked from one to the other, coming to rest on Kendra. "Kendra? We do not belong here."

She looked up at him with tears forming in her eyes. She glanced at Petera and Stant, seeing the same sad but determined resolution on their features. She could sympathize with Arness, but she also knew that she simply couldn't turn her back on the very real dangers that lie ahead. She smiled sadly at him. "I am sorry."

Arness shifted his stunned look to Stant. "Stant? Surely, you know this is insanity! Surely, you will not take their side over one of your own kind?"

Stant shook his head slowly. "It is not a matter of taking sides, Arness. It is a matter of survival. This is not just a human problem. This is a problem that we all must face who live within this realm." He shook his head again. "I cannot turn my back on it, nor can I ignore it."

Arness couldn't believe what he was hearing. He had fully expected the other three elves to follow him from the camp and the insanity. The fact that they let him walk away alone was like a sharp dagger being thrust into his chest. His bewildered and hurt expression finally came to rest on Petera. "Petera, surely you will come with me? We have much in common, and we have no need to die in this insanity. Come. Let us leave this behind us."

Petera could not raise his eyes to look at Arness. He was having the hardest time keeping his place. "I cannot leave, Arness. If Stant and Kendra feel this strongly about it, and if only a portion of what Devenshire says about these evil stones are true, then I can no more walk away from this than you can go along with it. We each must follow our paths and mine is to go with them."

Arness' eyes narrowed in growing anger, anger born of deception from the humans and betrayal by those of his own kind. They were elves and this madness had nothing to do with them. His face flushed crimson as his limbs began to tremble in the iron grip of his rage. He fixed each person with a heated glare of hatred, saving the most vicious for the elves. "To the fires of hell with all of you!" he shouted before turning on his heel and storming away.

"Arness!!" Kendra called out, taking a step toward his fleeting shadow. Stant gently took her arm and stopped her.

"Let him go. If his heart is not truly with us in this quest, then we are better off without him for he will be a hindrance," Stant said.

"Perhaps he has a point worthy of considering," Kendra argued her tear laden gaze searching the night for any sign of Arness, but he could no longer be seen.

"Listen to me, all of you," Devenshire said as he moved to the edge of the fire so that he could see everyone. "Arness is not acting out of cowardice by questioning us. He has a very valid point, and one each of us should consider carefully before continuing. What I am planning to do is madness, and perhaps my sanity has fled me, but I have seen the scrolls. I know what the potential is for what lies ahead, and I cannot follow any other path. My conscience demands no less.

"However, as my conscience binds me to this path, it cannot allow me to bind others to it. I have to do this, the rest of you do not. If any of you feel that you cannot continue, then depart with my blessings and know that I will hold no ill will toward you. Yet know this as well: if you decide to continue, make sure it is what you truly wish to do, for I will brook no further confrontations such as the one that has taken place this night. What lays ahead demands a unity of force and a focus of intention that cannot allow any dissention. If your hearts and souls are not wholly in this cause, then do me the favor of departing now for to continue with only half a heart will doom us all!" Devenshire paused to lock his eyes with each person, and in turn, showing each of them the depths of the conviction that drove him. He drained the remnants of his whiskey, his face tightening in reaction to the hard bite of the liquor. "I will depart into the woods for a short time to allow you to discuss this amongst yourselves. When I return, I will begin making further plans for the journey ahead, and I wish to only have those here who are with me without question, without doubt and with their fear properly managed."

With a final intense gaze at each person, Devenshire dropped the tin cup next to the fire as he walked away into the darkness. He could not shake the feeling that he had been too harsh with them, but there would come a time, very soon, when such dissention among them would spell certain doom for them all. As each determined step carried him deeper into the darkness, he found himself wondering if he would return to an empty fireside. A part of his mind hoped to find them all gone when he returned, yet another hoped to find them all still there. He was not sure which hope brought him the greatest joy and which the greatest dread.

~*~

"Well?" Armand demanded of the tracker. The sun was setting low in the sky casting longer and deeper shadows. The Captain's mood was running very much along the lines of the shadows.

The tracker knelt in the dirt, his skilled eyes searching for signs only he could see. "Five horses... two ridden by women... several hours ago."

Armand regarded the setting sun and turned in his saddle to Lordalise, who had moved up beside him while the tracker had studied the trail. "How long before Devenshire can begin to move again?"

Lordalise studied the horizon and the fading light. "Another hour, perhaps less," he answered. "If he is very careful, he could already be out and about."

"Which direction?" Armand demanded of the tracker.

The man rose from his knelt position and studied the trail before he began to scratch the stubble growth of beard upon his chin. "Still heading due north."

"We move!" Armand said as he gathered his reins.

"By your leave, Captain, but the men and the horses could use a rest. We have been pushing hard this day," the tracker said.

Armand fixed the middle-aged man with a cold stare that made the tracker lower his eyes from those of the captain. "The men are my responsibility and my worry. Yours is the trail. I will not concern myself with how you follow the trail, and you will not concern yourself with the men or their horses. We move!" Armand replied with enough frost in his voice to chill the warmest day.

"A moment, Captain Armand," Lordalise said as his face became a mask of concentration. The Hunters eyes were locked to the definite indentations of hooves in the loose soil of the trail before them.

"We do not have a moment. The demon will be on the move again very soon, and I wish to make up for lost distance," Armand snapped in reply.

"We may be riding right into a trap," Lordalise said, continuing to look about them. "There should only be four sets of tracks, not five. Devenshire has been holed up somewhere behind us."

"So they led the fifth horse to create the tracks," Armand replied.

Lordalise shook his head and shifted his worried gaze to the tracker. "Are any of the horses you are tracking not being ridden?"

The tracker shook his head. "No. All five have riders upon them."

Armand finally shook himself out of his aching frustration to understand what all of this meant. "Another trick?"

Lordalise nodded slowly. "Somehow they have either weighted the horse down to make it appear there is a rider or someone else has joined them."

"But why? Why go to the trouble of the deceit?" Armand asked.

"To keep us off guard, to rattle our nerves, and make us question our facts," Lordalise replied, his features creasing under the heaviness of his thoughts.

"I do not understand. Devenshire does not need to engage in such trickery. He simply has to swoop down out of the night and begin killing!"

Lordalise shook his head. "My dear Captain, there is still much you have to learn about the vampire. It is not simply enough for them to feed. That is easy enough for them. They relish in the game, the challenge of the hunt. To torment their prey and hunt them down as animals makes their fear increase, and the vampire loves fear nearly as much as they love blood. He is playing with us, Captain, as surely as the cat plays with the mouse before killing it."

"We should split our party. Part of us will continue on after the trail, and the others retrace our path to find Devenshire," Armand said.

"No. To split us will surely mean death for all of us," Lordalise snapped in reply. "We should continue on as we have been. My men and I will guard the rear, in case Devenshire appears from behind."

"Do you feel he will attack?" Armand asked.

"If he does not, it is because he has some other sinister plan. We must proceed very carefully, Captain. Take nothing for granted, assume nothing, and be ready for anything." Lordalise twisted the reins, turning his mount around before shouting out and digging his heels into the horses' flanks.

Bonzwa watched as Lordal rode back toward them and found himself still very uncomfortable being in such close proximity to the Royal Guards. He was a bandit, he stole for profit, and he stole for the pleasure of stealing. He was now being forced to ride and work with men who, just a night ago, were sworn to capture him and throw him in a cell. Such irony was not lost to Bonzwa, and he did not wish to appreciate it.

Lordal, or Lordalise as they had been instructed to refer to him, pulled up rein beside him. "The demon may be about to attack from the rear. Be alert!" he said in curt tones as he turned his mount and fell into step with him.

"Sire? Do you truly believe that Devenshire is the vampire?" Last night in Lirpa, Lordal had used the ruse that Devenshire was a vampire to secure the assistance of the Royal Guard, but increasingly, he sensed his leader now truly believed his own deception.

"Now more so than ever," Lordal replied tightly, his eyes continuing to study their surroundings intently.

"I am aware that you know how to battle these creatures, but the rest of us do not. We are bandits, not Hunters," Bonzwa said carefully.

Lordalise shifted his gaze to Bonzwa, studying him carefully. "You have something on your mind, Bonzwa?"

"It is simply that we are not trained as you are, Sire. We would be a quick and easy kill for a vampire," Bonzwa answered.

"You are afraid," Lordal said flatly. It was a statement of fact without question or accusation.

"Yes," Bonzwa answered without hesitation. "Any sane man would be!"

"Good," Lordalise said with a tight, short nod. "Fear can be your staunchest ally in a battle such as this. I have weapons that the demon cannot stand against. I will be here. He will not strike down many before I strike him down."

Bonzwa considered Lordal's words and found that he drew no comfort from them. He could not help but notice how Lordal had said that the vampire would not strike down many before he was struck down. That was all fine and good... unless you found yourself as one of the 'not many.' As with the night before, Bonzwa got the definite impression that Lordal was no longer acting as the bandit king, but as a Hunter, intent on only one goal: the destruction of the vampire Devenshire regardless of the cost. With a firming resolution, Bonzwa decided that he would not be one of the 'not many' that the vampire would strike down... regardless of the cost.

CHAPTER EIGHT

Devenshire walked through the darkened woods, only part of his mind taking in the beauty of the forest that could be found even in the pitch of night. The other part of his mind churned over the possibilities that lay ahead for him and his self-appointed crusade into uncertainty. Would any of his companions or the elves be at the fire when he returned? Would he suddenly find himself alone in the desperate attempt to stop something that might never even come to pass? He had to be honest with himself in the thought that perhaps he had acted out of haste. Maybe the old legends surrounding the Stones of Andarus had tainted his thoughts causing him to act out of fear instead of calm, organized, rational thought. While Xavier was a very powerful mage, the possibility existed that not even his great resource of power could break the secret of the Stones. There was the possibility that even if Xavier managed to tap into the Stones that he would be absorbed just as every other mage had ever been. Just as these thoughts occurred and tried to find permanent purchase within his mind, they were whisked away and dashed against the harsh walls of reality. He had read the scrolls of the Stones. He had performed the spell of Knowledge, and he had seen the Stones as they had been in the church of Shantira's village. He had sensed the terrible latent power within them. For Xavier to lead such a raid for the Stones could only mean that some truth could be found in the legends, and the chance for catastrophe was simply too great to ignore or leave to chance.

"Nice speech."

Devenshire spun, his right hand instinctively going for his sword. His eyes scanned the darkness and found Darkseed leaned casually against a tree, his arms folded across his chest and a thin cigar clenched between his teeth. Just enough moonlight filtered through the branches to make him partially visible.

"Damn you, Darkseed! That is a good way to get yourself killed!" Devenshire muttered as he forced himself to relax from the sudden start. It was then that he realized that his natural sense of the workings of the Mystical Arts had been sending its tingle up and down his spine. He had simply been so absorbed in his own thoughts. He quickly chastised himself for the lapse.

Darkseed studied him for a moment. "I would apologize for the start, but you know as well as I do that I should not have been able to surprise you." He smiled and shook his head making a tsk tsk sound. "Very sloppy, Daimion. Not heeding your senses is a good way to get yourself killed."

Devenshire could not argue the point or the logic. He relaxed and let his arm drift away from his sword as he scowled. "I am to assume you have a point?"

"I always have a point. You are preoccupied, and by your own assessment of our quest, such preoccupation could be deadly. Suppose I were an assassin sent by Xavier?" Darkseed asked with a mixture of hard reprimand and jovial humor in his tones. He knew he wasn't telling Devenshire anything he didn't already know, but he did so enjoy catching Devenshire in such lapse moments. For all of his qualities, Darkseed knew that Devenshire had a bad habit of taking himself too seriously at times.

Devenshire shrugged as he turned away from Darkseed, knowing that his friend was right and detesting the fact at the same time. "Then there would be a corpse here."

"Probably yours," Darkseed snipped in reply.

"Point made and taken," Devenshire replied shortly, wanting to leave this subject behind them.

"I have another question for you Daimion," Darkseed said, knowing he had made his point, and Devenshire was now berating himself far worse than anyone ever could.

"Go ahead." Devenshire sighed. He knew from long association with Darkseed that it would be quicker to allow him to ask the question than try to avoid it.

"The fight in the inn last night, what happened?"

"I was ambushed by bandits. We fought, I defeated them," Devenshire replied in clipped tones, not in the mood for an in-depth discussion on an event he still didn't entirely understand himself.

Darkseed sighed. "Must we do this dance yet again? You know that I know far more happened within that building than what you just told me. There was an incredible surge within the Mystical Tides. I could feel it half way across the city. I did not know you were involved until later in the night, but something on a large mystical scale happened. What was it?"

Devenshire sighed again. He did not wish to have this conversation right now. Yet he knew, deep down, that Darkseed might be able to shed some much needed light on it for him. Taking a deep breath, he began. "After our argument in the tavern I returned to the inn. A group of bandits laid in wait for me. I was able to disarm two of them when a third stepped through the door and fired a crossbow. I ducked out of the way, but the bolt felled one of the bandits. I rendered the crossbowman unconscious and then began fighting the other bandit."

"Were they bandits or Followers?" Darkseed asked.

"Bandits. I thought them to be Followers at first, but they admitted they were bandits from a group that had attacked us the night before," Devenshire replied as he resumed his story. "As we fought, the bandit that had taken the crossbow bolt to the chest suddenly rose to his feet." Devenshire paused because he knew Darkseed would react.

"Came back to life? A zombie?"

Devenshire nodded. "It appeared so. I tried to kill it with my sword and received a vicious backhand for my efforts."

Darkseed shook his head. "You cannot kill something that is already dead. You must counter the magic that reanimated it."

Devenshire nodded. "I was able to cast two spells which weakened, and finally, for lack of a better word, killed it."

Darkseed's eyes narrowed, his mind churning over what Devenshire was telling him. "Go ahead."

"Just when I thought the bandit was truly dead, a demon erupted from his corpse."

"What?" Darkseed asked incredulously. "You are going to have to be more specific than that. More details if you please."

Devenshire nodded. "The body began to spasm and jerk about on the floor. A mound formed in its chest and began to grow, swelling outward."

Darkseed focused his attention on every word. "What was your natural sense of the mystical tides doing?"

Devenshire chuckled dryly. "It was quite intense, painful even. It felt as though the entire length of my spine was being crushed."

"Did you recognize the pattern of the power being used? Surely, at that intense a level, you had to have some indication," Darkseed countered.

Devenshire shook his head. "No. It was a very strong aura and an intense presence, but I could discern nothing about whoever was casting the spell. It was very odd."

Darkseed's brow furrowed. "Odd indeed. Go on."

"The demon exploded from the bandit's chest and quickly grew in size."

"What did it look like?" Darkseed asked, stepping from the shadows of the tree to cross the distance between them.

"It was about four feet tall and bright red in color. The skull was round with a sharp jutting chin that came to a point. A row of boney spikes protruded from between its eyes and moved over the top of the skull to run down its spine. The mouth was large, had no lips to speak of, and had a lot of very sharp teeth. There was some kind of greenish ooze that dripped from the teeth. It was very slight of build, almost skeletal."

Darkseed nodded slowly. "Your description sounds like a Ganatu."

Devenshire looked puzzled. "A what?"

"A Ganatu. They are demons, Satan's little lap dogs, more or less. They are very tenacious little bastards, and nasty to boot. They kill their victims by starting to eat them while they are still alive. The greenish ooze you spoke of is sort of mystical venom that prevents the soul from departing the body in the usual way. Once death claims the victim, the soul is transferred to the Ganatu and then taken back to hell."

Devenshire nodded slowly. "It attacked the remaining bandit and began mutilating him, swiping at his face with its large claws. At one point, it took a large bite from his throat."

"It does indeed sound like a Ganatu," Darkseed agreed, and then shifted his gaze back to Devenshire's darkened silhouette, his eyes narrowing in deep thought. "What happened next?"

"I stopped it from killing the bandit. I tried two counter spells, but they did nothing but weaken it. It clawed my arm, causing a rather nasty wound, and I honestly thought I was finished. My sword was across the room, and I was losing a lot of blood quickly. I knew my sword was my only chance, and I put all I had into a spell to bring it to me, but my powers were drained." Devenshire paused and furrowed his brow as though he were trying to remember the next events. "The rest is a bit hazy. Somehow, just as it was about to swipe at my throat, my sword was in my hand." His words came haltingly as he tried to force the memories into sharper focus within his mind. "I sliced off one of its claws… it staggered backwards… I got up and started stabbing it… multiple times. Finally, I cut its head off. There was a bright flash, and I could feel a tremendous release of dark power… very overwhelming… then the head and body vanished, even its blood disappeared."

Darkseed nodded, his features set in grim understanding. "By beheading it, you canceled out the spell. A Ganatu can only be given solid, physical form through a spell cast by a Dark Mystic and then only one of respectable skill level." He paused a moment, taking a deep draw from his cigar. He removed it from his lips and studied the glowing tip as he exhaled the smoke, his mind churning over what he'd learned. He shifted his gaze back to Devenshire. "What happened next?"

Devenshire had also been deep in thought, trying to sort through the mystery. Darkseed's knowledge of the demon had answered several questions, but it left others a mystery. "I passed out. I awoke in the forest outside the city. My wounds had been tended to by a new acquaintance that, fortunately, had some considerable skill in the healing arts."

"Most fortunate, indeed," Darkseed commented absently. His mind was absorbed on other matters.

Devenshire shifted his gaze to the shadowy silhouette of his friend. "I know that tone. You know something you aren't telling me."

Darkseed shook his head. "Not at all. I am just curious as to who would summon a Ganatu."

"Xavier!" Devenshire answered without hesitation.

"You say that like you have no doubts," Darkseed commented.

"I have none. I do not know how I know it was Xavier, I just do."

Darkseed nodded again. "Then, if you are correct, it was a good thing."

"A good thing? The demon very nearly killed me," Devenshire replied tightly.

"Yes, but it did not, and now Xavier is taxed from summoning it. Even as powerful as Xavier is, summoning a Ganatu taxed his power, I promise you. That will be power he will not be able to use on the Stones of Andarus."

"Now all we have to do is hope we can use that to our advantage," Devenshire answered before taking a deep breath and blowing it out through puffed cheeks. It was more of a tension relieving gesture than anything else.

Darkseed continued to study Devenshire closely, his mind shifting to another topic, one he knew better than to broach, but one he felt as though he must. "I see you are still running."

Devenshire shifted his gaze to his friend. "What? Running? Running from what?"

"You are still fleeing your past," Darkseed said matter-of-factly.

Devenshire grew instantly tense, his mood plummeting rapidly. "I am sure I do not know what you are speaking of."

"Lie to the others, Daimion. Not to me. I was there. I saw what happened. I know what it did to you. Why will you not let it go? Why do you insist on keeping it alive within you?"

Devenshire's entire demeanor had shifted into something dark and angry. When he spoke, his voice was deep and fuming. "Why do you insist on prying into affairs that do not concern you?"

"Because someone needs to!" Darkseed snapped in irritated frustration. "Why do you insist on carrying this poisonous memory with you always? It burdens your soul. It darkens your being. Release it! Cast it off and get on with your life! By the Fates, Daimion, it was nearly sixteen seasons ago!"

"I will carry it with me to my grave!" Devenshire growled with his anger more evident than ever.

"Why?" Darkseed demanded hotly.

He spun on Darkseed so quickly, and so violently, that Darkseed took a step back, starting to reach for his sword. "So that it will not happen again! I will never allow it to happen again! Ever!!" Devenshire shouted in rage, his hands balled into trembling fists at his side as he towered ominously over Darkseed. "Now mind your own business!"

For several long moments, they stared at one another. Darkseed's gaze while angry was more filled with sadness for the black thing that had tainted his friend's soul. Devenshire's was livid and carried a very clear warning that this subject was not one to be debated a moment longer. Finally, it was Darkseed who backed down. He raised his hands to shoulder level and stepped back. "My apologies, Daimion. I only sought to help."

Devenshire wrestled with his anger, struggling to subdue the beast that had very nearly made good its escape from the iron will he worked to maintain on all of his emotions. He closed his eyes and took several deep breaths before answering. "If you truly wish to help, leave the past in the past and do not mention it again."

Darkseed nodded slowly, sadly. He had hoped that in the time since Devenshire had left Lirpa, he had found some way to reconcile the demons he insisted on carrying with him. It was painfully obvious now that not only had his friend not found a way to reconcile the demons, but also they had grown in strength and intensity. It was incredibly sad, but he knew Devenshire and knew that he had pushed the topic as far as he could without the need to defend himself from an attack. "As you wish," he said softly. He returned the cigar to his mouth and puffed on it as he waited for Devenshire to regain control of his anger.

"We should return to the camp," Devenshire muttered in the fading waves of his anger. "What has everyone decided?"

Darkseed smiled. "Come see for yourself," and with that he turned and began walking off into the darkness.

Devenshire shook his head. "Why must every question you answer be so dramatic? Can you not, just once, answer a direct question with a direct answer?" While he had regained control of his anger, his mood was still foul.

Darkseed turned and began walking backwards, extending his arms out beside him. "I could. But this is much more entertaining."

Devenshire sighed, shaking his head. He shook himself out of the remnants of his dark mood and set off behind Darkseed. "Ass!"

Darkseed did not respond as he turned back around and continued walking. His mind was churning over what he had just learned. It caused a great deal of trepidation within him. He had been telling the truth about the Ganatu, and he was sure that was what Devenshire had faced. What he didn't tell Devenshire was that a mage of his skill level should not have been able to cast a spell that would have been of any consequence to the demon. Devenshire's skill level should have prevented him from downing the zombie, to say nothing of battling a Ganatu. Darkseed acknowledged that he himself would have to use a considerable amount of power to cast a spell capable of weakening a Ganatu. The other, more troubling aspect to Devenshire's story was the ending. A Ganatu was a creature made up of dark energies and the power required to keep the demon in a physical form would be tremendous. Severing the demon's head would have caused an enormous, uncontrolled release of those dark energies. It would have been a release that Devenshire should not have survived.

Darkseed had studied the incident in the Inn while everyone had been running about trying to catch one another. He had delved into the Mystic Tides to learn what he could which was just enough to roust his suspicions about Devenshire's growing abilities. Those suspicions were only strengthened by the spell he had unleashed on Armand. Darkseed had cast the spell that had put Armand's men and the sheriffs to sleep, but had left Armand alone. He had a spell ready to stop Armand from harming Brianna should the need have presented itself, but he wanted to gauge Devenshire's response first hand. He had been amazed to say the least. The spell Devenshire used to free himself from the ropes was simple enough, and any apprentice mage could perform it. However, the bright blue orb of power that he had thrown at Armand, and very nearly killed him in the process, was seasons of study beyond Devenshire's abilities. After the battle in the clearing, Darkseed had questioned Devenshire about resuming his studies, and his response that he hadn't, only increased the trepidation. He would have to keep a very close eye on Devenshire for there was a power growing within him that not even he was aware of. Such power, unchecked and without proper discipline, could spell dark times ahead for everyone.

Devenshire was several paces behind Darkseed as they moved toward camp. He was about to increase his pace to catch up to him when something rippled through his senses briefly and was gone. He froze and took a moment to consider what the sensation had been and what it had meant. Although he could not be sure for the sensation had been far too weak and brief to identify, he could not help but feel that it had been a reoccurrence of the sensation of being watched that he had experienced earlier in the night as he had hunted. He turned in a slow circle, his eyes and senses searching for anything that might hint at the source of the flickering sensation, but found nothing. With narrowed eyes, Devenshire continued toward the camp, but his mind continued to search the woods around him. He silently vowed that he would catch whomever it was that insisted on this cat and mouse game with him. It would only be a matter of time and concentration.

~*~

When Devenshire walked back into camp, he saw that Zandorth, Brianna, Shantira, Darkseed, Stant, Petera, and Kendra all sat around the fire. Only Arness was absent, and Devenshire found that he genuinely felt no ill will toward the elf for his choice. He stepped into the circle of the fire and studied each face that looked back at him with resolute expressions. With a faint smile, he nodded. "Are you sure?" he asked them.

Zandorth made a sound of exasperation. "Sometimes, Devenshire, I wonder if your mind truly works at all! We are here, are we not?"

Devenshire arched one eyebrow at the warrior and nodded again, reading through the man's gruff words to the meaning he would never in a thousand lifetimes give words to. "Very well then. Let us tempt our fates," Devenshire said as he settled back down on a log near the fire.

Zandorth snorted as he climbed to his feet. "If you and Darkseed are even close to correct in what you say of the Stones of Andarus, tempting our fates will be easy." Devenshire smiled as Zandorth moved off from the fire. "Since this is your expedition, Devenshire, you can have the first watch. I am going to sleep," the warrior tossed back over his shoulder as he walked away.

"Perhaps you all should try to get some sleep. We will be leaving out early in the morning, and I do not know when we will have the chance to stop again. Unless I terribly misjudge Captain Armand, he has discovered our true trail and is on his way as we speak," Devenshire said.

Petera and Stant nodded in agreement as they rose and moved off from the fire, issuing biddings of a good night as they went.

"Darkseed, could I trouble you for that healing now? My arm is becoming quite bothersome," Brianna asked tiredly.

"Of course, I should have tended to it by now," Darkseed replied as he stepped over to sit down next to Brianna and began gingerly removing the thick bandage.

Shantira looked up at Devenshire. "If you wish, I could stand the first watch with you. I am not tired, not at all." There was a great deal of hope in her offered assistance. Brianna subtly watched Shantira and then shifted her gaze to Devenshire. With a twist of regret, she saw that he had completely missed the true meaning of her offer... or ignored it.

Devenshire smiled in gratitude. "My thanks, but that will not be necessary. You should at least try to sleep." He looked off toward the ridge where they had first spotted the crater. "I will be up on the ridge," he said as he began walking away. Shantira slumped and propped her chin in her hand as she watched him go, the disappointment evident on her face and in her bearing.

Kendra watched him go, and Shantira did not miss the way her eyes danced along his build. She saw the shimmer in her eyes that she had seen in other women's eyes in the tavern, and in Brianna's eyes, as well. Jealousy flared within her before she was even aware of it forming.

"He is not like other men, is he?" Kendra asked absently.

Brianna looked up from her wound to the Elven woman and smiled softly as she shook her head. "No. No, he is not."

Kendra turned her eyes to Brianna at the touch of fondness in her voice. "Is he yours?"

Brianna laughed. "No, no one holds Daimion."

Kendra's lips curled into a seductive smile as her gaze swept back to the spot where she had lost sight of him. "Indeed? Interesting."

"None hold him… yet!" Shantira quipped as she rose from her log, "Good night!" she snapped as she strode off into the darkness.

Kendra watched her go and turned her puzzled expression to Brianna, seeking an explanation. Brianna smiled and shook her head again. "Shantira is taken with Daimion. She will not admit it, not even to herself, but she is."

Darkseed snickered and shook his head as he continued to remove the bandage from Brianna's wound.

"What do you find so amusing?" Kendra asked.

Darkseed's smile widened as he spoke. "I have seen this so many times before that I cannot remember the count. Daimion has always had this way of attracting female attention. The odd thing is, he does not try to do so. Perhaps that is why it is so effective, he does not force it, it is simply something that happens, and he neither encourages it nor does he subdue it."

"Whatever it is," Brianna injected casting a quick glance in the direction Devenshire had gone, "it is quite effective." Her lips twisted into a fond smile.

"I see," Kendra replied as her eyes left Brianna's smile and returned to the spot she had last seen him. "How very interesting." Brianna and Darkseed exchanged knowing glances and merely smiled but made no comment.

Darkseed performed the healing spell on Brianna's wound and advised her to treat the arm with care for a few days until the latent power of the spell ran its course. He also suggested that as soon as possible, they should gather the ingredients for a salve to help aide in the healing. After a while, everyone retired to their blankets with the exception of Devenshire who stood watch on the ridge of the crater.

A figure stood in the shadows of the dying campfire. After a time, it moved silently through the camp, pausing over each slumbering form. It paused for a little longer over Darkseed and studied him intently. Next, it paused over Brianna's slumbering form and studied her for a considerable amount of time. With movements that made no more sound than the wind whispering through the trees, the figure moved halfway up the incline of the crater behind Devenshire. It studied him the longest. There was much to do and so little time in which to do it. With only the tiniest flicker of movement, the figure was gone.

CHAPTER NINE

"Halt! Thief!"

Beckellar Moon sat on a rooftop, idly cleaning out from under his fingernails with the tip of his dagger when he was startled by the sudden shout from the street below. He quickly tensed, searching the rooftop for any sign of someone coming up on him unawares. A quick scan of the rooftop reassured him that he was alone. With a quick, fluid movement, he rose and crossed to the edge of the roof. He lowered himself to his knees and carefully eased his head out over the edge to take a look. As he studied the street below, he mumbled to himself, "Surely they are not looking for me. I have not stolen anything... today."

The streets of Lirpa were settling into their mid-morning routine, and from his vantage point, everything appeared normal. With a wry grin, he continued to scan the streets as he mused that appearances could, indeed, be deceiving. Last night had been mysterious, horrifying, exciting, and singularly intriguing in every sense of the word.

A band of criminals had come to the city and set about carving a swath of bloody destruction through Lirpa as surely as driving a sharpened dagger through a fluttering heart. He had tried to follow the events of the night, but having to remain hidden from both the local sheriffs, as well as the famous Captain Armand of the Royal Guard, had kept him from investigating these newcomers for himself. He found he was always a step behind the fleeing criminals as he tried to discern their true nature for himself. Moon had heard the terrified rumors that one of the criminals was a vampire and was responsible for the deaths of Lorinda and Constable Liston, not to mention the horrid mutilation of two men within one of the local inns. Such terrified whispers were usually only a tiny fraction of truth doused with a healthy topping of irrational speculation and a dusting of fear.

He had managed to sneak into the inn and see the destruction for himself. In this case, at least, there had been no exaggeration. In fact, the truth was far more terrifying than the rumors. While he considered himself a strong man, what he had seen in the lobby of the inn had nearly made him retch. It wasn't only the sight of the mutilated bodies, the blood splattered into what seemed like every corner of the room and the bits and tendrils of raw meat scattered all about, but the smell also added a layer of grotesque clarity to the scene.

Later, he had happened upon Captain Armand and another man, by rumor a Hunter, surveying Lorinda's corpse. He had felt a deep twinge of regret at her death. She was a good woman despite her chosen profession, and on a strange level, she had been one of his few friends. They had shared many nights in merry revelry, and he had even purchased her services on a few occasions. Her passing would mean little to the bulk of the citizens of Lirpa, but to him and a handful of others who existed in the shadows of the city's dark underbelly, she would be sorely missed.

Moving on through the night, he had heard of Constable Liston's death at the hands of the same supposed vampire who had taken Lorinda's life. The regret he felt at Lorinda's passing was absent in Liston's. While the city mourned the passing of the dear constable and lamented at the passing of a so-called great man, Moon knew exactly what the realm had lost with his passing, and it wasn't much. Liston had convinced nearly everyone that he was a just and fair man, a man above reproach who executed the duties of Constable with the sterling white purity of the Fates themselves. Again, to those who existed in the darkness of the city's alter ego, Liston was a brigand who deserved every terrifying moment his death promised had been imparted upon him. His devious behavior, sadistic traits, and unique application of the laws of the land were widely unknown to the bulk of the people who lived on the fringes of society such as Moon did. Unfortunately, those people had no voice with which to be heard.

"Halt!" the shout came again and Moon snapped his head around in the direction it had come from. It was two streets over. Moon rose to his feet and began running toward the source of the shout. He was curious by nature and intrigued by his chosen profession.

Beckellar Moon was in his twenty-fourth season and stood over six feet in height. He was slight of build, but possessed a hidden strength that bellied his thin frame. His sandy brown hair flowed about his head to trail down below his shoulders. It was thick and shone with the luster of youth. He was dressed in black, knee-high boots, black breeches tucked into the boots, a black shirt that was a size larger than he normally wore, and a black cloak. He also wore a pair of fingerless gloves, black of course. The only hint of color to his attire was his skin and the silver of the short sword slung low on his right hip.

He crossed the rooftops with ease. It was a path he favored simply because he enjoyed being able to move freely about the city without having to worry as much about inadvertently running into a sheriff. None of the brigand sheriffs had the energy, proclivity, or the physical conditioning to run the rooftops. He also enjoyed the physical challenge that leaping from rooftop to rooftop provided. As he approached the street, he heard the pounding of hooves and the shouts of people below. He paused at the edge of a roof and peered over the periphery to see a man running down the street, a coin purse clutched tightly in his right hand. Shifting his gaze, he saw a mounted sheriff barreling down on him. The throngs of people in the street gave the advantage to the thief. He shifted his gaze back to the thief, and in a sweeping glance, knew this to be an apprentice thief, quite possibly on his maiden voyage into the underworld of crime. A wry grin twisted the corner of Moon's lips and he chuckled softly to himself. The blossoming thief was very green, and while part of the scene unfolding below him was amusing, that part of him that took pride in his profession found it twistingly painful. With a deep sigh, he rose and jogged onward, looking for a suitable place to drop to the street below. Normally, he would not involve himself in the affairs of others, but last night's events and their insinuating circumstances had left him restless and put his normally good mood in a bit of the doldrums. He needed diversion and the apprentice thief below promised exactly what he needed.

The man who had snatched the coin purse from one of the vendors ran full out in a desperate flight from the mounted sheriff who seemed quite determined to capture him. As he dashed through the streets, he risked a quick backward glance to find the sheriff struggling through the crowd, but still gaining on him. It would only be a matter of time before the sheriff caught him. His wide, panicked eyes suddenly broke from their intent gaze down the street to begin searching side to side in hopes of finding a path of escape. The weight of the purse clutched tightly in his right hand whispered to him, shoring up his faltering courage and determination. This was only his second foray into the world of the criminal, and he found the thrill of stealing offset by the sheer terror of being caught. His heart thrashed about in his chest while his stomach flipped in multiple somersaults inside his torso. Sweat coursed down the sides of his face and trickles ran down his spine. Fear rallied to wrestle control from his mind while exhilaration laughed with abandon within his mind. It was a confusing combination and one that could help him understand the allure of becoming a thief. Then there was the practical matter of taking care of his needs. The considerable weight in his right hand promised him many days of carefree living. It certainly was better than shoveling out the stalls of the livery for the mere pittance he was paid.

Another quick glance over his shoulder showed the sheriff had managed to gain more ground on him. The sheriff's shouts and the angry whinny's of his mount served to clear the path. He snapped his head back around and continued frantically searching for a path of escape. That's when he noticed the alleys. He felt suddenly foolish. How many had he passed? How many paths to escape had he looked right at and ignored?

"Ass!" he muttered to himself, and he suddenly peeled off from the main street and dashed for the secure gloom of the alley. Freedom was a matter of paces away and the lap of luxury beckoned.

Both quickly vanished from sight as a hand clamped down on his left wrist with surprising force. This was followed quickly by his running to the end of his arm and being snapped back. Before he could turn to look at whoever had grabbed him, his assailant used his momentum to propel him into a circular staggering path within the tight confines of the ally. As he was about to regain his balance he was suddenly released to be sent crashing into the wall of the building. His body bounced off the wall, causing him to collapse into the dirt. Instantly he was stunned, his breath exploding from his heaving chest and his perceptions dissolving into a kaleidoscope of dazzling lights of pain.

"Careless," a disembodied voice said through the loud ringing in his ears as he shook his head trying to clear his vision. He opened his eyes to find his spinning vision filled with a crooked view of the main street he had just left. The sight twisted and threatened to spin, which caused him to close his eyes tightly.

"Here, allow me to assist you," the voice echoed through the muck of his perceptions. The thief was dimly aware of a pair of hands taking him carefully by the arm and beginning to pull him up. He was able to force his legs to obey his commands and soon he was standing, albeit unsteadily, next to a shadowy figure.

"W-who are you?" he asked as he shook his head again in another attempt to clear his spinning vision.

"My name is of little importance. It is the message I have been sent to deliver to you is what should concern you," the voice replied.

In his stunned state, the thief momentarily forgot that he was being pursued by a sheriff for theft. "What message?"

Through his steadying vision, he could see the man look up one direction of the alley before quickly scanning the opposite direction as though he were making sure no one was within earshot. Satisfied that they were alone, the strange man looked at the prospective thief and smiled a wide, almost crazed grin before leaning in closer. "The Fates tell me they do not believe you will be successful in this endeavor."

The thief's brow furrowed in confusion, not entirely sure he had heard the man correctly. "The Fates? You speak to the Fates?" he asked incredulously.

The man's face assumed a thoughtful expression for a moment before he slowly shook his head. "Nay, it would be more accurate to say that they speak to me."

"I see. The Fates speak to you. Personally."

The man smiled widely again. His eyes shone with an expression that bordered on insanity while the toothy grin only served to shove the expression across the border. With a quick nod and a maniacal bounce of his eyebrows, the man replied with an enthusiastic, "Aye!"

The thief had managed to regain most of his senses. With the return came the realization that the sheriff couldn't be far behind by now. He stepped back from the strange man, nodding slowly. "I see. Well give them my regards and condolences on being wrong. I have every intention of being successful in this endeavor. Now, if you will excuse me I have..."

"Bug!" the man screamed before slamming a fist deep into the thief's midsection. He grunted heavily and doubled over from the force of the blow. He felt sure he was about to retch.

"My apologies," the strange man said as he jerked the thief upright and slammed him back against the wall. "I really hate bugs." The man stuck his face very close to the thief's and studied him with a very surreal intense gaze. "Are you all right? You look like you are about to be ill. Do you hate bugs as well?"

"You bastard... you did that on..." the thief tried to reply but was cut off by the crazy man cupping his hand and slapping it over the thief's mouth with enough force to slam his head back against the wall while busting both lips at the same time.

"Shhhh... The Fates tell me the brigand sheriff is very near! We must use stealth or you will surely be arrested!" The man removed his hand from the thief's mouth and absently wiped the blood from his fingerless glove to the thief's shirt. Suddenly the man cocked his head toward the street and the sound of approaching hooves. He suddenly stepped back and took the thief by the right wrist.

"Quickly! Hide over there!" he squealed as he planted his feet and swung the thief around to fly across the ally and crash face first into the opposite wall. He bounced off and collapsed to the dirt once again. The man scooped down and picked up the purse of coins the thief had dropped. "Oh my. You have dropped your purse. Here, allow me to assist you again."

"Hold!" came the deep shout of the sheriff from the entrance of the alley.

"Ah, sheriff! Thank the Fates you came along. I found this man running down the alley with this purse in his hands. I fear he may be a thief."

The sheriff studied him very closely before shifting his gaze to the semi-conscious thief moaning softly in the dirt. "Indeed he is. He stole that purse from one of our street vendors."

The man's expression shifted into shock as he looked down at the thief with disdain. "You are a thief! Oh my!"

"Who are you?" the sheriff asked with a glint of suspicion in his eyes.

The man bowed low. "Merely a subject of his majesty who wishes to only do his part to maintain the law and the peace of the land."

The sheriff dismounted and moved to the thief. "My thanks. I feared this brigand might make good his escape."

"And deprive one of our beloved citizens of their hard earned wealth? Surely the Fates would not allow such a thing."

The sheriff chuckled darkly as he roughly hauled the addled thief to his unsteady feet. "You must be new to Lirpa. If only more people believed as you, my job would be considerably easier."

The man extended his hand with the coin purse toward the sheriff. "Here. The bastard dropped his ill-gotten gain in the dirt. Please make sure the vendor gets it back. I am sure he needs every coin."

The sheriff took the coin purse and slipped it inside a vest pocket. "I will make sure the coins end up where they belong," he said with a shrouded look in his eyes that spoke loudly of what the man was not saying.

The man nodded, and his expression also saying volumes that his words were not. "I am sure."

The thief shook his head and slowly opened his eyes to focus on the man. His dazed expression slowly cleared and then began turning to anger. "You son of a bitch!"

The man's expression never shifted as he suddenly launched a short, vicious right jab that rocked the man back into the sheriff. The punch had come so fast that the sheriff wasn't entirely sure what had driven the criminal back against him.

"You do not know my mother well enough to call her a bitch!" the man replied. He smiled pleasantly at the sheriff who suddenly had to support the thief's unconscious form. "Will you be requiring anything else from me?"

The sheriff hoisted the unconscious form to his shoulder and studied the man with a renewed expression of admiration. "Nay. You have done enough, and you have the thanks of all of Lirpa for your selfless acts this day. You should consider becoming a sheriff. You have natural skills at apprehending criminals."

The man slowly smiled and raised his hands to shoulder level. "Oh, no. I am not worthy of such a lofty office held by such valiant men. I am simply glad I could do my part. With that, the man bowed, "I bid you a good day."

"Good day, sir and many thanks," the sheriff replied.

The man only waived as he turned and began making his way down the alley away from the sheriff who was carrying his latest arrest to his horse. He continued to stroll casually down the alley, crossed the next street, and entered the alley on the other side. Then, with only a casual glance around to make sure no one was watching him, he climbed up on a crate stacked next to a building with a low roof. He nimbly jumped, gripping the edge of the roof and then pulled himself up. He then traveled the distance to a higher roof and then crossed over several streets before pausing to lean against a chimney.

Beckellar Moon reached into his cloak and pulled out the purse the would-be thief had been carrying. He bounced the bag in his hand and nodded in approval of its considerable size and weight. There was a good portion of wealth in his hand, enough to sustain him for many days and, he smiled with great mischief, nights to come.

Moon's only regret was that he would not be present to see the look on the sheriff's face when he opened the purse he had handed him only to find rocks inside. It had been ridiculously easy to swap them. He pushed off the chimney and began strolling along the rooftop, whistling a merry tune and bouncing his newfound wealth in his hand. His thoughts touched briefly on the man he had stolen the purse from and felt a tiny sliver of sympathy for the fool. Not only had he lost his purse of coins, but he had also gotten a fair beating for his troubles.

The sliver quickly vanished, and Moon shrugged. "Apprentice!" he snorted before a merry chuckle rattled his throat. Now, with this boost to his wealth, he was free to pursue the criminals who had swept through Lirpa and had become legends overnight. Such a group bore closer inspection, closer assertion of their true designs. For any group of people to leave the sheriffs and the Royal Guard looking so utterly foolish was no small feat, and it spoke of their considerable talents.

In Moon's experience, considerable talents always led to considerable wealth... either earned or stolen.

CHAPTER TEN

"We are getting closer," the tracker said as he knelt in the darkness, studying the trail with the light from a sputtering torch he held overhead. "These tracks are not very old."

Armand studied the darkened trail before them with his eyes while his mind considered the darkened trail behind them and the possible specter of Devenshire hunting them, stalking them, and waiting for them to become vulnerable. He could almost feel the demon's eyes upon him, and it made his skin crawl. Armand found himself silently saluting the demons' tactics. The apprehension that each rustling branch, each snapping twig, each groan of a tree settling in the coolness of the night would herald the hellish attack that would kill them all was wearing on them, making them weary. Despite his desire to hunt the ghoul down quickly and dispatch him back to hell, Armand knew his men would soon need a rest from the darkened fears, both real and imagined.

"We will continue until dawn, and then we will make camp," Armand said. Any objections the men might have had remained unspoken as the tracker stood up and moved to mount his horse. "How far ahead of us do you think they are?"

With the sound of creaking leather, the tracker settled into his saddle and gathered the reins. He bit at the corner of his moustache as he considered the captain's question. "Five hours, possibly less," he finally replied.

Armand nodded. They had made good time after discovering Devenshire's false trail. The five hours that remained was time they could easily make up after a short rest come dawn. Perhaps if he gave the criminals another day of peace, they would believe that he had abandoned his search for them and grow careless. With a slightly devious smile, Armand nodded again, this time in agreement with himself. Yes. Let them think they had made good their escape. They will relax, and once they did, they would make the one mistake that would deliver them into his hands.

They rode on through the night. As the first gray fingers of dawn began spreading the curtain of darkness aside, the criminals' trail began to become easy to follow. With the increasing light and loose soil of this area, the criminals' trail was clear even to the untrained eye. The ground was growing more and more unleveled, indicating that they were entering the fringes of the Mt. Kil'tafore mountain range. The trail would get difficult from this point on. As they rode, Armand noticed that the criminals' trail veered off to the right and up a sharp, tree-choked incline. Armand followed the incline with his eyes until he found the top and slowly shook his head. "What in the name of the Fates are they doing?"

The tracker watched the incline as well, and his features took on the look of deep concentration. "There are deep craters scattered throughout this entire area. Perhaps this is one of those craters." He swung his head around and gave Armand a knowing stare. "It would make an excellent campsite if you were trying to hide from our position here. The rough terrain would make anyone skirt this crater in favor of easier passage."

Armand regarded the tracker for only a moment before the same thoughts that had been running through the tracker's mind ran through his. Of course! If this was one of those craters, and if the criminals had made camp there, then perhaps they had felt secure enough in their seclusion to still be there. A dark grin creased his features as he nodded once. He turned in the saddle to address his men, but kept his voice low. "The criminals have gone up there," he said pointing up the incline. "This could be a crater and the criminals could very well have set up a camp there last night. They could even still be there. We will dismount and make our way up on foot as to not make too much noise. Swords drawn, crossbows at the ready, and be prepared!"

The entire party silently dismounted, drew and prepared their weapons, and began picking their way up the incline, careful to keep the noise at a minimum. At this higher altitude, rocky terrain, and with the crisp morning air, sound would travel very far. It took quite a considerable time to navigate up the side of the crater with stealth. Once they had reached the top, they found that it was, indeed, a large deep crater. Armand and his men lowered themselves to their bellies and crawled slowly forward, looking through the brush to the floor of the crater below. It was quite peaceful looking. Thick, lush grass, heavy overgrowth around the edges of the clearing and along the lip, which would provide excellent cover and it even, hosted a small fresh water pond. Someone wishing to remain hidden for a long time would find this crater provided everything one could possibly need. Armand scanned the interior of the crater, but saw no signs of the criminals. After several long moments of searching, he decided that they were not here. With a heavy sigh of disappointment, he rose to his feet and motioned for his men to follow suit. "We can walk from here, but be alert! Just because we cannot see them does not mean they are not there."

After reaching the floor of the crater, it did not take them long to find their campsite. Although they had gone to great lengths to hide the evidence, Armand and the tracker found enough proof of their presence to know they had been here.

"They had a small fire here," the tracker said as he knelt before a loose mound of fresh earth. He sifted through the loose soil and found ash beneath. He used his fingertips to brush the ashes around before raising his fingertips, coated with ash, to his nose. He sniffed deeply, and then touched his tongue to the ashes. He nodded before looking about the clearing. "They ate mountain hares, several of them," he said after spitting out the ash that had stuck to his tongue and wiping his fingers off on his breeches leg. "They used logs here," he pointed to round indentations in the grass, "and here for seats. They removed them from here to further try to hide the evidence of their camp."

"How can you possibly know that?" Bonzwa demanded in disbelief. "You find some ashes under the cover of dirt and you know not only that they had built a fire, but what and how many of what they had eaten?"

The tracker regarded Bonzwa with a bored expression before turning his attention to Armand, as if Bonzwa and his question were beneath his notice. "The ashes are still warm and the drippings of roasting meat are thick in the ash, much thicker than they would be had they only cooked one animal." The tracker looked around the clearing. A wry smile pulled at the corners of his lips as he raised a finger to point at three black dots circling in the dawn sky. "Scavengers," his eyes drifted down from the buzzards to a wooded area at the far end of the clearing. He nodded to himself. "I am sure you will find the innards, skins and bones of the hares somewhere over there," he finished as he pointed at the area he knew the remains were located.

"How long ago?" Armand asked, shifting his gaze around the clearing, searching for any other clues he might need.

"Four hours, perhaps less," the tracker replied.

"Which direction did they go when they left?" Armand asked.

The tracker began walking about the crater, kneeling occasionally to check something that had caught his attention. After several moments, he returned to the men and pointed toward the northern end of the clearing. "They are still heading north," he paused a moment as he did a double take at the tracks he had been studying. "Odd," he commented as he knelt back down and continued to study.

"What is it?" Armand asked.

"Very confusing. It appears that at least three other people have joined them."

Armand frowned. "Are you certain?"

The tracker nodded. "Yes. There are three additional riders. Their mounts are smaller as are the riders, but there are definitely now eight where there had been five."

Armand sighed and nodded once as he continued to survey the crater. He wanted desperately to continue the chase, especially in light of the fact that Devenshire had added to his number of minions, but he also knew this was the best opportunity for his men to rest. He turned to the men and nodded once. "Gather our mounts, bring them up here, and then make camp. We will rest here for a short time before moving on. I suggest that all of you eat and sleep while you can and do it quickly. I cannot say when we will stop again."

The sound of so many men moving at once was nearly deafening in the calm morning air. He turned and began walking about the clearing, knowing that his men would pitch the camp quickly and efficiently. As he walked, he took the opportunity to walk out some of the stiffness from so many hours in the saddle.

Lordalise knew the stunned expression on his face was plain for all to see. He struggled to contain the protest that clawed at the back of his throat. Taking several deep breaths to regain his composure, he turned to Bonzwa. "You and the others bring our horses up. Make camp, but be ready to move at a moment's notice." Bonzwa nodded and turned to issue the orders to the others. Lordalise turned back around and set off after Armand. "Captain Armand," Lordalise called out as he strode quickly to catch up to him. "A moment, please."

Armand stopped and waited, watching the Hunter approach and knowing what the man was going to say. "Yes, Master Lordalise?"

"Dawn is upon us. The vampire will have to find a dark place in which to hide for the day. Would it not be more beneficial to push on, to attempt to catch up to them? We are only a few hours behind."

Armand stretched his arms behind him to work out more kinks while answering the question. "Perhaps, but this past night of constant fear that Devenshire might strike at any moment and from any direction has worn my men down. To say nothing of the fact that we spent the night before chasing them throughout all of Lirpa and then pushing onward through yesterday and last night without rest. My men are of hearty stock, Master Lordalise, but they are still human."

"I understand your points, Captain, but I would hate to lose any advantage all of the hard traveling we have done to this point. Surely we could ride on through today and make camp this evening."

Armand sighed and stifled a yawn as he twisted his torso at the waist. Several soft pops and cracks came from his lower back in response. "Now is the best time to make camp and rest."

"I do not follow your logic, Captain," Lordalise replied, trying valiantly to maintain his composure. It was madness to stop now, now that they were so close to catching up to them.

"By stopping now, while the sun shines, the men know that Devenshire cannot harm them. They will be able to sleep more soundly with that knowledge." He saw the protest forming in Lordalise's eyes. "Make no mistake. I want these criminals as badly as anyone in this party does, but when we take them, I want my men fresh, alert, and ready. I do not wish for them to be battling both an enemy and their own fatigue. It may also work in our favor to delay our strike, to let them believe they have eluded us. They may grow careless and thereby give us an advantage." Armand could tell by the set of Lordalise' features that the Hunter did not like that course of action.

"Devenshire and his minions already know we are after them, there is little chance of our regaining anything resembling an element of surprise. Surely your men are trained and disciplined enough to ward off fatigue and stress long enough for us to accomplish our goal," Lordalise countered.

Armand did not miss the sarcasm in the Hunters' voice and he found himself growing angry. Perhaps he had underestimated his own level of fatigue. He refused to allow Lordalise to provoke him into an angry confrontation. He reminded himself that they both wanted the same thing and this was simply a difference of opinion on how to go about achieving that goal. "My men are indeed trained and disciplined enough. But I see no point in forcing them into such a situation when it is not necessary. When the time for battle comes, Master Lordalise, you will find my men are unequaled to the task," Armand answered in tightly even tones.

Like they were in Lirpa? When you and your highly trained men allowed them to escape? Lordalise thought, wanting desperately to let the thoughts transform into words and fly out of his mouth. Instead, he bit back on the sharp sarcastic retort and forged ahead with his counter argument. "Every hour we delay is another hour that Devenshire has free reign upon our realm. Free reign to slaughter innocent people, possibly even perverting their souls into the very essence of evil that he represents! I have taken an oath to protect the citizens of this realm from hell spawned bastards like Devenshire and no amount of stress or fatigue will keep me from fulfilling that oath!"

Armand felt his patience growing thin. He was not accustomed to having his orders or his decisions questioned. While he acknowledged that the service Lordalise and those like him provided was beyond value, he could not go along with having even a Hunter question his command. He took another deep, calming breath. When he spoke, his voice was calm in volume, but there was a definite hard, chilled edge to his words. "Master Lordalise. Perhaps now is a good time to set things in their proper prospective. I am in command of this expedition. You are here to eliminate a ghoul that we are ill equipped to battle. Once Devenshire is found, I will yield to your expertise in that area. But until that time, I expect you to yield to my expertise in tracking down criminals. Let us not lose sight of our common goal and further blur that sight with impatience. Devenshire cannot slaughter anyone, or pervert their souls, so long as the sun shines. We will lose nothing by allowing ourselves a few moments of rest and respite."

The skin under Lordalise' eyes tightened and his jaw set in a hard line of growing anger. Armand reasoned that as unaccustomed as he was to having his command questioned, Lordalise must be equally unaccustomed to having his charge questioned. For a moment, Armand feared the Hunter would launch another argument to push on. After a few moments, though, Lordalise bowed slightly. "As you wish, Captain. Forgive my impatience. I see the wisdom of your decision and will abide by it."

Armand felt relief wash through him that he would not be forced into a power struggle with Lordalise, which would lead to more unpleasant confrontations between not only himself and the Hunter but his men and those of Lordalise. With a tired smile he placed a hand on Lordalise' shoulder. "Think nothing more of it. We are tired, angry, and thirsty for vengeance. Such a powerful combination can often lead to small bouts of irrational thought. I promise you that we will find them and swoop down upon them with the same fury and thirst that Devenshire has used on his unfortunate victims. He will pay for his crimes and pay for them dearly, both he and those who would travel with him."

Lordalise smiled and nodded, saying nothing else. Armand patted him on the back, then turned and continued walking toward the wood line. The captain did not see the smile on the face of Lordalise quickly twist into a scowl as the captain walked away. "You fool!" he hissed softly. He then turned and began walking back toward his men. Armand was thinking like a soldier, a soldier in pursuit of ordinary criminals. This was his mistake and such a mistake could get them all killed in short order. Devenshire was not an ordinary criminal, did not think like an ordinary criminal, and did not act like an ordinary criminal. If Armand continued to treat him as such, a very fatal mistake was in the works. Lordalise had faced too many vampires, had too many close brushes with death to allow his end to come now and because of a soldiers mentality. For now, he would let Armand lead this expedition, but he could see a time coming when he would have to take charge and save Armand from himself.

~*~

Arness stalked around the small campfire, his anger burning as brightly as the fire. That damned Darkseed! He had known what Devenshire had planned to do, and had known the impossible nature of challenging Xavier, and of trying to take those damnable Stones from him. Stant, Petera, and Kendra had swallowed Devenshire and

Darkseed's lies and were following them all into certain death. That was the part that angered him more than anything else. His kinsmen had not followed him out of that camp of the insane, and he felt betrayed. They were elves, just as he was. They were not human, and yet they had allied themselves with the humans and let him walk away. *To hell with all of them! May the fires of hell melt the flesh from their foolish bones.* He was not about to risk his life on a quest that had no chance of success. If he were destined to travel through this realm alone, then so be it. He would become rogue, traveling alone.

Kendra.

Her slim petite form came to mind, and he felt the longing he had always harbored for her double in strength. She was taller than most Elven females and her delicate features radiated a beauty and sensuality that Arness had never seen in another face. Blond hair, pale blue eyes, full red lips that always seemed on the verge of a playful pout, her graceful limbs, firm breasts, and the way her hips rounded into the most perfectly shaped legs he had ever seen. All these things combined to taunt him with visions of pleasures she could impart. More than once, her countenance had visited his fevered dreams. In his dreams, she was his and his alone. She would kneel before him, smiling up at him with an expression that spoke of passion and pleasure. She would submit herself to him, and he would take her with the blazing passion that seemed always to smolder within him.

He remembered the way she had looked at Devenshire, the way her eyes had lingered over nearly every inch of his frame. The appreciative smile she had tried to hide, but still played at the corners of her lips. Then her full red lips had parted, and the tip of her tongue had brushed ever so slightly over her top lip in an expression that left no doubt as to the nature of her thoughts. She wanted him. Badly.

Arness' face twisted into a vicious scowl as he recalled the look on her face and at whom it had been directed toward... Devenshire. *That bastard was trying to steal her away from him. She had started showing an interest in him and now Devenshire was using his charms to steal her attentions.* Well, he would not give up without a fight. He would have Kendra, somehow, someway. There had to be a way to eliminate Devenshire from her consideration and do so without drawing attention to himself. His mind shifted into full concentration on finding a path to the object of his desires.

Looking up at the sky, he could see the first hint of approaching dawn. Devenshire and his parade of lunatics would be packing up camp if they had not already done so. The best way for him to learn of a way to win Kendra's attention was through study and concentration. Devenshire had weaknesses, all men did. Finding his would only be a matter of watching him closely and learning all he could about the man's strengths. Once he knew Devenshire's strengths, his weaknesses would be easy to find and exploit. With a set expression of determination, Arness quickly snuffed out his small fire and strode to his mount. With a glimmer of new hope and a plan of action, he swung himself into the saddle and turned his horse toward the camp and his new path.

Arriving at the crater, Arness found it occupied by a large complement of Royal Guardsmen and others. Dismounting quietly and slipping into a small grove of trees, Arness studied the situation. The nearest complement of the Royal Guard was in Lirpa and Darkseed resided there as well. He knew Darkseed had a dubious reputation and had had several incidents with the local constable. Perhaps Darkseed had committed some crime in Lirpa and was now fleeing from the law. It would explain why a self-serving individual like Darkseed would suddenly decide to join a noble, albeit insane, cause. What better way to leave Lirpa and perhaps enlist assistance in hiding from the authorities?

Perhaps he could take it another step further. It was obvious that Darkseed and Devenshire had some kind of history together. It could be possible that Devenshire was just as self-serving as Darkseed and therein laid a possible course of action. If Devenshire was wanted for some crime, then there might be a way to serve two purposes here. If he helped in the capture of two possible criminals like Devenshire and Darkseed, then he would have the gratitude of not only the Royal Guard and the Constable of Lirpa, which was not a bad thing to have at all. Then showing Devenshire for the rabble that Arness believed he was would snuff out any interest Kendra had in the man, thereby leaving her attentions open for him to step into. Yet none of these things was certain. The Royal Guards below were definitely in pursuit of someone, but there was no guarantee that it was Darkseed or Devenshire that they were after. More information was needed and the only sources of reliable information lie below him setting up a camp.

CHAPTER ELEVEN

The sword blade pierced the air where Devenshire's back had been only a second before. Spinning to the left, Devenshire swung around behind his would-be assassin and quickly drove his right fist deep into the man's lower back. With a grunted squeal of pain and surprise, the man arched his back in reaction to the blow. Devenshire quickly took the man's hair in his right hand and jerked back and down, pulling his attacker off balance. As the man fell backwards, Devenshire turned and dropped the outside edge of his left hand into the man's throat while simultaneously jerking up on the handful of hair in his right hand. Once the chopping blow to his throat had been executed, Devenshire released the man's hair and allowed him to fall the ground. As he fell, the attacker forgot his sword as his hands grasped at his throat and the sudden lack of oxygen passing through it.

Devenshire quickly scanned the small clearing for any signs of any accomplices the man might have, finding none. He calmly knelt down beside the man and watched as he struggled to get air passing through what felt like his crushed throat. Resting his elbows on his knees, Devenshire regarded the man a moment, cocking his head to one side as the man gagged and wheezed, desperate for air. "You will be able to breathe in a moment. However, I am not entirely sure you will want to by the end of our conversation," he said matter-of-factly.

"Go... go to hell!" the man rasped out as he rolled from one side to the other trying to recover from the pain of his left kidney and severely bruised windpipe.

Devenshire smiled with a slight chuckle. "I will make sure you show me the way. Now, to the matter at hand, who are you and why did you attack me?"

"I will tell... tell you nothing," the attacker gasped.

Devenshire arched one eyebrow, and nodded slowly. "Then allow me to answer the questions for you. Your name is meaningless save to mark your grave. You are, more than likely, a Follower sent by Xavier to kill me. How accurate is that?" The man looked up at Devenshire but did not reply. No reply was necessary for Devenshire saw the truth in the man's panicked expression. "I see," Devenshire said as he slowly nodded and looked out across the forest clearing he had been standing in. He had been searching for a suitable campsite for the night as well as the most likely place to find fresh game for the evening meal. He had taken a moment to stop walking and soak in the calm, peaceful solitude of the clearing when he heard the unmistakable sounds of someone attempting to sneak up on him from behind. He had willed himself to remain absolutely still until he heard the man's sharp intake of breath as he prepared to drive the sword through his back. He looked back down at the man who was beginning to have more success breathing. "How many of you did he send?"

"I will not answer!" the man rasped defiantly.

"That would be a mistake. You have been discovered and captured by your intended victim. How much leniency and mercy do you expect me to show?" Devenshire asked the rhetorical question as his darkening gaze conveyed the very real threat he posed.

"You do not frighten me! There is nothing you could do to me that would make me betray my Master!"

Devenshire's lips twisted in a hard, cruel grin. "It is not my intention to frighten you. It is my intention to make you, with the proper persuasion, decide if your secrets are worth keeping."

The man stopped rocking back and forth to look up into Devenshire's eyes. "You would dare torture me?"

Devenshire's hard grin turned cold as he shrugged. "That is entirely up to you."

The assassin searched Devenshire's eyes, trying to determine if the man was telling the truth or simply bluffing. He did not like the answer he saw. In that instant, his blood ran cold for he saw the unwavering conviction in the man's eyes. "You would not dare torture me! My Master would surely make you pay!"

Devenshire chuckled. "If your master were truly so powerful, he would come strike at me himself instead of sending his inept lackeys. All he is doing by sending the likes of you is giving me time to hone my fighting skills. You are nothing but practice for me, and I can do with you what I wish. Your Master will do nothing but find another mindless slug to take your place."

Suddenly the situation changed and Devenshire knew it wasn't in his favor. It was something in the man's eyes, something in the sudden but subtle shift in his demeanor. Just as he felt the presence of someone behind him and ordered his muscles to respond, he heard the distinct whistle of an arrow slicing through the air followed by the meaty *thunk* of the impact. As another voice cried out in agony, Devenshire completed his spin, rising to his feet. He saw another Follower standing behind him, sword raised high. From the center of his chest protruded the thin shaft of an arrow. Devenshire instinctively reached for his sword as the Follower staggered backwards, his sword falling from his hands as they wrapped around the shaft. As his face lost all color and went slack in amazed pain, the

Follower looked up in the direction the arrow had come before slowly dropping to his knees, his face still a mixture of dawning pain and disbelief.

Devenshire turned his head to also look in the direction the arrow had come and found Kendra slowly lowering her bow, her eyes intently locked on the Follower as he pitched forward to the ground, driving the tip of the arrow out through his back. She shifted her intense gaze to Devenshire and held it for a moment. Slowly, a sultry smile parted her lips as she winked at him. Devenshire smiled and nodded his thanks before shifting his attention back to the Follower at his feet. "As you were saying?"

The man was staring at his fallen companion, his hand still on his throat, but not rubbing it any longer. The seriousness of his situation finally sunk in and he knew he was lost. It was of no matter, though. He had served his Master faithfully. He shifted his gaze to the man he had been sent to dispatch and chuckled softly, the sound very gravelly with the damage to his throat. "You can take a cup of water from a river and not weaken it."

Devenshire's brow furrowed as he tried to understand what the man was saying. He heard Kendra's light steps as she began walking toward him. "What?" he asked.

The Follower simply smiled and relaxed. "Kill me. I will tell you nothing else."

"What did he say?" Kendra asked still walking toward them.

Devenshire saw the resolution in the man's eyes and also saw something else. An eerie calm, an almost sardonic acceptance that he was about to die. With his brows knitting even tighter together, he dug deep into the man's words about a river. "You can take a cup of water from a river..." his voice drifted off as he raised his head to look at Kendra. Then his eyes drifted up over her shoulder to the woods behind her. His eyes grew wide and his blood ran cold. "But you cannot weaken it," he finished in a whisper. "Behind you!" he shouted, glancing at her and seeing a mirror image of his expression in her delicate features. That was when he realized that she had screamed the same thing to him that he had yelled to her. He spun to see two Followers coming upon him from behind.

A trap.

The first two Followers were simply bait, to see what type of opposition Devenshire would pose to an attack or to weaken him and make it easier for the three men emerging from the forest behind Kendra and the two closing in on his position to finish him. He tossed his sword to his left hand and quickly performed a quick gesture in an attempt to call on his powers. He tried to duplicate the spell he had used on Armand, but nothing happened. A second time, he dropped his hand to his side, willing the blue sphere of light to appear, but there was no sign of it. He was accustomed to feeling the echo of his powers within him, but now he felt nothing, as though his powers were gone. He shifted his focus as he drove the point of his sword into the ground to free up his left hand. Again calling on his powers, he thrust both hands, palms out, toward the attackers as he slammed the heels together. This had been the spell he had used on the demon inside the inn, but again nothing happened. He couldn't understand why he couldn't summon his powers, but he knew he didn't have the time to sort through the mystery at the moment. Grasping the hilt of his sword, he jerked it free of the ground and prepared to meet the attack head on. "Very well," he muttered, "we do this the old fashioned way."

Kendra had turned to see the three men easing their way out of the trees. Once they saw that they had been discovered, they abandoned stealth and bolted toward her, swords raised. She reached up over her shoulder and pulled another arrow free from her quiver. With the eased accuracy born of a lifetime of using the bow, she quickly nocked the arrow. Raising the bow while pulling back on the string, she lined up her shot with little thought to her action. The thumb of her right hand touched her cheek as she stared down the shaft of the arrow lining up on the chest of the center man. She puckered her lips and gave a light kiss as her fingers released the string. It slapped against the inside of her left wrist with a sharp twang as it sent the arrow whistling off toward her target. She felt the tingle in the fingers of her left hand as the string impact vibrated against the wrist guard. The man she had lined up her shot on tried to shift his path to avoid the arrow, but all he accomplished was to cause the arrow to pierce his chest off center. The impact was hard and caused him to twist his upper body as he cried out in pain. With his balance thrown off by the impact, he fell to the ground and bounced from the momentum of his charge. She shifted her gaze to the two remaining men and knew she didn't have time to pull another arrow. Dropping her bow, she pulled her short sword free and prepared herself to meet their attack. While she knew how to use a sword, she was not as comfortable with it as she was her bow.

Devenshire barely had time to get his sword free before he was forced to side step a harsh stab from the third man. With his balance off, he swung his sword around toward the man who easily shifted his sword up to block the swing. Devenshire held no illusions that it would have hit the man, but it forced him to defend the blow, and thereby giving him time to regain his balance. As he back peddled a few steps and balanced his stance, he saw the first man he had taken down with a blow to the throat roll to his stomach, preparing to rise. He risked a quick glance in Kendra's direction and saw her drop her bow as she reached for her sword. He shifted his gaze and saw one of the men in a crumpled heap, the shaft of an arrow protruding from his chest. He began sidestepping, keeping his sword at the ready. He was going to try to get closer to Kendra, and perhaps give them both an advantage. The Fates knew they were going to need it. The third man, the one who had slashed at him as he pulled his sword out of the ground, growled and launched his attack. Devenshire forced himself to remain calm as he met and countered the offensive. He kept himself on the balls of his feet and drew his senses to a razor fine edge. While he parried the thrusts of the third man, he kept the other two men within his field of vision. The man's face was a tight mask of concentration, and Devenshire knew he would have to be very alert for any weaknesses. This man had been trained in the finer arts of swordplay. It would be safe to assume all of Xavier's Followers had been, as well.

Kendra deflected a blow from the first man to reach her. She quickly spun out of the path of the next swing and lanced out, trying to pierce her opponent's side. Her blade was thrust down by a swing from the second man, saving his companion. She quickly propelled herself backwards, giving her space to form her next plan of attack... or defense, as it was turning out to be. The first man looked down at his side, amazed at how close he had come to being wounded. His gaze rose in smoldering anger toward her. "You pointy eared little bitch!" he hissed as he began to advance on her again. She let the slight roll past her. She was accustomed to such ignorant remarks, and they had no affect on her aside from the touch of sadness at the short sightedness of some people. In this instance, she actually welcomed the racist barb, because it meant the man was getting angry and would be fighting with his emotions instead of his skill. She tightened her grip on the sword as her eyes flickered between the two men as they advanced on her. The first man slashed at her as the second man postponed his attack to see which direction her defense would go. *Clever*, she mused. She brought her sword up to block his overhand attack while at the same time swinging her left arm around behind her to free the dagger in her belt. As she pivoted her right arm around to block a swing from the second man, she brought her left arm back around her body and swung it in a long arc, aimed at the first man's stomach. He saw the swing coming around and quickly bounced backwards, but not before the tip of the blade ripped through his shirt and the skin beneath it. Not waiting for the results of her attack on the first man or the next attack from the second, Kendra launched herself to her left. She landed in a shoulder roll that brought her to her feet several paces away from her attackers. It had all happened to so fast, she had to take a moment to gather her bearings.

The first man staggered back, his left hand slapping to the burning pain spreading across his midsection. The second man blinked several times, not entirely sure how his target had so quickly gotten away from him. The Elven woman moved with a swiftness he had not encountered before. He glanced at his companion as the man lifted his shirt up to see how badly he had been injured. His first instinct was to help his companion, but the Master's orders had been very clear, so he shifted his attention back to the woman and quickly advanced on her new position.

Devenshire deflected the attack of one man while ducking beneath the swing of a second. The man he had struck in the throat was on his feet now and was reaching for his sword. Very soon, it would be three on one. Devenshire knew he would have to even the odds very quickly. He swung his blade around, feinted a thrust at the fourth man before shifting his attack into a thrust at the third man who was trying to bring his sword around for another swing.

The third man saw the attack coming and scrambled backwards to avoid Devenshire's thrust. Before the fourth man could attack, Devenshire kicked out with his left foot, catching the man in the stomach. With a grunted expulsion of air, the man sank to his knees, hugging himself against the pain and sudden lack of air. Devenshire quickly brought his foot back down and balanced himself before launching into an attack at the third man who was just propelling himself into an attack. Devenshire saw the sword tip speeding toward him and quickly planted his feet, twisting his upper body to the right, and leaning back. The blade sliced neatly through the air his midsection had occupied just seconds before. The man had been braced for his sword to sink deep into his opponent's body. With Devenshire twisting out of the way, the man was thrown off balance and stumbled forward. Devenshire allowed himself to fall backwards to avoid the man's stumbling advance. As he fell, he recoiled his right arm and thrust his sword straight out. He felt the impact along his arm and heard the man's strangled cry before he braced himself for the impact with the ground. As he hit, he felt the man's feet stumble over his legs. Devenshire quickly rolled to his right and came up on his knees, his sword at the ready.

The man he had just wounded had been tripped up on Devenshire's legs, falling on his face. A quick glance showed Devenshire that the fourth man was struggling to his feet while the first man, the one he had struck in the throat, was advancing on him from his right side. Reaching beneath his cloak, he pulled a dagger free, flipped it over to grip it by the tip, and took aim at the fourth man, waiting until he was upright to throw the dagger. He was also painfully aware of the crush of time as the first man was closing on him rapidly. Snapping his head from one man to the other, he realized that the first man was going to reach him before the fourth man could present him with a suitable target. Time for a change of plans.

Kendra balanced herself and focused on the man advancing on her, keeping the wounded one in her peripherals. The first man bared his teeth at her before launching in a series of short quick jabs designed to put her on the defensive. She parried each thrust and moved backwards, keeping both men in front of her. She could hear the battle between Devenshire and the other men behind her, but she dared not look to see how he was faring. Fear drove a spike into her mind and tried to shred her concentration. She was not a skilled swordsman. She was an apprentice at best, and she would not stand for long against two opponents, let alone a skilled lone one. The man she was now locked in battle with was testing her skill while looking for the perfect moment to strike with a real attack. Kendra was honest enough with herself to know that such a moment would be coming quickly. Her breath was growing shallow in her throat, sweat was pouring down her face, and she could feel the rapid pounding of her heart in every extremity. Swallowing against the dry knot in her throat, and the fear rising up from her core, she willed herself to focus, to concentrate on keeping herself alive through the next attack. Then, she would worry about the next one.

Her opponent changed his attack from a testing flurry of swings and jabs to a more concerted one of probing lunges and stabs, poking at her defenses, searching for that one opening. All the while his burning eyes were locked to hers, searching for fear, searching for a flinch, anything that would tell him that his attack was wearing her down. She set her features in granite and forced herself to ignore the trembling vines of fatigue beginning to wrap around her arms and legs. There had to be a way to defeat this man, to survive. There just had to be. That's when the weight of the dagger in her left hand registered. Her thoughts raced through the fear-frosted edges of her mind and searched for what she could do with the dagger that would make a difference. Her arms were getting heavy, her lungs burned, and she knew she was running out of time. She had no idea how long the fight had gone on, but she knew her endurance was being taxed.

The man seemed to know, as surely as if he had read her mind. His mask of angered concentration was beginning to relax a little. He had won and he knew it. It was simply a matter of the formality of killing her. Kendra had tried to fight with calm intellect and that was failing. She knew it was time for an act of desperation. At least that would give her more of a chance of surviving than waiting for him to wear her down until she could no longer defend herself. With that, she released the reins of her control and abandoned herself to the primal need to survive. She narrowed her eyes, focusing on nothing but the man in front of her. She watched, waited, and prepared herself for any opportunity that might present itself.

Devenshire braced himself as the first man bore down on him, sword raised high and ready to strike. The fourth man had regained his feet and was retrieving his sword. In the hairs breadth of time before the first man reached him, he made his decision. He dropped his sword and dagger as he bounced to his feet, turning to fully face the first man. With as much speed as he could pour into his limbs, he reached up and grasped his attackers' wrists. Using the momentum of his opponents run, he fell backwards, while bringing his right leg up. As his back hit the ground, Devenshire drove his right boot deep into the man's stomach and pushed hard, swinging up with his arms. The man was pivoted into the air and flipped over. Just as his feet pointing straight up, Devenshire released his wrists and rolled to his right.

The man came down hard on his back, smashing every breath of air out of his lungs in a loud and pain riddled grunt. Devenshire rolled to his knees just as the fourth man reached him. Reacting out of instinct, he drove his right fist deep into the man's stomach while also ducking to the left, away from the downward swing of his sword. With a grunted hiss of forcibly expelled air, the man staggered back a step just before Devenshire rose, planted his feet, and drove his right fist up and into the point of the Follower's chin. The man's head snapped back as he stumbled backwards two steps before crashing to the ground. Stars and streaks of pain erupted inside his skull as he found himself stunned and unable to move. He knew he had to get up and strike a victory blow for his Master. Failure was not an option, and he would sooner die here at the hands of his Master's enemy than face his Master with news of his failure. Forcing his numb limbs to move, he tried to roll to his side, but he suddenly found himself pinned to the ground by a black clad knee and a harsh shove from a hand upon his shoulder. Though he could only make out a fuzzed silhouette hovering over him, the touch of cold steel against his throat was crystal clear.

"Who sent you?" came the harsh demand of his target.

"Go to hell!" he replied as his eyes rolled upwards in their sockets.

"You first!" He felt the steel drag across his neck a heartbeat later. There was only a little pain, much less than he would have expected from having his throat slit. He was vaguely aware of the hot splash of blood across his face and chest as the silhouette rose and vanished from his fuzzed vision. He found it very hard to breathe and his strength was fading rapidly. He knew he was dying, and the calmness he felt in accepting that fact was fascinating. He had expected his death to be a fear riddled, terrifying moment. As the sunlight beat down on his chilling face, he found himself calm, at peace. He would not have to face his Master with news of his failure. As his perceptions began to fade, he found it odd that he actually wanted to thank the man he'd been sent to kill.

Devenshire turned from the doomed Follower to find the man he had flipped into the air, the one who had started this attack, still trying to suck air into his deflated lungs passed his bruised windpipe. As he moved to retrieve his sword and dagger, his gaze fell on the other man, the one he had sliced across his side. He was sitting up, studying his wound, oblivious to anything else. Devenshire shifted his gaze quickly to see Kendra fighting two other Followers. He bent down and picked up his sword and dagger before running toward Kendra. As he passed the man he had wounded in the side, he raised his sword up over his left shoulder. "Your companion is at hell's gate waiting for you!" he hissed as he swung the sword around and very nearly decapitated the Follower.

Kendra saw her opening, her one moment of opportunity to survive this encounter as the man brought his sword back for another swing, leaving himself open. With a scream of fear and defiance, she planted her feet, closed her eyes, and swung her dagger upward with all her might. She felt the impact along her left arm all the way to the shoulder. She felt the hot flow of his blood across her hand and heard a strangled cry. She opened her eyes to see that she had driven her dagger up through the bottom of the man's jaw, through his tongue and lodged the tip into the roof of his mouth. She released the dagger and stepped back, watching the pain and fear explode within his eyes. He abandoned his sword as both hands reached up to grip the hilt of the dagger. As her chest heaved under her labored breathing and her nerves still tingled with icy fear, she watched the silent debate in his eyes of whether to pull the dagger free and the fear of the pain doing so would cause.

"Bastard!" she hissed as she coiled her right arm back and bringing the tip of the sword up. With a snarl, she drove the sword through the man's chest with all the strength she had left. The blade sliced through flesh, nicking ribs as it passed through to puncture his rapidly beating heart. For a brief moment, she honestly believed she could feel his heart fluttering around the tip of her blade. His eyes went wide and the dagger embedded in the roof of his mouth was forgotten as he collapsed to his knees followed instantly by Kendra falling to hers, her strength spent. They stared at one another for a moment, one about to die and one realizing just how close to death she had come. The man moaned softly as he fell to his left. Kendra simply released her sword and allowed it to fall with him since she didn't have the strength to pull it free. She slumped in place and closed her eyes. She wanted desperately to fall to the ground also, her strength gone from her in her last defiant blow against her opponent. She knew there was still one man left to face, and she honestly didn't know how to even begin to fight him. She was spent. She heard footsteps crushing leaves and twigs as they approached her. She heard the eerie silence that always follows an intense battle, and she realized that if she did not act quickly, this would be the last time she heard such a silence. She forced her eyes open and saw the first man advancing on her, his sword held tightly in his trembling right hand. She looked down and saw the hilt of her sword protruding from the Follower's chest. Though she felt as though there was nothing left within her, her spirit refused to let her simply kneel in the forest and accept death. She took hold of the hilt of her sword and pulled back, trying to free it from the dead man's body, but it wouldn't come. The sounds of the footfalls stopped beside her and she heard the man's harsh breathing. He was angry at having been wounded and now enraged at the death of his companion.

"Stay your sword, you little bitch! Your end is near and it is going to be excruciatingly painful!"

Kendra jerked on the sword again and this time it slipped free of his chest. She shifted her gaze upward just as the man raised his sword up and over his left shoulder. She realized he fully intended to decapitate her. She felt the weight of her sword in her trembling hand and quickly brought the blade up in an attempt to deflect his swing. She wasn't sure how she would fight him since she doubted her legs would support her weight at the moment, but she knew she had to try.

"I think not!" came another voice. She heard the distinct sound of a blade slicing deep into flesh. Despite her fatigue, she jumped in a start as the tip of a sword suddenly protruded out of the man's stomach. With dazed confusion, she saw the man's face pale as he looked down at the tip of the sword. It was bloody with tendrils of flesh and entrails hanging from it. Suddenly, the tip jerked back inside his stomach and he felt the tearing pain all the way through his body as the blade was finally jerked out of his back and the hard grip of a hand on his left shoulder roughly jerked him to the side. He fell to the ground, still not fully comprehending what had sent him to the Afterlife so suddenly.

Kendra blinked, not sure of what she was seeing. The man who had been about to attack her was tossed aside and Devenshire stood in his place, his bloody sword still at the ready. His burning eyes watched the Follower hit the ground before they turned to her. He was breathing heavily and the fire of battle still raged in his eyes. It was a frightening thing to see. For a moment, with his heated gaze on her, she felt a flicker of fear that he might actually kill her himself.

"Are you all right?" he asked.

"I think so..." she whispered, not really sure of the answer herself.

"Were you wounded?" he asked. Gone were the warm mellow tones of his deep voice that she was growing ever so fond of. The harsh edge of tightly controlled anger made his voice almost evil. Blinking out of the exhausted shock of nearly dying, she shook her head sharply to bring herself back to the world of the living. "No. I am fine," she replied. He nodded as he turned to the two Followers at his feet. He bent down and cleaned his blade on the clothes of one of the men. She shifted her gaze around the clearing, struggling to dispel the cold grip of the specter of death. That was when she saw the two bodies Devenshire had dispatched. A flash of movement caught her eye and she forced her attention to focus. She saw a third man moving off through the woods away from them. A survivor. A survivor that would quickly alert Xavier to their exact location. "Daimion! He is running!" she called out.

Devenshire spun around to see the very first Follower running into the woods. He looked down at Kendra. "Alert the others! I cannot allow him to escape!" he said a moment before he took off in a dead run after the man. Within a handful of moments, the woods on the far end of the clearing had swallowed them both. While she wanted nothing more than to fall to the ground and recover from the encounter, she knew she had to do as he instructed. Forcing herself to her feet, she sheathed her sword and then began the unpleasant task of jerking her dagger free from the Follower's skull, which nearly made her retch. Swallowing against the bile in her throat, she crossed to where her bow lay, retrieved it, and set off for the trail where the others were waiting.

CHAPTER TWELVE

Devenshire ran through the woods, shielding his face from low hanging branches and brush slapping at him as he ran. His eyes squinted into the gloom of the forest, searching for any sign of the Follower. He couldn't allow the man to escape. He would go back to Xavier with a wealth of information such as their numbers, their strengths and, most importantly, their exact location. Devenshire had to admit that he had no idea how much Xavier already knew through whatever spell he was using that allowed him to spy on them, but he wasn't about to simply sit back and hand the madman any new information.

He slid to a stop and forced himself to be still, to calm his ragged breathing long enough to listen for which direction the man was running. He could hear the crashing of the man's body through the woods to his left. Snapping his head in that direction he narrowed his eyes, just able to make out the man's fleeting silhouette in the distance. He was making good time. Devenshire shifted his direction and took off in a dead run in pursuit. If the man made it to a horse, the pursuit would be over. He wished he had taken a moment to summon his mount before setting off after the Follower, but it was a moot point now. As he ran, he tried to focus his powers to lock on the man, to give him a mystical guide to where the Follower was, but like at the onset of the fight, his powers were not responding to his commands. He couldn't understand why his powers had been so abundant and easy to control in Lirpa, but they had seemingly abandoned him on the trail. It was a disheartening problem but one he could not afford the mental energy to contemplate now. With his powers not responding, he would need to focus on his more traditional abilities.

He leapt over a fallen log just in time to see another log that had fallen across two other trees at head height. He just barely had time to throw his body backwards, kicking his feet out from under him. He slid under the log, just barely grazing his nose as he fell to his back and slid across the forest floor. Just as he slid to a stop, he barely had time to register the blade quickly descending toward his face and to force his body to react. Rolling to his left, he could feel the tip of the blade graze the back of his skull as he rolled away. He quickly rolled to one knee just in time to see the Follower launch himself at him, intent on impaling him on his blade. Devenshire had dropped his sword as he slid under the log so he had no choice but to gather his strength and launch himself to the left, twisting his body to land on his left shoulder and allowing the momentum to roll him to his feet. He didn't waste time going for his sword opting, instead, to launch himself at his opponent before he could regain his balance. The Follower staggered a few steps and then steadied himself. He turned to find his target only to see Devenshire's angry snarl a second before a fist filled his vision. The impact snapped his head backwards as the force of the blow numbed his senses enough to force the fingers of his right fist to open, dropping his sword. Just as he heard the sharp crack of cartilage, he felt himself driven backwards. It took all of his strength to remain on his feet as he slid to a stop. He felt the familiar burn across the bridge of his nose and knew it was broken. The warm flow of blood across his top lip only served to confirm his suspicions. He quickly wiped the back of his hand across his nose, which only inflamed the already burning pain of the break.

Devenshire approached and quickly launched a hard right jab toward the man's face. To his surprise, the Follower threw up his left arm to block the jab and countered with a hard right cross. Unlike Devenshire's punch, the Followers knuckles crashed into the right side of Devenshire's jaw, snapping his head around. His body followed the force of the blow and he was staggered. Tiny sparkles of pain erupted inside his skull as he felt the familiar numbness begin to spread throughout his body. He tasted blood and spat, feeling the anger rise within him and welcoming it as an old combat companion.

Through disorienting ripples in his vision, he looked up as the Follower approached. He spat blood again and twisted his lips into a harsh grin. There was a part of him that reveled in the fight that enjoyed the raw primal emotions that only a good fistfight could conjure. As the Follower closed in on him, he released himself to the thrill. The Follower threw a flurry of quick, short jabs, which Devenshire quickly pulled his arms in to block. The blows, while painful, only inflicted pain on his upper arms and elbows. The Follower launched a right uppercut, which Devenshire snapped himself backwards to evade. He quickly shot out a right jab that caught the Follower on the jaw and sent him staggering backwards. The blow had not done any significant damage, but it had thrown him off balance long enough for Devenshire to move off the defensive.

Devenshire stepped forward and snapped off a short hard left jab followed by a vicious right cross that sent the Follower sprawling to the forest floor. Devenshire wasted no time in advancing on the downed man and realized, too late, that the man wasn't as stunned as he had thought as the Follower's right foot shot out catching Devenshire in the stomach. Sharp lances of pain raced up his sides as his knees buckled from the force of the blow. Devenshire fell to his knees and doubled over against the searing pain in his lower torso. His breath was coming in short shallow gasps, which provided little to no air for his already starved lungs. He heard the solid footfalls of the Follower as he advanced on him. Devenshire shook the fuzz from his vision and snapped his head up to see the Follower raising a dagger to shoulder level, ready to strike. Devenshire gritted his teeth and drove his right fist out, not really caring where the blow landed so long as it bought him some time to regain his senses. He felt his fist sink deep into the soft mid section of the Follower and heard the man's sigh of suddenly expelled air. Reacting from instinct rather than any formulated plan, Devenshire rose to his feet and slapped his palms together, lacing his fingers. With a snarl, he unleashed a double-fisted uppercut, which caught the Follower just under the chin and sent him flying backwards, the dagger flying from his now numb hand.

The man hit hard on his back, instantly dazed. Devenshire unclasped his hands to rest them on his trembling knees as he took a moment to clear his senses. The Follower was in much better physical condition and much more seasoned in combat than he had anticipated he would be. He filed the information away for future reference since very rarely did someone get the opportunity to underestimate an opponent and live to learn from the experience. Breathing hard from the pursuit as well as the fight, he raised his spinning vision up to find the Follower struggling to regain his senses. His eyes were wide and disoriented as they stared up at the canopy of branches overhead. Devenshire knew his respite would be very brief. He stood upright and walked toward the downed Follower, stooping low to retrieve his sword as he went. He stopped beside the man and rested the point of his sword slightly to the right of the sternum. He swallowed hard once and leveled a hard gaze at the man. "How many travel with Xavier? Where is he now?"

The man's eyes rolled in his head as he struggled to understand what he was hearing. "What?" he rasped out between ragged breaths.

"How many travel with Xavier?" Devenshire repeated applying a little pressure to the sword.

The Follower blinked and looked up at him, his eyes revealing that he now understood that he had lost the fight and only had a narrow window of opportunity to save himself. "My Master commands an army! An army that will crush your paltry bones into powder!" the Follower hissed, summoning all the venom his disjointed mind could muster.

Devenshire shook his head slowly, swallowing again against the dry knot of thirst at the back of his throat. "I rather think not. If you and your companions are an example of the troops Xavier commands, we have little to worry about."

The Follower relaxed. "We are but a fragment of the might my Master commands. Go on! Assume you and your pathetic little band of misfits has even the slightest chance against my Master! It will make his ultimate victory all the sweeter!"

Devenshire found himself growing irritated at the cadence of the Followers. Their blind, unwavering devotion to Xavier was as confusing as it was infuriating. "Yes, yes, yes! I have heard all of this before and I grow weary of it! I will make this simple, simple enough for even your dull mind to comprehend! Tell me how many Followers travel with Xavier and his exact location, or I will kill you here and now!"

"My death will mean little in the ultimate conquest of..." the Follower never got to finish his sentence, as Devenshire drove the tip of his sword deep into his chest, cleaving the man's heart nearly in two. With a startled gasp and a violent twitch, the Follower moaned softly as he relaxed into death.

Devenshire watched the life fade from the man's eyes and shook his head. "If your life means so little to you then it means even less to me," he said. It was such a sad waste that these Followers were willing to die rather than betray a man who, in the same circumstances, would sell every one of them out to ensure his survival. For several moments, Devenshire leaned on his sword still buried deep in the Follower's chest, gathering his strength. Once the last of the disorientation passed, he stood upright and jerked his sword free of the body. He wiped the blood from his blade on the Followers clothes and then searched the body, looking for anything that would give him any information about Xavier. Around the man's neck, he found an amulet hanging from a small chain. As soon as he saw it, he felt the tingle run up his spine that told him this was mystical in origins. He held the amulet in his hand and felt the tingle intensify. He closed his hand around the amulet and jerked it free from the dead man's neck. He opened his hand and studied the amulet intensely as he rose to his feet. While he knew the amulet was magical in nature, he could not discern what its purpose was. He turned it over in his hand, studying it intently.

He regarded the dead Follower for a moment. "I do not suppose you will tell me what this is either," he rasped out from the dry knot in his throat. He returned his gaze to the amulet and that was when he noticed the intensity of the tingle in his spine increase. Along with the increase came the sensation of being watched. His gaze swept out around the forest, his eyes, as well as his senses searching for the source. The sensation was identical to the one he had felt in the Tavern the night this quest began. As his features took on a grim set, he knew Xavier was watching him. His eyes narrowed as he tried to pinpoint the exact direction the spell was coming from. He found an area above him that seemed to be the strongest source of the impression running through him. He glared at the spot and tried to conjure up Xavier's eyes looking at him. "Take a long hard look, Xavier!" he hissed as he gestured toward the body of the Follower with his left hand. "This is your future, you pathetic bastard! You are going to have to do much better than this if you plan to stop me from killing you!"

Without another word, he turned and began walking back toward the clearing where the attack had first begun. He would search the other Followers for clues and perhaps Darkseed could glean something of a mystical nature from the amulet.

~*~

Xavier strolled through the darkened forest, searching desperately for release in the sinister solitude. He had waited, impatiently, for the rest of the late afternoon to fade away so that he could submerge himself in the blackness of nightfall. The darkness, with only an occasional shaft of moonlight breaking through the canopy of branches overhead, reached in and lovingly massaged his soul, reinvigorating the blackness that lived there and soothing the fearful trepidation that threatened to consume him. A breeze would rustle a branch, an insect would call out or one of the many nocturnal animals would make some sort of a sound, but otherwise the night was silent and all encompassing. Just the way he preferred it.

However, this night found that he could not completely embrace the comfort his dark mistress always offered him. His mind was pre-occupied with other matters, specifically Daimion Devenshire. The fury, which had just started subsiding during his walk through the darkened woods returned with a white-hot intensity, pushing even the Stones of Andarus beyond his consideration. The attack had been perfectly planned. He had sent men to shadow Devenshire's group, watching and waiting for the perfect opportunity to eliminate the bastard. Through a detailed look through the Orb of Vision, he had seen Devenshire leave the others. He had watched as the bastard child of a filthy whore had isolated himself in the forest. Through a mystical amulet, he had given his attack force, he had directed their movements, and basically, handed Devenshire to them on a silver platter.

While the attack had been perfectly planned, it had not been perfectly executed. The fools! He had felt their deaths, both through the Orb and the amulet. He had been so sure of their victory that he was watching the attack through the Orb only to watch Devenshire and the Elven bitch dispatch his men. He had then watched Devenshire chase down the last man and kill him in short order. Then, with amazement, he saw Devenshire look directly at him through the magic of the orb. Though many miles separated them, Xavier had felt the anger radiate off the man as surely as though he were standing next to him.

"Take a long hard look, Xavier! This is your future, you pathetic bastard! You are going to have to do much better than this if you plan to stop me from killing you!" Devenshire had said before walking away. As angry as it had made him, it had also chilled him slightly. The absolute resolution he had seen in Devenshire's eyes touched a deep-rooted concern deep within him. He knew the stubborn bastard would not give up so long as he lived.

Xavier also found himself annoyed because he had not heard from Cyrus and was wondering what the wizard was doing. Why had he not eliminated Devenshire as he had ordered him to? He knew Cyrus would carry out his orders, but the insolent bastard would do so in his own time. Perhaps Cyrus had grown too arrogant, too sure of his standing. Perhaps the time had come to teach the wizard his proper place.

A distant rumble drew his attention to the sky. Xavier found himself so absorbed in his thoughts that he had not noticed he had entered a clearing deep in the forest. Xavier followed the distant rumble to the northern sky. In the distance, he saw a brief flash of light. Several moments later, the faint sound of distant thunder resonated through him. A faint smile touched his lips as he inhaled deeply the scent of coming rain. As much as he reveled in the darkness of night, he equally enjoyed a violent storm. The sheer destructive power of storms touched the same within him. Closing his eyes, he let his mind imagine the storm brewing far away, and he wished he could bring it to him, to let the slashing rain, blinding lightening and deafening thunder destroy the torturous thoughts and feelings trying to overtake him.

As a gentle breeze rustled his hair, a thought whispered into his mind. A storm. A powerful storm that would lay waste to everything in its path. Xavier slowly opened his eyes and fixed a hard glare into the distant thunderstorm as an evil grin spread his lips. A storm that would lay waste to everything in its path... even Daimion Devenshire.

CHAPTER THIRTEEN

Darius stepped into the dark, dank coolness of the cave just as the first graying of the sky overhead warned of the approaching day. With a snarl of irritation, he retreated into the far depths of the cavern he had found earlier in the night. While it wasn't the perfect place for him, it would have to do. With just the lightening of the night sky, he could feel his strength begin to wan, and he cursed the approach of another day. After he had scouted out this resting place, he had spent the bulk of the night watching over Brianna. He had wanted to feed, but to do so, meant he would have had to make do with wild animals or other vermin and that thought brought a soured taste to his mouth. While he could sustain himself on animal blood, it was the rich, invigorating blood of humans that brought him the greatest pleasure and the most power. In terms that a mortal could relate to, it was like being able to survive off just water, but the bite and tingle of liquor was much more enjoyable. He knew he could not afford to feed on one of the humans who were with Brianna, as he may yet have a purpose for them, and he knew he could not afford the time to go back to the soldiers chasing Brianna's group. He had fed well over the last two nights, and he knew he could hold off feeding again for a little while longer.

As he had watched over her, he let his mind wander back over time to when she had been his and the memories of a time when he was not as he was now. It had been a very long time since he had thought of his so-called life before receiving the Dark Gift, a time when he had been mortal. His pleasant memories of that time were hazy, and the warm feelings he had felt back then were now simply specters, shadows of emotions he remembered having, but did not remember exactly what they felt like. It was only the memories of his time with her that caused him the closest thing to regret for the loss of his mortality. He had gained so much in the exchange. Everything he had ever wanted had been his upon awakening in this new existence. She was the only thing he had lost and that caused a pang of painful regret deep in his cold, still chest. He knew, though, that soon she would be his again, and his dark existence would be complete.

Just as he was enjoying his trip through the massive expanse of memories stored within his mind, the dark evil that had brought him to her, to the burnt-out shell of a village flared up and demanded his attention. The power behind that sense of evil was staggering, even by the standards that had given him his new existence. Something sinister was happening, the dark tides of the night showed it to him, the wind whispered warnings of it to him, and he knew that his pursuit of Brianna was carrying him toward it. What did the mortals who traveled with her expect to accomplish? Stop the sinister evil power? That was laughable. The power at work here was far greater than anything mere mortal men could ever possibly hope to overcome. Darius was not even sure his awesome reserves of power would be a match for it and that alarmed him more than anything else. Anything that could possess that much dark power was dangerous, possibly too dangerous. Despite hours upon hours of meditation and deep delving into the Mystical Tides, he could not discern the true nature of the power or what its ultimate purpose was. But he would. He couldn't afford not to. He had left behind his territory not only to pursue Brianna, but also to confront this dark power and decide if it were something he should welcome as an ally, or defeat as an opponent.

Darius had created a comfortable territory back in Malfon Provence. He had invested many seasons in creating it. By moving secretly, feeding selectively and enslaving just the right people at just the right time, he had established himself in a nearly invulnerable position. All of Malfon province was under his control, whether the paltry mortals who lived there realized it or not. He had servants in nearly every village and city in the province, which helped in making sure that his presence was never known to anyone. It had been difficult at first, with much careful planning, and even more careful execution of his plans, had been required. On many occasions, he had very nearly made a misstep that would have led to his discovery. His first order of business had been the subtle removal of the Order of Hunters from the area. No vampire had occupied Malfon province or the surrounding area for nearly seventy-five seasons. That was not to say that there were not vampires there, but that they were simply few in number and were being very cautious in their activities. Darius had no desire to share his territory with another vampire and so he had actually aided the Hunters in removing them. Though destroying another vampire had marked him for elimination by the few organized Clans of Vampires, he could not afford for one of the few vampires in Malfon to make a mistake and thereby, reveal all of them to the Hunters. He knew that he would not be happy until Malfon had every appearance of being absolutely free of vampires... save for one anonymous vampire unknown to all but a very select, and very controlled, few. After many seasons, his plans had finally bore fruit. With all the other vampires removed, it had only been a matter of enslaving a few select, high-ranking officials. He had thought to enslave the governing Lord of Malfon, but he was inaccessible and he was a man of faith, which meant he always carried a sigil or charm of his faith with him. Such sigils and charms held no mystical power, but if the human possessing them believed strongly enough in their faith, they became powerful talismans which would keep his kind at bay. Fortunately, for Darius, not all of the governing lord's court was as devout of faith as he was and Darius had made do with enslaving a top advisor. Once this was complete, it was only a matter of a handful of seasons before the Order of Hunters was believed to no longer be needed in Prothtow. It had taken seasons, but finally the last Hunter had departed the area, leaving it wide open for Darius to step into and claim for his own.

That left the priests of the area. As much as he despised their ilk, and as much of a threat as they were to him, they were actually helping him maintain a tight grip on his throne of power. The priests of the area were unusually strong of faith and such priests were dangerous, much too dangerous for any large number of kindred to chance being discovered. So the Clans of vampires avoided the area, and the individuals who were foolish enough to attempt what Darius had succeeded at, were destroyed in short order. Occasionally, a vampire mercenary, hired by one of the Clans, would come looking to destroy him for daring to kill another vampire, but he always made short work of them. After such a long time in the area, he knew it like the back of his hand. Those who came looking for him did not. It was ridiculously easy. Malfon was the perfect place to hide in and almost be in plain sight. No one, not even a Hunter, would think to look for a vampire in the midst of such devout and powerful priests.

Now his kingdom was threatened. The evil presence he had sensed spoke of a threat to all he had worked to accomplish. He recalled the time before he took up residence in Malfon, when he simply roamed from area to area, feeding until he was discovered, and the Hunters would come after him, driving him on to the next area. While fleeing to another area he would be forced to feed on any source of blood. Mice, rats, snakes, frogs... whatever he could find. There were times when livestock had appeared as a feast to him and such memories sickened him. While the blood of animals would sustain him, it would do nothing to maintain his power. Only the blood of humans would completely rejuvenate and strengthen his powers. Once he had established himself in Malfon province, he had vowed to never again wander the countryside like a scavenger. Ever! So he would have to root out this source of evil, appraise it, and quite possibly destroy it. Yet, as arrogant as he could be, he knew his limitations well enough to know that he could not combat this evil alone. He would need help. As galling as that admission was for him to make, even more so was the only apparent source of help—the humans traveling with Brianna. They were on a direct course toward the source, and so he found, with an irritating sense of irony, he would have to rely upon, what was to him, food for help, and in the process, he would be helping them. Not a situation he neither liked nor was he accustomed to...

Finding a suitably darkened corner to hole up for the day, Darius knew that he would have to approach the humans and barter some sort of pact with them, enlisting their help while offering his services as well. As the strange sleep of the un-dead called to him, he honestly asked himself if studying this source of great evil was truly worth what he was about to pay.

CHAPTER FOURTEEN

"What do you make of it?" Devenshire asked as he sat on a fallen tree.

"It is made of amber," Darkseed said as he turned the amulet Devenshire had retrieved from the dead Follower slowly in his fingers, studying it intently. "The metal is of poor quality and would not be very conductive of mystical currents, and the amber is low grade as well."

"So what does that mean?" Brianna asked as she stood behind Devenshire.

Darkseed continued to study the amulet as he slowly shook his head. "It would not have been able to hold much power and any spell cast into it would soon begin to fade rapidly. This was no mystical artifact. It was more or less a cheap piece of jewelry that Xavier was able to use for a limited spell."

"What kind of spell?" Shantira asked as she eased up next to Devenshire and began looking at the red, swollen knuckles of his right hand.

"The kind that would allow his Followers to find us, follow us, and allow Xavier to tell them when to attack," Devenshire answered.

Darkseed nodded. "It would fit. That would be about all this trinket would be capable of doing."

"Can you not delve into the amulet and discover what Xavier used it for?" Stant asked, keeping a close eye on Kendra. While she had not been injured in the fight, it had left her shaken.

Darkseed bounced the amulet in his hand as he shook his head. "Any mystical energy stored in the amulet has long since dissipated. There is nothing left within it, I already tried."

Shantira gently slid her hand under Devenshire's right one and lifted it from his knee, her face twisting into an expression of pain at the bloody, bruised, and swollen joints. She looked up at his profile and saw no trace of pain in his features. "Does that not hurt?"

Devenshire turned his head and looked at her before looking down at his hand held gingerly in hers. "It has some sting to it," he said with a smile before turning his attention back to Darkseed. "Is there no way to use it as a method to track Xavier or find his location?"

"He would have been a fool to allow such a thing to fall into our hands," Zandorth grunted from his position behind Darkseed.

"What do you mean?" Petera asked.

"There is a reason this thing," he said jerking his chin toward the amulet in Darkseed's hand, "is poorly made. It would not hold much power, and what little it did hold was quickly gone. Xavier would have to assume that there was the possibility his men would fail and that this amulet would be captured." He paused as he regarded the amulet and nodded. "A very sound tactical maneuver."

"You admire him?" Kendra asked with chilling tones.

"I do not. Nothing will give me more pleasure than to rip his guts out and choke him to death with them! I simply acknowledge his tactical planning and forethought. It means he is neither overly confident nor careless, which makes him even more dangerous," he snapped in reply.

Devenshire nodded. "I agree. The tales surrounding Xavier would lead you to believe he is arrogant, cocky and over sure of his abilities. While he may very well be all of those things, you do not get to the level of power and control he has established by being ignorant. Xavier is careful and plotting. He is also very patient."

"There is nothing quite as deadly as a patient opponent," Darkseed added.

"Will there be more attacks?" Petera asked hesitantly.

"Probably, but not today," Devenshire replied wincing as Shantira dabbed at his bloody knuckles with a linen.

"He sent this group to try to kill one or more of us, but I would wager the bulk of what he sought from this attack was to gauge our strengths and weaknesses," Darkseed said.

"He did not learn much. The attack was centered on Devenshire. Why just on Devenshire?" Zandorth replied with a curious gaze in his eyes and a furrowed brow.

"I was attacked also!" Kendra snapped back.

"Because you went after Daimion instead of staying here like he instructed," Shantira pointed out with a hard edge to her voice.

"Had I not, we could very well be burying him right now!" Kendra replied through clenched teeth.

"Stop it, both of you!" Brianna snapped. "We have more important things to worry about!" She turned back to look at Zandorth. "That is a very good question. Why was the attack focused on you?" she asked the back of Devenshire's head.

Devenshire shook his head as he gently pulled his damaged hand from Shantira's painful ministrations, not missing the heated glare she threw back over her shoulder toward Kendra. He didn't have to look to know a similar expression was on Kendra's face as well. "I do not know. Perhaps he feels that killing me would dishearten the rest of you, and you would give up the quest."

"Perhaps, but I cannot help but feel there is more to it than that,"

Zandorth replied.

"Such as?" Darkseed asked.

The warrior shook his head slowly, his face lost in deep thought. "I do not know, but we must be prepared for any possibility, including the possibility of another attack happening sooner rather than later."

"Good point," Stant said as he nodded. "Xavier could be counting on us to not be expecting another attack so soon."

"But he might take that into consideration and not launch another attack knowing that we could be expecting it," Petera countered.

"Stop," Devenshire said as he slowly rose to his feet. The adrenaline from the fight had worn off and now his body ached and he felt fatigued. "This is exactly what Xavier wants us to do, second guess our every decision. We will continue on like we have been, but we just have to be more alert of our surroundings and be ready."

~*~

They traveled on for the next four days without further incident. Devenshire and Darkseed continued to examine the amulet, and they were able to speculate that even with the limited abilities of the talisman, it would have allowed Xavier to direct the movements of his men. It would have allowed Xavier to communicate with the wearer, not direct verbal communication, but rather subtle mental impressions. Darkseed had delved deep into the amulet and learned the spell had run its course as the mystical energies within had been exhausted. The amulet was useless now aside from a moderately attractive piece of jewelry.

Kendra had been shaken from the attack, but she had regained her composure quickly. While part of her had been mortally terrified at the near end of her life, another part reveled in the exhilaration of battle. Devenshire had wasted no time in both complimenting her archery skills and thanking her for her intervention that had surely saved his life. Zandorth had, naturally, been quite annoyed that he had missed the fight. Various discussions had continued while they rode about what the underlying implications of the attack might mean, but it was generally accepted that this was certainly not the last one. While Darkseed continued working on a mystical way to block whatever method Xavier was using to track their movements, it was agreed that they would simply continue on as planned.

Their path took them higher into the Mt. Kil'tafore mountain range, through terrain that was difficult to travel, but was plentiful with food and fresh water. While they had food reserves in their packs, they took full advantage of the availability of fresh game, vegetables, and even fish from one the many streams found on their path through the mountains.

Devenshire took the lead with Brianna, Shantira, and Kendra behind him. Darkseed and Petera followed the women with Zandorth and Stant bringing up the rear. The elder elf and the warrior seemed to find a common ground and spent most of their days riding together and discussing battles from the past. Devenshire's maps showed them that the quickest course to use to intercept Xavier was straight over the mountain range. While Xavier could move faster on the flat lands, he would have to go around Mt. Kil'tafore. Another advantage to the mountainous route was the difficulty Captain Armand would have in gaining any ground on them.

After the first few days, there was little to no conversation. Each member of the party was too preoccupied with trying to unravel the mysteries from their perilous trip through Lirpa. Each question demanded to be answered, and yet ignored the most stringent efforts to obtain those answers. Each person struggled to understand what exactly had happened during that terrifying night in the big city until their heads ached and their minds screamed for release and diversion.

They rode late into the night and rode out before sunrise each day. While this deprived them of sleep, it was the best guarantee they had that they would not only gain ground on Xavier, but put more distance between themselves and the party of Royal Guards pursuing them. Each night, Darkseed would perform a Spell of Knowledge to check on Armand's progress. Each day found them gaining a little more ground on him. Despite his best efforts to find Xavier within the ebb and flow of the Mystical Tides, the Master Mage was using a counter spell to thwart his best efforts. Several times throughout their journey, Devenshire's natural sense of the workings of the Mystical Arts would alert him with a sensation that they were being watched, very much like the sensation that had come over him that night in the Tavern and in the forest after the fight with the Followers. There was no doubt in his mind that, while they couldn't track Xavier's movements, the madman had no trouble keeping tabs on them.

Following their usual pattern, they found a suitable place to make camp for the night in an area that would allow them to build a small fire for cooking without broadcasting their location to their pursuers. A quickly prepared meal of venison from a deer Zandorth had downed the day before, and potatoes from their packs, settled their grumbling stomachs. Devenshire took first watch while the others rolled themselves tightly into their blankets as the chill of the night settled about them.

As the small campfire exhausted itself to smoldering embers, the night seemed to grow deeper, quieter, and to Devenshire, more peaceful. He sat at the edge of a grove of trees on a slight rise overlooking their camp. He had found a tree that had been bent over as a sapling, and had never straightened back up. It provided a perfect seat with another tree standing close enough to serve as an excellent back support. He sat with his back against the upright tree with his right leg pulled up so that his foot was perched on the bent tree. He laced his fingers around his knee and soaked in the dark peacefulness. He let his mystical senses expand out until he was sure that no one would be able to venture too close to them without his knowing it. With a deep sigh, he forced himself to relax. The days in the saddle had been riddled with concern for the threat pursuing them and fear for the evil they pursued. The seemingly insurmountable mountain of mysteries from Lirpa had been kneading his brain until he was sure that there was nothing left inside his skull except for a small puddle of slush. Tonight he refused to dwell on Xavier, Lirpa, Armand, Lordalise, the Stones of Andarus or any of the hundreds of other questions that each of those subjects stirred up. Instead, he forced his mind to find something else, anything else to fixate on, if only for a few moments. Tilting his head back he found the three quarter disc of the moon and stared at its glowing beauty, feeling the sense of serenity deepen. The moon, especially a full moon, always made him feel as if he could absorb just a fraction of the power and beauty of that orb, and doing so eased the turmoil of his soul. As he became lost in the beauty and power of the night, his mind began to wander through the forest of his thoughts.

Rachelle Tambrey drifted through his mind. Thick long blonde hair framing a delicate face that held a beauty that he was hard pressed to define. Her eyes, the strange way they seemed to look at him and through him to what lie beneath him. The way they seemed to glow with a light all their own. Then there was the pain, that ever present sense of some great inner agonizing torture within her. He recalled their last meeting in the clearing outside of Lirpa. The way she had sat next to him until he woke and the gentle cool touch of her hand as she had brushed a lock of hair from his forehead. There had been a definite spark of something in the air between them that he could not define any easier than her beauty. Then her mood had suddenly shifted, and she had become very distant and almost short with him, as if he had offended her in some way. Why, he wondered? What had he inadvertently touched that caused such a shift in her manner? Even the mysteries surrounding her made her that much more appealing, and he found he wished for her company, her soft melodious voice in his ear, and the chance to learn more about her.

As his mind continued to wander, Brianna's countenance swept into his thoughts, and his smile grew as he recalled various different memories surrounding the woman. The nights in the tavern when they would play their sensual little teasing games with one another, each determined to best the other. The way she would call him a bastard when he scored a particularly clever remark, and the way she could appear so stunningly beautiful that his breath would catch in his throat. He would try valiantly to suppress his reactions to her, but he always knew that he could never hide them deep enough or quick enough to prevent her from knowing of them. Each time she would smile and briefly lower her eyes when such reactions to her burst to the surface.

Just as with Rachelle, there were many mysteries surrounding Brianna, as well. There was some tragic memory that forced her to keep her heart under close guard and any prospective suitors at bay. Something terrible had happened to her in her past, and Devenshire only had hints and shadowy speculations about what that event might have been. Just as she tried to delve into his past and failed, so had he with her. Each subtle attempt to learn more was gracefully, gently, and skillfully side stepped as only Brianna could do. Memories of their lovemaking came, as they often did when he thought of her. The passion between them was as unique as their relationship. It was more intense than any he had ever encountered, and it formed some of his fondest memories. Brianna surrendered to her passions more completely than any woman he had ever known. Just as with everything else with Brianna, she did nothing half way. She had a unique ability to immerse herself in the fires of their passion, losing all control and inhibition, and giving herself to the moment, and yet always seeming to be in total and absolute control. Making love to Brianna was a passionate journey through the highest peaks of pleasure and the deepest oceans of passion, with no hint of ever returning to the earthly plain of the everyday.

Then, without warning and without his bidding, the only other passion of such deep all consuming nature came to his mind, and instantly, the peace and serenity of the night and his thoughts were shattered. *Her* memory came. The memory blasted through the inky surface of his deepest thoughts and soared through his mind, searing all the pleasant thoughts with the fire of its refreshed agony. The pleasant and peaceful thoughts flared brilliantly before turning dark and sinking from his mind as the dark memory took dominance. *Her* face loomed before his mind's eye, and he squeezed his physical eyes shut tightly, hoping to bar her image from his mind, but to no avail. Pain, sorrow, and anger flared up brightly throughout him with the intensity of a raging forest fire. He sought some way to use the anger to force the memories back down and out of his conscious thoughts. Feelings and memories of feelings that her face brought surfaced on the heels of her image, and he found himself suddenly adrift in a swirling sea of hopeless despair. He swam with the urgency of someone who fears he is about to drown, while the current of the dark memory pulled him down, forcing his mind to face the tides of his past. Feelings of coldness, emptiness, and loneliness closed in upon him, pushing him further down. Just as he feared he would lose himself to the memory and be forced to endure the consequences of losing to the recollection, he found the one emotion that saved him, had saved him so many times in the past, and he clung to it as though it were his only source of salvation.

Hatred. Pure, burning hatred flared, and he embraced the fire, taking it deeply into him and letting the heat burn away the dark memory and send it fleeing back. Even as the pain and memories retreated, he was not content to merely drive them back. The pain had been as fresh as the day it had been inflicted on his soul, and he wanted retribution. With flames in his mind's eyes, he forced her face back to the forefront. With all the venomous vengeance he could muster, he forced her to become engulfed in the flames of his hatred. He watched in sadistic glee as she writhed in agony as she was consumed slowly... painfully... totally. She screamed, cried out, begged for forgiveness and mercy. He gave neither. With a mental scream of rage, he gathered the fire of hatred about him and flew headlong toward her image, feeling the fire burn through him, spilling out of his eyes, through his skin, from every pore. With all his mental might, he expelled the fire from his body and directed it toward her image, which now cowered before him in mortal fear. The flames raced from his eyes, his fingertips, his very being to swallow her whole. His mind heard her screams, her pleas for forgiveness, and he felt a near sexual gratification sweep over him as he did nothing to stop the flames from consuming her, taking her silken skin and turning it black before melting it from her supple and graceful limbs.

With an evil smile of satisfaction he watched her memory burn, felt the heat of the intense fire upon his mind, and he reveled in its warmth. Then the screams and pleas faded, the fire grew cooler, and the radiant light of the flames dimmed. As he watched, the fire burned itself out leaving a smoldering pile of bone and ash, which a wind quickly whisked away.

Such purging never comes without a price. As the last particles of her ashes were whisked from his mind, he felt the old familiar chill descend about his essence. He had forced her horrid memory back into the deepest recess of his being, but now he was cold, bitter, and empty. Spent far beyond any means of the mere physical exertion could manage, and he sagged as he opened his physical eyes, looking out at the night which now seemed as cold and empty as he felt inside. He desperately sought something in the night around him that would return to him the peace and serenity he had felt only moments ago, but they were gone, seeming to have been burned away with the memory, and Daimion Devenshire wondered if he would find a moment of such peace and calm ever again.

"Daimion?" a soft voice called out to him tentatively.

Although he had been far too distracted to sense anyone's approach, he was not startled by the sudden sound of another voice.

He was simply too drained to be startled, too empty of will to care who approached or what their purpose was. With a tired sigh, he did not turn to face the source of the voice behind him. "Yes, Shantira. What is it?" he asked in a deadpan tone of voice.

There was a pause before her soft voice came again. "My apologies. I am disturbing you. I will depart."

"No. You are not disturbing me. As a matter of fact, I could use some company at this moment," he replied softly.

He felt her hesitation, her uncertainty in whether to approach or turn and go back to her blankets. Finally, he heard her soft footsteps and felt her step up beside him. Her eyes were studying him, searching for the source of his odd tone of voice.

"What is wrong? You look disturbed," she observed.

With a tired sounding chuckle, he shook his head slowly, his eyes staring off into the darkness. "It is nothing. I simply find no comfort in the company of my own thoughts at the moment."

"Is it anything I can help with?" she asked.

"No," he answered with no emotion in his voice.

"Auntie Lucinda always told me that when you find no comfort in the company of your own thoughts, it is time to seek out the company of another's," she offered.

Devenshire turned his head to look intently into her blue eyes. "Lucinda was indeed a very wise woman."

Shantira hugged herself against a chill that had little to do with the night air. Her expression darkened with the intense sadness the death of her village had inflicted on her being. It was a pain that would fade, would become manageable in the seasons to come, but it would never, ever go away. As her sad expression looked out into the night, he felt a sharp twinge of regret that someone so young and so innocent would be marred so badly. She drew in a deep slow breath, and nodded slowly. "Yes, she was."

Silence reigned between them for a time as each dealt with their mental phantoms. The insects continued their nightly song and the winds whispered through the trees. While the setting should have been nothing short of absolute peace laced with a heavy undertone of romance, neither found anything but cold darkness. Finally, Shantira took in a deep breath and tilted her head back, shaking her hair out of her face. "What mental ghosts have arisen to haunt your mind, Daimion?" she asked, forcing the pain back under a control she thought she would never truly master.

Devenshire had to quickly shift his gaze forward. The motion of shaking her hair back had lent her a very alluring demeanor, and he did not wish to battle not only the after effects of the dark memory but his own natural impulses as well. "The usual assortment of mental demons who take great delight in tormenting me. Yourself?" he asked, quickly shifting the focus to her, wishing for anything to divert his attention from his own battle-ravaged thoughts.

Shantira stared up at the half moon, and her eyes seemed to grow distant as she considered her own thoughts. "I am not sure I should even voice them," she finally answered.

"You will find that I am a very good listener. The very best kind of listener, as a matter of fact," he said with a warm smile.

She smiled fondly as she shifted her gaze from the moon to his smile. "What makes you the best kind?"

"I hold the one trait that separates a good listener from a terrible one," he replied.

"What trait is that?" she asked with a warm smile.

Devenshire arched his right eyebrow. That simple act ignited the mischief in his eyes and deepened the warmth of his smile. The flood of strange emotions and sensations coursed through her again, and she felt her cheeks flush.

"A short memory."

Shantira laughed, and Devenshire found himself transfixed by the musical chime of her laughter. It was a very pleasing sound, and despite the soul rending after effects of having to deal with the dark memory, he laughed as well.

"You have a very nice laugh. Very pleasing," he said as their laughter subsided.

The blush that had already begun spreading across her cheeks deepened several shades instantly as she quickly dropped her gaze to the ground, wishing to hide both her face and her feelings as quickly and as deeply as possible. "Thank you," she whispered.

Devenshire nodded once. "My pleasure."

She looked up and their eyes met. For an instant that could not be measured by any means of time keeping, they simply looked deep into each other's eyes. The moment consumed all — the night, him, her, and the inner turmoil that tore at both. In that moment that knew no limit of mere time, two tortured souls found a moment of respite and each brushed all too briefly against that which each sought, and that brief brushing touch eased the fear in both of them that what they sought was forever out of their reach. Finally, it was Devenshire who found himself and gave her a warm smile as he turned his eyes back to the night. He had no wish to do so — in fact, he wanted to continue to gaze into the deep blue of her eyes, to see where this encounter might go and what it might bring. He wanted to lose himself in that brief flicker of comfort he had seen so deeply within them. It had whispered of a release of the pain he continually ran from and yet never seemed to gain any distance over. Yet as promising as that brief flicker had been, he knew he could not pursue it, could not risk what it would cost him to achieve and what it could cost her in the end. He had to protect himself, and more importantly, he had to protect her from emotions she was ill equipped to deal with for now.

Shantira felt a stab of disappointment at Devenshire turning his gaze from her. Ever since the first time she had seen him, she had wanted his warm gaze upon her. The memories came without her calling them—the day he had saved her from certain death in the woods, the night in the tavern when they had danced and he had looked so deeply into her eyes that she had felt bare and open to him. Then the night on the balcony of the tavern when she had sought to apologize to him and she found his eyes upon her, felt the odd combination of heat and chill race through her at his glance. The other sensations he caused in her, the ones she could not put a name to, the ones she could not understand, at least not until that night in Lirpa. As she had walked the streets of the dark city, she had finally understood what that sensation was, finally knew what it was he stirred in her... desire.

Yes. She desired him. She wanted his touch on her skin, wanted his body as close to hers as possible. She wanted to feel the sensations that she had only heard about, the intense passion and abandon that she had heard Brianna speak of on numerous occasions. She wanted to experience for herself what she had only heard and dreamt of, and she wanted Devenshire to help her experience it. She felt closer to him now more than ever. It was as though she were standing on the precipice of gaining that which she sought, and yet she was too terrified to step off. He was hers. For this tiny fragment of time, he was hers, and she wanted nothing more than to steal him away and keep him all to herself. Brianna's warning of pursuing such a path with him tried to force its way into her mind, but she refused. She took a deep breath, and while in her mind, she lifted one foot off the edge and began to lean forward, ready to step into the terrifying unknown. "Have you ever been attracted to someone and not know how to let that person know?" she asked hesitantly.

Instantly, she knew she had asked the wrong question. The warmth that had permeated him only a heartbeat ago was gone. She could almost feel his emotions shut down, quickly buried beneath his iron control. "Once. A long time ago," he answered in monotone.

She desperately searched for a way... any way... to erase her question, to bring that incredible warmth within him back to the surface. The damage had been done, and now she found that she no longer wanted to discuss the subject. "I am sorry. I did not mean to dredge up any painful memories," she whispered.

Devenshire's gaze was locked deep into the inky blackness of the night as he shrugged. "You had no way of knowing," he suddenly took a deep breath and let it out in a sigh, shaking himself, at least partially, out of the dark mood. "It matters not. It was a long time ago."

He stood up and turned to face her. "Shantira, if you love someone, tell them," he said matter-of-factly, cutting to the heart of her question, amazing her with his ability to know such things so quickly.

It was Shantira's turn to gaze off into the night, lost in the turmoil of her emotions. "It is easy to say such a thing, but much harder to do."

He smiled. "Nonsense. It is very easy to do."

She gave him a sideways glance that said she didn't agree with his assessment. "What if the other person does not feel the same?"

He took in a deep breath and shifted his gaze upwards toward the moon. With a shrug, he replied, "Then at least you will have released the burden. The truth will be out and your soul will not be plagued with a lifetime of unanswerable questions about scenarios that will never come to pass. If the other person does not feel the same," he paused a moment to shake his head, "then there is nothing you can do about that."

She smiled up at him as she slowly shook her head. "You make it sound so easy."

He chuckled. "Once you realize the consequences, it is very easy to do. The hard part is learning how painful the consequences can be."

"You speak from experience?"

The smile dampened as he swung his head around to lock his gaze deep into hers. In a brief flash, she saw the flickering, tearing edge of his pain, as she was taken aback by the intensity. "Always," he answered softly.

Almost without her realization, her right hand began to rise from her side, intent on gently stroking his cheek. She wanted to do anything she could to eradicate, or at the very least, ease the intense pain she had glimpsed in his eyes. She caught herself midway and quickly dropped her hand back to her side. "So much pain..."

He brought his hands up and rested them lightly on her shoulders. "Shantira, there will always be pain. You cannot walk this life without it. It is a grueling taskmaster whose snapping whip will seem to be your only companion at times. However, you need the pain. It molds you, it forms you, and it makes you appreciate the few fleeting moments of happiness that come your way. Such is the harsh reality of our existence."

Tears welled up within her eyes as she searched his, desperately wanting to see that what he spoke of with such conviction was a lie. "What are we to do?" she asked in near desperation.

He smiled again. "What was it Brianna told you? Hope?" he nodded. "Hope is sometimes all we have and all we need. There will always be torment within your life. In one form or another, something will always tear at your soul. There is no escaping that one basic fact of life. Shantira, our time within this realm is short. Too short to spend torturing yourself with burdens that you cannot control. The Fates know there are enough of those as it is. If I have learned nothing else, I have learned that it is best to take the chance. If you risk nothing, you gain nothing. The Fates are a peculiar lot. One can never say with any certainty, which way their favor will swing. But if you stop and consider it... it is one of the things that make life worth living."

It was Shantira's turn to sweep her gaze out into the deep darkness and ponder what he had said. With a wistful sigh, she merely shook her head, uncertain of what to do next. For many moments, Shantira stared off into the darkness, her features nearly unreadable as she considered his words. She knew the truth of what he had said, but her courage would not allow her to utter the words her heart demanded her to release. The moment had come and then had departed, and she had not acted. Sadly, she stepped back from his hands, and smiled softly. "You have given me much to ponder, Daimion. I will consider it." She turned and began walking away, and Devenshire watched her go. She stopped after several steps and turned back to look at him, and smiled. "Thank you."

Devenshire gave her his warmest smile and a brief nod. "You are welcome, Shantira. Good night."

"Good night, Daimion," she replied before turning and fading into the darkness.

After he was sure she was gone, he returned to his seat on the bent tree. Letting his breath out in a long, slow sigh, he shook his head—too much emotion in too short a span of time. Fighting his emotions always drained him and left him feeling vulnerable. It was a very dangerous situation and one he was always wary of. Shantira was a beautiful young woman, and he could not ignore his own desires toward her. However, his desires were purely physical. He knew enough about young women to know that any reactions she may have would be purely emotional and that would be dangerous. He knew he could not act upon his desires for she was still an innocent, and she would have no control over her emotions. He knew he could not give her what she would want, even if she were not aware of what she wanted. To take her innocence from her, and then refuse her what her heart would yearn for afterwards, would be more devastating than if a stranger attacked and took her innocence by force. A dark flicker of a memory caught the edges of his thoughts and reminded him of a time when such considerations would have gone ignored by him and his ensuing vow to never, ever act in such a way again.

With a weary sigh, he turned back to the night and his own dark thoughts—those inspired by the unexpected release of memories he had sooner not have considered. This night would be long, far longer for him than the others, and he knew that the days to come would be made up of not only the trials of their journey, but his own internal struggle to gain back lost distance on a past that refused to remain there.

CHAPTER FIFTEEN

The cold gray dawn found the small campfire resurrected and a boiling pot of coffee gurgling on one of the rocks circling the fire. The deep, rich aroma quickly spread across the camp, stirring the exhausted travelers with the lustful promise of a pleasant awakening. Darkseed had taken last watch, and as the blackness of the night sky began to lighten, he had stirred the nearly dead embers of the fire and put on the pot of coffee. Normally, they would wake, break camp, and set out for another long day upon the trail. This morning, however, Darkseed had decided they could afford enough time for a cup of coffee, and as he smiled around the smoldering cigar between his teeth, a good smoke.

Brianna was the first to step up to the fire, her blanket wrapped around her. She smiled pleasantly at Darkseed as she took up a seat on one of the upended logs. "Good morning, Rav."

Darkseed smiled, and nodded once as he extended his chilled fingers toward the fire. "Top of the morrow to you, M'lady. I trust you rested well?"

Brianna stretched, and he could hear the distinct pop of several vertebrae in her back. Each pop caused her to wince and then relax in relief, as the knot was released. "Not at all. I feel as though I spent the night upon the rack." She twisted at the waist as far as she could one way before turning all the way in the other direction. Each movement was accompanied by smaller snaps and cracks. Finally, she faced forward again and smiled down at the pot near the fire. "The coffee smells delightful."

Darkseed knelt down and retrieved a small tin cup from a stack of them next to the fire. He took up a thick rag and carefully lifted the pot from the rock before pouring the thick black liquid into the cup. With a smile, he set the pot back down and extended the cup toward her. "It is very strong and very hot."

"Just like the way she prefers her men," Devenshire added as he stepped up to the fire from the thinning shadows.

Brianna snapped her eyes up at him and did a poor job of concealing her smile as she took the cup from Darkseed. "Indeed? Then why do I spend time with you?"

Darkseed didn't even try to conceal his cackle of laughter, as he had to pull the cigar from his mouth quickly. Even Devenshire smiled and replied without missing a heartbeat. "You are, obviously, a woman with very refined tastes and an excellent sense of passion, and you know the best places to find it."

"Oh, please!" Darkseed scoffed as he clamped the cigar between his teeth and squatted down to pour two more cups of coffee.

Brianna cupped the tin between her hands with the edge of her blanket wrapped around it to protect her from the heat. She smiled and shook her head as she held the cup close to her face, soaking in the smell and the heat. "Who also has a continued proclivity for associating herself with bastards."

"Here," Darkseed said as he stood upright and extended one of the cups toward Devenshire. "Drink this so we do not have to hear you praise yourself any longer."

Devenshire chuckled as he took the cup with a nod. "My thanks."

Darkseed lifted his cup to his lips and blew across the surface of the coffee. He watched as Brianna and Devenshire locked gazes and simply stared at one another for a few moments. At first, he thought he was seeing two people who deeply loved one another sharing a tender moment. Then, Darkseed realized who he was looking at and knew he was seeing something he wanted to see, not what was actually happening. While he knew very little about Brianna, he had seen enough to know that her control over her emotions was every bit as rigid as Devenshire's. He sipped at the hot coffee as he continued to study them, fascinated by the silent play of words between them. They were sharing a moment that no one else would understand, and many would misunderstand, was something neither of them was capable of. He shifted his gaze to Devenshire, studying his friend's eyes intently. He knew Devenshire cared for Brianna, probably more than anyone in recent history, but he did not love her. Likewise, the Lord of Prothtow cared deeply about him, yet she did not love him, at least not in the traditional sense of the word. How sad, he reflected. These two people insisted on traveling through this life alone. Right before each of them was a very solid prospect of finding love and happiness, everything everyone else craved with an insatiable hunger. Yet, standing in the cold gray dawn, Darkseed knew that whatever lies ahead in the seasons to come for these two, it was not each other. He cocked his head to one side as he finished his study of them. With sad clarity, he realized that these two would continue to enjoy each other's company, and then they would part ways never to see one another again.

How very sad.

Brianna broke the intense stare first as she sipped her coffee, closing her eyes against the warmth. "The coffee is wonderful."

Darkseed bent at the waist in a half bow. "Many thanks, M'Lady."

Devenshire sipped his coffee as well, but his eyes were fixed on the horizon and the approaching sunrise. "How far ahead of Armand are we?" he asked.

Darkseed shrugged. "We have a solid days lead on him, perhaps more."

Devenshire nodded as he shifted his gaze to another point on the horizon. "Have you been able to break Xavier's spell that keeps him hidden from you?"

Darkseed shook his head as he puffed on the cigar. "Not as of yet. It is a very complicated incantation."

"He has been watching us. He knows exactly where we are," Devenshire said lifting the tin cup to his lips.

Darkseed frowned. "I have sensed no spells being used to observe us."

Devenshire shifted his eyes to Darkseed, letting the full meaning of his next words sink in. "I have."

Brianna shifted her eyes between the two of them. "How is it that you can sense Xavier's spell but Darkseed cannot?"

"I have a natural sense of the workings of the Mystical Arts. I can sense when magic is being used in proximity of me," he answered.

"Tis true. Daimion's natural sense of the workings of the Arts far exceeds any detection spell I have ever seen," Darkseed added.

"So it is not a spell?" Brianna asked.

Devenshire shook his head. "No. It is much more like a sense than magic, like eyesight or hearing."

"Interesting," she commented as she returned to her coffee.

Slowly, the others joined them at the fire and gratefully took a steaming cup of the coffee. Conversation was minimal as the group of travelers stole a few moments of peace and relaxation. Devenshire took a few moments to assess the overall condition of his companions. Zandorth's eye had reopened but still looked terrible as the deep black and blue around his eye had begun turning yellow as the deep bruise healed. The slash on his right forearm was healing well despite his refusal to allow him or Darkseed to use a healing spell. He had used herbs to make a salve that protected the wound from infection and aided in healing.

Brianna's arm was nearly completely healed aided by a combination of herbs and magic. The smaller cuts and scratches from their frantic flight from Lirpa were diminishing as the days past. Shantira's physical injuries from Lirpa were nearly healed, but the gaping hole ripped through her soul from the destruction of her village was as open and raw as the night it was inflicted. The quest to stop Xavier was giving her mind something to occupy itself with, and had helped her deal with the grief slowly, but he knew some wounds would never heal.

The group as a whole looked haggard. The night in Lirpa, the ensuing frantic flight from the city, and the determined pursuit from

Captain Armand, was wearing on them. They needed a break from the pursuit and the flight. They had at least a one-day lead on Armand, and he knew that while they didn't know exactly where Xavier was, their path over the mountain range would close the gap between them immensely. Perhaps they could afford a few hours of rest before heading out again. Sipping his coffee, he continued to ponder the thoughts. The ground they would lose to Armand and Xavier could easily be made up and the rewards were great.

"We will not head out right away this morning. We can afford a few hours of rest," he announced. Their faces instantly brightened at the prospect of not having to immediately climb back into their saddles. Smiles beamed at the prospect of delaying another day of monotonously passing miles.

Everyone's face, save for one.

"Foolish, Devenshire," Zandorth protested. "Armand will not be taking such breaks in his pursuit of us, and Xavier will not wait for us to catch up to him."

Devenshire smiled slightly. "Armand is a day behind us, perhaps more. Xavier has to go around the mountain range while we are going over it. Any loss will be minor and easily made up. We can afford a few hours respite from the trail."

"How do you know Xavier is going around? Perhaps he is going over as we are," Stant asked.

Devenshire shook his head. "Unlikely. He is traveling with a large complement of his Followers and there are wagons being used. He will not be able to traverse the mountains with wagons."

"And how do you know he is using wagons?" Petera asked.

Zandorth nodded slowly in approval as he realized Devenshire's thought process. "Because I picked up their trail as they left Nelton. There were wagon tracks. Devenshire is right; they cannot be going over the mountains."

"It would seem you have considered all options," Kendra commented with a smile and poorly hidden attraction in her eyes.

"He always does," Shantira injected quickly with more than a slight edge to her voice.

Darkseed chuckled as he tossed the remnants of his cigar into the fire. "Since we have some time, I am going to find a nice quiet place to relax and simply exist."

"We should use this time to make battle plans!" Zandorth injected. "If we are not prepared, then we are doomed to fail."

"I have to agree with him," Stant added. "It would be better to be prepared."

Devenshire arched one eyebrow as he shifted his gaze to them. "I can think of no better men to undertake such a task," he said as he stooped to drop his empty coffee cup next to the fire. He straightened, turned, and began to walk away.

"What are you going to do?" Brianna called after him.

"There is a stream nearby. I am going to bathe," he paused and turned to regard the group around the fire with mischief blazing in his eyes. "Something some of the rest of you might consider." A slight smile tugged at the corners of his lips as he turned back and continued to walk away.

"Did he just say we stink?" Petera asked with a slight edge of anger in his voice.

"He did." Darkseed answered with a tight grin and a slow shake of his head.

"He can certainly be a rude bastard when he wants to be," Stant remarked with an offended tone to his voice.

Brianna giggled as she watched him walk away. "Yes, he can."

~*~

"Captain! You should see this!"

Zebadiah Constance turned and walked to where one of his men stood looking over the carcass of a horse. They had traveled through Lirpa, and they were now on the outskirts trying to pick up Brianna's trail. As he walked toward his man, he considered how his angry concern for Brianna had very quickly escalated to a point where his blood ran cold in terrified worry for her. After assembling his entire regiment and dispatching a courier to Castle Nightwind to alert King Lordoran of the situation that had meant enough to Brianna to abandon her post to pursue it, they had arrived in Lirpa two days after Brianna and her group had passed through. As they had moved through the city, they had heard tales that troubled him deeply. A visit with several sheriffs and a hastily appointed replacement for Constable Liston left him utterly confused and mortally terrified for Brianna. Wild stories of death and mutilation, of vampires and harrowing escapes from the city, all focused on Brianna and the group with whom she was traveling.

He finally reached his man. "What is it?" he asked.

"Lady Standish's horse, sir," the guard replied indicating the swollen carcass. Constance studied the corpse intently. The tack had been removed before the animal had been dragged out of the city to allow it to decompose. At first, he didn't recognize the animal as belonging to Brianna, but then his eyes spotted the brand burned into its hip. There was no mistaking it. This was Brianna's mount. Cold dread gripped his chest as he shifted his gaze to the puncture wound, which had caused the animal's death. Someone had run the horse through with a sword or spike. The next immediate thought was whether or not Brianna had been hurt... or worse.

"What do you think happened to her, sir?" the guard asked softly.

Constance continued to stare at the body, ignoring the rancid smell of decomposition and the nearly deafening buzz of the thick cloud of flies swarming the carcass. His mind poured over the multiple options of what had become of Brianna. The tales he had heard in the city did nothing but cause his imagination to run rampant. Three men murdered and mutilated inside one of the local inns, the very real possibility of a vampire being on the loose and responsible for the death of Constable Liston, a local whore and a young woman found in the cellar of Liston's residence, and an unbelievable tale of a pursuit through the streets of the city that left Constance wondering if he would ever learn what had become of his mistress.

The soldier in him tried to squash the fear, to force him to view the situation objectively and logically. The part of him that looked upon Brianna as a father would of his daughter, felt cold terror dissipate his blood as it ran through his veins. Taking a deep breath, he forced the soldier to the surface. "I do not know. She survived her trip through the city even, if her mount did not," he said as he turned to survey the surrounding forest, his eyes squinting in the sunshine. "If we are to take the stories we heard as true, then she is being pursued by a detachment of the Royal Guard, and they are heading north."

The guard looked about the area, his voice dropping to a near whisper, "What of the vampire?"

Constance snapped his head around to fix the man with a heated gaze that left the man withering. "There is no proof of vampires! Just the hushed terrified whispers of ignorant folk who are scared far too easily! I will not complicate this journey with ghost stories that will have us jumping at every sound like scared children! Do I make myself clear?"

The guard snapped to attention. "Very clear, sir!"

Constance held the heated gaze a moment longer to drive his point home before shifting his gaze to the clearing. "They left the city heading north. We will head to the northern most edge of the city and begin searching for their trail. Have the men mounted and ready to move out immediately."

"Yes sir," the guard replied as he hurried off to carry out his orders. Constance took a few more moments to study the area before his gaze returned to the carcass. His eyes narrowed as they locked on the dead horse. "Where is your mistress? What has become of her?" he whispered.

Silence was the response.

Constance wiped a thin sheen of sweat from his forehead before setting his hat back on his head. He turned from the corpse and began walking toward his mount. Despite his best efforts and the iron discipline of the soldier within him, he found himself wondering how they would find Brianna and battle a vampire at the same time.

CHAPTER SIXTEEN

"We are losing ground on them," the tracker said as he looked up at Armand.

The Captain shifted his weight in the saddle and looked down on the tracker as he knelt in the dirt and grass, searching for signs of the criminal's trail. The task was complicated by the fact that the further up into the mountain range they went, the harder it was to follow their trail. The soft dirt of the flatlands gave way to a more compact soil and loose gravel.

"How is that possible?" Lordalise demanded. "We have been pursuing them non-stop since leaving Lirpa."

The tracker lightly brushed his fingertips across the faint indentation of a hoof print in the hard ground. "This track is at least a day old, perhaps more," the tracker said, ignoring Lordalise's question. It had been established early on that the tracker did not care for the Hunter and would not answer any direct question from him.

"Are you sure it is the right trail?" Armand asked making a sign to Lordalise to not agitate the situation any further. The Hunter opened his mouth to say something, but quickly clamped it shut. The heated glare he directed at the tracker was intense.

"This track belongs to a large breed of horse. One of the criminals rides such an animal, and we have been following this track since leaving Lirpa. This is the print of the same animal," the tracker answered as he found another hoof print and measured the distance between the two with his eyes. "Same gait, same weight indentions… it is the same animal with the same rider."

"How have they gained so much distance on us?" Armand asked.

The tracker stood up while his eyes continued to study the ground before him. He shrugged. "They are riding further into the night, perhaps sleeping only a few hours before setting out again. Judging from the strides of the animals, they are using a very effective speed. It crosses many miles while minimizing the wear on the mounts. They are also making very good use of the rugged terrain where a small number of people can pass while a large party such as ours must take frequent detours." The tracker paused as he studied another area of ground, his experienced gaze showing him signs that none of the others could see. With a barely perceptible nod of appreciation, he smiled slightly. "Whomever we pursue, they are no apprentice to the arts of eluding pursuit."

Armand didn't miss the smile on the tracker's face. "You speak as though you admire them. Need I remind you they are murderers?"

The tracker never looked up as he shook his head. "Trust me, Captain. I want nothing more than to deliver you to them so that they may face justice for their crimes. However, that does not mean that I cannot admire their skills, no matter how wasted such talent is."

"We must double our efforts, Captain," Lordalise said. "We are losing them."

Armand sat still for several moments, his eyes studying the trail and then the path ahead of them. After several thoughtful moments, he regarded the tracker. "How difficult will it be to keep track of them? How old will their trail have to be to prevent you from following them?"

The tracker removed his hat and wiped the sweat from his forehead. "I would not let them get much further ahead of us. The higher they go into the mountains, the harder it will be to track them."

Armand sat in thoughtful silence for a few more moments before a tiny sliver of a smile touched his lips, as he nodded once. "We will continue along this path and at this pace."

Lordalise felt his jaw drop open. Armand didn't seem to be the least bit concerned that Devenshire and his band of demons were slowly leaving them behind. Had the captain lost his passion for justice? Had his vow to avenge Constable Liston been negated? Or was it something else? "With all due respect, Captain, I advise against this course of action. Need I remind you of the dangers of allowing Devenshire to roam free?"

Armand's tiny smile broadened as he shifted his gaze to the Hunter. "Rest easy, Master Lordalise. There is a method to my madness, and I assure you that Devenshire will not make good his escape."

"May I ask what suddenly has you so confident?" Lordalise asked.

Armand chuckled as he urged his mount onward. "You may ask…"

Lordalise watched Armand ride away and felt concern spike within him. Armand was acting strange. His anger and thirst for vengeance, which had him driving hard to overtake the criminals seemed to have cooled, and their pursuit had slowed considerably.

Bonzwa steered his mount up next to Lordalise. He joined Lordalise in watching the captain of the Royal Guard ride slowly onward. He switched his gaze to the former Hunter turned Bandit King turned Hunter again. "What troubles you, sir?"

Lordalise never took his eyes off Armand's retreating back. "The good Captain seems to have had a change of heart in regards to our quest."

"How so?" Bonzwa asked.

Lordalise continued to study Armand as he absently chewed on the edge of his bottom lip. His eyes narrowed as he considered all the possible explanations for Armand's change in behavior, and what it would mean for his duty to destroy Devenshire. Finally, he shook his head slowly. "He is acting like a man who has either far more information than he is sharing with us or a man who has lost his interest in the hunt. Either scenario does not make me very comfortable." Lordalise paused as his mind continued to churn over the new mystery Armand's behavior presented. After a few more moments, he shook his head slowly again. "Be alert, Bonzwa. The time may come when we may have to re-examine our alliance with the noble Captain Armand, and the separation may not be peaceful."

Bonzwa didn't welcome the cold spike of dread Lordalise's words drove into his mind. It was already bad enough to be in such close proximity to the Royal Guards, let alone working with them. The thought of having to fight their way free of them wasn't any better of a prospect. "Fight a regiment of the Royal Guard, sire?"

Lordalise swung his head around to look at Bonzwa. "Who said anything about fighting? There are many ways we can separate ourselves from Captain Armand and his gallant Royal Guardsmen." he gathered his reins and urged his mount forward. "Remember who we are, Bonzwa. Devenshire is not the only creature who can take advantage of the dark of night."

It was Bonzwa's turn to sit in the saddle, watch Lordalise ride away, and ponder exactly what he was doing. Were his loyalties to his men? The bandits who had made him a very wealthy man? Or were they to the Order of Hunters? A group he had not been a member of in many seasons? Bonzwa had to honestly admit that for the first time since meeting Lordal, or Lordalise or whatever his true name really was, he wasn't sure where the man's allegiance lay. One thing was certain: he would not end up standing before a Tribunal Lord for any number of the multitude of crimes he had committed. He took up his reins and nodded after Lordalise. "No, sire. No, he is not."

~*~

Shantira moved through the forest, her eyes searching intently for berries, herbs, wild vegetables, or anything else that they might be able to use to bolster their food reserves. She welcomed the chore for it forced her mind off the tragedy of her loss or the torturous thoughts and feelings Devenshire stirred.

It also kept her mind off Brianna.

Ever since Lirpa, she had been experiencing strange thoughts over her and it was deeply troubling. She caught herself staying as close to Brianna as possible, even making sure her blankets were close to Brianna's as they slept. The overriding concern for her safety was very powerful and incredibly hard to shake. It was manageable during the day, and she could almost convince herself that it was gone, but once night returned, the desire to stay close to Brianna and ensure that no harm came to her was overpowering. She even found herself waking in the middle of the night to sit up and keep watch over her. It was maddening. The desire to keep Brianna safe was natural, as it would be with anyone she cared about, yet there had been no increase in her concern for the others, even Devenshire. She knew that this drive to keep Brianna was stronger than any desire she had to keep him safe which, given her preoccupation with him, was very strange. She could not explain it any better now than when it had first appeared in Lirpa when she had nearly strangled the guard who had used Brianna as a tool to force hers and Zandorth's surrender. She paused as she realized that she had let her mind wander yet again, and she wasn't paying attention to her search for food. Just as she was chastising herself for her lack of attention, she heard a splash up ahead. She knew there was a small pond nearby, but she hadn't realized she had ventured so close to it.

Suddenly, her breath caught in her throat as she also realized that Devenshire was bathing in that pond. Her knees began to tremble as she considered what to do next. The talk with him the night before had been magical, and while she had not been able to give flight to the words her heart and mind demanded she release, she did feel closer to him. She had seen the echoes of pain in his eyes in the pale glow of moonlight and had also seen that damnable charm that always made her feel as though her insides had turned to mush. She knew she should turn around and walk away, but her feet refused her command. She squeezed her eyes shut and shook her head. This wasn't right. What she was thinking wasn't proper behavior. She bit her bottom lip as she continued to struggle with herself. Her mind tried to remind her of her upbringing, of how such thoughts, let alone actions, would be frowned upon. Her heart and soul, recently liberated by her experiences in Lirpa, demanded she continue on, to satisfy the itching curiosity about him that taunted her almost every time she looked at him.

The sound of rippling water echoed in her ears, almost like a siren's song drawing her to certain moral doom. She turned her back on the pond and forced her heavy legs to propel her away, to save her from her sinful desires. This was the proper path, the way Lucinda had raised her, the way a proper young lady behaved. Two steps turned to three, then four and then five. Every step was difficult to make, but made her mind praise her for taking the higher moral path.

Her steps slowed and became less determined as her darker side taunted and teased her with mental images of what might be waiting for her in the pond. She forced herself to move, to place one foot in front of another hoping against hope that distance would take the edge of the temptation. Finally, she found herself once again standing in the forest, battling herself, and listening to the sounds of a very naked Devenshire, just yards away. Finally, she stomped one foot and let her breath out in an explosive sigh as she turned and began moving back toward the pond. "Damned moral high ground should not be so high!" she muttered.

She used every bit of stealth she possessed to approach the pond. Through tree branches and brush, she could make out the sight of someone floating in the water, but the undergrowth was too thick at this point to make out any details. Her eyes grew wide and her breath shallow as she concentrated on not making a sound as she approached. She came to a break in the brush and found Devenshire's soaking wet clothes laid out on a boulder. Obviously, he had dove into the pond fully clothed, and then took them off and laid them out to dry. *How clever*, she mused. He could bathe and wash his clothes at the same time. The sound of movement in the water jerked her head up and her wide eyes looked out across the pond. Devenshire stood in a shallow part of the pond where the water came to the points of his hips. He was facing her, but was not looking at her. He was slicking his long wet hair back from his face giving her an ample view of his torso. While her heart pounded in her chest, she found her lungs had seized and her eyelids simply refused to blink.

Whatever images of what he might look like unclothed she had held in her mind did no justice to what she saw before her now. His arms were muscular and very well defined. They weren't the bulging masses of muscle that Zandorth's arms presented, but it was a very well defined muscular tone that was incredibly attractive. His chest looked like it had been chiseled out of granite. Through a thick covering of hair, she could see the definite bulge of pectoral muscles. The hair, while thick on his chest, thinned as it moved toward the tight knots of muscles of his abdomen. Her eyes widened even further as she felt like her chest was contracting on her heart, threatening to seize it as it had her lungs. She felt dizzy, disoriented and couldn't understand why his appearance was having this affect on her. She had seen other men without their shirts on, many of them had been better muscled than Devenshire, but yet the sight of him before her made her knees weak, her stomach flutter, chest tingle, and her mind swim. There were other sensations in other areas that she had experienced before, but not to this magnitude.

Devenshire lowered his arms back to his sides and lowered his head. His eyes closed as he simply stood there in the water. For several moments, both he and Shantira were motionless. The only sounds were the water droplets falling from his wet hair to the pond's surface and the usual sounds of the morning. She wasn't sure which terrified her more: that he would walk further out of the water and reveal more of himself, or that he wouldn't.

In another annoying turn of her confused thoughts, she found herself praying for both. Instead, he turned slowly until his back was facing her as he began walking into deeper water. What she saw on his back turned her blood cold. His back was a solid mass of crisscrossed, twisted, knotted scars. They were thick corded masses of scar tissue that indicated that the wounds had been both numerous and deep. There was no doubt as to what had caused the scars. She had seen them before. He had been flogged, and the whipping had been severe. What had he done to warrant such a beating? The crime must have been ruthless given the solid mass of damage across his entire back. The scars were also old which meant the flogging had occurred long ago. The sheer brutality of the beating told her that someone had intended for him to never, ever forget his crime or his punishment.

Where a moment ago she had been transfixed by his ruggedness, she was now transfixed by the fear of his past. What could he have done? What crime had he committed and what did that mean for the type of person he was?

"It is a bit cold to be swimming," a soft voice echoed from the far side of the pond. Shantira's eyes snapped to the source and found Kendra standing on a boulder on the far side of the pond. Her hands were clasped together before her, and she gently swung herself back and forth from the waist. She made no attempt to hide the fact that her eyes were admiring him, and her wicked little smile left no doubt as to the thoughts that consumed her mind.

Devenshire smiled as he swung his head in her direction. "I find it invigorating." He made no attempt to cover himself. His demeanor was the same as if he had been fully clothed while talking to her.

She felt her anger spike as her eyes narrowed on the blonde Elven woman. She had no business being here! Devenshire was simply trying to bathe, not be a spectacle for a woman who could not control her primal urges. With a sickening realization, she understood that the same could be said of her and her covert efforts to admire Devenshire's form, but she pushed those observations aside. What was worse, Kendra wasn't even trying to hide. She was being both upfront and open about her attempt. With growing guilt and mounting anger, she realized she had to retreat. There would be no logical explanation for her hiding in the bushes while Devenshire bathed.

"I can most definitely see where it would be incredibly invigorating," Kendra said with a definite purr to her tone.

Bitch! Shantira's mind screamed out.

Devenshire didn't reply as he simply stared at her, that wicked mischief again lighting his sultry eyes. Shantira found herself praying that he would tell her to go away, to let him bathe in peace.

"Would you like some company?" she asked coyly.

Devenshire arched one eyebrow, and smiled. "The water is quite cold," he warned.

With a twisted smile, she reached up and began loosening the closures on her shirt. "I find it quite invigorating. I am sure that the water will warm up once I am immersed in it."

Shantira knew she had a decision to make. Either leave now or dive into the water and drown the little tramp bitch elf. Clamping down on her anger, she slowly backed away. After she was convinced that she was well hidden by the underbrush, she turned and carefully chose her path away from the pond.

A few moments later, she heard the splash of Kendra diving into the water. With gritted teeth, she prayed for a very large and vicious sea creature to devour the whore.

Slowly, of course.

CHAPTER SEVENTEEN

Darkseed moved through the thick woods, searching for the perfect spot. The bonus time presented by not immediately hitting the trail gave him a valuable opportunity to delve deep into the Mystical Tides and seek answers to many questions. Primary among them was Devenshire's unexplained increase in mystical skill. The spells he had cast in Lirpa were seasons of study beyond his ability. He should not have survived the battle with the demon in the inn, and he certainly shouldn't have been able to unleash the spell he had used to down Captain Armand. Such unexplained increases in skill and power were dangerous for someone who has not undergone the discipline of learning them. A subtle probing of Devenshire about details of the fight with the Followers had revealed that his powers had failed him. This was also troubling for it meant that the latent powers within him were growing and directly linked to his emotions. That level of power, uncontrolled by a lack of discipline, was unpredictable. Tie that power directly to Devenshire's emotions, which were equally unpredictable, and you had the makings of epic disaster. If his powers continued to develop without the proper training, he would be susceptible to the allure of the Dark Arts. Very quickly, the Dark Mystics would become aware of him and would begin to lure him to their side with great powers and abilities. The Dark Mystics were masters of finding promising students of the Mystical Arts and grooming them for inclusion to their ranks. They would promise great power and gifts of incredibly powerful spells. This path was definitely more attractive than the seasons of study offered by a retreat of the Mystical Arts. Darkseed had seen it before and it was terrifying. Once a person surrendered to the allure of the Dark Arts, their soul was forever lost to the hellish domain of the underworld.

While Devenshire was quite possibly the most disciplined person he knew, Darkseed could not simply rely on that trait. The allure of the Dark Arts as presented by the Dark Mystics could be very tempting. They would eventually find one of Devenshire's weaknesses and attack, wearing him down until he would gladly surrender to the allure of dark magic. Only the discipline taught at a retreat could make it possible for a practitioner of the Mystical Arts to resist. Even with all the training offered by the Adepts, there were still those who crossed over to the darkness and were lost. This was to say nothing of the dangers of Devenshire's powers being unleashed without the proper control. A spell could go in any number of directions if the caster was not in absolute control of the powers being used.

Darkseed remembered the many occasions the Dark Mystics had sought him out, trying to win him over to their side. He had seen what happened when someone surrendered to the Dark Arts and what they became was sufficient evidence of why he would never surrender. That did not stop them from making the attempt on numerous occasions. While they had not tried to convert him recently, he was constantly on the watch for any sign that they had launched another attempt.

Aside from the concerning mystery of Devenshire's growing powers, there was the problem of Xavier and his ability to block himself from Darkseed's most potent observation spell. It had been a very long time since anyone had been able to block Darkseed's powers, and while it was annoying at first, it had become a challenge that he was growing to enjoy. He also needed to check on the spell he had cast on Armand and his company. It was a small spell and one that could easily be overcome, but it had served its purpose so far. The spell altered their perception of time so that their actions were delayed a few moments. They would not actively perceive the change, and it had been the primary reason they had gained so much distance over them. Each morning when they broke camp to pursue them, their movements had slowed tremendously, almost freezing them in place. Their perception of time was altered so that their movements seemed perfectly normal. To them, they were breaking camp and back on the trail in a matter of moments when it was actually taking them much longer. Eventually, one or more of them would realize the deception, and the spell would instantly be broken for the entire group, but it had bought them some valuable time.

Finally, he found himself in a small clearing. He was far enough away from the camp to ensure he would not be disturbed. He would need complete and uninterrupted solitude for what he was about to attempt. He sat down on the ground and folded his legs to him. Lowering his head, he closed his eyes and forced his body to relax. Breathing deeply, he focused on blanking his mind, of forcing his attention on each breath in and each breath out. He forced himself to tune out the sounds of birds in the trees, the whisper of the wind, and the rustle of leaves caught in the fleeting caress of the passing wind. Slowly his surroundings faded away, his body lost sensation as though it were slowly dissolving away. As his mind entered a trance-like state, the physical realm melted away, and for a while, he was in complete limbo. There was no sight, no sound, no smell, and no sense of touch. It was as though his mind had been taken from his skull and cast upon the black emptiness of non-existence. As trained as he was in making the terrifying journey from the land of the real to the insubstantial arena of the Mystical Tides, he still found the crossing disturbing, and his instincts fought against the suspension of his earthly body.

His mind's eyes began to perceive pinprick dots of light, very much like stars in the darkest night sky. A sensation that resembled a moderate breeze swept across his perceptions, and he knew the transition was almost complete. Streaks of blue light flashed past followed by lazy blue ribbons of glowing mystical energy began to swirl about him. Tingling warmth settled about him, and he felt total relaxation as if he were in a hot bath. The blue streaks of light flashed passed in multiple directions, and the swirling ribbons grew in number and intensity until they resembled a mystical stream, hence the name of the Mystical Tides. Maintaining the tedious balance of concentration and relaxation, Darkseed immersed himself further and further into the swirling tides of mystical energies. The further he immersed himself, the more he could learn, the more he would be able to do. Such total immersion into the tides was very difficult for someone of even Darkseed's skill level. For Devenshire to have immersed himself deeply into the tides to learn of the Stones of Andarus was another indication of the unexplainable and concerning growth of his powers. Though the sensations he was feeling were not real in the physical sense, to his mind they were very solid. In his mind, he was now floating serenely in the gently rolling tides of florescent blue energy. His eyes were closed and his breath was so slow it did not appear that he was breathing at all. Tight muscles from days in the saddle loosened their vice-like grip, and the tensions of the quest melted away. With one final mental command, he let himself sink below the surface, now fully immersed in the Mystical Tides.

The swirling blue ribbons gently turned his 'body' as they moved past him. The bright blue streaks were now more subdued, almost gentler as they shot past him. The warmth was tinged with an occasional chilled breeze, and pale blue orbs of intense light drifted around him in numbers far too high to ever count. While his mortal perceptions told his mind that he was under water, his mind knew that he had left his physical body behind and these perceptions were simply basic reactions from his mind. He squelched these sensations and forced more concentration into sifting through the fleeting, twisting, swirling strings of knowledge that now encompassed him. The blue orbs were bits of knowledge. To learn what a particular orb possessed involved mentally joining with it, very much like taking a book off a shelf and opening its cover. His mental eyes searched each orb closest to him, his mind searching for the orbs that would reveal what was happening with Devenshire's powers.

He frowned as none of the orbs responded to his search. He could usually find answers quite easily once he was this far into the tides. He relaxed a little more and forced himself to remain calm. Only calm and orderly thoughts could find answers within the tides. Any overt emotion would cause the connection to the tides to weaken. He searched again and found nothing regarding Devenshire at all.

Odd. There should be something within the tides regarding him. Every person in the realm had a knowledge orb within the tides, and if your concentration was sufficient, you could access that knowledge. It was as though all traces of Devenshire had been removed from the tides, and that was impossible. Darkseed doubled his efforts and continued to swim through the tides, searching for any trace of Devenshire. After an exhausting search, he could find nothing. Darkseed realized that he was tensing up, and that was leading to fatigue which would shorten the amount of time he would be able to remain in the tides.

Forcing himself to relax, he stopped searching for information regarding Devenshire. Something was very wrong here. No one could hide or remove information from the Mystic Tides. Even when someone died, their essence and knowledge could be found within the tides. By the very nature of the Mystic Tides, Darkseed should have been able to, with the proper discipline and concentration, find out any answer he needed. No Adept, no Dark Mystic, no one could tamper with the structure of the tides and yet the information he sought could not be found. He should have found Devenshire's essence easily given his long association and close connection with him. It was clear that someone of respectable power was going to great lengths to mask Devenshire's essence within the tides. Up until this moment, Darkseed would have thought such a feat was impossible.

He had expended a great deal of energy in searching for clues about Devenshire's growing abilities. His time within the tides was growing short, and he still had much to do. He decided to let the mystery of Devenshire's missing information stand for now. He mentally shifted his course through the tides and began trying to locate Xavier, and attempting to break through the veil that he was able to put up in order to shield himself from Darkseed's most stringent attempts to locate him. In the distance, he spied a flickering red orb. It stood out in sharp contrast to the blue orbs and swirling tides around it. He focused on the red globe and knew, on an instinctual level, that he had found Xavier. The Mystical Arts were always blue in color while the Dark Arts were red. Even though Xavier had mastered both forms of magic, his intentions in using them were evil, therefore his essence within the tides would be more red than blue.

Careful to suppress a spike of joy, for even positive emotions could disrupt his tie to the tides as quickly as negative ones, he moved toward the orb. It was puzzling how he had been able to so easily find Xavier in the tides when all previous attempts had been frustratingly futile. He had been able to locate Xavier's essence in the tides before, but he had been able to cast a veil over his essence that Darkseed had been unable to break. Now, however, it appeared that the veil surrounding his essence was gone. Darkseed slowed his approach to the orb. Something was not right. It should not have been this easy. Had his enhanced spells finally been able to negate Xavier's veil? Or had the demented mage canceled out his veil? Or was the madman casting a spell so powerful that it made maintaining his veil impossible?

Moving carefully, he moved closer to the red orb, which much to his dismay began glowing brighter. Wherever he was, Xavier was casting a powerful spell. He tentatively began probing, searching for the answer. He had to know what Xavier was up to. Suddenly, the red orb split open and a red bolt of mystical lightening shot out, striking Darkseed in what would be his forehead. Instantly, his senses were over loaded with intense energy. He felt himself caught in the hidden protection spell Xavier had cast about his essence, and he chastised himself for being so careless. It was so obvious and something he would have done in Xavier's place.

Darkseed quickly threw up his own defensive spell and quickly sought to sever the painful tie that Xavier's spell had on him. A lesser mage would have been consumed in Xavier's spell. Their mind would have quickly been stripped of all defenses, which would have left it powerless to navigate the strong currents of the tides. In essence, they would be forever trapped in the tides while their physical body would become a mindless shell of barely living tissue. A very frightening prospect, and one Darkseed was determined would not become his fate... not this day. His counter spell quickly threw up a protective shell about his essence within the tides. Xavier's spell was not intended to overpower an Adept, so Darkseed was able to protect himself. Just as the last tendrils of Xavier's spell were cut off by Darkseed's protection spell, he was able to catch a brief glimpse of the spell Xavier was casting...

In the quiet clearing, Darkseed's body sat slumped on the forest floor. It looked as though he were unconscious. His breath was very shallow and his pulse very faint. To the average passerby, Darkseed would appear very near death. Such was an illusion, and the illusion was short lived. With a startled gasp Darkseed suddenly shot backwards, hitting the ground hard as his extremities shot out in all directions. His eyes were wide in terror as they stared up into the sky, and his breath came in ragged gasps. His entire body trembled with pain and fear.

"No!" he gasped as he struggled to force his mind to absorb the very sudden transition from the tides back to the physical realm. He could not discern if what he saw was from his physical eyes or mental ones. Was he truly lying on the forest floor, or had his mind been expelled to another dimension? For a moment, all he could do was lie on the ground and look up into the growing dark clouds forming in the sky.

"No!" he rasped again as he struggled to regain control of his body. That last instant of contact with Xavier's counter spell had been tremendous. A subtle layer of the spell had been triggered by Darkseed's counter spell, which had forcibly expelled him from the tides. He had not been prepared for such a maneuver, and the resulting ripping of his mind from the tides had left him nearly catatonic. The trip out of the tides was supposed to be as slow and controlled as the entrance. Being thrust out of the tides had left him unprepared to re-assimilate himself with his physical body, and the shock had left him paralyzed. Now was not the time for such paralysis. He had seen what the spell was that Xavier was casting, and he had to warn the others. The boiling clouds that rolled overhead with ever darkening color were tied directly to the attack Xavier was launching.

Move, damn you! His mind screamed at himself. Time was short, dangerously short.

Finally, after what felt like an eternity, the middle finger on his right hand twitched. It wasn't much, but it was enough to allow him to focus on regaining control of his body. The index finger moved next. The ring finger followed, and finally, he was able to curl his fingers into a fist, a trembling fist that began shaking loose the paralysis.

That is it! Move, you sluggish swine! Move your ass! He screamed at himself within his mind. His eyes blinked as a flash of lightening flared overhead. The following rumble of thunder shook the ground and drove the spike of fear deeper into his chest. As the wind picked up, hurling leaves and twigs about the clearing, he was able to roll onto his side and pull his legs up to him. He rolled up onto his knees and forced his agony-riddled joints to move as he pushed himself up on all fours. Giant drops of rain began to pelt him, almost painfully. He raised his head and looked up through the canopy of branches and saw that the blue sky was completely gone now, dominated by the nearly black storm clouds that had nothing to do with any natural occurrence of weather. He staggered to his feet just as the distant roar became barely audible. Breathing heavily from his struggle to regain control of his body, Darkseed watched the storm continue to grow. He was terrifyingly aware of what the roar was—he just hoped he was fast enough to reach the others and that he had enough power left to fight it. As he broke into a staggering run back toward the camp, he realized he didn't like the answer to either question.

~*~

Brianna sat at the fire, enjoying the solitude and another cup of Darkseed's strong black coffee. She had contemplated visiting the pond for a swim with Devenshire, but had seen Kendra sneaking off in that direction. With a twisted grin, she hugged her blanket about her. If the Elven woman were as bold as she presented, it would be a swim she would not soon forget. Perhaps for Devenshire as well.

Darkseed had ventured off on some mystical mission she didn't even pretend to understand. Zandorth had mumbled something about battle practice, which had intrigued Stant who invited himself along. Shantira had gone off in search of berries and wild vegetables, and Petera was simply enjoying a peaceful morning stroll through the forest. The result was a perfectly peaceful morning alone. She enjoyed these moments when she could simply exist. No demands of her office, no demands of those around her, and no trepidation about the mystery they had left behind in Lirpa or the danger of what lie ahead of them with Xavier. Just a few lovely moments with herself.

With a deep sigh, she closed her eyes, lifted the tin cup to her lips, and sipped the coffee. She slowly opened her eyes and gazed up at the piercingly blue sky. It was going to be a beautiful day. She heard the crash of brush followed by hard footfalls. She lazily turned her head toward the sound and saw Shantira moving toward her. The hard look in the young woman's eyes, the clenched fists at her sides, and the way she nearly stomped out each step, told Brianna that the peacefulness of the morning was about to come to a screeching halt on the heels of the ravaging storm of Shantira's emotions.

"Oh, well," she whispered to herself. "It was nice while it lasted." She arranged her features into a pleasant smile while she waited for her friend to arrive.

Shantira plopped down on a log and leaned forward, resting on her knees as she glared into the fire. The tightness of the skin under her eyes, the angry, defiant jut of her jaw, and the waves of anger that rolled off her was palpable.

"I take it you are not having a pleasant morning?" she asked innocently.

"I am fine! It is of no matter!" Shantira muttered in reply.

"Very well, then," Brianna replied as she returned to her coffee. She silently counted down the moments to what she knew was coming next.

"Dirty little tramp!" Shantira spouted. "She has no right!"

Brianna suppressed a smile. "I am assuming you are referring to Kendra?"

"She does not deserve any name other than tramp, or perhaps

whore!"

"Oh my. Pray tell what has this *blight on humanity* done now."

Shantira snapped a glare toward Brianna. "Do not placate me, Brianna! She is an evil temptress!"

"And who is she tempting?" Brianna asked absently, knowing full well what had transpired.

"You know damned well who she is tempting with her whorish charms!"

Brianna let the venom roll past her. It was not directed at her, but since she was the only one present, Shantira had to vent it somehow. She also knew she had to disarm the fury before it drove her to do something foolish.

"Why you, naughty little minx! I did not think you had it in you," Brianna said with a coy tone and a sultry smile.

Whatever Shantira had been expecting, Brianna's response was not it. Her fury was momentarily halted as she stared at her with confusion. "What?"

Brianna smiled as she nodded. "I may make a woman out of you yet."

"What are you blathering on about?" Shantira demanded, her fury now back in motion.

"Kendra found out Daimion was taking a swim and decided to join him. For you to be this angry means you saw her at the pond with Daimion. That also means you were at the pond watching what I have to assume was a very wet and very naked Devenshire." Brianna giggled as she raised the cup to her lips once again. "Searching for berries, indeed."

"That is not..." Shantira started to retort and caught herself. "What I mean is that is not the same. I was not..." She paused again as she realized that she was no more innocent than Kendra.

Brianna smiled pleasantly, her expression patiently waiting for the explanation to the trap she had caught herself in. "Yes? Go on."

"I did not deliberately go to the pond to spy on Daimion! I was looking for ber–... fruits and other vegetables." She quickly corrected her use of the word berries.

"Yet you found yourself at the pond, and Daimion is not an easy man to miss, especially naked. You could have easily made a retreat, but I would wager that you stayed and observed for a bit," Brianna replied.

"It is not the same!" Shantira fired back, but it lacked conviction, as she knew her anger had led her to betray her behavior.

"How so? You could have easily joined Daimion instead of Kendra."

"Impossible! Ladies do not do such things!" Shantira fired back and almost instantly winced for she knew she had, once again, trapped herself.

"Ladies also do not hide and watch naked men bathe. Women, however, do. There is no shame in following your nature, Shantira. Society may not approve, but you know my feelings about society."

"She has no claim to him!" Shantira shot back, trying to ignore Brianna's words.

"Nor do you," Brianna replied gently but with a layer of firmness in her voice. She watched with regret as that singularly harsh truth was, once again, rammed into her consciousness. "Nor do I. No one has claim to him. I told you this in the beginning, and it is more true now than then. You must learn to govern your emotions concerning him, or you will be fighting many battles that you have no firm purchase on gaining any form of victory."

With her last statement, Brianna had diffused her anger, had made her understand that she had no right to be this angry, and the reason she had no right to be this angry made her sad. The child in her wanted to remain angry, to be told that she had every right to be this furious, and that the small statured Elven woman should die a slow, agonizing death for her actions. The adult understood with growing sadness and clarity that the child was, once again, wrong. With the anger dissipated, her posture slumped in defeat. "You are right, of course," she said in a dull, defeated tone. Her eyes dropped to the fire. "I am a fool!"

Brianna shrugged out of her blanket and set her tin down. She leaned over and placed a warm hand over one of Shantira's. "You are not a fool. You are a young woman who is being forced to learn control of her emotions. It is one of the most difficult lessons to learn, and there is no way to make the lessons painless."

Shantira struggled to recover her composure and put her wild rampant thoughts into some semblance of order. She had thought she had conquered her jealousy, but this morning had shown her just how little control she had gained. The deep conversation with Devenshire the night before had lulled her into thinking that she had made some kind of emotional connection with him and that he felt the same for her. She had not been at all prepared to learn that whatever feelings she had garnered from their conversation, they were not shared by him—at least not to the depth she had felt them. She sighed as the last of the fury left her. It was a fight she had no hopes of winning and one that she now felt embarrassed for engaging in. She slowly lifted her eyes to see Brianna smiling softly at her, her expression full of understanding for her plight. "Once again you have dragged me back from the edge of madness."

Brianna squeezed her hand, and smiled warmly. "What are friends for?"

Suddenly the temperature of the air dropped dramatically as odd shadows began to track across the wide-open clearing they had camped in. Both women looked up to see dark, ominous clouds roll in from what appeared to be nowhere. The wind picked up and the calmness of the morning was suddenly erased, being replaced with what promised to be a very nasty storm.

"Odd," Brianna commented as she released Shantira's hand and stood up slowly, scanning the building storm with her eyes. "There was not a cloud in the sky."

Shantira also stood, studying the sky and not understanding what she was seeing. "Tis not the season for such storms and certainly not this quickly."

"Take cover!" came a deep shout from their left. Both women turned to see Zandorth and Stant break into the clearing in a dead run. The wind began to whip their hair about their faces and they had to continuously wipe it away. Leaves and other debris began to swirl about the clearing as the wind increased in velocity. Flashes of lightening began to light up the dark clouds followed almost instantly by deep bellows of thunder.

"I have never seen a storm like this," Shantira commented as she alternated her gaze from the dark rolling clouds and the two men running toward them.

"Take cover!" Zandorth bellowed out again as he poured on more speed. It was surprising to the women to see such a massive form propelled with such swiftness. Stant, who was smaller in build and stature, was having trouble keeping up with the warrior. Concern at the sudden storm turned to fear as the danger it represented became very clear. This was no ordinary storm. The conditions to give it life had not been present. As the first giant drops of rain began to fall, dread flourished within them. They looked at each other, unsure of what the storm meant or what exactly they were to do next.

From their right, another figure burst from the tree line. They spun their heads in that direction to find a shirtless Devenshire running toward them. His shirt, cloak, and sword clutched in one hand as he sprinted for the camp. Kendra emerged from the tree line several paces behind him as she shrugged into her shirt.

"Take cover! Now!" Devenshire bellowed as his head turned toward the north and the darkest part of the storm clouds.

Zandorth slid to a stop next to the women, his sword in hand. "We must find shelter!"

"Where?" Brianna asked, not liking the deep dread that spread through her. "We are in the open!"

"I am not about to seek shelter under a tree with all of this lightening!" Shantira added, her eyes nervously scanning the clouds. She knew that a tree was the absolute last place she wanted to be with all the lightening.

Suddenly, a flash of lightening flashed across the sky and then streaked to earth several paces ahead of Devenshire. The ground erupted with a tremendous explosion that left a large crater in the ground and carried Devenshire off his feet and back in the direction he had come. He landed hard and rolled, knocking Kendra off her feet as he rolled under her. He came to rest several paces behind her and was still.

"Daimion!" Shantira shouted as she moved to run to him. Zandorth's steel grip stopped her.

"No! It is too dangerous!" he said.

"Let me go! He is hurt!" she screamed at him.

"No, Shantira. Stay here!" Brianna added.

From directly behind them, they heard another crash of something breaking free of the tree line. They spun to see Darkseed in a staggering run toward them. His features were pale, almost waxen, and his balance was uncertain judging by the way he half ran and half staggered. He shouted something at them, but the howl of the wind drowned him out. The rain was falling heavily now, which forced them to huddle against the sting of the giant drops. Shantira shifted her gaze from Darkseed to Devenshire and saw him climb slowly to his feet. He moved sluggishly toward Kendra and helped her up. He was disoriented, but alive. He urged a dazed Kendra on and began to run, taking her by the wrist, and dragging her behind him. Another flash of lightening splayed itself across the sky in a brilliant display of power before a large bolt broke away and struck the ground near the campfire. Again, the ground exploded into a shower of charred earth and waves of violently released energy. Those around the now extinguished fire felt the impact of the wave of energy, and they had to brace themselves to remain on their feet. The pounding rain, violent wind, and dangerous lightening left them disoriented.

Devenshire arrived to the group first and made sure Kendra was safe in their numbers. He spied Darkseed running toward them and then saw Petera emerge from another point around the clearing. He was clearly confused, and a little scared from the sudden appearance of such a violent storm, but he had the presence of mind to run toward them.

"What the hell is going on?" Brianna demanded. "Where did this storm come from?"

Devenshire shielded his face from the horizontal sheets of rain to focus his gaze toward the north and to what appeared to be the heart of the storm. "It is not a storm! At least not a natural one!" he shouted over the howling wind.

"Xavier!" Darkseed shouted as he reached the group. He paused to bend over, resting his hands on his knees as he tried to catch his breath and recover from the after effects of being ejected from the

Mystical Tides with such force.

"Yes!" Devenshire concurred. "And he is sparing no power! This is only the beginning! The worst is yet to come! We must find shelter!" he shouted over the din of the storm.

"There is a cave over there!" Zandorth bellowed as he pointed in the direction he and Stant had come from. "We may just be able to make it!"

A lightning bolt struck the ground near them, and the resulting explosion threw them all to the ground with a sickening splash of the water that had already accumulated. They quickly climbed back to their feet, wiping the mud and debris from their faces, their skin tingling with the close proximity of the energy release.

"That was entirely too close!" Kendra shouted.

"We are easy targets here! We must move!" Stant added.

"Darkseed! Can you throw up a shield around us as we move to the cave?" Devenshire asked loudly.

"My powers are taxed, but I will try! I do not know if it will be sufficient to protect us!" Darkseed answered, his eyes telling Devenshire the truth of what he meant.

"Something is preferable to nothing!" he shouted in reply.

Darkseed stepped into the center of the wet, huddled group and took a moment to compose himself. As the storm raged around them, he made a series of hand and arm gestures, which ended with his cupped hands at waist level. He opened his eyes and they glowed with a blue aura. A pale blue sphere formed around them and began to strengthen. As the shield gained strength, the wind began to grow weaker and the rain seemed to lessen.

"Good! A little more!" Devenshire shouted.

"Almost there," Darkseed muttered, as his face became a hard mask of intense concentration. The blue light in his eyes intensified until his pupils, iris, and corneas were gone, replaced by the intense blue glow of Darkseed's powers.

As the last of his shield formed, the storm was successfully sealed outside. The storm continued to rage, but it could not penetrate the shield. "The shield is in place, but I cannot hold it for long. We must move now!" Darkseed grunted.

"Lead the way, Zandorth!" Devenshire said. He winced as another wave of spasms raced down his spine. His natural sense of the use of magic had alerted him to the forming storm, and as it grew in strength, the tingle had grown into full-blown spasms. Now, with added use of magic from Darkseed to form the shield, it was increasing the intensity, and the pain. Slowly, they began to move. They had to move slowly to allow Darkseed to be able to walk and maintain the incredible power needed to hold the shield in place. Another lightning bolt struck the ground near them and the resulting shock wave caused the blue glow of the shield to flicker with red. Darkseed winced in pain as he absorbed the feedback from Xavier's magic. "Damn!" he muttered through clenched teeth.

"Let me help!" Devenshire said as he dropped the items he'd been carrying and prepared to throw his powers in with Darkseed's.

"No!" Darkseed shouted. "It is a meticulous balance! You may disrupt the shield and cancel it out completely!"

Devenshire nodded once, his features growing grim with the realization that there was nothing he could do. They continued the torturously slow pace. Several lightening strikes threatened them, but Darkseed's shield held. It was an odd sight to see the rain bouncing off the shimmering blue sphere. Inside the sphere, it was still, with the only sound reaching them being the muted sound of the storm. Occasionally, they would have to pause while Darkseed made an adjustment to the spell.

Suddenly, a lightning bolt arched across the sky before splitting off into multiple streaks. Instead of fading, however, they pulled back toward each other forming one massive, throbbing bolt, which shifted its path and shot toward the ground. This time it found its mark, striking Darkseed's protective shield dead on. Darkseed hissed in expelled breath as he struggled against the onslaught of power. His lips peeled back to show his clenched teeth as his arms trembled under the tremendous power he had to expend to maintain the shield. The blue aura turned red as the power of the lightning bolt momentarily assumed dominance. His arms trembled violently as he slowly pushed them up from his waist and spread them to encompass more power. "No, you will not, you bastard!" he hissed as he fought back. His knees trembled, and he looked as though he were about to collapse under a tremendous weight.

"Raven! Let me help!" Devenshire pleaded.

"No! Do not interfere! No matter what happens!" Darkseed grunted in reply.

Slowly, the red began to flicker and speckles of blue light began to re-appear on the surface of the sphere. Sweat poured down Darkseed's already drenched face as even the muscles in his face trembled with the effort he was exerting. The blue light emanating from his eyes began to dim.

"Come on!" he hissed. "Is that all you have?"

"I do not know if I would be taunting him!" Petera commented as he watched the tremendous struggle going on before him.

"He is not taunting, Xavier," Zandorth commented as he watched Darkseed. "He is taunting himself."

Finally, the red light was being pushed back, the blue light returning to dominance within the surface of the sphere. A faint breeze formed within the shield, and a few drops of rain penetrated its surface, but the power of the lightning bolt was held at bay. With a distinct and very sharp crackle of collided energies, the red light winked out.

"Good work, Darkseed!" Stant shouted.

"Do not celebrate just yet," Darkseed grunted. "I will not be able to hold off another one."

"You will not have to…" Devenshire's voice injected. There was an odd tone to it that made everyone except Darkseed shift their gazes to him. He was staring off to the north, and his face paled. "By the Fates…" he whispered with dread.

One by one, each set of eyes left him to see what he had seen that would cause such a reaction, and one by one, each jaw dropped open with shock, and then terror. What they saw made the storm to this point seem like a spring rain shower.

A massive Wind Devil spun from the bowels of the darkest storm cloud and instantly reached the ground. The spinning winds formed a very large finger that reached out, uprooting massive trees, tearing a massive swatch of destruction through the ground. Massive boulders were picked up and tossed as though a child were attempting to skip a stone across the surface of the water. Each of them had seen Wind Devils before, but none as large or as violent as this one. It filled the sky with its unbridled fury as lightning bolts flashed all around and through it. It was as if the funnel were drawing the lightning to it, gathering its energy to attack.

There was little doubt what the target would be.

CHAPTER EIGHTEEN

"Darkseed, drop the shield!" Devenshire said, his eyes locked fast to the massive Wind Devil that continued to chew up trees, rocks, and earth in its menacingly slow path toward them.

All eyes snapped to Devenshire, and many expressions conveyed their concern that he had lost his mind. "Are you mad?" Petera asked.

"It is the only thing protecting us!" Darkseed muttered, the whole of his concentration on maintaining the weakened orb surrounding the group.

"We are easy targets!" Devenshire said. "Darkseed's shield will not hold up to another lightning bolt! We need to split up, present more than one target."

"Daimion, we cannot out run lightning bolts!" Brianna injected, her worried gaze alternating between Devenshire and the Wind Devil.

"We are doomed if we remain packed together like this!" Devenshire snapped in reply, never taking his gaze form the funnel cloud. "The longer we stand here and debate this, the more time Xavier has to target us!"

"He is right," Darkseed agreed. "I cannot maintain this shield for much longer, and it is too weak to protect us from anything harder than the rain!" He closed his eyes and lowered his arms back to his side. As the sphere faded out of sight, Darkseed sagged, almost going to his knees from the release. Instantly, they were pounded with the full fury of the storm. The winds had grown in strength, and now they all had to lean into the gale to maintain their footing. Eyes were squinted or shut against an onslaught of driving rain and swirling debris. Added to the cacophony was the horrible roar of the giant Wind Devil as it slowly bore down on them.

Devenshire raised his arm to shield his eyes as he tried to maintain sight on the Wind Devil. "Split up! Run for cover, and be sure to zigzag your course! Do not run in a straight line! Try to confuse him as much as possible! Move!" he finished as he bolted off to his right. Almost instantly, the others followed suit. It took Darkseed a little longer to move since he had been taxed from the protective sphere. Suddenly, a large bolt of lightning streaked from the Wind Devil to strike the ground where they had all just stood. The massive explosion sent a column of seared earth and debris straight up into the air to be caught by the winds and whisked away. Darkseed caught the fleeting edge of the blast, and he was tossed into the air. He sailed through the maelstrom for a few feet before hitting the ground. His body bounced and rolled from the momentum to land in a crumpled heap.

Devenshire slid to a halt at the sound of the explosion and turned back in time to see Darkseed flung aside. "Darkseed!" he shouted, gritting his teeth against the pummeling storm, and his concern for his friend. "Damn!" he swore and shifted his position and sprinted for Darkseed. A moment later, another lightning bolt smashed into the ground where he had stood. With a growing dread, he realized Xavier was getting more accurate with his strikes. As he drew closer to Darkseed, he spied Zandorth also running toward the downed mage. "No, Zandorth! Seek cover!" Devenshire shouted, trying to waive the warrior off. Zandorth either did not hear him or was ignoring him because he continued to run toward Darkseed.

Another lightning strike crackled as it shot to the earth, blasting another hole in the ground and showering Brianna with debris. She shouted in pained surprise, and she threw her arms up in an attempt to protect her head. She stumbled and fell as the force of the blast pushed her off balance.

"Brianna!" Shantira screamed as she shifted her course and ran flat out for her.

"No! I am all right! Go to cover!" Brianna screamed at her as she staggered back to her feet. Using both hands, she slicked her soaked hair back out of her face and blinked against the onslaught of driving rain. Through the sheets of water, she could see Shantira still running toward her.

Shantira reached her and quickly tried to shield her, glaring up at the Wind Devil. Brianna shrugged out of Shantira's protective embrace. "Shantira! Stop! I am all right!"

"I will not leave you alone out here!" Shantira screamed in response.

"Fine! Let us go!" Brianna snapped in reply. This was not the time or place to argue over Shantira's bizarre behavior when it came to Brianna's safety. Together, the two women set out for the tree line and the cave that Zandorth said was in this direction.

The lightning strikes were coming with more frequency and greater destructive intensity. As Devenshire knelt beside Darkseed's crumpled form, he knew that none of them would survive a direct strike. A second later, Zandorth arrived, also kneeling beside Darkseed. "Is he alive?"

Devenshire rolled Darkseed over to his back and saw that he was slowly rolling his head back and forth, trying to roust himself. "He is alive. We have to get him out of here!"

"I will carry him!" Zandorth said as he stood, sheathed his sword, and bent over to easily hoist Darkseed to his shoulder.

Devenshire froze for a moment. His eyes snapped up to the Wind

Devil, and his expression went pale. "Oh no..." He suddenly planted his feet and turned toward Zandorth. "Move!!" he shouted as he pushed Zandorth in one direction before he dove in the opposite. The warrior knew enough not to question but simply react from instinct.

It saved his and Darkseed's life.

Using the momentum of Devenshire's shove, Zandorth twisted his body in the direction Devenshire had pushed them and pumped his massive legs for all the momentum they would give him. A split second later, a massive lightning bolt tore through the spot they had occupied only a few seconds before. He could feel the hair on his body stand on end from the close proximity to the energy of the lightning bolt. His body felt as though millions of ants were crawling all over him, feasting on his flesh. Then the massive explosion came, and he felt himself become airborne as the shock wave carried him off his feet. He felt himself take the brunt of the barrage of earth and debris thrown up by the eruption. He tightened his grip on Darkseed's body over his shoulder and tried to orient himself to the hard landing he knew was coming.

Devenshire took a handful of steps and then launched himself into the air in an attempt to put as much distance as he could between himself and the lightning bolt he knew was coming. As he had helped load Darkseed onto Zandorth's shoulder, the tingling running up and down his spine shifted, changed, and he knew what was coming. He could not explain how he knew, but it was enough that he did. The explosion was massive, and the shockwave caught him in the middle of his dive, flipping him through the air to slam him into the ground with stunning force. He was only dimly aware of his body bounding and rolling across the ground, and the debris that pelted him was lost on his dimming perceptions.

Kendra grabbed the rapidly approaching tree and used it as a pivot to swing herself around and behind it. She held on to the tree as she took a moment to calm her ragged breathing. She knew the dangers of hiding behind a tree in a lightning storm, but remaining in the open was definitely not an option either. With her blood running cold in her veins, she quickly swiped at the soaked tendrils of hair in her face, brushing it aside so she could see what was happening. Her wide eyes saw Brianna and Shantira disappear into the tree line off to her left. She shifted her gaze around and squinted through the driving rain to see the massive bolt strike the ground where Devenshire, Darkseed, and Zandorth had just been. The flash of bright white light, as well as the horrendous crash of angry thunder, caused her to squeal in surprised terror as she quickly dropped to a crouched position, throwing her arms over her head. It was an automatic reaction that she wasn't even aware she had performed until after it was done. She lowered her arms and raised her head as her terrified eyes searched the clearing. She was sure she would see three smoldering corpses where the men had been only a moment before. Surely, there was no way they could have evaded such a devastating strike.

To her relief, she could see all three of them. Zandorth and Darkseed were closer to her, and it looked like Zandorth was trying to get to his feet. Devenshire was lying face down on the opposite side of the massive hole that had been blasted into the ground from the strike. He was not moving. "No…" she whispered. Something caught her eye off to her right, and she turned her head in time to see Petera dash from the protection of the tree line toward Zandorth. Moments later, Stant appeared from further down as he, too, dashed toward the fallen men. She swallowed hard against her fear and shored up her determination. She could do no less than her kinsmen. Taking a couple of quick, deep breaths, she launched herself into the clearing and ran as hard as she could toward Devenshire's motionless form.

Brianna staggered to a stop as they entered the tree line. She took a moment to try to catch her breath. She was aware of Shantira right next to her, and the concerns about her bizarre behavior returned. This time, the concern was mixed with anger as she realized the young woman had very nearly gotten herself killed. She sorely wanted to lash out at Shantira, but her breath heaved in her chest, and she found she could not speak.

"Daimion!" Shantira shouted as she took several steps away from Brianna and toward the clearing.

Brianna straightened up, no longer concerned with chastising Shantira. Even above the terrifying howl of the storm, she had heard the dread and concern in Shantira's voice. Stepping up beside her, she squinted out into the clearing and what she saw caused her blood to run cold. Devenshire was a motionless heap on one side of a massive hole that had been blasted into the ground while Zandorth and Darkseed lie on the opposite side. She took several steps toward the clearing. "We have to help them!"

Shantira grabbed Brianna's arm. "No! It is too dangerous! You may get hurt!"

"Enough!" Brianna shouted as she turned and jerked her arm free of Shantira's grip. "I do not know why you are acting this way, and at this moment, I do not particularly care! Our friends are out there!" she screamed as she leveled a heated glare at Shantira and jerked a finger toward the clearing. "They are hurt and need our help! You wish to stop me? Kill me!" Brianna paused only a heartbeat as her angry glare drove the undeniable meaning of her intentions home to the young woman. She then turned and dashed out into the storm.

Shantira was stunned as her eyes drifted to the ground. She hadn't realized that the strange urge to ensure Brianna's safety above all else had driven her actions. Of course, Brianna was right, and she was growing more and more fearful of the strange thing within her that forced her to behave this way. Raising her stunned expression from the ground, she saw Brianna running out into the horrible storm. Just beyond her, she could see Devenshire's body sprawled in the mud. Blinking twice, she realized she was still standing in the trees. Pushing her confusion and fear aside, she ran out into the storm as well.

Devenshire grunted as he raised his face out of the muck. The ringing in his ears was giving him a headache, and he was slowly becoming aware of the numerous nicks, cuts, and bruises that his unprotected torso had taken since the onset of the storm. Shaking his head against the dizzying disorientation, he forced himself to his knees. He knew he didn't have the luxury of taking time to recover his senses. The storm was only growing in intensity, and he knew Xavier would not stop now, not when he had them stunned and disoriented. He shook his head again and shifted his gaze around the clearing, squinting against the driving rain, the continual swirl of debris raked by the massive winds, and the deafening roar of the Wind Devil that continued to bear down on them. As his eyes swept the clearing, which looked very fuzzy from the intense rain and wind driven debris, he felt his eyes widen. "No! Damn!" The others had left the safety of the tree line. They were running back out into the storm in order to help him, Zandorth, and Darkseed. He bounced to his feet and began trying to wave them off, shouting at them to go back. Of course, they ignored him as they kept running toward them. He felt a tight spasm along his spine, which made him wince. Just as with the last strike, he knew what was coming. His wide gaze shifted to the Wind Devil.

"No! You bastard! No!!"

The Wind Devil paused, simply sitting in one place as it spun with incredible destructive force. It was almost as if it were taking a moment to consider the multiple opportunities presented below in the dashing forms converging on one spot. With an incredible roar of rumbling thunder, a lightning bolt shot from the Wind Devil and struck the ground in front of Brianna and Shantira. With an ear splitting crackle of released energy, the ground erupted in an incredible explosion. Both women, while they had not been hit by the bolt itself, were close enough to take the brunt of the explosion. They were caught in the blast and hurled backwards.

Devenshire watched in terror as their bodies hit the ground hard and then were tossed like discarded refuse across the storm ravaged clearing. Their bodies came to rest near the tree line and did not move. He tried to reach out with his powers to see if they were alive, but his concern for them mixed with his fear from the storm was causing his emotions to spiral out of control. He couldn't focus his powers. He knew he needed to calm himself, to force his mind back into the orderly patterns of working the Mystical Arts, but in the middle of the hell-spawned maelstrom, the task was impossible. He took a handful of steps toward the women when he noticed Zandorth had managed to get back to his feet. He wasted no time in bending over to retrieve Darkseed's limp body and was in the process of lifting it from the ground when a small boulder, hurled by the force of the wind, struck him in the side of the head. Devenshire winced at the force of the impact as the warrior was carried off his feet by the blow. He landed on his side, rolled to his back, and didn't move again. With growing dread, Devenshire knew there was very little chance Zandorth had survived such a massive blow to the head.

The anger came almost without his bidding. One by one, Xavier was targeting his companions and was doing his best to kill all of them. The anger seethed, throbbed, pulsed within his veins, replacing his blood with lava. His eyes turned black as he turned toward the Wind Devil. "I am here, you gutless bastard! Strike me! I am the one you want! Strike me!" he screamed into the storm.

Brianna moaned as she slowly became aware of the storm again. Her head buzzed, and her ears rang unmercifully, but at least she was still alive. Opening her eyes, she forced herself up on one elbow, taking stock of what had happened. Several feet in front of her was a smoldering crater where the lightning bolt had struck, very nearly hitting her. Shaking her head again, she shifted her gaze around to see Shantira in the process of gathering her wits as well. She felt relief wash over her at the sight.

Looking out across the clearing, she saw Zandorth sprawled out next to Darkseed. His body was in a different position than the last time she had seen it, which led her to wonder if the warrior had risen, and then had been struck down again. Petera and Stant were very close to Zandorth now, and Kendra looked as though she were trying to reach Devenshire. Then she shifted her gaze toward him, and what she saw terrified her.

Devenshire was glaring up at the Wind Devil and shouting something at it. She could not make out his words over the wail of the storm, but the look in his furious expression left little doubt as to what he was saying. "Daimion! No..."

Darkseed thought at first that he was dead. Then the onslaught of pain convinced him that he was still very much alive. His head pounded as though someone were trying to crack his skull open with a rock. His muscles trembled with fatigue, and there was a very good chance that he would retch if he tried to set up. He knew, however, that he needed to move and do so quickly. The fact that he had not been cooked alive by one of the lightning bolts while he'd been stunned was amazing. Opening his eyes, he was greeted by a spinning kaleidoscope of the storm, which only made the urge to vomit stronger. Squeezing his eyes shut, he forced himself to roll to his side and then rise up on one elbow. Opening his eyes again, his sight slowed and then steadied to show him Zandorth sprawled just a few feet away. There was a large gash on the side of his head and blood coursed down his face. The blood mixed with the hard rain had caused the wound to look much worse than it probably was. He looked around in time to see Petera kneel down beside him. The Elf's lips were moving, but he could not hear him over the howl of the storm and the intense ringing in his ears. Stant followed as he dropped to his knees next to Zandorth, examining the warrior. He was dimly aware of Petera's hands on his shoulders, urging him to stand. Slowly, he allowed the man to help him to his feet, and he was instantly struck with how weak he felt, as though all of his physical strength had been siphoned away.

"Darkseed! Are you all right?" He finally heard Petera's voice over the noise. He managed a brief nod as he started to turn to check on Zandorth. A distant shout in the storm caught his attention instead, and he turned back to see Devenshire walking slowly toward the Wind Devil, shouting at the storm.

"Daimion! No!" he shouted after him, but he knew it was pointless. Even if Devenshire heard him, he would ignore him. He was trying to draw Xavier's attention, making himself a target to buy the rest of them escape time. "I will be damned!" he muttered as he shrugged out of Petera's grip and moved with staggering steps toward Devenshire.

"Darkseed, you cannot!" Petera called after him.

"Get Zandorth and get to cover! Now!" Darkseed shouted back over his shoulder as he struggled to get his strength back.

Kendra ran up to him and grabbed his arm. "Are you all right?" she screamed over the howl.

"I am fine," he lied. "Help the others get Zandorth to safety. He is badly hurt."

"What of you?" she asked before turning her gaze to Devenshire. "What of Daimion?"

"I will take care of Daimion. You must get Zandorth to safety! We do not have much time!" Darkseed replied as he brushed Kendra's hands off his arm and continued staggering toward Devenshire.

Devenshire felt the heat of his fury take him, and he welcomed it. It would give him the courage to do what he knew he must. He would take the brunt of the storm to buy his companions... his friend's time to escape. "Come, Xavier! Strike out at me, if you have the courage!" he screamed out at the Wind Devil. The more he considered the pain and suffering the madman had already inflicted, as well as the chaos he threatened to unleash with the Stones of Andarus, the more his anger grew. At this moment, he wanted nothing more than to get his hands on the mage, to beat him to a bloody pulp, and then wrap his hands around his throat and watch the light of life leave his eyes slowly.

"Come on, you bastard child of a whore! Strike me!" he screamed.

The answer was almost instantaneous.

The bolt shot from the center of the Wind Devil straight for Devenshire. Out of instinct, he growled and waved his right arm as though he were blocking a punch. The bolt sheared off and struck the ground several feet away. That was when he felt a surge of something deep within him, a feeling very much like the connection to his powers, but much more potent, much more powerful. It was very much like the feeling that had flared up within him that night outside of Lirpa when Armand threatened to kill Brianna. The fury had claimed him, and he had simply lashed out blindly. Not truly understanding where the feeling came from, Devenshire blindly opened himself up to it, embraced it, did everything he could to absorb it. He didn't care what it was or where it came from, so long as it helped him destroy the Wind Devil and the bastard who had spawned it. As his eyes began to glow with an intense blue light, he snarled in a crazed grin at the Wind Devil. "Is that the best you can do? Surely, the great and powerful Xavier has more in his pitiful arsenal than that!"

Again, a massive lightning bolt shot from the Wind Devil, heading straight for Devenshire. With a hiss, Devenshire snapped his right arm up, his palm facing the oncoming lightning bolt. A shaft of blue mystical energy shot from Devenshire's palm and caught the lightning bolt head on. A tremendous fireball erupted from the colliding energies, sending red and blue sparks rocketing in all directions.

Darkseed ducked at the loud explosion of the two energies canceling each other out. "What in the name of hell?" he muttered, unsure of what he had seen but very sure that it shouldn't have occurred as it had. Devenshire should now be a smoldering lump of charred flesh and bone.

"Come on, you pathetic son of a bitch! You can do better than that!" Devenshire screamed as he snapped his right hand down to his waist, his hand forming a cup. A bright blue orb appeared in his hand, and he gripped it tightly, tiny blue lightning bolts dancing around the surface of the orb, around and through his fingers. "Let us see how you like my lightning bolts!" he snarled, and he brought his arm back and then hurled the blue orb toward the Wind Devil.

The orb rocketed from Devenshire's hand, moving with eye blurring speed toward the center of the Wind Devil. Two lightning bolts lanced from the Devil in an attempt to pierce the orb, but missed. The orb, which looked tiny in comparison to the massive twisting Wind Devil, hit and almost instantly, the entire side of the Wind Devil facing them flared with a brilliant blue light, tinged at the edges with red. Sparks of blue and red expelled mystical energy, exploding from the point of impact, and the air seemed to crackle with the colliding energies canceling each other out. The sound of the Wind Devil changed. It had been an ominous roar of wind before, but now it sounded strangely like an unholy howl of agony, as if the storm was feeling pain from the attack. Not possible, Darkseed knew, but that's how it seemed. Then, to his shock, it seemed as though the intensity of the storm had decreased somewhat. The wind didn't seem as strong, the rain less painful as it struck skin. Was it possible that Devenshire's attack had weakened the storm? Normally, he would have said no, but watching Devenshire lost in his fury and launching spells that were far beyond his abilities, he could not argue the possibility. In the impossible, Darkseed saw their one chance for survival.

"Again, Daimion! Hurl your powers at it!" he shouted, no longer advancing on him.

Another lightning bolt shot from the Wind Devil. Devenshire threw his arms up, crossing his forearms in front of him, the blue glow of his eyes intensifying. The bolt struck his crossed arms. With a grunt, Devenshire staggered back several steps as the bolt dissipated.

Devenshire slowly lowered his arms and glared up at the storm, his face a twisted mask of insane fury. A cruel smile curled his lips as he stared up at the Wind Devil. "My turn!"

Devenshire brought his hands up to slap them together in front of his face. Closing his eyes, he slowly drew his hands apart, a blue beam of light connecting his palms. As he brought his hands apart, the blue beam of light grew in intensity. When his hands reached shoulder width, the beam separated and snapped back into each hand, engulfing it in a swirling blue light, almost as though his hands were covered with blue fire. Very slowly, Devenshire brought his hands out to his side, the strange blue fire growing in size. He opened his eyes, which now glowed even more brightly. He fixed his strange gaze on the Wind Devil as he began walking toward it again. The Wind Devil launched multiple lightning bolts that hit all around Devenshire, but never exploded nor hit him. Darkseed could not believe what he was seeing. While the sight assured him, they now had a chance of surviving the storm, his earlier concerns about Devenshire's growing powers tripled.

Brianna watched in awe as Devenshire advanced on the Wind Devil, his hands engulfed in strange blue flames, and his eyes glowing in that unholy light she had seen that night outside Lirpa when he had stopped Armand from killing her. As malevolent as he had looked that night, he was downright evil looking now, and a chill passed through her that had nothing to do with being soaking wet in a terrible storm.

"You are going to have to do better than this if you are going to stop me, Xavier!" Devenshire growled into the Wind Devil. "I will find you! I will stop you! I will kill you! I know you are too deranged to listen or believe, so take this with you on your journey!"

With a terrifying scream of rage, Devenshire threw both hands up, slamming the heels of his hands together and forcing his arms out toward the storm. A massive shaft of blue light shot from Devenshire's hands and slammed into the Wind Devil. The two mystical energies collided, and the air crackled with the tremendous release of power. Lightning bolts shot from the Wind Devil at random, shooting off into the sky, lancing out at the forest, but none having any impact, nor coming close to hitting any of the people.

Devenshire's face was a horribly twisted mask of furious concentration as he poured all he had into the release of power. His entire body trembled from the exertion. The wind howled in that uncanny sound that resembled pain as more lightning bolts shot out. The wind began to decrease in intensity, and the Wind Devil actually appeared to grow smaller. There was a pulsing in the air that was not sound, but rang in everyone's ears. Devenshire's mask of fury shifted, as he had to put more effort into maintaining the spell. There was less fury and more concentration, more exertion in his face. Blood began to trickle from his nose and the blue light in his eyes began to dim.

Come on Daimion! You almost have him! Do not give up now! Darkseed called out in his mind. He wanted to help, but also didn't want to disrupt Devenshire's concentration. The release of energy was tremendous, and it was rapidly taking its toll on Devenshire.

Devenshire's expression slowly began to shift from fury to pain as his knees began trembling, threatening to buckle. The strength of the wind decreased, and the rain had slowed to merely a gentle shower. There were breaks in the dark clouds overhead that allowed blue sky to peek through. Darkseed glanced up at the Wind Devil to see that it had shrunk considerably in size. It seemed to fight back against Devenshire's attack, but it was expending all of its energy to do so.

Blood now poured from Devenshire's nose as the blue light dimmed even further. Now the iris, pupil, and cornea could be seen through the dimming light, and Darkseed knew Devenshire was at his limits. Devenshire closed his eyes briefly and gritted his teeth tighter together. "No!" he hissed as he gathered his waning strength about him.

He forced his knees to straighten and forced his twitching arms up further. "No!" he shouted louder as he snapped his eyes open again and locked on the center of the Wind Devil. The blue light flared briefly as he drew his arms to him and then shot them out straight again. "Go to hell!" he screamed, and he hurled everything he had left into one last blast.

The Wind Devil rotation, which had been steadily slowing, now seemed to stop. In a bright flash of red and blue light, the Wind Devil dissipated with the last remnant tendrils of its form being whisked away by the dying winds.

Devenshire collapsed to his knees, his chest heaving under his labored breathing. His eyes were their normal color and appearance now, though wide and glazed over. He was very pale and his jaw hung slack while blood continued to trickle from his nose. He clumsily ran a trembling hand across his upper lip, smearing the blood. After several moments, his eyes rolled upward as he pitched forward into a limp heap in the mud.

All was silent in the clearing, and the silence was almost as deafening as the storm had been. The dark clouds quickly began to dissipate as the rain slowed and then stopped. Within the span of a few moments, the clouds had disappeared, and the sunshine returned, bathing the soaked travelers in what would have been welcomed warmth were it not for the terrifying ordeal they had just endured.

CHAPTER NINETEEN

Was this death? Had the Fates finally opened the gates to the earthly realm and pulled his soul into the Afterlife? He felt as though he were in a strange sort of limbo, as if he were adrift in a realm with no sight, no sound, and no substance. He found the memories of his life blurred and fading quickly. He was even having difficulty remembering what his name was. Whatever this void, featureless place was, he was definitely lost within it. In a strange sort of way, it was almost peaceful here. No worries, no stress, no pain... nothing. There was absolutely no trace of the intense pain he had experienced... how long ago? He could not remember. It could have only been moments, but again, it could have been seasons. He was not sure. Was this the Afterlife? If so, he found it very disappointing. He had heard that the Afterlife was a place where he would be reunited with loved ones and companions who had passed before him. It was a place of rich colors and warm sensations, a place where the cares of the earthly realm were nothing but a distant memory.

He had not expected a blank, empty void where every passing moment threatened to swallow him into oblivion. He tried to take a breath, but no air came. As a spike of concern pierced the calmness of this unremarkable place, he realized that his body no longer responded to his mental commands. This was puzzling, for if this were the Afterlife, he shouldn't need air. Yet his lungs, which should have been left behind in his earthly body, were screaming for it.

Concern turned to fear as he struggled to force his chest to expand and his lungs to fill, but this blank place was also devoid of air of any sort. He was suffocating, but if he were already dead, how could he suffocate? Pinpricks of light began to speckle his vision and his limbs began to tingle as if they were waking up after having gone to sleep. The pinpricks of light began to streak across the blackness, leaving multicolored trails of brilliant light in their wake, which seemed to ignite a dull throbbing pain within his skull. Each streak of light also seemed to increase the tingle in his limbs until they were throbbing painful stabs of a reality he thought he had left behind.

Slowly he became aware of the pounding throb of his heartbeat in his ears. The pulse was rapid, reflecting the fear, consuming him as he struggled to breath. He opened his mouth and tried to force his lungs to expand, to draw in the only thing that would save him now. Yet, despite his staunchest efforts, the air would not come, and he knew he was doomed. The excruciating pounding of his heartbeat became faster and faster as his terror grew. He found it frustrating that his life would end in such a fashion. There were so many grand plans for the future, so many things left to accomplish and a legacy to build that would stand the test of time. All of that cancelled out because of… his memories were fading as his life ended. He forced his dying mind to focus on what it was that was had cancelled out his existence. What horrible thing had left him in this place? The blackness was now filled with bright tendrils of light that seemed almost akin to lightening. They streaked and flashed across the black canvas of this place, painting a brilliant kaleidoscope of color while simultaneously igniting terror and pain with each occurrence. Several tendrils of the light snaked through his body igniting a burning trail of pain where they passed through. Each flash of light grew in intensity and threatened to blind him as the pain that lanced his entire body obliterated the peaceful calm he had first been aware of.

What had landed him in this horrible abyss?

He dredged through the dying layers of his mind for the answer, to at least know why he was dying. The pain in his skull began to grow from his efforts to remember, but he forged ahead, determination becoming all he had left in these fleeting moments of existence. Dark, blurry images finally began to respond to his search. Clenching his resolve, he forced all he had left into forcing these images into clarity. Three gray circles emerged from the black clouds of his mind. Very slowly, they began to shift and change, morphing into three rocks. The images stroked a dying memory, and it flared brilliantly back to life.

Rocks?

No… stones!

The Stones of Andarus!

The Stones of Andarus! Of course! How could he have forgotten them? They were an integral part of the legacy he had wanted to leave.

A tiny tendril of oxygen slipped into his lungs as though passage had been granted with the first solid memory he had been able to recall. Unfortunately, the tiny wisp of oxygen instantly ignited a fiery pain deep within his lungs, nearly seizing them in a spasm of unimaginable pain. Yet, as painful as that tiny gasp of air had been, his lungs clamored for more. His fading mind clung to the image of the Stones, desperately hoping that a firm grip on this memory would give him access to other memories.

What had happened to him? What had put him on the brink of death? He poured the last of his will into dredging up the memory from the black depths of his dying mind. Another larger grey orb drifted up for his consideration. Even though the pain in his head made him fear his skull would split open from the pressure, he forced his dying essence to reveal what would, most probably, be the last image he would see before passing into oblivion.

With agonizing slowness, the orb began shifting, taking on recognizable features of a man's face. As the blur sharpened, the image of a man's face peered out at him. At first he didn't recognize it, but a tiny fragment of recognition sparked within his dying brain and again ignited a nearly dead memory. When that memory flared, so did the fury, and it was the fury that saved him.

Devenshire!

In a forest clearing dappled with sunlight, Xavier's prone form suddenly bolted upright with a horrifying gasp, as he was finally able to breathe. His wide, terrified eyes glared up into the blue sky, unsure of what he was seeing or where he was, or even if he were truly still alive or was now a plaything for Satan. As the air poured into his lungs, they ignited with a hell storm of fiery pain, and that first lungful of air was expelled in a loud scream of agony.

As the scream echoed off into the forest and began to fade, he fell to his side, quickly curling himself into a fetal position. His face was a twisted mask of agony, and his breath came in short, shallow quick gasps as he fought against the pain. He considered for a time that his entire body was being pierced simultaneously and repeatedly by millions of swords, daggers, and lances. Squeezing his eyes tightly shut against the onslaught of a pain he didn't think the human body was capable of withstanding, he struggled to keep himself conscious and to battle back against the pain, to conquer it as it tried to conquer him. Through blinding pain, he forced his breathing to slow and become deeper. The quick, shallow gasps would do nothing but make the pain worse, plus the discipline of slowing and deepening his breathing would force his mind under control. He would need that control to wrestle back ownership of his body from the pain. He continued to breathe slowly and deeply, wanting nothing more than to simply enjoy the feeling of air swelling his lungs, even if it meant it caused his limbs to throb. The inside of his skull was a maelstrom of pain as his brain, and its dying cells were injected with a sudden and violent infusion of oxygen. With agonizing slowness, the pain began to subside. Slowly, his body uncurled and began to relax. After a time, he rolled onto his back and simply allowed himself time to recover. The knot of his brow brought on by the intense pain began to loosen, and his breathing slowly became more normal. Finally, with the pain properly under control and beginning to evaporate, he turned his attention to what had gone so disastrously wrong with his plan.

The plan had been foolproof. There should have been no way for any of Devenshire's party to survive, let alone the malignant bastard himself. At the very worst, perhaps Darkseed might have saved himself, but the others should now be smoldering piles of ash or chewed up bits of raw meat and bone cast afield by the Wind Devil. Yet every last one of them survived. How? The incredible power Devenshire had unleashed was far beyond his paltry abilities, and yet he had cancelled out the spell sustaining the storm. Darkseed, at his very best, might have been able to weaken the storm to a significant level, but even with his considerable skill in the Arts, he should have been the one who had done what Devenshire had accomplished. Slowly he opened his eyes and gazed up through the canopy of branches to the bright blue sky overhead. He squinted against the brightness as he continued to let his body recover. He forced his throbbing mind to contemplate where he had miscalculated, what vital piece of information had he missed that allowed him to make such an error? The answer lingered at the back of his mind and vied for consideration, but he refused. It couldn't be that. It just couldn't.

Your arrogance was your mistake! His subconscious chided.

No, it was not arrogance! It was some trick of the Fates or intervention from someone else that allowed Devenshire to survive! He argued.

It was the secret of the Scrolls, and you know it! His subconscious snapped.

No! It cannot be that. I will not consider it! His consciousness replied.

Then you are doomed, and you will fail, and Devenshire will destroy you! Was the instant answer.

He slowly raised himself up on one elbow, wincing in pain from joints that were not ready to move yet. His brow furrowed from the intense throbbing inside his skull as he slowly swept his blurred gaze about the clearing. He found it incredibly strange that the clearing would be so calm and peaceful in the aftermath of the intense clash of mystical energy that had very nearly killed him. Swallowing against the dry knot at the back of his throat, he spied the Orb of Vision lying on its side halfway across the clearing. The white crystal was black and tiny wisps of smoke drifted from its surface. A sense of deep dread quickly spread through him, as he feared that the backlash of power might have destroyed one of his most prized artifacts. He had been watching the events surrounding the storm through the Orb, guiding the storms' movements and launching his lightening attacks. Controlling the Wind Devil had been much more complicated, and combined with manipulating the storm, and the lightning strikes, it had taken all of his mystical might to maintain the balance of power needed to control the storm and the Orb of Vision at the same time.

Grunting against the onslaught of pain, he forced himself to his knees, and eventually his feet, his arms hugging his torso against new stabs of pain as he staggered toward the Orb. When Devenshire had unleashed his final furious attack, the two forms of their magic cancelled each other out and the backlash of power had been tremendous. It had poured through the Orb of Vision, engulfing him in pain and tossing him halfway across the clearing. His last vivid memory before waking in the dark abyss had been a brilliant flash of light, a loud crack of thunder and a sensation that his body was covered in millions of flesh hungry ants. Once he reached the Orb, he slowly sank to his knees and sat back on his heels, taking a moment to gather his waning strength. Breathing heavily, he forced his eyes deep into the inky depths of the artifact, hoping against hope that it was still viable. He tried to use his powers to gauge the level of damage, but his abilities were taxed to their limits. He was drained, and he knew it would be hours, if not days, before he would be capable of the most basic of spells. All he could do was wait and hope the power of the white crystal could repair itself. There was a very faint lightening of the black at the very center of the Orb, and he felt hope spring up. Very slowly, the very center of the Orb began to lighten further and further until a tiny speck of white could be seen deep in the center. Xavier slumped over partly due to relief that the Orb was recovering and partly due to the constant attack of pain. Closing his eyes, he allowed himself to relax. His powers were drained, but intact. The Orb of Vision had been damaged, but was repairing itself. With tremendous reluctance, he forced himself to face certain truths, regardless of how galling it was to do so.

First, he had underestimated Devenshire's level of skill. Obviously, the bastard was in command of greater levels of power than he had first thought. How he had managed to keep himself hidden for all these seasons, and also train himself in the mastery of the Arts, was a mystery to him. Devenshire should be dead now. Xavier had plotted, planned, and executed the act many seasons ago. Yet he lived... and prospered. Xavier had made it his personal business to track all practitioners of the Arts through his ties to the Mystic Tides. He had honed his mystical abilities to the point that he could locate anyone he wished. He had used this ability to keep track of all the practitioners of the Mystical Arts, to know who the major talents were, and thereby, who he would have to keep an eye on and who he would have to have destroyed. He had killed many mages once their abilities reached a level that might prove to be a threat to him. He had been able to track Raven Darkseed, gauging his skills and levels of power. Once it had become obvious that Darkseed was on the path to becoming an Adept, he had made three separate attempts to have him killed, but all three had failed. Once Darkseed had left the retreat and lapsed into his sluggish lifestyle of self-fulfillment, Xavier had simply left him alone, figuring that his levels of skill and power would decline once he abandoned the disciplines of the retreat. Such, however, had not been the case, and now he found himself questioning the decision to not make a fourth attempt on his life. Darkseed would prove to be a problem if he survived to reach him.

The bigger mystery was how had Devenshire been able to not only survive, but also hone his skills in the Arts without his knowing it? True, he realized that he had assumed Devenshire dead and had not spent time searching the Mystic Tides for his essence. However, Devenshire's growing strength within the workings of the Mystical Arts should have become known to him within his search in the Tides. Yet it had not. Why? The answer led him back to the topic his subconscious had scolded him about, the content of the Ancient Scrolls and the one tie that would leave him vulnerable. While he had read the scrolls, studied them, memorized them, and used their guidance to eradicate all possible obstacles to his path of greatness and domination, he had to admit the truth of the situation and doing so angered him. A deep-seated part of him had already acknowledged the truth, but the arrogance within him had refused to admit it.

Opening his eyes, he stared at the ground, forcing his mind to conquer his body, to push aside the pain and recover his strength. It had been a mistake to attack Devenshire with such a powerful spell. He had wasted valuable energy on the attempt, energy he would need to tap into the Stones and then control the power once it was released. Now he would have to wait weeks, perhaps longer, to make the attempt to breach them once he learned how to. It was a delay he could ill afford, especially with the equinox approaching and Devenshire coming for him. He would have to alter his plans and alter them quickly. If he had been critically drained from the mystical battle, then Devenshire must also be. He would have to strike again quickly while Devenshire and Darkseed both were weakened.

His mind began working on plans and accelerated timetables. He struggled to his feet, picking up the Orb of Vision. The tiny white dot that had appeared at the center of the Orb was growing, slowly filling in the Orb, and wiping out the blackness. Time was growing short and the time for decisive action was quickly passing him by.

He picked up the canvas bag and slipped the Orb inside it, tying it securely. Taking his time for his legs still threatened to betray him, he began making his way back toward his caravan. There were plans to form and death to deal to an annoying blight that should have been eradicated seasons ago.

Somehow, Devenshire had survived that first attempt...

Not the second time.

~*~

Dylena sagged against a tree, pausing to wipe the fresh wave of tears from her eyes and to try to summon enough strength to continue. How long had she been walking? She wasn't sure, but it wasn't nearly long enough to take even the faintest edges from her pain. With tear blurred vision, she looked about the forest, searching for something… anything that would speak of peace, beauty, and serenity, to numb the jagged edges of her grief and to provide her with just the whispered promise that there was still a reason to go on. Red rimmed, tear-swollen eyes searched and found none of these things.

Malcolm was still dead.

Her life as she knew it was still gone.

How long had it been now? A season? Could it be that she had endured an entire season of this grief and pain? She slowly shook her head, how had she managed even one day, let alone an entire season without him? Her eyes gave up their search for peace and serenity as they drifted down to the ground and her bare feet. If it had been so long, why did it feel like she had just found his body in the fields a few moments ago? Why did if feel like the months of anguish she had endured had been for nothing? Everyone had told her that the pain would ease, the grief would become manageable and that soon she would be able to smile with fondness at his memory. Her face twisted into an angry snarl. Everyone had lied! True, there were times that it seemed as if the pain was a little less, a tiny bit more manageable, but these fleeting moments were soon eradicated by the violent sweeping return of a grief that knew no limits.

Unbidden, the memories returned, not that they ever ventured too far from the forefront of her mind. Malcolm had been her first and only true love. They had been together for many seasons and there was no doubt in her mind that the Fates had made him for her, and she for him. While their existence was poor with each day being a struggle to survive, it was also rich beyond compare with the deep warmth of friendship, companionship and an all-consuming love. He was so kind, so gentle, and so completely devoted to her that she had never been able to find the words to express what he had meant to her. With a fresh wave of tears, she looked up at the canopy of branches overhead and realized that she never could now. As the pain in her chest twisted with fresh grief, a sob broke through her trembling lips she hoped… prayed that somehow he had known, or at the very least, knew now.

"Malcolm…" she whispered, with a trembling voice into the emptiness of the forest around her. "My dear sweet, Malcolm. I never told you how much I truly loved you. Oh, I told you many times a day that I loved you, but I never made you truly understand just how deep and true my love for you ran." She paused to draw in a shuddering breath as her trembling fingertips brushed through a low hanging branch. Her fingers found a leaf, and her red, swollen eyes fixed on it. "You were everything to me. You were my sunrise, my sunset, and all the moments in between." She stifled a sob as she looked up into the sky. "How in the name of the Fates am I supposed to go on without you?" Her voice broke and a hard sob wracked her chest as her face twisted into deep, hard grief. "How can I continue to live when my heart is so shattered that it scarcely beats without pain?" She shook her head slowly as another wave of tears came, and her voice cracked under another tremendous sob. "What is the point? I have no direction since you died. I have no dreams, no ambitions, no desires… nothing. I care not to tend the crops, I care not to tend our empty home, I care not to do anything save mourn you." Her eyes drifted back down to the leaf still gently clutched between her thumb and forefinger. Her brows knitted together as she studied the leaf through a blurring wall of tears.

Life. It was all around her. In the trees, the plants, the birds, the animals, and the people surrounding her, and yet she felt anything but alive. Her chest was heavy with sadness and her soul a dark wasted pit where nothing lived. With a scowl, she jerked the leaf free from the branch and wadded it up within a trembling fist. "Die! How dare you!" she hissed. After a moment, the anger faded, and its fire extinguished through another wave of tears. Her trembling fist subsided as it dropped to her side, her fingers uncurling and letting the leaf slip from her grip. She slowly shook her head. She couldn't even maintain enough fury to kill a leaf, to say nothing of the monstrous grief within her.

For a while after he had died, she had been able to fend off the worst of the grief with intense anger, but now she could no longer sustain it. She was tired, weary to her soul of the grief and fighting against it. She knew where her answer lay now. She knew, just as she had known from the moment his death registered on her mind, she knew what she must do. She released a shuddering sigh as she lowered herself to her knees. Hugging herself against another onslaught of grief, she looked skyward again. "Please take me from this cursed existence. I cannot go on. I have tried and I cannot. Please bring me to where you are. I beg you! If you ever loved me, do not let me suffer any longer! Please end this horrid existence and allow me to be at your side again." Her weeping eyes searched the sky desperately. "Please!"

Only the chirping birds answered her hopeless plea. Red-rimmed eyes continued to scan the canopy overhead, wishing with every fiber of her being that the Fates would grant her wish, to end this wretched existence and reunite her with the only love she had ever known and now knew she would never know again.

"Malcolm? Please?" she begged. "Please bring me to you. Do not leave me here like this." After several moments, it became clear that neither Malcolm nor the Fates were going to answer her. Her brows twisted as a new wave of intense pain lanced her being. Slowly, her eyes fell from the sky, and she leaned forward to rest her forehead against the ground as the grief wrenched sobs from her already wracked body. She knew she had only one option left to her, and she despised the fact that she would have to resort to it. She would take her own life. It was the only relief from the pain left to her. While it would condemn her to an eternity in hell, far from her beloved Malcolm, surely an eternity in hell could not possibly be worse than the hell she was living in now.

"Perhaps there is another way," a deep timbered voice whispered softly through the forest.

Dylena didn't respond or give any indication that she had heard the voice. Having accepted the fact that the only release from her prison of pain and grief was death, there was no longer anything to fear from this realm. If the deep voice belonged to a bandit, perhaps he would be merciful and kill her. She was even willing to submit herself to the horrors of being raped if death came at the end of the act. If she died at the hand of another, she would be reunited with her husband, and this horrid existence would be a fading memory in his embrace. Drawing in a shallow breath, she replied without moving from her position. "If you have come to do harm, do your worst. I only ask that you kill me when you are finished."

"You would prefer death?" the voice asked.

"Without hesitation," she responded instantly. "So take what you want from me but only if you intend to kill me afterwards."

"You are willing to throw away the precious gift of life without as much as a token resistance?"

Finally, she found the strength to move and she sat upright, while remaining on her knees. She found the tall man standing before her, studying her with intense blue eyes. He was just over six feet in height with long black hair, streaked with tendrils of white and tied at the nap of his neck. A full beard, also streaked with white, covered the lower half of his face, but enough remained to show her how lean his features were. He was considerably older than she was, quite possibly in his sixtieth season or more. His cheeks were hollow and the dark circles under his eyes leant his face a drawn, exhausted appearance. He was dressed in black boots, dark tan breeches, and a lighter brown shirt. A dark cloak hung from his spare shoulders and draped about his frame to almost touch the ground. His clothes appeared to be several sizes larger than he was. , and if he were armed, she could not see his weapon, nor had he drawn one. His hands hung at his sides as his intense gaze studied her. Taking a slow, ragged breath, she shook her head as she answered. "This life is no gift and it is certainly not precious, at least not any longer."

A genuine expression of pain flashed across his features as he continued to stare at her. "How sad. Such pain. It resides deeply within you." He paused in his study of her as his features twisted in painful sadness and tears gathered in his eyes. "Pain, loneliness, and despair are your constant companions now." There was no question in his tone. His words bore the hard edge of conviction.

She sniffed as she drew the sleeve of her dirty dress across her nose. She had not bathed nor changed clothes in many weeks, the pungent stench was thick about her, and she did not care. Her brown hair hung in tangled clumps about her shoulders. Her tattered dress hung loosely from her frame as she had lost a lot of weight in the months since Malcolm's death. "What do you know of such things?"

A slight and sad smile touched the corners of his lips. "I am an expert in such things. Pain, suffering, loneliness, grief, and despair are my specialties."

Her brow drew together in a confused expression as she looked up at him. "How so? Who would want to be an expert in such things?"

"I am an expert in alleviating them, of making them go away, never to torture people again," he answered softly and the warm, gentle tones of his voice gently stroked the ragged edges of her pain, and actually soothed them... somewhat.

A harsh chuckle rattled her throat. "Nonsense! No one can just make such things vanish! Do what you came here to do and kill me, or leave me be, but do one now!" she demanded tiredly. She was exhausted, truly to the depths of her entire being.

He nodded slowly. "I am doing what I came here to do, or at least I am trying to. You seem a bit reluctant to have your pain conquered."

She shook her head, growing impatient with this bothersome stranger. With exaggerated motions, she spread her arms out to her sides. "Then work your magic and make my pain vanish!"

He shook his head, and he began to walk a slow circle around her. "It is not magic, at least not in the conventional sense. It is more like a cleansing, a deep eradication of the source of the pain."

She sighed in frustration. "Then get on with it!"

"You do not believe me," he said with conviction.

She scoffed. "Of course I do not!" she dropped her arms back to her sides and lowered her head. "Such things are not possible! You are some type of brigand come to steal from me, or a bandit intent on robbing and possibly raping me. In either case, get on with it or leave me to my suffering!"

"I assure you, I do not wish to steal anything from you, nor do I have any interest in raping you. All I want is to relieve you of this horrible pain and suffering you are enduring, but to do so, you must believe in what I can offer you."

She slowly shook her head, exhaustion settling in to displace a fragment of the grief. Sleep had been a vanishing rarity since Malcolm had died, and the tiny moments when she would pass out from exhaustion, were the only breaks from the suffering. She felt such a moment coming upon her, so her interest in this bizarre conversation was waning rapidly. "Fine. I believe. Now take the pain from me."

He chuckled softly. "No, you do not. You are only humoring me."

"Whatever it takes to make you go away! The only way to take my pain from me, and release me from this cursed existence, is to slit my throat! I would loan you the knife to do it, but I do not have one with me!"

He paused in his circular walk around her and looked down on her bowed head. "There is another way."

"Here," she spat as her hands began reaching behind her to loosen the ties of her corset. "I will make it easier for you to rape me. My charms mean nothing to me any longer since the only man I wished to give them to is no longer here! All I ask is that you kill me once you are finished. I do not even care if it is done quickly or slowly, just so long as it is done!" She gave no indication of hearing his last comment as she struggled to untie her dress.

"Dylena?" came another voice into the clearing, and she froze in the act of disrobing. Her eyes grew wide as she recognized it, and while part of her wished to spin around to verify what she heard, another part held her fast in place, fearful that this was just a figment of her fragmenting mind.

"No! Do not toy with me so! Do not do this to me, I beg of you," she pleaded, her eyes filling with fresh tears.

"It is no trick. I would never toy with you so. I have come for you, as you asked," the ghostly familiar voice replied.

"I cannot!" she hissed, squeezing her eyes tightly shut, her hands abandoning the ties of her corset to clutch together at her chest.

"Why?" he asked.

"Because if I look and you are not there... I cannot bear the thought," she whispered.

"Fear not," the voice said, with warm, inviting tones. "I am here."

With wide, terrified eyes, she slowly turned her head, half-fearing that he would be there and half-fearing that he would not be. Then she completed her turn and there he was, standing not five feet from her and looking as tortured and grief-stricken as she was.

"Malcolm?" she asked so softly that she wasn't sure she had actually uttered the name.

"My dear wife! Oh, how I have missed you!" he replied with tears and a deeply stricken look in his eyes. His arms rose from his sides and spread out, inviting her to come to him. "Let me hold you. Let me sooth your grief, if only just a little."

A sob broke through and rocked her body as her trembling hands rose to cover her mouth. How could this be? How could he be standing there looking as real as the last morning she had seen him alive? She wanted to rise to her feet and run to him, but she feared that any movement she made would make this illusion vanish. She could not speak as more sobs convulsed her throat, making it hard to breath.

"Dylena, my love, I am so sorry for leaving you so suddenly! I would never willingly do such a thing to the only love I have ever known or wanted. I have tried so hard to return to you, but the Fates would not allow such a thing."

"My precious Malcolm!" she whispered through the trembling sobs. "The Fates know how deeply I have missed you, how hard I have mourned you. I have wanted nothing more than to join you! I can scarcely believe you are here now. This must be some illusion, some trick of my grief come to torture me further."

Malcolm smiled through the tears flowing down his cheeks. "No, my love. No illusion. I am here. Come to me and let me prove how real I am."

Whatever hesitation she had before had vanished as she climbed to her feet and began a slow walk toward him, her eyes riveted to him, terrified he would vanish with the next beat of her heart. When she was within three feet of him, she dared to believe that he would not vanish. "Oh, Malcolm," she sobbed as she dashed to him and fell into his arms. As they folded about her, she buried her face in his chest and cried. She could smell his scent just as she remembered it. The feel of his arms around her was exactly as she remembered it. All the pain and grief came rushing to the surface and she released it, wanting to finally be rid of it, free from it. As the bone-jarring sobs racked her body, she felt the first feathery fingers of release stroke and smooth the raw and jagged edges of her grief.

"How?" she asked through the sobs, her voice muffled in his chest.

"Naiop has made it possible."

"Who?" she asked.

"The man who just came to you. His name is Naiop, and he knows how to breech the barrier between the living realm and the afterlife. He can bring a soul back from the beyond. I have been watching you suffer and have wanted nothing more than to come to you and ease your pain, to assure you that everything was all right and was going to be all right."

She continued to cling tightly to him, her arms squeezing him with all the strength she had. She had him in her arms, and she was not about to release him for anything in this realm. She heard his explanation of how he had come to be here, but she didn't contemplate it for long. All that mattered at this moment was the fact that the part of her that had been so savagely ripped from her upon Malcolm's death was now within reach.

"I have missed you so..." she said as she sobbed into his shirt. "I cannot eat, cannot sleep, and cannot do anything but be crushed by this horrible pain!"

"Release it, my love. Release the pain. Give it to me so that you no longer have to bear its crushing weight upon your dying soul," his warm, rich voice soothed into her ear. She did as he asked. She held nothing back as she threw open the deepest wells of her being and allowed the pain to rush forth. As his hand gently caressed her shoulder, she could feel more sweet relief slowly spread through her as more and more pain faded.

"Oh my love! To have you here now, to have you holding me, is all my heart has yearned for. Please take this wretched pain from my breast to curse me no longer," her muffled voice sobbed into his chest.

"Give your pain to me, love. I will take it from you and give you peace and serenity in return. Your suffering is over. Your trials upon this realm are complete. You may rest now. You may now join me. You have but to release all of your pain to me, and our final journey will begin."

There was something odd and quite ominous in his words, but she could not find the will to care. The more pain she released to him, the more warm peace she found flowing through her. He was here and holding her close. Nothing else mattered.

She began to notice an odd sensation drifting through her. It was as if she were growing lighter, ready to float upon the wind. Her body began to fade from her perceptions and a sort of numbness began to spread through her. She had been so caught up in the fact that Malcolm had, somehow, been returned to her and his warm embrace was soothing her grief and pain, and that by the time she realized that the new sensation should concern her, there was nothing she could do about it. She tried to pull her head from his chest, but found she could not. He was not holding her head to his chest. She simply did not have the strength to move. "My dear? I feel strange. What is happening?"

"Shhhh. Do not concern yourself with it. It is merely the euphoria of finally being free of the pain," his soothing voice answered, but it did not sound like Malcolm's voice. It took her several moments to realize that the voice belonged to the strange man who had managed to reunite her with Malcolm. Panic tried to flash through her, to alert her to some sort of danger she had been unaware of, but it was too late. She felt her body fading from her awareness and even her awareness was dimming.

In the forest, the man known as Naiop held Dylena tightly to him as her body slowly dissolved into a fine powder. As the last of her crumbled within his arms and was whisked away by the wind, he tilted his head back, closing his eyes as the raw, savage pain from the woman soaked into his being. He sighed in refreshed delight as her pain rejuvenated him. He lowered his head and opened his eyes to reveal black orbs. He smiled in satisfaction as he consumed the last of the grief and pain. His face flushed and his body filled out, the grey left his hair and beard and his clothes now fit properly, giving the strong, healthy appearance of a man many seasons younger than he had been only a moment ago.

Slowly, his eyes returned to their normal blue color and he looked about the clearing. While any pain would sustain him, grief was always his preferred feast. The pain within grief was so raw and so primal that it would maintain him for weeks to come. Now that he had fed, it was time to continue pursuing the dark magic he had sensed many nights ago near the city of Lirpa. He had been searching for another source of pain when he had felt a shudder pass through him. Something incredibly dark and powerful was passing through. He quickly set after it with earnest. Whatever this new source of power was, it was evil, and evil always lead to pain and suffering. This dark power definitely promised to leave a feast of pain and suffering in its wake. Adjusting his cloak about his shoulders, he set off toward his mount.

The dark evil was heading north, and therefore, so was he.

CHAPTER TWENTY

"Is he going to die?" Shantira asked with deep concern as she stared down at Devenshire's pale features. She watched his chest slowly rise and fall, and it was the only thing giving her any hope that he still lived.

"No," Darkseed answered softly from his position next to Devenshire across from Shantira. "He will not die, but I do not know what he will awaken to be." Like her, his eyes moved from Devenshire's pale features to the slow movement of his chest.

"What do you mean?" she asked with trepidation. She felt like there should be something she could do to help him. With anxious frustration, she did the only thing she knew to do as she reached down to brush a damp lock of hair from his forehead. His skin was cold and clammy. They had moved Devenshire, Darkseed, and Zandorth from the clearing and into the cave that they had found earlier. They had quickly built a fire at the back of the cave and stretched the wounded men out. They had thought to cover them with blankets, but they were all rain soaked and now were stretched out on the cave floor in an attempt to let them dry.

Darkseed had regained consciousness first, and despite a massive headache, he appeared to be none the worse for wear. He had examined Devenshire and determined that there was nothing either physically or mystically that could be done for him. He was in a sort of coma brought on by both the tremendous release of power and the backlash of mystical energies from the two sources of magic cancelling each other out... violently. He left Devenshire in care of Brianna, Shantira, and Kendra as he set about dressing the nasty gash on the side of Zandorth's head. He determined the warrior would survive, thanks in no small part to the extraordinary thickness of his skull. Petera and Stant kept a vigil next to Zandorth, making sure the warrior continued to breathe.

Darkseed's features were grim as he studied Devenshire's pale face. "He released a tremendous amount of power, far more than he should have been able to. Such a release is dangerous and might have left him... altered."

"What do you mean *altered?*" Brianna asked with short tones.

Darkseed looked uncomfortable. "Daimion was not a skilled practitioner of the Mystical Arts. He did not have the discipline or training for the powers he was wielding out there." He paused as he continued to search for the right words. "I cannot say what happened to his mind in the backlash of power that felled him."

"Stop with the mystical double-speak! What are you talking about?" Brianna demanded. She was struggling with several emotions at once, and her patience was wearing thin. The unexplained obsession Shantira had with her safety was now deeply troubling her. Whatever was happening with the young woman was no longer an odd occurrence, and it bore further scrutiny. It was now an ominous problem that she wanted answers for immediately. She was also deeply concerned for Devenshire, both from the fondness she held deep in her heart for him as well as the fear she had felt in the clearing. As with the night they had escaped from Lirpa, she was at a loss to understand or explain what she had seen in the clearing. The spell he had unleashed on Armand outside Lirpa had been troubling, but the release of power he had displayed in the clearing was frightening. While she didn't know all that much about the Mystic Arts, what she did know said that what she had seen Devenshire do was impossible.

Darkseed took a deep breath, carefully considering his response. The answer was not simple to explain, even for an Adept. He had to find the words that they would understand just how close Devenshire had come to death, and the fact that if he regained consciousness, he could be far from what he had been before. "What makes it possible for someone to manipulate the Arts is tied directly to their life force. Using the powers of the Mystical Arts requires a great deal of concentration and focus. Without that concentration and focus, there is little control of the power that is released, and conversely, there is little control of the drain on the life force. The power Daimion released was seasons beyond his capabilities, and therefore, he had no discipline to control such a release. The drain on his life force was considerable, perhaps too much so."

"So he could still die?" Shantira asked with deep concern etched deep into her words as her fearful expression dropped back to his face.

Darkseed shook his head slowly. "No. If he were going to die, he would have done so already. He will continue to live, but if he awakens, he may not be the same as before."

"Wait! You mean he may not wake up at all?" Kendra asked.

The hard lines of concern in Darkseed's face answered the question before his words did. "It is possible that he will live out the rest of his days as he is now. If too much of his life force was drained, he may not have the will or the strength to awaken."

Each of them slowly shifted their gaze to Devenshire's prone, motionless form. Even his breathing was shallow and slow. The silence within the small cave grew tangible in the aftermath of

Darkseed's statement. Each of them tried to imagine continuing the quest to stop Xavier without him and none of them liked what they saw. Devenshire had been the driving force behind their efforts to stop the madman. Who would lead them if he could not? What would they do with him if he could not awaken?

"And if he does awaken?" Brianna asked softly, not really wanting to voice the question or hear the possible answers running through her mind.

"He could be as he was before, or he could not remember anything of his life before awaking in this cave or any measure of situations in between. One thing is certain, no matter what state he awakens in, his days of manipulating the Arts is over. No one can experience that type of release and retain their abilities," Darkseed replied as he reached into his vest pocket and withdrew a cigar. It was soaking wet and ruined. A deep frown etched itself into his features as he tossed the wet cigar into the fire.

"Is there nothing you can do for him? You are an Adept, you command greater powers than Daimion," Brianna pointed out.

Darkseed shook his head. "My powers were taxed in the attack. It will be many days before I will be able to work my craft again. I could not even conjure a tumbler of cognac at this moment." He looked down at Devenshire. "It is up to him at this point. His strength of will determines his path now."

Brianna smiled softly at Devenshire. "If that is the case, he will awaken as big a bastard as he ever was."

"How long have we been in this cave?" Zandorth's deep voice demanded from the opposite side of the fire.

They all jumped in a start and turned to find the warrior on his feet gazing at them expectantly. Petera and Stant had become so engrossed in the discussion about Devenshire's condition that they had stopped watching Zandorth. As his intense gaze shifted from one person to another, the only indication that he had even been injured was the makeshift bandage tied around his head.

"How are you feeling?" Stant asked.

"I am fine," he replied as he reached up and pulled the bandage from his head, "How long have we been here?" he repeated.

"A few hours now," Darkseed replied.

Zandorth shook his head. "We must move! We cannot afford this time. Armand will be gaining on us, and we are losing ground on Xavier!"

"Daimion is injured and so are you. We can afford a few hours of respite," Brianna countered.

"Devenshire can be lashed to his mount, and I am fine. We must move out!" Zandorth snapped in reply.

"We have a two-day lead on them, Zandorth. We can afford a few hours to gather our wits and tend to our wounded," Darkseed replied.

"My wits are fine and the wounds have been tended. By your own admission, Devenshire may already be lost to us. If such is the case, we cannot allow him to hinder our progress. We must move to prevent Xavier from gaining any more of a lead on us or to allow Armand to gain any further ground on us!" he grumbled.

Brianna felt her eyes widen at the warriors willingness to discard Devenshire so callously. She knew, deep down, that she shouldn't be surprised. He had been more than willing to leave Devenshire behind in Lirpa, but coming face to face with the warrior's rigid thinking always stunned her. She opened her mouth to protest when she caught Shantira rising to her feet in her peripherals. She turned her head to see the growing anger spreading across the young woman's face, and it gave her a touch of relief. Finally, she was showing concern for someone other than her.

Shantira's eyes narrowed as she rose slowly to her feet. "Am I hearing you correctly? Are you actually suggesting that we leave Daimion behind in this state?"

Zandorth fixed his hard gray eyes on her, the conviction of his words plain in his expression. "He will only slow us down and will be of no use to us in this state."

"You cold hearted bastard! You would leave one of us behind like this? Vulnerable to any means of attack?" Shantira snapped, astonished and angry at the brutality on display before her.

Zandorth shifted his hard gaze to Shantira, his expression unchanged from before her outburst. "I would expect nothing less in his place."

Shantira snapped a trembling finger down toward Devenshire. "Daimion is not like you! He would never, ever leave you behind like that!"

The granite set of Zandorth's features never shifted as he shrugged. "Then he is a fool!" Zandorth quipped in return.

Darkseed rose from his seat, his hands raised, and palms out in what was intended as a calming gesture. "Rest easy. This gains us nothing. Fighting amongst ourselves only strengthens our enemies." He shifted his gaze to Zandorth. "We are not leaving anyone behind." He tried to put a combination of a hard edge, and yet a reassurance in his voice to reach the warrior in a way that would not antagonize him.

It failed.

"You do not command me, mage!" Zandorth grumbled in a tone that clearly carried the conviction of his belief and the resolution of his position.

Darkseed sighed heavily, knowing that the fight was upon him now. "Perhaps not, but I can promise you that we are not leaving this cave without Daimion. You do as you wish, but before you rush out to confront Xavier on your own I hope you are ready for your journey to the afterlife."

"At least I will die with honor!" he snapped in reply before motioning toward Devenshire. "I would rather stand alone before Xavier's army in defiance than kneel before the headsman's block because of foolish sentiment!"

"Caring for your comrades is not foolish sentiment!" Brianna said in the tight confines of her efforts to control her anger.

Zandorth shifted his cold gaze to her. "Of course it is! In this state, Devenshire will only slow us down which will allow Armand to catch up to us, allowing Xavier ample time to unleash his hellish plans! I can promise you that neither Armand nor Xavier will take such sentiments into account before delivering our fates to us!"

"How can you be so cruel?" Kendra asked softly, truly astonished at the hardness of the warriors thoughts.

The question hit a nerve with the warrior as his gaze shifted into a harder glare, his eyebrows pulling together almost as if something had pained him. His massive hands slowly curled into fists at his sides as his gray eyes bore into the Elven woman. "Because this realm is a cruel place! There is no softness here! There is no warmth here! This realm is a harsh, cold, empty taskmaster that wants nothing more than to hold you down and strip the life from you, one tiny fragment at a time until you are empty, hollow, and dead inside! Any warmth or comfort you find is an illusion, dished out by the Fates to lull you into a false sense of peace and security! There is only life and death in this realm, and if you want to avoid the second one you had damned well better fight for the first! You are born into this hellish place naked and defenseless! You will leave the same way! Every moment in between is a struggle. You have to fight to remain alive, and you have to constantly be ready to face any number of opponents who wish only to deprive you of life and freedom! This is the harsh truth of our existence, and the sooner all of you embrace that truth, the greater your chances of surviving to fight another day! To win one more tiny victory over the taskmaster!"

Zandorth paused as he realized his emotions had escaped the tight confines of his control. He closed his eyes and took in a deep breath, letting it out slowly while his fists gradually relaxed. He opened his eyes and surveyed each of them, the intensity of his gaze softening from before. His tone was more subdued as he continued. "Know this: If Armand catches up to us, surrender will not be among the options he will offer us. We have shamed him, made him look foolish before his men." Zandorth shook his head. "There are many accidents that could befall us on our way back to the tribunal in Lirpa. Also, know that each moment we delay is another mile Xavier gains toward his retreat and his intentions for the Stones of Andarus grow closer to reality. I do not intend to die at the hands of the Royal Guard or in the aftermath of whatever Xavier has planned simply because one man can no longer carry on the quest! Make your decision and make it quickly!" He swept the others with his hard stare for a moment before he stepped around the group and exited the cave, vanishing into the growing shadows of the late afternoon.

For a time, silence reined in the cave, save for the crackle of the fire. As harsh as Zandorth's words had been, they each knew that, at their core, they were right. Each moment was an advantage for those chasing them as well as the ones they chased.

"As much as I hate to admit it," Petera finally said, "he is right. We dare not allow Captain Armand to catch up to us, and we dare not allow Xavier to make his retreat."

"We cannot leave Daimion behind. He will surely die!" Kendra argued.

"We may not have a choice," Stant replied reluctantly.

"I do not believe what I am hearing!" Brianna injected. "Are we seriously debating on whether or not we will leave Daimion behind? Is this what I am hearing?"

Petera and Stant's faces shifted into uncomfortable expressions as they looked up at her to see the smoldering anger building in the depths of her eyes. "Zandorth makes several good points," Stant countered.

"I do not give a damn about his good points! You two are seriously talking about leaving behind the one man who began this quest! The first one to see the very real danger Xavier posed to this realm and ushered us into action! I have had this argument with Zandorth before, and I am perfectly fine with having it again here! I will not leave him behind! Armand and Xavier and the Stones of Andarus be damned!!"

Darkseed watched the group, watching their actions and reactions to the situation. Petera and Stant were siding with Zandorth and the women were devout in their resolution not to leave Devenshire behind. It was an interesting dichotomy.

"I will stay with him," Shantira volunteered. "If he recovers, we can rejoin you."

Another touch of relief passed through Brianna at Shantira's willingness to put someone else's well being ahead of hers. Perhaps whatever had spawned the odd behavior in Shantira was passing.

"As will I!" Kendra added. No one missed the tightening of Shantira's expression as she fought against the anger toward Kendra.

Darkseed shook his head. "We cannot split the group like this. We are already at a disadvantage as it is. To split us up will only hurt us and leave us more vulnerable."

"Then we are weak," Brianna injected, "because I am staying with him as well!" Her chin lifted in hard defiance as she locked eyes with Darkseed.

"A sweet sentiment, but not one I am willing to have on my conscience."

They all snapped their eyes around to find Devenshire watching them through swollen eyes.

"Daimion!" Shantira exclaimed as she quickly knelt down next to him again, her hand coming to rest on his chest. "How do you feel?"

Devenshire grunted as he shifted his position. "Like I was caught in a stampede of rampaging bulls." His voice was gravelly and very rough.

"What do you remember?" Darkseed asked, more than just a little relieved that his friend had regained consciousness.

Devenshire paused for a moment, his eyes drifting to the roof of the cave as he tested his memory. Finally, he groaned as another stab of pain lanced through him. "Everything. The Stones, the night in Lirpa, the storm... everything."

Darkseed caught Brianna's eyes and nodded slightly, the relief showing in their depths. In return, Brianna briefly closed her eyes and visibly relaxed. When she opened her eyes again, she smiled at Darkseed and returned his subtle nod.

"I was very worried about you," Shantira said softly, smiling down into his face.

"We all were," Kendra added, kneeling down on the other side of him, opposite Shantira. No one missed the venomous glare Shantira shot at the woman as she settled down beside him.

"Ladies, please. With this much female attention, Devenshire may never recover, feigning his injuries for twice the time they will afflict him." Darkseed sighed heavily.

"I agree," Brianna amended with a poorly concealed grin. "We need to let him rest and recover his strength. We cannot remain here much longer."

Stant and Petera rose from the floor and made their way toward the cave entrance followed by Darkseed. Kendra and Shantira reluctantly rose and began moving out also. Brianna watched them move out through the cave entrance before she knelt down beside him, placing her hand over his resting on his chest. She smiled down into his eyes. "Are you truly well?"

He smiled up at her and nodded slowly. "I just need a few moments to regain my strength."

She bent over and placed a light kiss on his forehead. "You had me worried, you bastard! Do not do it again!"

He smiled tiredly, and chuckled softly. "I will endeavor to do as you wish, M'Lady," he answered softly, his gaze locked tightly to hers.

She nodded once, and rose to her feet, making her way out of the cave.

After she had gone, Devenshire's face lost the warm smile and took on a more serious expression as he gazed up at the cave ceiling. He didn't really see the ceiling as he considered what he had felt within the grip of the maelstrom. He knew Xavier had cast the spell. He had felt his essence within the power of the storm as surely as he had felt it in the burned out ruins of the church in Shantira's village. He had known Xavier was a much more skilled practitioner of the Arts than he was, but he had not been prepared for the level of power he had sensed within the storm. Xavier was much more powerful than he had originally thought, and for the first time since beginning this quest, he found himself questioning their chances for survival, to say nothing of success. Perhaps Darkseed had been right in his argument that night in Lirpa, and maybe there was no way to truly defeat the mad mage.

Conceivably, the entire realm was nothing more than a plaything for whatever twisted whims Xavier had once he commanded the power of the Stones. He shook his head hard shaking off the doubts within him while also stirring the throbbing headache to a new level of intensity. His whole body felt battered, bruised, and broken. He would honestly be surprised to find no broken bones. He was also disturbed by the fact he could not feel his powers. It was as if his mystical abilities had been ripped from him, and he feared that what few skills he had acquired within the workings of the Arts were gone. While he was nowhere near Xavier's level of skill, what few powers he had possessed were a comfort to him. He withheld the hope that his powers would return, but he knew enough of the workings of the Arts to know that such an expenditure of power he had unleashed never came without a price. The thoughts were troubling, and he desperately wanted to banish them from consideration, but he knew they would haunt him for a long time to come.

Devenshire didn't know how long he had been lost in thought, but when he finally shook himself from the morbid and troubling thoughts, he noticed that it was getting late in the day. Time was working against them, both in regards to the group they ran from and the group they chased after. He tried to sit up and found that any movement racked his body with burning pain. He was in no condition to ride, but he knew they didn't have the time for him to regain his strength. Hugging his torso against the onslaught of pain, he forced himself to a seated position, grunting against the assault. Taking a few moments, he bowed his head and forced his breathing to calm.

"Daimion! You should not be trying to rise!" Shantira's voice came from the entrance.

He smiled and slowly shook his head as she came to his side. "We cannot afford the time for me to recover completely," he replied as he forced the pain from his expression before looking up at her.

"How do you feel?" she asked, the concern etched deeply into her features. Her eyes scanned his body, searching for any sign that he was as well as he appeared to be or if there was something that required immediate attention.

"I am none the worse for wear. I need to consult my maps to get a bearing on our path. Could you retrieve them from my pack?" he asked nodding toward the bag situated against the back wall of the cave.

"Of course," she replied as she rose to retrieve his pack.

Soon he had his maps spread before him, studying them in the flickering light of the small fire. Shantira sat beside him, her left leg upright as she rested her chin on the back of her hands on top of her knee. She watched intently as Devenshire traced paths on the maps, and then he would retrieve another map and unroll it on top of the first to study it intently as well.

"What are you looking for?" she asked softly, not wanting to disturb his concentration.

He placed his finger on a spot on the map he was studying. "We are here, in the mountain range. Lirpa is here," he said as he moved his finger to another spot on the map. She nodded slowly. They had covered a significant distance since leaving Lirpa.

"Where are we going?" she asked.

Devenshire paused as he studied the map. He reached up and rubbed his temple against the throbbing headache. "We are here," he indicated by pointing at the spot of the map he had noted earlier. "I would guess that Xavier and his travelers are somewhere in this area," he said drawing a circular pattern on the map with his finger, which was far to the right of the area Devenshire said they currently were.

"Why are we here and he is there? Why did we not follow him?" she asked.

"He is traveling with a large group of men which requires wagons to carry supplies. They will not be able to traverse the mountain range and will have to divert to the east to the Gillman Pass."

"Are you sure he would travel that far out of his way?" Darkseed asked from the entrance of the cave.

"I do not see where he would have a choice," Devenshire answered.

Darkseed moved up to the opposite side of Devenshire from Shantira and knelt down to study the maps with him. He placed his finger on the spot Devenshire had identified as Lirpa and drew a line to the northwest. "There is the Skey Pass to the west. It is much closer and would get him through the mountain range sooner."

"True, but the trail from Lirpa to the Skey Pass is mostly forest and would be difficult to traverse with a large party. He would lose more time by trying that path," Devenshire pointed out.

"The Skey Pass would allow him the opportunity to come upon us from the rear," Zandorth's gruff voice resonated as he entered the cave. He crossed to stand behind Devenshire and studied the map. He pulled his sword and used it as a pointer, placing the tip on the area where they were currently located. "We will exit the mountain range here," he said tapping the map. "We would then proceed directly north in the hopes that we have closed the distance on Xavier's caravan. However, if Xavier uses the Skey Pass, he will emerge from the mountain range behind us in this area." He used his sword to trace the pattern on the map. "That will put them in an excellent position to attack us from the rear."

Devenshire and Darkseed's faces grew stern as they studied the prospect Zandorth posed. It was very clear that Xavier could use just such a tactic, and it would, indeed, leave them vulnerable to an attack from the rear. They exchanged a brief worried glance before returning to the map.

Finally, Devenshire shook his head. "Xavier had a tremendous lead on us. I doubt he would throw that away by trying to catch us from behind. He has the Stones and will be very anxious to begin trying to tap into them." Devenshire shook his head again. "He will be heading toward the Duvall Retreat with all haste."

"We cannot discount the possibility that he may have sent some of his Followers to ambush us from behind," Zandorth countered.

"No. No, we cannot," Devenshire agreed. He continued to study the map intently, searching for the correct path. It was bad enough trying to stay ahead of Captain Armand and his party, but now to have to worry about a detachment of Followers as well complicated things a great deal. Devenshire's bloodshot eyes scanned the map in the area they were currently located, and he forced his mind to ignore the intense headache and pain that racked his body and to think through his options.

"What if we cut through this area?" Shantira asked, drawing an imaginary line from their current location to an area just ahead of the Gillman Pass. It was a diagonal line straight from their location.

Darkseed shook his head. "That is very rough terrain, even on horseback."

Devenshire studied her suggested path intently, his eyes darting from one area of the map to another, and back again. A slow smile began tugging at the corners of his mouth, which Darkseed noticed. "Come now, Daimion. You cannot be seriously considering that path."

"It would give us a tremendous advantage in fleeing from Armand, catching up to Xavier, and taking us out of where any detachment of Xavier's Followers might try to ambush us."

"True, but you must consider that route," Darkseed argued. "It is filled with steep slopes, deep canyons, and very treacherous footing for even the most disciplined horse."

"I agree with Devenshire," Zandorth said as he nodded once. "It will give us the best tactical advantage considering what we face."

Darkseed looked up at the warrior. "It also gives us the best opportunity to break our necks if we are not very careful."

Zandorth regarded Darkseed intently. "If the path is too dangerous for you, perhaps you should return to Lirpa."

Darkseed's eyes snapped around to the warrior and narrowed with growing anger. "You are questioning my bravery or my skill?"

Krahl shrugged. "I question nothing. I let the obvious speak for itself."

Darkseed studied the warrior briefly before a dark grin lifted the corners of his mouth. "You select the path, big man. I will be right behind you. If you are very nice, I will even assist you should you fall."

Krahl's face took on a dark mischief. "That will be the day."

Shantira sighed in irritation. "For the love of the Fates! I am about to suffocate from the press of male ego in here! Could you two put away your members, and let us get back to the task at hand?"

Devenshire snickered in spite of the pain wracking his body. He regarded Shantira as she shook her head and shifted her attention back to the map before her. He could clearly see that the young, naïve village girl was changing, becoming something more than even she was aware of. He could clearly see Brianna's influence on her as well. He could almost hear Brianna's voice saying something very similar.

Darkseed looked at Shantira as though he were seeing her for the first time. It was clear by his and Zandorth's expressions that they had not expected such a brash statement from someone more than half their size. Devenshire saw Zandorth's jaw jut out in anger, and he quickly stepped in as the warrior opened his mouth to issue a retort. "I agree. We must select our path quickly and move out. We have lost too much time as it is." He relaxed as he saw Zandorth snap out of whatever angry reply he was about to issue and return his focus to the map.

"The path Shantira suggests is dangerous, but I believe it will give us the best advantage," Devenshire pointed out.

"I agree," Zandorth added.

Darkseed studied the map, and the growing frown spreading across his face revealed his concern. After a moment, he slowly shook his head. "It will be treacherous at best." He pointed to an area along the intended path. "This area here is thick with trees and undergrowth, and the path is barely wide enough to accommodate a person on foot, let alone someone on horseback. One wrong step and you will be plummeting to a certain and a very painful death."

"Agreed," Devenshire replied with an unwavering look into Darkseed's eyes.

"Let us not forget that Gryphons are rumored to nest here as well." Darkseed injected.

"I do not see where we have much choice," Shantira injected, her eyes intently studying the map.

"Nor do I," Zandorth agreed. "But it will, indeed, be a most dangerous trail."

"Darkseed?" Devenshire asked.

After several moments, Darkseed released a sigh. "Why not? We may as well continue pressing our luck." He rose to his feet and stretched his back. "Hell, we should not have made it this far. When do we leave?"

Devenshire nodded. "Agreed. We should break camp immediately. We have already given the good Captain Armand plenty of time to cut our lead on him."

"Are you well enough to travel?" Shantira asked Devenshire, her hand coming to rest on his forearm.

Devenshire smiled tiredly. "I will be fine," he lied. He wondered how he would be able to simply sit astride his mount to say nothing of actually navigating him through such a treacherous path.

"I will prepare the mounts," Zandorth said as he moved toward the cave entrance.

"I will inform the others," Darkseed said as he fell into step behind Zandorth.

Shantira remained where she was as Devenshire began rolling his maps up. She studied his profile in the flickering firelight and felt the strong feelings and sensations tugging on her. She was continually amazed how being so close to him both made her feel safe and terrified her at the same time. She leaned slightly closer to him, not entirely sure why, but her eyes were focused on his lips. She caught herself at the last minute and shifted her position just as he turned his gaze to her. "Is something wrong?" he asked.

She smiled slightly and tucked a strand of hair behind her ear. "No. Just lost in thought is all," she lied.

He paused in rolling up the last map. "Which thoughts?" he asked, his voice seeming to grow deeper.

She knew she had to shake herself out of this moment. There was no time to pursue these feelings with him, regardless of how badly she wanted to. Her mind quickly worked to come up with a suitable response. She looked down at the map in his hand, and she asked a question she had been asking herself since she had learned just what they were dealing with in the power of the Stones of Andarus. "What will we do if Xavier is successful?"

Devenshire's eyes dropped to the cave floor as he contemplated the question. She had the sense that it was also a question he had been asking himself as well. "We will have to find a way to survive in whatever twisted reality Xavier creates, providing he can control the power of the Stones once it has been released. In either case, we will not be able to remain in this area."

Shantira nodded slowly, his answer matching the one she had already come up with. "Where would we go? What area in the entire realm would be suitable?" The fear was clear in her voice and even more so in her eyes as she searched his. This time she wasn't looking for reciprocal feelings, but a genuine warm reassurance that everything was going to be okay.

Devenshire held her gaze for a moment before he shifted his attention to the map in his hand. It was a map of the known areas of the realm and he laid it back upon the floor, smoothing it out and using rocks to hold it flat. He then turned to the campfire and took up a charred piece of wood from the outer edge of the pit. He turned back to the map and leaned closer to her as he made a black dot on the map with the charred end of the wood. "We are here right now."

She nodded, noticing how tiny this representation looked in comparison to the map they had used to plot their next move. He began drawing a dotted line due north. "If we fail to stop Xavier from unleashing the power of the Stones, and we manage to survive our encounter with him, I would head due north."

She watched as the black dotted line continued toward the top of the map and an area that contained no drawings, no indications of anything existing there. She knew that such an area was unexplored and had never been charted. Her eyes grew wide as he continued the dotted line until it disappeared off the edge of the map. She looked at him briefly before shifting her gaze back to the map. "What is there?"

Devenshire's face grew hard as he studied his path. "The Wastelands."

"What are the Wastelands?" she asked.

Devenshire sighed heavily. "Some say the edge of the realm. No one has ever been there, or at least, no one has ever returned from there. It is a land of great mystery, myths, and legends. Some even say that this is where the Afterlife begins." he paused as he considered the myths and hushed rumors. "Regardless of what is there, if there is any place within this realm that one could escape the power of the Stones, it would be there."

"It sounds frightening," Shantira said, hugging herself against a slight chill.

"No more so than what the Stones will do to our realm," he replied evenly. Silence reined in the cave for a time as each considered the renewed horrors of what the coming days and weeks would bring. The prospect of fleeing to an unknown region that had never been explored was terrifying to her, but as Devenshire pointed out, it could not possibly be worse than whatever the power of the Stones would do to the rest of the land.

Finally, she shook herself out of the fright. "I should help break camp."

He nodded as she rose to her feet. She fixed her concerned gaze deep into his eyes, searching for that warmth and security she always found there. He smiled warmly up at her. "Fear not. We have not been defeated yet. As long as we have life within us, there is always a chance."

She tilted her head slightly as she studied his face. There was no attempt at soothing her fears in his eyes. He honestly believed what he said. She smiled warmly. "You say that with such assuredness."

He nodded. "That is because I believe it, with all that I am. I am not defeated until I die. True, I may have to retreat and regroup from time to time, but you truly never fail until you quit trying," he shook his head, "As long as I live I am not defeated."

She took a moment to consider his words and his conviction in saying them. Some of the fear diminished as she replayed what he had said over in her mind. She nodded slowly and gave him another warm smile before turning and walking out of the cave.

Devenshire watched her leave and as soon as she was out of sight, his face lost the warmth of a moment ago. While he truly believed what he had told her, he found himself growing more concerned at their ability to stop Xavier. His battle with him through the storm had revealed just how great the power was that Xavier commanded and it had spawned a tiny sliver of doubt within his mind. He looked back down at the map and its path to nowhere. His brow furrowed as he studied the map, knowing that what he had drawn was a last ditch option. None knew what was in the Wastelands, but whatever was there had to be better than what would happen to the realm if Xavier were successful. Wouldn't it? With a deep sigh, he removed the rocks holding the map down and began rolling it back up. He could not answer that question and that troubled him. Would what Xavier unleashed upon the realm truly be so horrific that he would take his chances with the edge of the realm?

He paused in the act of placing the map in his pack with the rest of his maps. He studied the rolled up map and felt irritation growing within him. The path to the Wastelands was a gesture of surrender and cowardice. His flight into the Wastelands was nothing more than his fear manifesting itself within his mind. While he had drawn the path north, he had actually seen himself riding his mount flat out toward the Wastelands, fleeing whatever horrors the Stones brought.

He shook his head sharply. He would not flee. He would not surrender and allow Xavier to remake this realm, or if he could not control the power of the Stones, surrender to the twisted power of the Stones of Andarus. The map became a symbol of his fear, and it disgusted him. He would have none of it! If he failed to stop Xavier, he would rather die in the attempt than flee from the results.

Looking around the cave, he spied a crevasse in the back wall. He rose and moved to it, slipping the map deep inside of it, hiding it from the realm and from himself. It was a token gesture, but it helped him shore up his resolve. He was weak from the battle with the storm, his powers were drained, and he was in pain. Pain and fatigue were notorious for sapping a man's resolve and courage. He gathered his pack, and using his boot, scattered the firewood, making sure none of it landed outside the ring of rocks used to contain it. Satisfied that the remnants of the fire would soon burn itself out, he headed for the cave entrance, feeling slightly refreshed at the gesture of leaving his fears behind in the cave.

Failure was not an option. It couldn't be.

CHAPTER TWENTY-ONE

Hesax paused before the massive wooden doors of the great hall, his thick hands resting reluctantly on the hoops that waited for him to pull on them. He took a deep breath and let it out slowly as he bowed his head, staring down at his hands frozen in place on the openers. He could not recall ever being filled with this much dread at the prospect of entering the great hall. In fact, he reflected, every single occasion he had been called to enter had been a merry time filled with revelry, fellowship, and genuine camaraderie.

Such was not the case this time. He must deliver some very disturbing and disheartening news to the council, and he would sooner jump from the highest precipice in the realm than utter the words he was about to tell. He still could not believe what he had learned, nearly refused to believe it. Something must be horribly wrong if what he had learned were true.

Taking a deep, steadying breath, Hesax shored up his resolution and raised his head, locking his steely gaze forward as his massive forearms pulled back on the hoops. He was a warrior, and warriors never shirked their responsibilities, regardless of how unpleasant the task. The hinges on the double doors groaned in protest as they were forced to bear the weight of the oak doors, as they slowly swung outward. Feeling a similar squeal of protest within his mind, Hesax squared his shoulders and strode into the great hall, his shoulders back, his head held high.

The great hall was just that, a great hall. A massive room dedicated to the fellowship of a vanishing breed of men who valued honor, integrity, and the preservation of the realm above all else. His boot heels clicked sharply on the stones of the floor, worn to a smooth shine from the passage of countless feet. The click echoed off into the massive expanse of the room. There was absolutely nothing small about this hall, from the furnishings to the decorations to the men who occupied it.

The massive fireplace occupied most of the wall, measuring nearly ten feet in width, seven feet in height and nearly six feet in depth. It was capable of burning an entire cord of wood at a time, though this was only done in the dead of winter. On one side of the fireplace was a large steel pole hung on a hinge with a hook on the end. This was designed to swing out from the fireplace where a pot could be hung on the hook, and then the pole could be swung into position over the fire for cooking. Above the fireplace was a solid oak mantle that was carved from a massive tree. The craftsmanship was amazing, and Hesax never entered the great hall that he did not pause to admire the mantel. It had been stained to a deep luster that caught the light and gently reflected it back in subtle shades.

Massive tapestries hung from the walls, reaching nearly from ceiling to floor, each portraying a different chapter in the history of their guild. Thirty torch sconces were placed symmetrically along all four walls of the room providing ample lighting while a giant chandelier made from deer, elk, and moose antlers hung from the highest point of the pitched ceiling from a large chain. Upon each tine of each antler was a lit candle. As with the fireplace, Hesax was always enthralled with the chandelier, not with just the magnitude of it, but the sheer beauty, as well.

The walls were large planks of mahogany reaching from the stone floor up fifteen feet to the edge of the ceiling, which was made of large square beams of solid oak reaching up to the pinnacle of the room some eight feet higher up. Two large banquet tables were situated on each side of the room forming a sort of aisle down the middle. Another even larger table crossed the back of the room, turned to form a head table of sorts. Long benches ran the entire length of the smaller tables while elegantly crafted high backed chairs sat behind the larger head table.

On the wall across from the fireplace hung numerous locks of hair tied tightly at one end and allowed to hang down loosely. The lengths varied as did the colors and each was tied with a different swatch of cloth. This was the wall of memory, a place to honor all members of their guild who had fallen in battle or given their lives in the line of what their code demanded of them. When one was killed, a lock of their hair was cut and tied with a piece of cloth from whatever they were wearing. This formed the memorial that was hung upon the wall to honor their lives and their passing. When the tradition was started, it had been suggested that the swords of the fallen be hung upon the wall, but it was quickly and clearly determined that a warrior was to be buried with their sword, no matter what. The locks of hair were a simple, yet dignified salute to those who had gone before.

Hesax gave a brief nod of salute to the row of memorials and gave a silent prayer of gratitude and respect for every man represented on that wall. He shifted his gaze back forward and tried to ignore the multitude of eyes upon him as he strode toward the head table. Each of the smaller tables were occupied with men, each watching his every step, trying to discern if what they had heard was true, and if it were true, what that would mean for their next action.

At the head table, five men sat waiting. The man in the middle sat back in the largest chair, his elbows resting on the arms of the chair and his hands clasped together, fingers interlaced and pressed against his upper lip. His hard gaze was locked fast to Hesax as he approached, his gaze expectant, almost earnest in its intensity.

Hesax knew that he would be the most eager of all to hear his news. As leader of the guild, Hadran would be the one deciding what course of action they followed next, and given what he was about to tell them, Hesax did not envy his task.

Hesax walked up to the head table and planted his feet firmly into place, legs spaced wide. He drew his broadsword and held it up until the blade was right in front of his face, his eyes locked intently with Hadran's eyes. He then spun the sword around and placed the tip on the floor, folding his hands together over the pommel and bowing his head to Hadran.

"My life is my service," he said in the customary form of greeting.

Hadran studied Hesax intently, searching for any indication that his worst fear... their worst fear... was a reality. For a long time, he sat frozen in place, watching Hesax and measuring how to proceed. Each of the men at the head table, as well as every man seated at the long tables, watched and waited, their eyes darting back and forth between Hadran and Hesax. There was hesitation within Hadran and that was nothing short of a rarity. Hadran was a man of decisive action, showing no hesitation or doubt once his was locked to a course of action.

"You have news?" Hadran finally asked, the only part of his body moving being his lips as he spoke. Several in the room had to study Hadran closely to make sure he was even blinking.

Hesax raised his eyes to Hadran and gave a short, quick nod. "I have."

Hesax glanced at the two men to Hadran's right and then shifted his gaze to the two men on his left. These were Hadran's lieutenants, his most trusted advisors. They, like the others, stared intently at him, waiting for his report. "Do you wish for me to give my report now?"

Hadran's eyes glanced to his left and then quickly to his right before snapping back to the center and locking again on Hesax. "We have no secrets here! You know this!"

Hesax nodded. "Yes, I do."

Hadran's eyes darted quickly to the tabletop before returning to Hesax's again. With his doubled hands, he took a breath and nodded once. "Report!"

Hesax took a deep breath, pausing a moment hoping against hope that something... anything, would interrupt him before he had to report on what he had discovered about one of their own. When the interruption didn't come, he forged ahead. "It would seem our earlier fears are realized."

There was a collective gasp that rippled through the room like a chilled winter wind. Heads along both tables huddled together and hushed whispers were exchanged. Yet, even whispers, when there are so many at once, can be quite cacophonous. Hesax welcomed the muted roar of so many whispers being exchanged at once. It meant he had a few more moments before he had to give the details he knew Hadran would demand. Hesax turned at the waist until he could see the empty spot along the table to his right. The object of his report was supposed to be sitting in that spot, joining his brethren in the communion of their cause, not the subject of this hastily called gathering of their guild. Furrowing his brow, he let his eyes dart form man to man, seeing each one steal a glance at the suddenly ominous empty spot amongst their ranks.

"Silence!" Hadran shouted above the din, his eyes slowly slid along the gathered members of the guild, letting them know he would brook no further interruptions in these proceedings. Once silence returned to dominate the great hall, he shifted his hard gaze back to Hesax and nodded. "Continue!"

Hesax sighed and nodded. "As you command. It appears that our brethren was, indeed, involved in the night of wickedness that struck Lirpa two nights ago."

Hadran remained motionless. "To what degree was he involved?"

Hesax shifted his gaze to the floor and took a moment to try to find a way to utter the next words in a way that were not as final as they seemed in his mind.

There had to be some kind of mistake. There had to be. His thoughts shouted deep within his mind. But his deeply rooted belief that this was wrong and that the man at the center of this meeting was incapable of the disgraceful behavior he was being accused of was not enough. There was the matter of the dishonor that this man had not only brought on himself, but their guild, as well. Such dishonor could not and would not be tolerated.

"Completely from what I have learned, he assaulted members of the Royal Guard, allied himself with criminals and…" he paused, unsure if he would be able to utter the next words even under the threat of dishonor and disciplinary action. It was inconceivable that any member of their guild would behave in such a way, but especially *this* member, "…aligning himself with a vampire."

This time there was no rippling of whispers that were being subdued but an all out, unified shout of defiance and disbelief as every single man along the secondary tables shot to their feet nearly simultaneously. Hesax winced under the deafening roar of so many outraged voices exploding at once. The five men at the head table slowly scanned the crowd of outraged men, the uncertainty in their eyes about how to restore order… in all their eyes save for one…

Hadran slowly unclasped his fingers, separated his hands, and rose to his feet in careful, measured movements. His hard gaze slowly swept the room, his expression set in stone and unreadable. Hesax did his best to try to discern what was in his leader's thoughts, but only the hard set of his features greeted his searching eyes. He braced himself for the bellowed order of silence he was sure Hadran would issue.

Hadran slowly raised his hands from his sides, his palms out and pointed down, his fingers casually extended outwards. He raised his hands to chest level and bounced them repeatedly in a motion asking for silence instead of demanding it. It was such a simple and lackluster gesture, but almost instantly, the deafening roars of protest began to subside. While the shouts dwindled, Hesax could feel the waves of outrage rolling from the gathered men.

Once the noise subsided, Hadran addressed the group in a calm voice. "I will have order." He looked down at Hesax. "What proof do you have of these allegations?"

"I have spoken with several sheriffs of Lirpa as well as many citizens, and while there are some variations in the story, they all tell the same core theme."

"And that theme is?" Hadran asked.

Hesax took a deep breath and launched into his report. "Three men were murdered inside a local inn, their bodies rent far worse than any butcher could do. Our brother was detained for questioning in the matter when it was discovered that a vampire was within the city. It is believed that the vampire aided our brother and the other criminals in their escape from the city jail. Other reports indicate that Constable Liston, a local whore and a young woman at the constable's residence were all killed in the manner of a vampire. It is said that our brother led the criminals in their escape from the city and fought alongside them against the Royal Guard, injuring many soldiers."

"Impossible!" one man shouted in defiance.

"I will not believe such a lie!" another man shouted.

Several other voices began shouting their disbelief of the story, and Hadran, again, raised his hands in an indication that he wanted silence. "I know how you feel. I feel the same. There is a part of me that refused to believe that Zandorth Krahl could be guilty of these charges. Yet we have the unified word of Lirpa sheriffs and citizen accounts of the events. Such a report, regardless of how we feel about it personally, must be addressed in accordance with our charter."

"Zandorth Krahl is a warrior among warriors! He is the embodiment of our charter! I will hear no more of these lies!" one warrior shouted.

"He has saved my life on numerous occasions and has fought valiantly for our realm since his inclusion amongst our ranks! I, too, shall not believe this tale of lies!" another man chimed in.

"I must say that I am not at all surprised," said the man to Hadran's left. Almost instantly, an eerie silence descended upon the great hall. None had expected such a comment... none save Hesax. He would have been more surprised if the comment had not come.

Hadran turned slightly to regard the man. "Speak your mind, Sylus." As one of Haran's lieutenants, Sylus Lorenthal's counsel was given considerably more weight than others.

"I mean no disrespect to Zandorth, but he has always been..." Lorenthal paused, Hesax was sure for dramatic effect, before continuing, "...different than other warriors."

"There are no rules against being different," Hadran replied.

Lorenthal nodded. "True, but Zandorth has always existed on the fringes of our guild, always a member but never truly involved in our movements."

"Again," Hadran said with a distinct edge of disapproval in his voice, "there are no rules against being such."

Lorenthal pursed his lips as though he hated what he was about to say. "Tis true, my Lord. However, as your chief advisor, it is my duty to point out all matters of consideration on any given situation. Zandorth is one of us, but he lingers on the peripherals of our guild and, therefore, how do we truly know the man he presents to us?"

Again, the room erupted into a loud chorus of descending, and in some cases, angry shouts at Lorenthal's subtle accusations. Hesax didn't join in the chorus of defense of Zandorth's honor, opting instead to study Lorenthal. His eyes narrowed as he watched Lorenthal study the men and saw the tiny, nearly invisible crack of a sinister smile at the corners of his lips. It was no secret that Sylus Lorenthal hated every fiber of Zandorth's being. Some great feud had begun between them seasons ago, and none seemed to know how it started, but one thing was certain: it would undoubtedly continue until their time upon this realm was over... and quite possibly into the afterlife beyond. Hesax knew this was some carefully orchestrated campaign Lorenthal was launching to either attempt to get Zandorth ostracized from the Warriors of the Ancient Class or to have him killed for disgracing the guild.

"It is no secret that you hate Zandorth!" Hesax shouted, trying to be heard above the din of the crowd. Lorenthal didn't so much as look his direction, and Hesax doubted the man could hear him over the noise.

"Silence!" Hadran shouted into the crowed, raising his booming voice, so that it would echo off the walls and pitched ceiling of the hall. Slowly, the angry roar began to subside.

"You had something you wished to say, Hesax?" Hadran asked once the noise had subsided.

Hesax leveled a heated glare at Lorenthal. "It is no secret that you despise Zandorth! How do we know these arguments you raise are nothing more than your attempt to have him discharged from our ranks?"

Lorenthal's face twisted into a look of shock and dismay, and Hesax knew there wasn't one single iota of sincerity or truth in the expression. "Brother Hesax! I am deeply troubled by your accusation!"

"I am sure!" Hesax snapped in reply with every ounce of sarcasm he could muster.

"Hesax! That is enough!" Hadran snapped fixing him with an irritated look mixed with an effective level of reproach. "Lorenthal will be given a chance to answer your accusations."

Lorenthal smiled at Hadran and bowed his head as he rose to his feet. "Thank you, Hadran." He slowly shifted his eyes out toward the assembled warriors, their steely depths paused only a fraction of a moment on Hesax, and in that fraction of a second, a deeply rooted and even more deeply disguised look of treachery passed through their depths. "It is true that Zandorth and I have never gotten on well with one another. I will even go so far as to admit that seeing him ostracized from our ranks would bring me no sorrow. However, it is not my personal feelings that drive me this day, but rather the matter of our honor. As Warriors of the Ancient Class, our honor is everything to us. It is what drives us and what unifies us against the infinite injustices that challenge our realm. Without honor, we are nothing!

"Zandorth has fought bravely and has upheld our charter well for many seasons, I will not deny that. He exists on the edges of our guild, shunning our gatherings, missing crucial meetings to discuss new threats and tactics with which to confront them. While he has been a member of the Warriors of the Ancient Class, he has never truly been one of us, at our core. How can any of us truly know the real Zandorth?"

"What is your point, Lorenthal?" one man shouted.

"My point?" Lorenthal repeated as he rose to his feet. "My point is that deceit, treachery, and evil take on many shapes in our realm. It assumes many guises in its dark quest to conquer our land and our souls! What better disguise could it assume than a warrior among warriors? What better way to weaken one of this realms' staunchest defenders than by infiltrating its ranks and destroying it from within?"

"This is madness and slanderous! I will hear no more of it!" another man shouted as he stepped away from the table and began walking toward the doors.

"Hold, Rowan!" Hadran said with a hard edge in his voice.

Rowan spun and leveled a trembling finger at Lorenthal. "Nay! I will hear no more of this brigand's lies! He hates Zandorth and is exploiting this situation to gain a victory in his feud with him!"

"You will stay, and you will listen and we, as a group, will decide what our next course of action will be!" Hadran replied in even harder tones.

Rowan's eyes narrowed in building rage as he glared at Hadran, his massive muscles bunching under the tightening knot of his rage. Hadran met his glare and did not flinch. There was no give in either man's intense stare, and Hesax wondered how long this stare down would last.

Finally, Rowan's lips pursed into a tight line as his hard gaze shifted to Lorenthal and part of his upper lip lifted into a snarl. "Very well! I will listen to his dung heap of lies, but know this Lorenthal: you have questioned the honor of a Warrior of the Ancient Class, and a friend of mine... nay... a brother of mine! If you are proven wrong, I will see to it personally that you give Zandorth the chance to reclaim his honor, and I will take great delight in watching him slaughter you!" He spun on his heel and returned to his place at the table, his glowering rage tightly focused on Lorenthal.

"Do not make empty threats, Rowan!" Lorenthal shouted in what was supposed to be a warrior's rage, but it lacked the strength of conviction.

Rowan smiled a cruel smile. "That was not a threat... it was a promise, and far from an empty one!"

"Enough of this!" Hadran barked. "Nothing is to be gained from this childish squabbling."

"I agree, Hadran. We should..." Lorenthal began but was cut off as Hadran snapped his head around to fix him with just as hard a glare as he had used with Rowan.

"I said that would be enough! I have heard all I need to hear!"

Lorenthal's eyes narrowed in anger, but he had enough sense not to snap out a reply, opting instead for, "As you command."

Hadran shifted his hard, and now, troubled gaze back out into the assembled warriors. "This is indeed a dark day. A day I had not thought I would see in my time as a warrior. One of our own stands accused of horrendous crimes... both against the realm we were sworn to protect and against us, his brethren." He paused to look up at the row of massive tapestries that lined the walls. "Our history is rich with brave and noble men who unselfishly took up the mantle of defending this realm against all who would do it harm. These men who called themselves warriors carved out the true nature of what it takes and what it means to be a Warrior of the Ancient Class. To them we owe a debt of gratitude that can never be repaid. They have shown us the way a man should live his life, they have given us a code of conduct that defines what a warrior is and what a warrior should always aspire to be. With their blood, sweat, and every last drop of their souls, they defended this realm, and then passed it on to us, to treasure it, to defend it with our dying breath if need be." His eyes left the tapestries and shifted to the men gathered before him. "Each of you have proven your worth and your honor, and each of you have proven your bravery, many times over."

"As has Zandorth!" a man shouted from the group.

Hadran nodded slowly. "Aye, as has Zandorth. Zandorth Krahl has always displayed the traits every warrior should aspire. He has fought in countless battles and has never shirked even the most tedious of tasks when it comes to defending the honor and well-being of this realm. But, as Sylus points out, he has always kept his distance from the core of us, has lingered on the fringes. It is not for me to judge what this means, but it is for me to judge what he is accused of, and like most of you, my instincts tell me that these are lies or misconceptions of true events. However, I, as your leader, do not have the luxury of allowing my instincts to be the final judgment in a matter this serious. I must address this from the position of what is best for the Warriors of the Ancient Class. More importantly, I must address this from the position of what is best for the realm... our earthly mother who it is our dying responsibility to nurture and protect." He paused and leaned forward, his fists resting on the table before him. "We must treat this situation as any other we would face. The fact that one of our own is the threat we must deal with changes nothing." His face twisted into a mixture of rage and regret. "Nothing!"

Each man in the great hall exchanged nervous glances. They knew all too well that Hadran spoke the truth in that regardless of how each of them felt on a personal level, they must act in accordance with the codes of conduct of the Warriors of the Ancient Class. Eventually, slow nods started appearing along the lengths of each table. Even Hesax had to admit that, while he didn't for a minute believe Zandorth was guilty of the crimes he was accused of, they had to treat it like any other threat.

Hadran stood upright again, squaring his shoulders, and it appeared, shoring himself up for the task at hand. With his course set, he looked down at Hesax. "Where were these criminals going?"

"They are heading north. That is all I was able to learn." Hesax answered.

"And Zandorth is with them?"

Hesax paused only a moment. Hadran had shown them the true path every warrior must follow in this situation, and he would not shirk it now, regardless of how he felt about it personally. "Yes."

"Then you, Rowan, Lorenthal, and I will set off in pursuit of them within the hour," Hadran said.

"Me?" Lorenthal nearly squeaked out in disbelief.

Hadran turned his head to fix him with an unflinching stare. "Yes you! Were you not the one who brought up the very real possibility that Zandorth could very well be guilty of these crimes?"

"Well, yes, Hadran, but I do not see where that requires me to…"

"You know the code, Sylus. You have made the accusation, so now you must prove it or give Zandorth the opportunity to reclaim his honor before the guild," Hadran shot back.

"I feel my talents would be better suited to remaining here and commanding the garrison in your absence," Lorenthal argued, wondering how his position had so suddenly thrust him into a direct confrontation with Krahl.

Hadran swept the men in the hall with his massive left arm. "Any one of these men could stand in my steed. I trust each of them with my life and my charge! You will ride with us, and we will seek out the truth for ourselves. Be ready to ride within the hour!" With that, he turned to his left and quickly strode from the room, his shoulders squared, and his step sure. There was no doubt from anyone in the room that Hadran would track Zandorth down and find the truth of this situation regardless of what it took to do so.

Hesax shifted his gaze from the door Hadran had disappeared behind to Lorenthal who looked truly angered. Hesax smiled slightly as he moved around the head table and up next to Lorenthal as the other warriors broke into smaller groups to discuss what had just transpired. Lorenthal was chewing on his thumbnail as his eyes stared straight ahead. Hesax knew that whatever he was looking at, it wasn't anything in this room. "Are you prepared?"

Lorenthal jumped as if in a start and spun to look at Hesax. "What do you mean?" he asked angrily.

"Are you prepared to face Zandorth when he reclaims his honor?" Hesax asked.

Lorenthal's eyes narrowed in anger, and it was then that a tiny sliver of cold fear touched the base of Hesax's spine. What he saw in Lorenthal's eyes was anger mixed with enough fear to make him dangerous, very much like a cornered wild animal. "You need not concern yourself with Krahl's honor. You should be more worried about surviving this quest!"

Hesax clamped down on the sliver of fear and forced a danger of his own into his return stare at Lorenthal. "Are you threatening me, Lorenthal?"

Lorenthal smiled, and there was nothing but coldness in the expression. It very much reminded Hesax of a serpent. "Not at all. Consider it…" he paused to glance out at the gathered warriors, singling his gaze on Rowan who was staring back at him with the same level of vehemence, "consider it a friendly warning." Lorenthal shot Hesax one more angry glare before stepping past him to leave the great hall.

Hesax turned to watch him go and wondered just how many of the dangers they would face in their journey to find Zandorth would come from inside the group he traveled with.

CHAPTER TWENTY-TWO

"They are being pursued. There is no doubt," the soldier said as he continued to study the ground.

Zebadiah Constance sat his mount and studied the soldier tracker. "How many?"

The soldier studied the trail. "Hard to say, sir. Twenty, perhaps more."

"How many travel with Lady Standish?" Constance asked.

"I make out six or seven."

"How far behind them are we?" Constance asked intently.

The soldier sighed heavily as he slowly looked up at Constance. "Four, possibly five days, at least."

Constance's brow furrowed as he absorbed the news with frustration. Whomever Brianna was traveling with, they were making very good time, even over the Royal Guard. There were several troubling trains of thought that vied for the captain's attention. Primarily, what had happened in Lirpa that branded the governing lord of Prothtow province a criminal? If he caught up to Brianna at the same time as the Royal Guard, he knew he would not be able to prevent her from being arrested. While he was charged with Brianna's safety, he knew enough about protocol to know that he would have no authority to keep the Royal Guard from arresting her. To further complicate matters was what he would do if he caught up to her before the Royal Guard. He was bound by the same laws as the Royal Guard, and he knew, under the strictest dictates of his office, he would have to place her under arrest and turn her over to the Royal Guard. Not even her title and standing within the Lordship would prevent her from being arrested. There was, of course, the possibility that any number of politically driven deals could be made behind the scenes that might lead to her hand in whatever crime she was charged with being conveniently forgotten. While Constance was a soldier and avoided all things political, he knew enough to know that he could not base his faith in that to be able to save her.

Beyond that, however, was what had caused her to take off as she had. He had known Brianna since she was a small child, and he knew her well, perhaps better than anyone else did. She was wild and impulsive, but she was not completely irresponsible. Despite the wild abandon that she lived her life with, there was a strong sense of duty and honor within her. She would not have abandoned her post unless the circumstances were dire indeed. He had read and re-read her final missive to him multiple times since the day she had turned up missing. He had analyzed each word, each phrase, searching for some clue that would give him an advantage over not only those who pursued her, but the terrible thing she had gone off to face. He knew nothing of the Stones of Andarus, had never even heard of the myths surrounding them. He was a soldier, a man rooted in the harsh reality of the ordinary day-to-day. He was not given to flights of fancy or the insubstantial elements that made up the fringes of the realm. He believed in only that which he could see and touch. While in Lirpa, he had spoken to a couple of scholars about the Stones of Andarus and what they had told him amounted to nothing much more than a childhood ghost story. Three rocks that held the power of creation? That could destroy the realm if that power was ever released? Ludicrous. Beyond belief. Yet Brianna had believed in the tales enough to set off in pursuit of them.

The other piece of this maddening puzzle was not a myth or a legend. Xavier and his demented Followers were well known. He had single handedly cut a swath of evil destruction across a large portion of the Northern Province before being stopped by the Mystics of Solmentoli and the Warriors of the Ancient Class. Reports said that Xavier and the bulk of his Followers had been killed in the massive Battle of Duvall many season ago. There was always the possibility that Xavier had survived the battle and had returned to re-establish his sick Order. These were things he was familiar with, the hard, the substantial, the provable, and the tangible. If Xavier was on the loose, then he must be stopped, and if Brianna was determined to stop him, then whatever threat he posed, imaginary or not, had to be put down like a rabid animal.

Regardless of the circumstances and the real or imagined attributes to this mystery, he owed it to the crown, to the province, and to the Lady Standish to investigate, gathering all the facts that he could gather, and act accordingly. He would seek out Brianna and her companions. He would listen to their story and then decide for himself which path to follow: Arrest her and her companions as criminals against the crown or forsake his office and join her. He had been a soldier long enough to realize there were times and situations that overshadowed the harsh rules and protocols of the law.

Withdrawing from his deep thought, he looked about the landscape, taking in a deep breath. "We will stop for a short time and consult our maps. I want the shortest patch found between ourselves and the Lady Standish."

As the men began dismounting and maps began being pulled from packs, Constance dismounted and walked a short distance away from the rest of them, facing due north. The harsh lines of his face cut deeper as he searched the sky. "Where are you, Brianna, and what, in the name of the Fates, have you gotten yourself into?"

~*~

Backellar Moon slipped back through the forest as silently as the breeze. He had just observed a group of men in military garb stopping to examine the trail of the Royal Guard and the criminals they pursued. Judging from the coat of arms emblazoned on their tunics and saddle blankets, they were the Honor Guard for Lady Standish of Prothtow Province. Very curious. Why would Standish's Honor Guard be this far out of their province? What were they chasing and what did it have to do with the criminals and the Royal Guard? This little adventure was taking on an entirely different light with each day that passed. He had thought, at first, that he was trailing some very talented criminals that had managed to relieve the fine citizens of Lirpa of the tremendous burden of some of their gold. Yet as he watched and listened, he was beginning to see a much grander scheme begin to take shape... and a much greater opportunity for wealth.

Moon stepped into a clearing and crossed to his recently acquired mount. It was a skittish animal, which was nothing he could not handle for the short term. However, he knew he would have to trade someone at the next opportunity for a calmer animal. As he swung himself onto the animals back, he considered what he knew and what path he should follow next. One of the criminals was someone of substantial status. Rumor was that she was a member of King Lordoran's Lordship. Highly unlikely, but worth keeping in mind, nonetheless. The members of the Lordship were lazy pigs who lavished themselves with great creature comforts at the cost of the common folk. They fed their hedonistic lifestyles with the blood, sweat, tears, and broken bones of the citizens they were supposed to lead.

He had heard rumors that Lady Standish was not like the other members of the Lordship, but he had always dismissed this as propaganda from the crown, designed to restore some sort of belief in the structure of the Lordship. If Standish was one of the criminals being sought, perhaps there was another way to increase his profits from this venture. He absently wondered what the going ransom for a member of the Lordship was these days.

Moon was acutely aware that he was venturing into something that was far more than it appeared on the surface. Such things were always dangerous, and as luck would have it, the most profitable. He decided to keep following these people, learning as much as he could about their true stories. Only then would he know which path to follow and which path would give him the highest possibility of profit.

Devenshire and his party made short work of breaking camp and loading up their mounts. Within a short span of time, they were moving out, following the harrowing trail Shantira had suggested. Each person had been told of the dangers and to be on the lookout for dangerous footing from here until they exited the mountain range.

As nightfall cast them into complete darkness, they relied on Zandorth to lead the way. Warriors of the Ancient Class were very well adapted to traveling in the deepest, darkest nights. Even with Zandorth's skills, the going at night would still be slow.

Shantira steered her mount up beside Brianna. She was troubled by her behavior during the storm. She felt the need to discuss it with Brianna and try to understand what was happening.

"How are you feeling?" Shantira asked hesitantly.

"I feel better. I am still a little weak, and my arm is sore, but I am better." Brianna answered, her voice saying just how irritated she still was with Shantira.

"I am sorry for my behavior earlier. I do not know what came over me."

Brianna turned her head to study her young friend. "I do not understand what is happening with you. Why must you always center your concern on me? I am not the only member of this group. Is there something you are not telling me? Has something happened that I am unaware of?"

"No," Shantira answered softly, unsure of how to proceed. "I cannot explain it. I just feel the ever increasing need to protect you."

Brianna studied her profile, searching for any indication of what was causing the odd behavior. All she could see was the sincere regret for her behavior and the deep confusion it was causing her. Her brow furrowed as she considered what was happening within her young friend. She had endured much in the past days. She had lost her home and family, been caught in Devenshire's mysteriously seductive aura and had been thrust into this desperate pursuit of a madman with the capabilities and resources to effectively destroy the realm. She sighed softly. "I suppose there are worse things to be guilty of than worrying over the wellbeing of a friend." She smiled warmly as Shantira looked over at her. "Maybe we should discuss this with Darkseed or Daimion. Maybe there is something mystical at work here."

Shantira was silent as she shifted her gaze forward. The suggestion was a sound one, one that made sense, and yet she felt resistant to it. Why? Why did the thought of letting them use magic to answer this annoying question trouble her so? As with everything else in her life now, there were no answers. She didn't want to arouse any more concern within Brianna so she forced a tight smile to her lips as she shifted her gaze back to her friend. "We should consider it, I think."

At that moment, Kendra steered her mount up on the other side of Brianna, a pleasant smile on her fair features. "May I join the conversation?"

"Please do," Brianna answered. She could instantly feel the tension within Shantira double. It was clear that Shantira did not like Kendra, and the source of that dislike was the man leading this quest. While a part of her wanted to spare Shantira the discomfort of being around Kendra, another part knew that Shantira had been warned of the situation surrounding Devenshire. She had been warned of his nature, and the way women were drawn to his mysterious aura. Brianna regretted the pain Shantira was feeling, but she also knew that it was past time for Shantira to accept the situation with Devenshire and find a way to combat her emotions.

"I spend most of my time with men and find their company a bit boring at times. I was hoping to join in with some female conversation," Kendra said.

"I understand. The male train of thought can be a bit single minded of purpose," Brianna replied with a warm smile. "Feel free to join us."

"My thanks."

"Where do you hail from?" Brianna asked.

"My homeland is across the great ocean to the east," Kendra replied.

"The Elven Forests?" Brianna asked.

"You have heard of it?" Kendra asked.

"My father has told me stories of it. He visited it once during the Goblin Wars," Brianna replied.

"Yes, that is where I hail from. Like most of my people, we journey to the human lands, at some point in our lives, to see for ourselves what we have heard of humans," Kendra answered.

"And what have you heard about humans?" Shantira asked shortly, trying to hide the ice in her voice, but failing.

Kendra regarded Shantira briefly, her expression telling of her growing irritation at the young woman's blatant hostility toward her. "Nothing bad. Just that you are different. That you have different ways and customs, some of which seem bizarre to us, but that does not mean they are bad, just different."

"What brings you to our area? The Great Ocean is many miles away," Brianna asked quickly, trying to intercept any short, snapped reply from Shantira.

Kendra shrugged. "Just curiosity. I have to admit that I have found life in your lands much more exciting than that of my own home. I have been contemplating remaining here."

"Really? What about our land do you find so interesting?" Brianna asked, genuinely interested. She had met several elves in her life, but had never really talked to one to any great length.

With a twisted grin, Kendra looked at Brianna. "The men. They are much more bold and brash than Elven men. There is a quality about them that I find very interesting. Take Devenshire, for example. There is something about him that I find very interesting. He is not like any other man I have met since I have been here."

Brianna was looking at Kendra, but she could feel Shantira stiffen at her mention of Devenshire. Brianna had to honestly admit that a deeply hidden part of herself did not like the sudden interest the Elven woman was showing in him.

"You will not find any other man like Daimion," Brianna answered. While she could admit not liking Kendra's interest in Devenshire, she was well enough in control of her emotions that it was of little consequence. She knew that all the anger and jealousy in the realm would not stop what would come to pass between them.

"There is a dark mystery surrounding him. The way he moves, the way he speaks. It definitely stirs the imagination," Kendra commented, her eyes having drifted forward to find the object of her conversation. "I am truly surprised no woman has claimed him yet."

Brianna smiled. "No woman will claim Daimion. He is not one to be claimed."

"How so?" Kendra asked, shifting her puzzled expression back to Brianna.

Brianna shook her head. "He does not give his heart. He does not fall in love."

Kendra regarded Brianna with a slight smile. "Forgive my prying, but do you speak of this from experience or hear say?"

Brianna returned her smile. "A combination of both."

"So you have had him?" she asked eagerly.

Brianna and Shantira both were taken aback by the directness of her question. Their eyes widened with shock at the bluntness with which she had asked. Kendra looked at both of them, and her expression shifted as she realized that she had stepped over some line that she was unaware existed. "Forgive my forwardness. I sometimes forget that ladies in this realm do not ask such questions. I fear that I forget my place at times. You do not have to answer such a crude question." She looked quite embarrassed.

Brianna found herself smiling. While such a question was completely within the realm of something she, herself, might ask, it had stunned her to hear such a brash question from another woman. "No apology is necessary. Not with us, at any rate. But with other so-called 'ladies' of our region, you would do well to use a bit more tact in asking such a question."

"I fear my forwardness has gotten me into trouble on more than one occasion. I fear my heart is still a bit wild, and I have yet to gain the discipline I have been told that women here have over their hearts and emotions. Plus, as I have said, I have been in the company of men for a long time."

"That does seem to be a question worthy of most men." Brianna giggled. "They do tend to think of little else."

Kendra laughed softly. "Yes. It does seem to dominate their minds."

Silence reined for a moment before Kendra cast a sideways glance at Brianna. "So you are involved with Devenshire?"

Brianna smiled warmly. "I hold no ties over him, and he holds none over me. We have a unique relationship that could best be described as close friends."

Kendra nodded, catching the meaning Brianna did not speak aloud. "Very close friends, I would venture to say."

Brianna's eyes sparkled with hidden humor. "Yes. Very close at times."

Both women began to laugh. Their laughter irritated Shantira, and she found herself waging a losing battle with her anger. The way they were speaking of Daimion angered her. It was as if they were sharing a hidden joke at her expense. Even her knowing that this was not the case would do nothing to ease her anger at not only Kendra, but Brianna, as well.

Finally, she could bear the grating sound of their laughter no more. "You two are speaking of Daimion as two drunken men would a bar wench!" she snapped.

Brianna turned her head to look at Shantira. "Why not? Have you not seen your share of drunken men talking about a woman in such a way?"

"You are not drunken men, and Daimion is not a bar wench!" she replied shortly.

"Unlike the men you speak of, though, we mean no disrespect to Devenshire. He is simply a very attractive and interesting man, and we are merely admiring his attributes. There is no harm in that, is there?" Kendra asked.

Shantira felt her anger mounting, and she continued to struggle with it. She knew she had no right to be upset and could even agree with Kendra in that there was no harm in discussing Daimion in such a way, but to hear them carry on about him seemed to rake her nerves and stir a jealousy she knew she had no right to feel. She could find no answer to Kendra's question, so she remained silent.

Kendra looked from Shantira to Brianna, question in her eyes. Brianna shook her head slightly and smiled tightly, letting Kendra know that this was not the time to discuss Devenshire any further. Kendra's eyes took on a mischievous glint as she turned them back to Shantira, and Brianna felt herself tense up, knowing that the Elven woman was about to stir the flames of Shantira's anger a little more.

"I have enjoyed our talk, M'Lady Brianna. Perhaps we can continue it later. If you will excuse me, I think I will journey ahead and speak with Devenshire for a while." With that, she nudged her horse on ahead.

Brianna fought the smile that begged for release as she looked at Shantira from the corner of her eyes. She could see her bristle under Kendra's parting statement. Part of her wished Kendra had not taunted Shantira in such a way, while another part knew that this was what Shantira needed—a harsh taste of the reality of the situation. While she may have strong feelings for Devenshire, she had to realize that she had no claim to him, and that his ability to attract female attention was something she had better get used to, and the sooner the better.

"Tramp!" Shantira hissed at Kendra's back.

"That is a harsh thing to say about someone you barely know," Brianna observed.

"She has no right to carry on such about Daimion," Shantira replied while her eyes continued to throw daggers at Kendra's back.

"Then am I to assume that I am a tramp, as well? I was carrying on such about Daimion, too." Brianna asked, a definite chill entering her words.

"You are different. You are involved with Daimion," Shantira replied.

"No, I am not! I have no more claim to him than Kendra does," Brianna paused only a moment before adding, "or than you do."

Shantira's eyes fell, and her shoulders slumped slightly as Brianna's words reminded her of something that she already knew, but did not wish to face. The harsh truth was laid out before her, and she knew she was failing at accepting it.

"Listen to me, Shantira. I see what is happening within you. You are taken with Daimion, and I can understand that, but I warned you that night in the tavern not to fall in love with him or expect him to do the same. I warned you of the perils of that path. If you are going to become confrontational with every woman who shows interest in him, then you will be fighting countless battles in which you have no ground to stand upon to claim victory. I am not trying to be harsh, just realistic, and I am hoping to help you understand the true nature of the situation."

"I know. I do, but I cannot help it. I cannot get him out of my mind. I have tried and tried but I cannot fight the feelings he stirs within me," she replied despondently, and Brianna felt sympathy swell inside her for the younger woman's turmoil.

"Then perhaps distance is what you need. Separate yourself from Daimion, and give yourself room and time to put your feelings into the only perspective that will spare your heart."

"Like yours?" Shantira asked looking up at Brianna, tears forming in the corners of her eyes.

Brianna nodded slowly. "Yes, like mine. I have to constantly remind myself what lies ahead for me if I allow my feelings to run away with me. It is not easy, this I know, but it is necessary.

"How? How do you do it? How can you make love to him and not be in love with him? How do you separate your heart from your body like you do?" Shantira's tone was filled with the desperate need to find an answer, the near panicked desire to find some ease to the torment within her.

For a moment, Brianna's expression became distant as if her mind had suddenly gone to a deep place in her memory. When she finally spoke, both her voice and her expression were darker, guarded almost. "I can do it because I know from experience what kind of pain will come of our relationship if I do not. Trust me on this, Shantira. That kind of pain will make the pain you have now seem like nothing. It is a pain that I pray you never have to experience and it is one that you should avoid... at all costs."

"But in doing so, you cheat yourself out of the beauty of being in love. Of finding a mate and creating something with someone that only two people in love can create," Shantira argued.

Brianna considered this for a moment then shook her head. "No. I do not feel as if I am cheating myself. I have become independent, far too independent for most men's taste. They pursue me at first, play for my attentions, and yearn for me. But once they discover that I am not one to be mastered, that I am not one who needs a man in my life for any sense of completion, they quickly lose interest. Those who do not lose interest are eventually scared or irritated away by my own headstrong ways. Most men are looking for a woman to yield to them, to become their mates, bear and raise their children, maintain their dwelling for them, and be at their *beck and call*. I am not such a woman. I love my life as it is, and would not trade it for any other. I fear falling into the traditional roles of a woman of our time would cheat me out of the life I have, the life I have spent a very long time building."

"But what of love? What of having that one special someone in your heart?" Shantira almost begged. She tried to avoid the memories of the night she had joined Devenshire on watch, and the way they had talked, the way he had looked at her, and the feelings that she was all but certain had flared within him. There had been something between them that night, and it had almost become... what? What would have happened if she had spoken what her heart screamed at her to speak and her mind yelled at her not to? She had returned to her blankets, but she had not slept. Images of Devenshire, and what might have been between them, drove away any possibility of sleep.

"What of it? I have love in my life. I have very fond memories of special men I have known, and I cherish each of their memories dearly. Shantira, just because I do not love in the traditional sense of the word does not mean that I do not love at all. In some very special and very different way, I love Daimion. But it is a tightly controlled, carefully hidden type of love that will not hurt me in the course of time to come. The way I love Daimion is known only to me, and I revel in the secrecy of it. It is something private to me and to me alone. It is something that I can enjoy without having the additional burden of having others know and react to, when no reaction is necessary. Do not think me wrong simply because I am different."

"I am trying to understand. I truly am," Shantira replied softly, sadly.

Brianna smiled. "Do not worry. There are times I do not understand it myself. It is merely something within me that has caused me to become the way I am. It is the way that allows me to live my life to the fullest with minimal risk of being hurt. I am not saying my way is the right way... it is simply the right way for me."

"I do not know if I can be as you are," Shantira said softly.

Brianna's brow furrowed in sympathy. "Oh, Shantira, do not try to be as I am. Be as Shantira is. You must find your own path through the perils of life. It will not be an easy path to find. It will be found through trial and error, and there will be much pain and suffering in the search for it. Once found, however, it is the most fulfilling, most enriching thing in all of creation."

Shantira sighed heavily. "It does not sound very easy at all."

Brianna smiled softly. "I did not say it would be easy. It will, however, be worth it. Once you find it, you will find a way of living that best suits you and no one else. In an odd way, it is the quest for the path that helps mold the path itself."

Shantira looked at Brianna askance. "Now you are speaking in riddles."

Brianna laughed softly, placing a hand on Shantira's shoulder. "Perhaps. But is not life one of the largest riddles of all?"

Shantira considered her words for several moments before she sighed in exasperation, finding truth in her words, but nothing that eased her turmoil.

"I hate riddles."

CHAPTER TWENTY

THREE

Captain Armand felt his jaw go slack as they rode into the clearing. The destruction was incredible. Massive trees had been uprooted or simply laid down as though a giant hand had pushed them over. The ground was a soupy mess of churned mud. The entire clearing was littered with debris from what could have only been a massive storm. "What in the Fates?" he asked softly.

Lordalise pulled up rein next to him and took in the devastation. "A terrible storm must have passed through here, perhaps even a Wind Demon."

"Impossible!" Armand countered as he continued to study the clearing. "'Tis not the time of the season for such storms."

"And yet here is the proof," Lordalise replied sweeping his left arm across their view of the clearing.

Armand had to admit to the harsh facts despite the impossibility of such a storm at this time of the season. He turned in his saddle to address the tracker. "You are certain they came this way?"

The tracker nodded. "No doubt, sir. Their trail leads directly into this clearing."

Armand nodded as he returned to face front, taking in the debris field again. "Perhaps they were caught in the storm," he theorized aloud.

"Perhaps," Lordalise agreed. "It would not have affected Devenshire, but his minions are human, and one or more of them may have been caught in the storm and killed or injured. If they are injured, and Devenshire did not have them killed, they could be nearby. A most fortuitous find should we be able to find them."

Armand understood what Lordalise was saying and nodded once. "I want search teams to break away and begin looking for survivors or bodies," Armand ordered. "Tracker, I realize picking up any trail in this muck will be difficult, but if they survived, I want to know which direction they went."

"Aye, sir," the tracker said as he dismounted and began walking into the clearing.

"Master Lordalise, I would like for you and your men to search the surrounding area for any sign of survivors or new victims of Devenshire's," Armand said.

"Of course, Captain," Lordalise said as he looked up into the sky. "I must point out that it will be dark soon, and it would be unwise to have our numbers scattered across the area."

Armand looked at the fading light of the day and nodded. "Of course," he turned to his men. "Begin your search but return here before night fall."

The soldiers acknowledged the order and began breaking up into smaller groups to better facilitate the search. Lordalise gathered his men around him and gave a short series of instructions before they began to move out. Just as they were entering the tree line, Lordalise looked back over his shoulder into the clearing. The tracker was hard at work trying to sort through the muck and locate a trail. He shifted his gaze to Armand just in time to see him walking toward the darker shadows at the opposite side of the clearing alone. His brow furrowed as he considered what Armand was doing. His behavior had been odd since they had located Devenshire's first camp outside Lirpa. What was happening with him? Why would he frequently make treks into the woods alone? Something was amiss with the good captain, and he intended to find out what. While it was highly unlikely that Devenshire had converted him to one of his minions, he had to keep the possibility open for nothing was impossible when it came to the dealings of a vampire.

Bonzwa moved up beside Lordalise and joined him in watching Armand walk into the woods. "What troubles you, sir?"

Lordalise continued to watch the tree line even after Armand had disappeared from view. "The good captain is behaving oddly. He has a secret that he is not sharing with the rest of us."

"Such things speak of dishonesty, of deceit," Bonzwa replied, also watching the tree line. This was the first break he had seen in the link between Lordalise and Armand. Up until recently, they had formed a bond that seemed unbreakable and now that a chink appeared in that link, he began to hope that perhaps it could be severed, and he would have his leader back. Not Lordalise the Vampire Hunter, but Lordal, the Bandit King.

Lordalise chuckled at first, and then laughed. "Only a bandit would make such an observation."

Bonzwa allowed a tight smile to form across his lips. "It is what I am best at."

Lordalise nodded. "Indeed. Then I take it that you are as disquieted by Armand's actions?"

Bonzwa considered the question carefully. He knew that if he moved too quickly to sever the bond between them that it would fail. He knew he would have to work carefully, subtly opening the crack between them a little at a time. "As you pointed out, sir. I am a bandit. I know the deceitful things a dishonest man thinks. I make no harsh judgments about Captain Armand, but I do recognize the behaviors of a man who is hiding something."

Lordalise nodded. Bonzwa knew such thoughts had already occurred to his leader, but he hoped hearing them voiced aloud would sink them more firmly into his mind. "Indeed. I would very much like to know what tasty little secret the good captain is hiding from us. Keep a close eye on him as well as the rest of the Royal Guard. I doubt our true identities have been discovered. However, only a fool does not plan for every possible outcome. If they begin to show signs of moving against us, we will need to move quickly. Spread the word to the others, but show now outward sign of suspicion. We need their numbers to help track down Devenshire and destroy him, but I will not allow them to capture us."

A tiny sliver of relief crept into Bonzwa's mind at his words. Finally, the man was once again showing signs of being the bandit king. It disappointed him that Lordal was still intent on his hunt of Devenshire, but the fact that he was beginning to consider separating them from the Royal Guard was promising. He would, indeed, do as Lordal instructed, with pleasure.

~*~

Xavier sat in a plush chair within his tent, a goblet of wine in one hand, his other hand absently stroking his forehead. His eyes were locked intently on the Stones of Andarus. Even as drained as he was, he could still feel the power of the Stones. It reached out to him, begged him to come closer and lose himself in the depths of their unimaginable power. He still cursed himself for expending so much energy on the attempt to kill Devenshire and his band of misfits. He should have been conserving his power, saving it for the task of tapping into the Stones. Now, drained as he was, he could perform only the simplest workings of the Arts. He did not even have the power to immerse himself in the Mystical Tides to see what had become of Devenshire nor could he see what had become of Cyrus the wizard. He had been tasked with killing Devenshire, and yet he had heard nothing from the wizard.

Taking a drink from the goblet, his eyes never left the Stones. While he could not tackle the problem with his powers, he still had his mind, and he would continue to work through the problem of accessing their power without being reduced to a pile of ash.

"You are a fool!" a harsh voice echoed out of the shadows. Xavier simply blinked as he continued to study the Stones. He had been expecting this visit virtually from the moment he had been cast out of the storm by the backlash of power.

"Such is your view, Baldar. You will understand if I do not share it," he replied with boredom.

The Dark Mystic stepped from the shadows of the tent and moved up to stand on the opposite side of the table holding the Stones from Xavier. "You have exhausted your powers and put our prize further out of our reach!" The reddish glow of his eyes boring into Xavier from deep within the hood of his cloak.

Xavier's gaze never left the Stones as he replied with an apparent lack of interest in the conversation. "A minor setback, at worst. My powers are regenerating, and I will be back at full strength within days."

"You wasted precious time and energy on Devenshire, and now your plans are ruined!" The Dark Mystic hissed in mounting anger. His growing rage radiated from him in invisible waves.

Xavier finally shifted his gaze from the Stones to the glowing eyes of the Dark Mystic. "My plans are not ruined. I am still in control of the situation and I will break the secrets of the Stones," he shrugged. "The only thing that has changed is the time table."

"We will brook no further delays! We have waited an eternity for this power!" Baldar hissed, his gray fists trembling at his side. He knew that in his weakened state that he would have to proceed carefully, for he was, at this moment, no match for the Mystic.

Xavier nodded slowly. "Indeed. You have waited an eternity. Will a few extra days make that much difference?" Xavier rose from his seat and moved to the table holding the Stones, his free hand resting lightly on its edge. "At any rate, my powers are useless to me at this juncture."

Baldar's head cocked to one side. "What do you mean?"

Xavier chuckled before taking a sip from the goblet, his hard eyes never leaving the Dark Mystic. "I must first learn the nature of the mystic barrier surrounding the Stones. Any mystical energy directed at the Stones will activate the barrier and doom the caster to certain death. The solution to the problem of the barrier will have to be found without the use of mystic energies. In fact, my powers being drained may be a carefully hidden blessing. While they are drained, I cannot inadvertently activate the protective barrier. So you see? You have churned yourself into a frenzy for nothing," Xavier concluded with a dark smile.

Baldar was silent for several moments as he contemplated Xavier's argument. Finally, his glowing gaze dropped to the Stones, and he tactfully changed the subject. "What of Devenshire? You failed to destroy him yet again. He still lives and still poses the greatest threat to our plans. He also serves as a distraction for you. How do I know you will not strike at him again once your powers return?" Baldar formed the question into a demand as a way to negate the fact that Xavier had completely defeated his argument about his powers being drained.

Xavier's dark smile deepened as he ran a finger lightly along the edge of the box holding the Stones. "I have dispatched a wizard to kill Devenshire and his companions. I will not strike out at him again, unless I have no other choice."

Baldar nodded slowly, his eyes lifting slowly to Xavier. "Yes. I know. You dispatched him days ago, and yet Devenshire still lives. What has become of your magical assassin?"

Xavier felt the rage ripple through him with amazing speed as his eyes snapped up to glare at Baldar. "You dare spy on me?"

The spark of anger in Xavier seemed to calm Baldar as an eerie dark chuckle echoed from the black depths of the hood. "Yes, we do."

"How dare you!" Xavier hissed.

The mounting rage within Xavier seemed lost on the Dark Mystic as he extended his right arm. From the sleeve of the robe came a gray-scaled hand with long fingernails that almost looked like talons. With deliberate slowness Baldar drug the nail of the index finger along the top edge of the box's opened lid, mimicking Xavier's action from a moment before. The red eyes remained locked with Xavier's heated gaze. "With this much at stake, we will do whatever we deem necessary to ensure the success of our plans. Much time and effort has gone into this endeavor, and we will not have it squandered away by your petty human weaknesses."

Xavier's eyes narrowed dangerously. "I will not tolerate such deceit!"

Baldar chuckled. It was a dark and ominous sound. "You have no choice! What will you do? Strike out at me? Your powers are depleted." It was very clear in his bearing and manner that the Dark Mystic was taking great joy in the exchange.

"My powers are not the only weapon at my disposal, mystic!" Xavier replied in a cold, deadly tone.

"What other weapons? Your swords and daggers? Do you honestly think your mortal weapons will have any effect on me?"

The calmness that descended over Xavier was quick and extraordinarily eerie. He slowly set the goblet down next to the Stones as his left hand dropped into the pocket of his robe. His right hand rose to gently rest on the edge of the box while his heated gaze rose to lock with the shimmering red glow of Baldar's. "No. Swords and daggers would do no harm to you."

With a dark smile, he looked down at the Stones as he casually traced a pattern on the center stone with his fingertip. "There is something very invigorating about the Stones. Even when no magic is used, you can feel their awesome power. It is a very deep hum that strums into your body." He looked up at Baldar. "Can you feel it?" Baldar's eyes narrowed as he stared at Xavier, his expression still haughty, but tinged with a touch of concern.

Lacking an answer from the Dark Mystic, Xavier continued. "No? A shame. There is nothing like feeling the presence of unbridled power, to know that such power exists, and that it is well within your grasp."

Baldar glanced down at the Stones and Xavier's finger lazily moving across the surface of them. "You are now going to threaten to cease your work on them?" he asked, his voice more calm, the anger not quite as evident.

Xavier chuckled as he slowly shook his head and looked back down at the Stones. "Oh, no. I would never threaten that. I want this power as badly as you do, if not more so. I will never stop working on a way to tap into their power."

"Then what are you speaking of? What is this great weapon you have to use against me?"

In a flash of movement, Xavier suddenly reached across the table and grabbed the Dark Mystic by the back of the neck and jerked him across the table. The table tilted, and the lid of the box holding the Stone's slammed shut. The goblet of wine spun and then crashed to the dirt floor of the tent. Before Baldar could understand what had happened, Xavier's left hand reappeared from the pocket of his robe holding an amulet. With a vicious snarl, he shoved the amulet very close to Baldar's face as the Dark Mystic suddenly hissed with a sound that would make the most dangerous snake recoil in fear.

"You dare lay hands upon me?" he hissed. "I will take great pleasure in…" His voice trailed off as he realized that the amulet was glowing in a sickly yellow light.

"You recognize this?" Xavier asked with a dangerous low tone. "It is the Amulet of Sansuri. Proximity to it for any length of time is certain death for a Dark Mystic. Do you not feel your very life ebbing from you as each grain slips past the center of the hourglass?"

Baldar struggled to free himself from Xavier's grip, but the amulet was already draining him. "You dare? Do you know what you risk?" His voice was becoming rough and horse.

Xavier chuckled, and the sound was very dark and ominous as he tightened his grip on Baldar's neck, giving it a hard shake. "Do you?"

"Stop this at once! Do you think even this amulet will protect you from all of us?" Baldar fought against the panic rushing through him. The amulet was not only draining his mystical abilities but his life force, as well.

"No," Xavier answered feeling the Dark Mystic's power and physical strength fading rapidly. "Just you. Your fellow Dark Mystics seem content to allow me to work in peace, and within my own time. You are the only one who ever appears to annoy me."

"My death will be avenged by the full fury of all the Dark

Mystics!" Baldar's voice rasped. His mind frantically searched for some method of escape, but the amulet had already taxed his powers to the point that he could not even call out to the other Dark Mystics for help. With sickening clarity, he realized he was completely at Xavier's mercy.

Xavier laughed as he pulled the amulet back a little bit. "Death? Come now, Baldar, who said anything about killing you? I simply wished to demonstrate that I am not completely helpless, even without my powers."

"Remove that cursed thing from me!" Baldar hissed. How had he not sensed the presence of the amulet? The crystal that made up its construction was deadly to Dark Mystics and prolonged exposure would prove fatal as it was their mystical abilities that made it possible for a Dark Mystic to exist within the realm of the humans.

Xavier bent over, pulling the amulet further away from Baldar and bringing his lips close to the Dark Mystic's hooded head. "Know this: I will brook no further interference from you! I will continue my work on the Stones, and I will be successful, and then we will all have that which we seek! If you threaten me again, I promise you that I have other means at my disposal that will make you beg for exposure to the Amulet of Sansuri. Did you honestly think I would willingly enter into a pact with the Dark Mystics without means to protect myself?"

Xavier allowed several more moments to pass before he released Baldar and stepped back, slipping the amulet back into his robe pocket. Baldar slowly stood upright and took several steps back, reaching up to absently rub the back of his neck. His eyes glowed with the concentration of his fury and bore into Xavier with an intensity that made him wonder if he would be forced to use those other means at his disposal. "You have gone too far, human!" Baldar hissed.

Xavier shook his head, the confident air of victory hanging about him as an aura. "I believe I have gone just far enough to prove my point. I would say we have reached a stalemate."

Baldar continued to glare at Xavier for several moments as he was forced to admit to the absolute truth in his words. "You have made an enemy this day!"

"As if we were friends before?" Xavier laughed a few more moments before bringing his dark mirth under control and fixing Baldar with a hard look and a slow nod, accepting the absolute truth of what Baldar said. "It is something I am accustomed to."

Baldar forced himself to relax in the trembling aftermath of exposure to the amulet. It was very unsettling to have been suddenly thrust from his position of superiority to one of subjugation. The anger within him for Xavier began laying down the foundation for a deep-rooted hatred that would continue to build long after this confrontation had passed. Taking another step back, Baldar reached up and jerked on the edges of his robe, settling it back in place around him. With disdain, he cleared his throat and set about the purpose of his visit. "I have come to tell you to make arrangements."

Xavier's brow furrowed. "Arrangements? For what?"

"We have decided to use our powers to transport you back to your retreat. This will better expedite your study of the Stones. On the trail, there are too many distractions, too many opportunities for something to happen to you." Baldar replied, still trying to compose himself.

Xavier looked down at the Stones and considered Baldar's offer. Being back in his retreat, behind the safety of the walls and his Followers, would definitely expedite his study of the Stones. While he didn't like being told what to do by the Dark Mystics, in general and Baldar specifically, he could find no reason not to accept their offer. He had considered how he could return to his retreat sooner and had not found a way that would not require an incredible expenditure of power. He lifted his guarded gaze back up to Baldar. "What of my men?"

Baldar shrugged. "They are of no concern to us. We will not expend the power to transport all of you back, just you. Send them in an en masse attack against Devenshire. Perhaps one of them will strike a lucky blow and remove him as an obstacle to our plans."

Xavier nodded slowly. He knew the Dark Mystic wouldn't care about his men, but he had to admire the idea of sending them all against Devenshire. As much as it galled him, he had to admit that Baldar was also right in thinking that maybe, just maybe, one of them would strike the blow that would end Devenshire's annoying existence. "When would this plan take place?"

"Now." Baldar answered.

Xavier considered the plan for a few more moments before nodding. "I will send my men against Devenshire. Give me time to lay out my plan to them, and I will be ready."

"Make it soon. You must still take time to recover your powers and whatever other arrangements you have to make to tap into the Stones. Time is not on our side. The optimal time for the attempt is fast approaching. If we miss it, we will have to wait another three seasons before we can make another attempt."

Xavier nodded with boredom. "I am aware of the Queleck's Equinox. I will be ready long before it occurs."

Baldar took a step toward Xavier and leveled a very dangerous glare into his eyes. "See that you are. Failure will not have a pleasant outcome for you."

Xavier grinned as he slipped his left hand back into his robe pocket and wrapped around the amulet. "Are you threatening me again, Baldar?"

Instead of uncomfortable fear, Xavier saw that Baldar's sinister grin matched his. There was no fear and no concern, and that troubled Xavier a little. "Not at all." The grin faded, replaced with harsh and hellish venom. "I am promising you!"

CHAPTER TWENTY-

FOUR

Lordalise paced about the camp like a caged animal, bristling at being restrained. This was madness, pure, raw madness, he reflected as he watched the scene before him. Nearby, lounging about a large campfire, the body of the compliment of Royal Guards, including Captain Armand, sat laughing and talking following their large meal of mountain hare and wild vegetables. A bottle of whiskey had suddenly been produced and was now being passed around. Each time the bottle made the circle, the laughter became louder as the festive mood increased.

The rest of the Royal Guards either had turned in for the evening or were milling about the camp. Nearby, his men sat huddled around a smaller fire, looking very uncomfortable. They were, after all, bandits and had no desire to be too close to the Royal Guards. Indeed, many of them were now closer in proximity to a Royal Guardsman than they had ever been before. Their talk was more subdued, their laughter more hushed, as if trying to maintain their front without drawing too much attention to themselves. Even the sight of his own men engaged in idleness angered him even more.

Lordalise could almost feel the moon sear a path across the sky, and with each tiny amount of distance it traveled, he could feel Devenshire slipping his grasp. The ghoul was gaining ground and would continue to do so. Whatever distance they made up during the day was soon lost by Armand stopping and camping each night. The captain seemed to have lost his sense of urgency in the pursuit of Devenshire, and that, above all else, irritated the vampire hunter even more.

"You do not seem to be in as festive a mood as the rest of us, Master Lordalise." Armand's deep, rich voice sounded, breaking him out of his angry pace.

"I see little to be festive about," Lordalise snapped back over his shoulder, not even bothering to turn and face them.

"We have survived the trek thus far. We will soon be joined by another detachment of men from my garrison. I have also summoned a brigade of Warrior's of the Ancient Class, and Devenshire is gradually falling further and further into our grasp. I see plenty of reasons to be festive," Armand replied with the thick slur of alcohol upon his words. While Armand was not drunk, he was clearly not the picture of sobriety either.

"Is that how you see things, Captain?" Lordalise growled as he turned to face the captain as he stood from his upended log.

There was only the briefest of pauses before the answer came. "Yes. That is how I see things," Armand answered with only a tiny lightening of his festive mood. "You see them differently?"

Lordalise clenched his fists in an effort to ward off the fresh wave of fury that was building within him. "Yes, I see them quite differently," Lordal replied in snipped tones. He paused to study Armand intently, searching for the answer to the mystery of his sudden lackadaisical approach to their pursuit. Surely, the deaths in Lirpa had not already drifted from Armand's mind, especially the death of his friend, Constable Liston, and the pain it had caused. He could not fathom that the torture of Liston's death had already eased from his soul. His frantic, ravenous, and burning desire to apprehend Devenshire seemed to have calmed. His air was more relaxed now as though he already had the demon.

"Perhaps you would enlighten me as to what perception of things I am not seeing." Armand replied smoothly.

Lordalise turned slowly to regard the captain. "Is that really necessary, Captain? I am sure you know all too well of what I speak."

Armand was poised, relaxed, that annoying good-natured smile plastered across his face. "Humor me."

"Very well. Devenshire is not falling into our grip but rather is making good his escape! We travel by day while he sleeps in death. Then we rest by night, while Devenshire's powers are at their peak, and he can cover far greater distances than we can. Whatever minimal gains we make during our daylight travel are lost, and the loss is added to each time we let the night pass us while we sit idle."

Armand smiled and shook his head slightly. "Rest easy, Master Lordalise. Things are not as they appear. Fear not, I have not lost my thirst for vengeance. Devenshire will pay and pay dearly for his crimes. I will not dally with rights for the accused or trouble a tribunal with having to decide his guilt or innocence. Devenshire will not escape us. These final nights he roams upon this realm are nothing more than a final sample of what will soon be lost to him after we send him back to the fires of hell."

Lordalise studied Armand closely for several moments. Where had this sudden assuredness come from? What tiny piece of information did the Captain have that made him so sure in his grip upon Devenshire and those who traveled with him?

"You are assuming that Devenshire has not already eluded us,"

Lordalise replied cautiously, testing the unknown waters of this new element of Armand.

"He may very well have eluded us, for the moment. But I feel certain that, within a matter of days, he will be ours," Armand replied with a controlled smile. Yet in his smile, Lordalise saw a flicker of something, some secret knowledge that only Armand was privy to, and his earlier suspicions were secured into absolute fact.

Lordalise's eyes narrowed, and he tilted his head to one side, studying the captain even closer. "If I may ask, what makes you so sure?"

Armand smiled broadly, his hands rising slowly from his sides slightly. "Let us just call it... a feeling."

Lordalise's eyes narrowed suspiciously. A feeling? No. There was much more to it than that... much, much more. Despite the apparent like of eagerness for the pursuit of Devenshire, Lordalise sensed something within Armand that made his hopes spike.

"A feeling? You are risking the blight of Devenshire's continued being on this realm upon nothing more than a feeling?" Lordalise asked cautiously.

Armand smiled, and he extended his right hand, which held the whiskey bottle by the neck. "Join us for a drink, Master Lordalise."

Lordalise stood rock still, his narrowed eyes studying Armand intently. The intensity of his stare caused Armand to chuckle as he stepped forward to place his left arm around the Hunter's shoulders. His right arm rose to offer the bottle, which Lordalise absently took, still studying him closely.

"Come, Master Lordalise. Let us take a walk and allow me to tell you about my feeling. I think you will find it most enjoyable."

Lordalise took a sip from the bottle and allowed Armand to steer him off into the darkness, away from both campfires.

Bonzwa watched the brief exchange between Lordal and Armand with growing unease. It was already too much to be so close to a full complement of Royal Guards, much less to actually be riding with them. Now his leader was becoming quite friendly with the captain.

Lordal, or Lordalise as he was becoming more often referred to, was establishing a report with the leader of the guards that sent alarms ringing out in his mind. Bonzwa already feared for his leader's sanity, now he found himself questioning Lordal's allegiance. What if, in the course of his ruse as a Hunter, Lordal found the qualities he had known before becoming a bandit? What if all these noble deeds reawakened the memories of what it was like to have once been a law-abiding citizen of the realm? What if the promise of the massive reward posted for each of their captures suddenly gave Lordal a means by which to reclaim the life he had lost? Bonzwa could easily envision a time when, if all these things came to pass, Lordal would easily hand the entire lot of them over to the Royal Guard.

A flask of whiskey was passed to him, and he drank deeply of it, his eyes never leaving the two figures who now spoke just far enough away for their words to be unheard. He absently passed the flask along as he continued to consider what was happening before his very eyes.

Putting Lordal's allegiance aside, Bonzwa contemplated another possible scenario coming to pass. What was to say that Armand had not already discerned whom and what Lordal and his men really were? Such a thing would not be beyond the realm of possibility. Rumors of Captain Armand were widely known, especially among the ranks of bandits who operated near Lirpa. He was shrewd and merciless in his pursuit of criminals. It was said that Armand had the ability to think as a bandit, to predict how a bandit would act and react. Such ability, in the hands of a Royal Guardsman, could be disastrous to the continued freedom of many bandits in the area.

Perhaps Armand had already learned whom and what they were, and he was merely biding his time, using Lordal's knowledge of vampires and weapons to combat them with to pursue and destroy Devenshire. Once the vampire was destroyed and its companion's dead, what was to say that Armand would not immediately have them all taken into custody to be taken back to Lirpa to stand before the tribunal?

Bonzwa shook his head slowly as Armand and *Lordalise* walked slowly into the darkness. Just as he had vowed to continue living in spite of the pursuit of Devenshire, he also vowed to remain free. The time for his departure from the ranks of his fellow bandits was drawing near.

~*~

Nightfall found them making camp again. The days of travel through the treacherous terrain had left them, once again, eager for the chance to get off their horses and stretch their legs and relax their nerves. As the nights before, Zandorth tethered the horses while Darkseed scrounged for the makings of a small fire, and Devenshire set off to hunt for a source of food. This night, Stant and Petera joined him, taking their bows. Elves were renowned for their seemingly natural skill with a bow, and Devenshire had welcomed them in the hunt.

Brianna, Shantira, and Kendra set to the task of looking through the surrounding brush for berries and herbs that could be added to their limited rations of food. The day's travel had carried them higher into the mountain range, and in this area, food would be plentiful. They knew, however, that once they left the mountain range, they would be getting into a wasteland that bordered the Coledecci and food would become scarce. As scarce as food would become in the days ahead, fresh water would be even harder to find. Zandorth remembered a place not too many miles out of their way where a stream flowed through the denser range of the mountains.

Devenshire, Stant, and Petera returned to the camp a short time later carrying four large mountain hares. These were even larger than the ones taken previously, and since none of them had eaten since the night before, little time was wasted in preparing them and spitting them over the fire.

The women had found a literal horde of berries and plants that shored up their stores and provided enough to go along with the evening meal. Since a source of water was close, no objections were presented when Shantira offered to make a soup out of one of the plants she had discovered. While the hares roasted, and Shantira's soup simmered, the weary travelers sat around the fire and discussed the journey ahead.

"Just how dangerous is this Coledecci?" Stant asked popping one of the berries into his mouth.

"All I know of it is what the rumors speak of," Devenshire answered as he chewed on the root of another plant the women had found. "Rumors speak of a rogue Dark Mystic who has turned the Coledecci forest into his domain. Legends speak of hideous creatures who roam the forest in search of specimens for his experiments."

"What type of experiments?" Petera asked with a definite edge of trepidation in his voice.

Devenshire shrugged. "Again, all I know are the legends. It is said that he takes great joy in experimenting on humans, finding new and more hideous ways to strip their minds and souls from them to feed some never-ending hunger for destruction and fear. It is said that his dark magic has conjured all manner of creatures to aid him in his quest for more specimens and that none who have ever entered the Coledecci have ever emerged again... at least not in the form that they had entered. They say he delights in mutilating his specimens and seeing how long he can keep them alive. It is also said that he feeds on fear much like a vampire feeds on blood."

Silence reined in the small camp after Devenshire finished speaking. Even the fire seemed to have subdued itself to keep from being too loud. Each person glanced around the group before fixing their gazes to the fire, trying to ignore the distinct chill that fell across them.

Kendra felt the ripple of fear dance up her spine and she shuddered. She looked up at Devenshire and saw a distinct lack of fear about him. He continued to rest his elbows on his knees and gaze into the fire. "You speak as though you do not believe these rumors."

Again, Devenshire shrugged. "I do not believe them blindly. I have discovered that there is always some manner of truth within any rumor. At any rate, we would be foolish not to proceed with caution."

"Why do we not simply circumvent this forest range?" Stant inquired finally able to shrug out of the frightened chill. He retrieved another berry and tossed it into his mouth, trying to appear nonchalant in the act.

"It would take many weeks to travel around it. I fear we may not have the time to spare for such a course. Fortunately, our path will take us through the narrowest area of the Coledecci so we should not have much to worry about," Devenshire replied as he carefully turned one of the roasting hares over to allow the flames to gently lick at the other side of the night's meal.

"How much time do you think we have?" Darkseed asked.

Devenshire shook his head. "I do not know with any certainty. What Xavier is attempting will require him to proceed with great caution, and such caution is time consuming. He will surely have read and heard of the other failed attempts to tap and harness the power of the Stones and will be taking great care to ensure that such a fate will not befall him. Yet with his skill and power, combined with those of the Dark Mystics? There is no way to know how long it will be before he makes his attempt."

"Perhaps he will make an error and fail as the others have," Zandorth observed with a touch of what might have been hope in his voice.

"It is possible. But what is at stake is simply too great a risk to leave to chance," Devenshire answered.

"I agree," a deep voice echoed from the woods.

They all jumped with a start and spun to face the source of the new voice. Devenshire, Darkseed, and Zandorth had their swords drawn before completing their turns while the Elves had suddenly found their bows and had arrows nocked into them with surprising speed. Brianna and Shantira both drew their swords as well, but their start at the sound of the new voice had delayed their reactions slightly.

From the shadows of the woods materialized the dim silhouette of a tall thin man. He moved with a grace and ease that made them all wonder if he were truly a man or simply a part of the night that had taken on the form of a man. There had been no rustling of underbrush, no snapping of twigs, no indication at all that someone had been approaching. The man stayed to the shadows, not moving close enough to the fire for anything of his appearance to be seen.

"Announce yourself!" Devenshire demanded to the darkened form, tightening his grip on his sword.

"I mean no harm. I come in peace," the silhouette answered, his hands emerging from the folds of his cloak to spread wide from his body to show he held no weapons.

"Who are you? What is your business here?" Devenshire

demanded, his voice edged with nervous anger. He had been taken by surprise and that irritated him very much. Although he had been engrossed in conversation, his powers should have alerted him that someone was approaching, and yet this man had masked his approach with apparent ease.

"My name is Darius. I wish to join your quest."

"What do you know of our quest?" Devenshire asked suspiciously.

"I know you go to face an evil presence. An evil presence that has the potential to destroy our realm as we know it. I wish to join you and be of whatever assistance I can be," he answered. There was a strange tone to his voice, a subtle undercurrent of something that almost put them at ease, yet at the same time, it stroked a sense of alarm within each of them.

"How do you know this?" Darkseed asked.

"Many nights ago, I sensed an evil presence within the flow of the Arts. I have been studying it in the attempt to learn its true nature, , and intentions. They have led me in this direction, and I believe, to you," Darius replied calmly.

Devenshire's eyes narrowed as his suspicions mounted. "You are a practitioner of the Arts?"

"Aye. I have studied the Mystic Arts, in all its forms, for many seasons."

"Am I to assume that also includes the Dark Arts?" Devenshire asked.

"Yes. I have also studied the Dark Arts, as well," Darius replied calmly as he absently picked at something hung in the threads of his cloak as though the object in his cloak and the subject of the conversation were both of secondary importance.

"Then you are aligned with the Dark Mystics," Devenshire stated more as a matter of fact than of accusation.

There was only the briefest of pauses before Darius turned his strange ice-blue gaze back to Devenshire. Devenshire's eyes narrowed as he peered deep into the odd color of the man's eyes and tried to discern what lie beneath the very calm and composed exterior. As Darius's eyes met his, he felt the distinct impression that there was nothing he could hide from the strange man. His gaze seemed to be able to penetrate any barrier. With the same, unnerving calm from before, he answered, "No. I am aligned with no one. I have had no need to be. Not until now."

"Step into the light. Show yourself!" Devenshire ordered.

"As you wish," Darius replied and his form began moving forward. As a course of second nature, Devenshire felt his grip tighten further on his sword as the stranger drew nearer. As the light of the fire dispelled the shadows that seemed to surround the man, more of his features came into detail.

He was elegantly dressed, more so than one would be for a journey of this length and duration. The dark cloth of his suit was only offset by the splash of red from his silk shirt. Even his cloak was the color of pitch, which would make seeing him in the dark with even a full moon to light the way difficult at best.

His features bore the pallor of illness, yet there was an incredible sense of strength and power about him. His jet-black hair hung to his shoulders and disappeared down his back, and his eyebrows seem to almost sweep upward, giving his face an almost satanic characteristic.

But his eyes were the most striking feature of all. They were ice blue in color and seemed to see far more than ordinary eyes should be able to see. They almost seemed to glow with a power all their own as if he could instantly look at someone and learn their deepest, darkest secrets, fears, fantasies, and dreams as if he were reading them from a printed scroll. Almost without conscious thought, Devenshire found himself strengthening his mental shields and also found himself wondering if any amount of shielding he could generate would protect his mind and soul from this man.

Then Devenshire realized his source of unease about this man. There was a presence about him that he had felt even before seeing his features. There was something dark and very sinister about him. It oozed from him, surrounded him, and seemed to drift forth to try to surround those around him. Whatever this man claimed to be, Devenshire knew he was evil, perhaps the essence of pure evil.

"What are you?" Devenshire asked even before he was aware that the question had formed upon his lips.

Darius seemed to almost smile at his question, as if he derived some dark satisfaction from arousing the sort of fear that would spawn such a question. "What do you think I am?" he asked in reply.

"I think you are far more than you appear to be. Far more than you represent to us now," Devenshire answered carefully.

Darius nodded slowly. "A very wise observation. I can see you are a man who does not fully trust all that he sees. You are one who accepts what he sees, but does not trust it until he has more information. Very good."

"And you are a man who enjoys bantering with subterfuge and facts crouched in riddles," Devenshire answered.

"As do we all. To one degree or another," Darius replied with a breathy chuckle.

"Since we seem to have a good understanding of each other's natures, then you will not be surprised when I say that I do not trust you," Devenshire stated flatly.

"You would be a fool to do otherwise," Darius replied just as flatly.

"Indeed. Just as I would be foolish to blindly accept your offer of assistance without knowing more of your true intentions."

"So you are rejecting my offer?" Darius asked with mild surprise.

"Yes," Devenshire replied evenly and without hesitation.

Darius shook his head slowly and smiled. "Unfortunate. I would make a very valuable ally in the battle you are about to wage."

"So you claim. I have no desire to face what is to come and have to worry over what motivates those with me," Devenshire replied, locking his steel gaze with Darius.

"So you will cast off an advantage simply because you know not of its source? Perhaps you are more foolish than I thought."

"Or more clever than you gave me credit for," Devenshire offered. "In either case, I will not travel or fight with those I do not trust."

For a moment, they locked eyes. Ice blue and blue-green locked in a battle of wills, each man trying to learn the true nature of the other, yet failing, each daring the other to falter, to slip, for either of them to let down their guard, and thereby giving the other an advantage. Such did not happen and finally, it was Darius who spoke, but it was not a submission, yet only a strategic change of tactics.

"As you wish. But let me give you this warning. You are ill prepared for what you are about to face. None of you can comprehend the magnitude of the evil that awaits you. In such times, you may find that you will have to suspend a great many things that you have believed in. You may very well face the day, and soon, that you will wish you had this night to live over again and the decisions you have made here to make again."

With that, Darius turned and strolled away into the shadows, becoming a silhouette, and the silhouette dissolving into the darkness of the woods beyond. Devenshire focused his powers and tried to track the man's movements, but as soon as his physical eyes lost sight of him, so did his powers. He sensed nothing from the woods in which he looked. It was as if Darius had simply vanished into the night with no trace left behind to confirm that he had ever truly been there.

CHAPTER TWENTY FIVE

They all stood frozen in the wake of Darius' departure. Each of them considered the sinister presence that had just departed, and each of them seemed to know that this was not the last time they would see him.

Devenshire kept scanning the tree line with his eyes and his powers, searching for any sign, any hint of the presence of Darius and found none. It would take considerable power for someone to mask, not only their presence, but also their approaching presence from his powers. Although his skills in the Mystic Arts were limited, some part of his natural ability made his senses stronger than most. He had always, even without conscious effort, been able to tell when someone was approaching him. But he had had no warning, no clue that anyone was approaching the camp.

Summoning his mental powers, he reached out for Darkseed's mind. *Did you sense his approach?*

No. Not at all. Darkseed replied, and Devenshire could feel his own unease reflected in Darkseed's thoughts.

I did not either. Nor can I find any trace of him now.

I cannot either. I tried a Spell of Knowledge while you spoke to him and found nothing. Darkseed answered.

If he possesses the power to mask his approach from both of us, then reflecting a Spell of Knowledge should prove no less difficult for him.

You do not understand, Daimion. I found nothing. No trace of anything. It was as if he were not there at all. No good, no evil, no happiness, no anger, no fear... nothing. It was as if you were talking to a corpse. I could not even find a trace of his life force, and that is impossible to mask, regardless of one's power or skill.

Devenshire felt his skin turn cold under Darkseed's thoughts. What kind of dark power did this Darius possess that would allow him to hide himself so completely from their powers? Someone with enough skill might accomplish such a feat with Devenshire and his limited abilities, but with Darkseed and his mastery of the Arts? The implications were appalling.

"What in the name of all that is holy was that?" Stant asked, finally breaking the cold silence that had descended upon them.

Devenshire shook his head slowly. "I do not know."

"A construct, perhaps," Darkseed speculated aloud.

"No. I would have sensed the use of any magic such as the kind used for constructs," Devenshire answered finally forcing his tensed limbs to relax as he stood upright, letting his sword drop to his side.

"But your powers were drained by the battle with the storm," Kendra answered, her fearful gaze still scanning the area of the darkened forest where Darius had vanished from sight.

"My natural sense of the Mystical Arts has nothing to do with my powers. Even without my powers, I should have still been able to sense workings of the mystical energies," Devenshire replied, also still scanning the blackness for any sign of the demon that had just left their presence.

"A demon,." Zandorth growled in echo of Devenshire's thoughts. "A pawn of Xavier or Satan himself."

"Possible," Devenshire replied. "If he possesses the power to hide his presence from us, then almost anything is possible."

"Not of Xavier," Darkseed said. They all turned to look at Darkseed, silently urging him to continue his speculation. "He did not attack us, did not try to learn anything of our intended plans. If his intentions were to spy on us to gain information for Xavier, then he has chosen the worst possible means with which to contact us and ease his way into our trust. I do not believe he is in league with Xavier."

Devenshire nodded in agreement. "It would stand to reason that if Xavier sent him to spy on us then he would have used more subtle means."

"But you are speculating on Xavier's actions with a reason that only the sane possess. Who can truly know what drives a mind as demented as Xavier's?" Zandorth asked. "Darius' intentions may not have been to spy but to disrupt. To un-nerve us."

Devenshire's eyes flickered with sudden understanding at what point Zandorth was trying to make. "To keep our minds disoriented? To keep us busy speculating about Darius instead of concentrating on Xavier and how to stop him?"

Zandorth nodded. "A very effective ploy. One that has been used in battle since time began."

"Very clever," Darkseed commented. "Keep us off balance, pondering Darius and worrying our minds to a frazzled edge trying to learn his intentions, and thereby, keeping us from concentrating on our true goal."

"What are we to do?" Kendra asked, fears tingeing her words.

Devenshire sighed heavily as he turned and sheathed his sword. He eased himself back down on the log where he had been sitting, and looked up at the others. "We proceed as we have been. We do our best to put Darius out of our minds and keep our minds focused on the task at hand. If the opportunity presents itself, then we may try to capture Darius, and hopefully, learn of his intentions, but we will not actively plan for such a thing. We keep our minds locked to our goal of stopping Xavier."

As they began recovering their composure and continued preparing the meal, a cold silence dominated the campsite, each person too engrossed in their own thoughts and fears to engage in conversation.

Brianna eased her sword back into its scabbard as she sat down, her mind a whirlwind of thoughts and fears that she knew she could not voice even if she had wished to. The moment that Darius' face had come into view she had felt her breath catch in her throat and felt her heart seized in a grip like that of cold steel. Her first impression was that she knew Darius, and yet she knew that she had never before laid eyes upon the man. It was a conflicting thought that worried at her mind. To look upon someone's face and seem to know them, yet know, without doubt, that she had never seen him before this night. Blurred memories tried to surface, memories that felt as if they belonged in her mind, yet felt as alien as any thought anyone could project into her mind. They were her memories yet not her memories. She concentrated on the badly blurred mental memories, trying to force them into sharp focus. They refused to obey her mental commands. Occasionally, an image would snap into a clear image only to quickly begin to swirl and ripple, much like a reflected image on the surface of water would when a stone was cast into it. A face or a room or the landscape would come, and none of them looked even vaguely familiar to her, and yet she could not shake the feeling that she should know every one of them by heart.

Memories of her nightmares returned—the nightmare that plagued her sleep far more often than not, the nightmare had been torturing her since her youth, and the one she had yet to make sense of. There were times when the nightmare would leave her be for months at a time only to return and haunt her sleep with a vengeance. Because of the nightmare, Brianna rarely slept and only in brief naps born of exhaustion. Even though the nightmare never changed, never altered in any detail, she could not become used to it or dispel the cold sweaty fear that held her for hours upon waking from it.

She looked down and saw that her hands had begun to tremble and she knew, as surely as she knew her own name, the specters of her nightmare, complete with the soul twisting fear, would visit her the next time she slept and would be just as terrifying as ever.

Shantira watched as Brianna sank back to her place and became lost in what was clearly disturbing thoughts. She wondered if Brianna's thoughts were any more disturbing than her own. The moment she had seen the pale strangers face, she had an eerie sensation of having seen him before… and recently. But she could not forge the time or the place from her memory. As she returned to her own seat, her right hand found her temple as she tried hard to place where she had seen those ice blue eyes before. She had the impression that she had encountered this man twice within the recent past, but she could find no reliable memory to support that feeling. The overriding sense of concern for Brianna's safety, which had been fading over the past two days, suddenly returned, and she found herself putting her own mental mystery aside and turning to face her friend. "Brianna? Are you all right? You do not look well."

Brianna looked up at Shantira and smiled her usual warm smile. But in the tiny span of time between the moment she looked up and then smiled, Shantira could see that her mind, if not her very essence, was being tortured. "I am fine. Just a little shaken up by the sudden appearance of our visitor," she replied, and Shantira knew it was a lie.

"You look as if you are deeply troubled. I am here. Let me help you if I can," Shantira pleaded.

Brianna's features only flickered a moment before her radiant smile returned but in that flicker, Shantira saw fear, confusion, pain, and a thousand other combinations of emotions that seemed to tear at her with the ferocity of a wild beast. "Tis nothing of consequence. I was simply startled at the sudden appearance of that man. But I thank you for your concern."

Shantira reached out and took one of Brianna's hands into both of hers. She felt the chill of her skin, felt the tremble that Brianna struggled valiantly to suppress. "You have been a true friend to me. One of the few true friends I have known in my life. You have always been there for me, lending me an ear or stern advice, whichever was needed at the time. Please, allow me to return the favor."

Brianna maintained her warm smile and patted Shantira's hands. "Tis nothing worth the effort to worry over." Then Brianna did the one thing Shantira feared she would do. With the skill that only Brianna possessed, she sidestepped the subject, and in doing so, put it out of the reach of further discussion. "I do not know about you, but I am starved," she said as she gently pulled her hand from Shantira's grip and rose gracefully to get something to eat.

Shantira watched her and somehow knew that food was the last thing that occupied Brianna's mind, but she also knew that once Brianna sidestepped a subject, it was pointless to pursue it any further. While she reflected that her concern for Brianna was genuine, she also felt that something else was directing her in acting upon that concern. It was the same feeling she had in Lirpa when the Royal Guard had threatened Brianna. Shaking her head to try to rattle something resembling order to her thoughts, she wondered if perhaps her sanity had begun to falter. With the destruction of her home, the mad dash from Lirpa, this odd behavior that seemed to be dominating her, the ominous threat of what they were riding into, and of course, her raging emotions over Devenshire, she found herself truly fearing for her sanity.

~*~

Darius strode through the night, seeing things that no human could possibly hope to see even with the brightest of moons overhead. He saw the physical things such as trees, brush, dirt, grass, flowers, and so forth. He also saw the ebb and flow of the tides of power that linked every living thing to the realm. He could see the tendrils of power as they flowed through the realm like the wind. He could see the rodent scurrying about in the dark searching for food and could also see the energy of its life force flickering from it like a candle flame. He could hear its tiny rapid heartbeat as well as the whispering sound of blood racing through its veins. A short distance away was a serpent, its useless eyes staring unblinking into the night, its forked tongue tasting the air, knowing that the rodent was nearby. With the silent skill of a predator, it moved forward, closing the distance between it and what would be dinner in short order.

However, none of these things truly registered on his consciousness. His mind boiled in rage at the recent turn of events. He had underestimated the caliber of people who traveled with Brianna and that, as much as the insolence of the one called Devenshire, nearly enraged him beyond his ability to control. How had he missed such obvious indications in how to proceed with them? Had he allowed his concentration to become so focused on Brianna that he had missed them? Devenshire was a minor mage, but the latent power that resided within him was formidable. Darkseed was a master of the Mystic Arts, and the skill he sensed within the Adept startled him. Darius had been surprised at the level of power he had to use to mask himself from their powers, and such levels of power never went unnoticed by him.

The Elves were of little consequence. They possessed no special gifts aside from their proficiency in combat, which would be of little use to them against him. The one called Zandorth was a warrior, and his greatest strengths also lie in the way of battle. While his physical strength and will were stronger than any he had encountered in a while, they were useless against one such as him.

Devenshire and Darkseed were the greatest threats to his plans. Darkseed, while he could never hope to match his own level of power or skill, could prove to be a problem. Other Adepts he had faced in the past were rigid in their thoughts and actions, to the point of being predictable. Those who followed the paths of the Mystics followed the dictates of their respective orders with a reverence that rivaled that of most religions. They had their holy scrolls and dictates that they followed blindly. The poor fools truly believed the doctrines that the old Adepts pounded into their minds and left each new class of mages more crippled than the ones before them.

But such was not a weakness of Darkseed. The man was a rogue. He followed no doctrines save those of his own desires, which changed from moment to moment. The man had somehow found a way to master the Arts while not loosing himself in the religious babble of the Order. In essence, Darkseed had the best of both worlds. He had the power of an Adept and the freedom of an ordinary human. That made him unpredictable and very dangerous. There would be no way to reliably know from which direction or in what form Darkseed would direct his powers. But there was a weakness, and Darius had only to wait patiently to exploit it should the need arise. While Darkseed possessed formidable powers and the skill to use them, in casting off the traditional roles of mages within his Order, he had lost some of the discipline that was needed to attain even greater power. Darkseed feared his power mastering him instead of the reverse, so he strived to keep from using his powers when he could. He also was immersed in the pleasures of mortal men, and the pursuit of them often distracted him. These two weaknesses along with the fact that, despite his powers and skills, Raven Darkseed was merely a mortal man combined to give Darius a weapon to use against him. All that was needed to best Darkseed was vigilance and patience. With a twisted snarling grin, Darius reflected that the long seasons of his existence had given him an abundance of both.

Devenshire. Within him, there was another problem, and perhaps an even greater threat to him than Darkseed. Devenshire was complex, more so than any man Darius had ever encountered in many seasons. With a galling self-admission, Darius realized that he had sorely underestimated Devenshire. The man's mind was sharp, clear, and missed little. He possessed a control over himself and his emotions that amazed Darius and went unrivaled in his memory. Another aspect of Devenshire was his ability to shroud his mind from within. The moment that Darius had looked upon each of the humans, his powers had filtered through their minds, seeing all he needed to see to know each of them as though he had known them for seasons, but not Devenshire. Even the passive mental shields he maintained were far stronger than those of concentrated mental shields. Once he had realized that Darius had come upon them unawares, he had strengthened his mental shields, and Darius found that he could not penetrate them without using powers that would have alerted Devenshire and Darkseed to his true nature.

Yet, in that instant before he strengthened his shields, Darius had gotten fleeting impressions. There was a dark memory deep within Devenshire. The nature of the memory he could not find, but it was something that drove the man to great lengths to avoid. Darius had also glimpsed the rigid self-control Devenshire maintained over himself, and such tightly bound coils of control were often difficult to break. There had been other impressions, but they were shadowy and fleeting. However, Darius did not discard them from his consideration. While they may not mean anything to him now, they might prove useful in the future, and he vowed to keep them nearby should any more lapses in Devenshire's shields reveal more to him.

With anger, Darius realized that his own lack of discipline had complicated his plans far more than Devenshire or Darkseed could have. Had he taken a little more time, studied the humans more closely before making his presence known to them, then his plans would not now be in the shambled state of disarray they were. Great care and planning would be needed now to gain entry into their ranks. He had aroused Devenshire's suspicions, and those would be the hardest to overcome. With growing dread and disgust, Darius realized the path he would have to take to align himself with the humans. He wondered if his dark nature, the multitude of seasons of being absorbed in the stark truth of his nature, would allow him to do what he now found he would have to do. The demands upon him would be great. With a scowl, his mind reached out to the image of the one called Xavier. It was this mans action that now placed him in this most disgusting of situations, and he promised himself that this one would pay dearly for what he was about to submit himself to.

Suddenly he stopped. Something was wrong. Something in the night was calling to him. He felt strange as dizziness swept over him. Placing his hand to his temple, he forced his mind to sweep out for the source of the sudden alarm that permeated him. Like a wild animal that did not know if it were predator or prey, Darius froze, willing himself to become nothing more than the empty breeze of the night. But as suddenly as the sensation came, it vanished, leaving the night once again as it had been... his domain.

For long moments, he did not move, his mind searching with a near frantic pace for the source of what had alarmed him. He knew the sensation well and it had saved him on countless occasions. There was only one thing that could cause this feeling... another vampire was near.

Vampires could sense each other's presence, could feel it in the tides of the powers that made up their being. It served as both warning and welcome, but Darius used it more as a form of warning. Vampires, by their very nature, were lone creatures and did not get along well with each other. There had been attempts in the past to form clans and organize the sparse vampire population throughout the realm, but each attempt failed resulting in the destruction of many vampires. He searched for the brief fleeting sensation, but found no trace of it. More than likely, the other vampire, or kindred as they were often referred, had just briefly entered the sphere of his senses.

Darius made a mental note to be on alert moving forward. He was far outside his realm, and he could no longer count on the knowledge of being the only vampire around as he had in his home province. He added this new factor into his ever-changing plans, plans that had a dual objective. One was to rid himself of the threat of this insane mortal named Xavier. The other was to eliminate the growing threat of Devenshire, Darkseed, and the others on the way to his ultimate goal: claiming Brianna as his again.

As she had once been...

...as she would be again.

CHAPTER TWENTY-SIX

Xavier stood in the center of his empty tent, the wooden box containing the Stones of Andarus tucked tightly under his left arm. He surveyed the interior of the tent and contemplated what was to come. Within the hour, the Dark Mystics would transport him back to his retreat to allow him uninterrupted study of the stones. They would open a dimensional portal, and once he stepped through it, he would instantly appear within his keep. A transportation spell like this one was very difficult and extraordinarily taxing. He had tried to perfect a spell like it, but the power required to execute one was enormous. It was also a very delicate piece of spell work. The tiniest variation in the mystical energies used to create it would result in a wide and very horrific range of consequences for the person stepping through the portal.

He had gathered his men around him and laid out his orders for an en-masse attack on Devenshire and his group. The orders were specific: kill the men, capture the women, and bring Devenshire's head back to him. The two women would make exhilarating additions to his stable of slave girls while Devenshire's preserved head would bear witness to Xavier's triumph and Devenshire's failure. Very poetic, Xavier mused.

As he hefted the comforting weight of the chest, he contemplated the one other piece of unfinished business: Cyrus. The wizard was overdue, and Devenshire obviously still lived. While his powers were taxed, they had regenerated enough for him to lightly enter the Mystic Tides. While it was highly unlikely that Devenshire had discovered and killed Cyrus, Xavier was leaving nothing to chance. Lowering himself to the dirt floor of the tent, Xavier forced himself to relax, clearing his mind of all thoughts. Slowly, he closed his eyes, summoning what remained of his powers and focused them on seeking out the Mystic Tides. It was extraordinarily difficult, but he was finally able to establish a connection with the tides. After even more difficulty, he was able to locate the wizard's essence within the tides.

Cyrus! You are late. What detains you?

Almost instantly, the essence replied as if it had been expecting this communication and was prepared for it. *I was not aware of any constraints of time upon the completion of my mission, Master.*

There it was—that ever present underlying sense of insolence from the wizard. In no other Follower was such a thing permitted. The only reason Cyrus was able to accomplish it was because of the wizard's incredible level of power and solely because of his value as a reluctant ally rather than an enemy. Only from Cyrus did Xavier allow such insolence, and this solely because of the wizard's power and value as an ally rather than an enemy. *Do not banter clever words with me, Cyrus! You know damned well that when I issue a command I expect it to be carried out as quickly as possible. Now answer me. What detains you?"*

There has been a complication, Master. Cyrus replied through the mystic tides of energy. There was no fear in the man, no sense of awe at the power Xavier wielded — even knowing this power could reduce him to a bloody pulp with but a single thought. All of the other Followers feared Xavier, and he fed upon that fear as a sustaining sustenance of his continued rule.

Explain! Xavier demanded.

Devenshire has been joined by an Adept. Raven Darkseed. Cyrus replied.

I am well aware of that! Darkseed joined Devenshire days ago! Besides, Raven Darkseed is not an Adept! Xavier snapped back. He had heard of Raven Darkseed as he kept up on the students of the Mystic Arts. Granted, Darkseed held great power and had, at one time, been believed to hold the potential of an expert, but he had left the Order before being adorned as an Adept.

I beg to differ, Master. While Darkseed has never been officially ordained as an Adept, his level of power and skill are those of an Adept. It is simply a matter of syntax. Cyrus replied.

Are you saying that his skill exceeds yours? Xavier replied, taking joy in trying to get some sort of irate response from the arrogant wizard. As with all the others times he had made such an attempt he was disappointed for there was no such response from Cyrus.

In some ways, his power and skill do exceed mine. However, I do not feel he could best me in a direct confrontation. Such an occurrence should not be used as a basis for action however. Darkseed is a random element and such random elements are best handled with extreme caution. Cyrus replied with the same nerve-racking calm that he approached everything else. Xavier found it more and more galling each time he was confronted with it.

I do not care about random elements or caution! I want the women and I want Devenshire's head, and I want them both now! Xavier commanded.

As I have already told you, Master. You shall have that which you seek. While you may have nothing to fear from Darkseed, and while I intend to serve you as I have sworn to do, I do not wish to end my existence within this realm. It was the closest thing to outright defiance that Xavier had ever experienced from one of his Followers. Cyrus had all but said that he would carry out his orders, but in his own manner and his own time.

Are you daring to defy my wishes? Xavier shouted into the tides.

"No, M'Lord. I would never be as foolish as that. I am merely stating that to carry out your wishes, I need to proceed in a fashion that will slightly delay my return with what you seek.*

Xavier had the very distinct impression that Cyrus had just tested the boundaries of his service. Xavier was aware that the wizard took delight in seeing just how far he could take his insolence, and he knew that the wizard had just, again, brushed up against the edges of the boundaries. Xavier could see the day approaching when he would have to destroy the wizard. The man's insolence and independence were beginning to outweigh any value his service was to him. To allow Cyrus to continue to test his might against Xavier's would only lead to a time when the wizard would think himself capable of taking on Xavier and defeating him. While such a thing was not likely, Xavier was not foolish enough to simply sit idly by while the wizard increased his power base and skill for just such an attempt. Best to destroy a potential enemy before the enemy knew he was in a position to strike. In the back of his mind, he acknowledged the same state of affairs between himself and Baldar. The similarities were fascinating and concerning at the same time.

Very well. Proceed. However, know that I have sent my Followers against Devenshire with the same instructions I have given you. You would be well advised to complete the assignment first. Be warned: I will not wait any longer.

With that, Xavier severed the link and withdrew his powers from the tides. Let the arrogant bastard consider that for a moment.

~*~

"Well what have we here?" the voice boomed from the dark shadows of the forest surrounding the clearing. Backellar Moon froze in the saddle for a moment, his mind already rushing ahead to formulate plans. It was very rare that anyone could come upon him unawares, and it never ceased to amaze and annoy him when it happened. What vital clue had he missed? Had he let his thoughts become so wrapped up in other matters that he had missed the obvious? He pulled up rein and began a slow sweep of the clearing with his eyes. It was getting on in the afternoon, and the shadows were growing deeper. He resisted the urge to reach for his sword or any one of the multiple daggers he had hidden about his body. It was too late for that. The resolution for this problem would have to be more hands on.

Three men emerged from the shadows of the tree line, swords drawn. Moon scanned the men, and instantly, knew a great deal about each of them. Their clothes were made of a heavier material and the stitches were thick, designed for life out in the open expanses instead of the comfortable confines of a village or city. Their hair was un-kept and greasy. Their faces were unshaven with a heavy accumulation of beard growth. His eyes flickered over their weapons as he continued to quickly study and assess them. Their swords were poorly made and even more poorly maintained. The blades were dull with multiple nicks and chips in them. Their faces and bodies were dirty as confirmed when the wind shifted directions briefly, catching their odor. It was clear — these men were bandits. Moon smiled and resisted the urge to chuckle: Bandits attempting to rob a thief. If the situation weren't so perilous, it would be funny. Moon dropped the reins and leaned forward, propping his right arm on the pommel of the saddle as the bandits continued to approach. The situation might turn out to be funny, after all.

"You find something amusing?" one of the bandits asked, seeing the smug smile on Moon's face. "You laugh at us?"

Moon simply sat in his saddle and shifted his humor filled eyes from one man to another.

"Now you disrespect me by ignoring me?" The man asked, feigning a level of insult that he truly did not feel.

Moon finally locked eyes with the middle of the three men. Assuming this one was the leader simply because he was the one making the most noise. "What would you have me do? Pee myself in fear of your approach? Thank you for attempting to rob me?"

The leader frowned for a second, stunned by the fact that his intentions had been so clear to the lone traveler. "Now you accuse me of being a thief! I should run you through!"

Moon chuckled as he swung his right leg over his mount and gracefully bounced from the saddle to the ground, which caused the bandits to stop their direct advance on him. "Let us be honest with one another, shall we? I have made no false accusations, and you are not truly offended by anything that has happened thus far." Moon let his arms hang at his sides, making no move to reach for his weapons.

The leader looked to the man on his left before shifting his gaze back to Moon. The expression in their depths said that he was clearly not as confident in his position as he had been just a breath ago. It always unnerved thieves when their plans were discovered prematurely. Moon knew this all to well. "You are an arrogant ass, are you not?"

Moon's smile deepened as he nodded. "So I have been told."

"Perhaps it is time someone cut some of that arrogance out of you!" the leader said with a deeper edge to his voice.

Moon's smile remained etched into his features but his eyes took on a more menacing gaze. "You are more than free to make the attempt!" He said as he folded his arms across his chest and leaned back against his mount.

The leader's filthy face cracked into a wide grin. "Oh, it will be much more than an attempt!" he said as he began quickly advancing on Moon. The other two bandits fell into step with him, slightly behind him. Moon's face remained locked in the joyful expression as his eyes danced from one man to another, his mind formulating his next moves quickly. He felt his heart begin to pound faster and felt his extremities begin to tingle with the infusion of adrenaline into his blood. He felt the old familiar rush of excitement into his brain that no amount of alcohol or herbs could ever duplicate. One thing was certain about Backellar Moon... he loved the fight.

"You should know that the Fates have told me that you will not be successful in what you are about to attempt," he injected as the men advanced on him.

The leader halted his advance as his brow furrowed in momentary confusion, "What did you say?"

Moon shrugged slightly. "The Fates say you will fail."

The man's confused expression twitched into a fairly amused one. "You speak to the Fates personally?" His companions also stopped their advance, seeing their intended target in a new and unsettling light.

"Of course I do. Do you not?" Moon replied easily.

"No, I do not speak to the Fates, and they have never seen fit to speak to me. Have you taken leave of your senses?" the bandit asked.

Moon's face twisted from a good-natured smile to a maniacal glare. "Perhaps! Why not come find out for yourself?" There it was. What he had been looking for. The leader's expression shifted subtly into uncertainty. It was one thing to attack an arrogant bastard and make him suffer the consequences of his over indulgence. It was quite another to tangle with someone who was insane. Moon's claim of speaking to the Fates combined with a little bit of acting was usually enough to dissuade people from attacking him, but he wasn't foolish enough to put all of his faith in that one tactic. If his apparent insanity wasn't enough to dissuade a would-be attacker, he was prepared with other methods.

The bandits exchanged apprehensive glances before all three locked their gaze to Moon who still stood with his arms folded and leaning against his mount. They were weighing their options, and had finally decided that even if the man were insane, he was still outnumbered three to one. They launched their attack suddenly. Moon willed himself to lock eyes with the leader, his first target and remain absolutely still until the last possible moment. Just as the leader was upon him, Moon tightened his grip on the short club under the fender of his saddle. With one quick movement, he pulled the club free and threw himself into a clockwise spin, his right arm reaching out catching the lead bandit on the side of his upper leg. The man yelped in surprised pain as he tried to compensate for Moon's sudden movement. Once Moon had folded his arms across his chest, and leaned back against his mount, he had slightly twisted his body to put the club in reach. He had a short club hidden under each fender of his saddle.

As the leader lurched to one side from the force of the blow, Moon planted his feet and shifted his turn in the other direction, bringing the club up over his head and gripping it on each end as the other bandit's sword came down. The metal bit deep into the wood, and Moon let his shoulders and elbows absorb the force from the blow. Pushing up on the club, he stood upright, bringing the second bandit's sword up with it. Not wasting a moment, he quickly brought his knee violently up into the man's groin before quickly spinning away, jerking his short staff free from the sword, and putting himself out of the path of the charging third bandit. The second bandit grunted and then squealed in pain as his knees slammed together in an automatic reaction to the blow. He would have naturally sunk to his knees, but the third bandit crashed into him, taking them both to the ground.

Moon planted his feet again and took a moment to evaluate his position. The leader had fallen to the ground and was in the process of getting back up. He had shifted his sword to his left hand so that his right hand could try to massage the massive knot out of his upper thigh muscle. The second bandit was rolling back and forth, hugging himself against a pain only a man would truly understand. A distant part of Moon could actually feel a fragment of pain in his groin area from blows he had taken before. It was a pain that once experienced, was never ever forgotten. The third bandit was scrambling to his feet, his right hand tightly fixed on his sword. Moon made a series of short, quick steps to swing his staff in an upward, underhand blow that caught the bandit across the bridge of the nose. A wet crack told him the bone had been snapped.

The bandit, who had just gotten his knees under him, was thrown backwards from the force of the blow, his back arching. Moon spun the staff around and delivered a hard blow to the back of the bandit's head, which jerked the man's head forward, halting his backwards fall. As his body lurched forward, following the force of the blow on the back of his skull, Moon snapped the staff around and buried one end of it deep into the man's mid-section before pivoting it over his left hand to deliver a crushing blow to the back of the bandit's head. The man collapsed to the ground and did not move again. Moon took a moment to verify that he was still breathing before shifting his attention to the leader. His attack on the third bandit had been fast, but the leader had managed to recover enough composure to launch an attack. Moon saw there was no time to formulate anything fancy as a defense so he relied on his instincts. He arched his back and leaned out of the way of the swinging blade. Just as he was about to lose his

balance, he twisted his body and quickly snapped his left leg up
under him to secure his balance. Reacting out of a sense he was hard
pressed to define, he pushed off with his right foot, pivoting on the
ball of his left. Reaching out with the staff, he smashed the leader
across the backs of his knees before pushing himself forward off both
legs into an upright position. He heard the leader's cry of pain as he
turned to watch him fall to his knees and then onto his stomach. He
rolled to his side and brought his knees up to hold them with his
hands. It was an odd-looking fetal position, and Moon paused,
cocking his head to one side to watch it.

Suddenly, he felt himself tense as he heard heavy footfalls coming
up from his left and slightly behind. Moon tightened his grip on the
club and quickly spun around to face the second bandit. Moon silently
saluted the man for his ability to get back to his feet so quickly after
such a crippling blow as he tightened his grip on the staff.

The bandit's angry snarl shifted slightly into angry surprise at the
sight of the intended victim spinning around to face him. His plan of
attack had been simple, catch the target with his back to him, and
drive his blade deep into his back. The bandit slid to a stop and
shifted into a defensive posture. Moon smiled slightly as he continued
to look deep into the bandit's eyes. The pain from the blow to his
groin was still raging through him. Moon could see it in his eyes as
clearly as if the man were still rolling around on the ground hugging
himself. The bandit's eyes shifted to his leader who was still nursing
his smashed knees and then switched to the third bandit who was out
cold. His eyes returned to Moon who was smiling at him, waiting
patiently.

"Bastard! I will kill you for this!" he hissed.

Moon tilted his head to one side and then looked skyward, his
expression looking like he was listening to someone else speaking. He
shifted his eyes back to the bandit and grinned as he shook his head
slightly. "The Fates say no."

The bandit hissed in anger and launched himself at Moon, his
sword already swinging around for a slashing strike. Moon stepped
back half a step and brought his club up to deflect the blow. As soon
as the bandit's sword was sent back from the impact with his staff,
Moon launched into an eye-blurring attack. In a string of very fluid
movements, Moon lanced out with the staff, cracking the bandit
across the wrist of the hand holding his sword. With a yelp, the
bandit's fingers involuntarily released their grip on the sword. As the
bandit's left hand wrapped around his right wrist, Moon's staff
snaked out and cracked the point of his left elbow sending painful
sparks of pain racing out from the joint. Moon spun the club around
and jabbed the end of the staff into the man's sternum. As the man
howled out and staggered backwards, his hands going to his chest,

Moon stepped back and swung the stick around to knock the man's legs out from under him, causing him to crash to the ground on his back. The bandit was clearly addled as Moon stepped across to straddle him. Moon took his staff by the center and bent over, quickly pivoting the staff back and forth, each end striking the bandit on each side of his head in a rapid succession of blows. The man's eyes rolled up in their sockets and a soft moan whisperd from his lips as the ends of the staff obliterated his consciousness.

Moon stepped over the unconscious bandit and focused on the leader who was still massaging his knees. His pained expression shifting to take in the sight of Moon advancing slowly toward him, his expression now calm and amused. Moon slammed one end of the staff into the ground near the leader's head before squatting down on his heels next to him. Moon studied the man's pained expression as he vigorously massaged his own damaged knees with delight before shifting his gaze back to the leader. "I have never been one to gloat when I am proven right in a situation, but I did tell you that the Fates said you would not be successful."

"Go to hell, you bastard! Kill me, and be done with it!" the leader hissed.

"Kill you?" Moon asked incredulously. "Why in the name of the Fates would I kill you? Why would I go to all the trouble of thrashing you so thoroughly, and then deprive myself the joy of watching you suffering through it, by killing you?" Moon shook his head as if it had been the silliest thing he'd ever heard.

The bandit watched Moon, not entirely sure of what to expect. "Then what will you do?"

Moon's pleasant smile turned dark and maniacal as he reached over and began patting the man pockets. "Exactly what you intended to do to me."

Almost an hour later, Backellar Moon exited the forest and shifted his course toward the north, his pockets a little heavier. While the bandits didn't have a great deal on them or on their scraggily horses, it was more than what he had begun the encounter with. As for the bandits, they would all awaken soon with some black and blue, swollen and cracked reminders of their encounter with him.

CHAPTER TWENTY-

SEVEN

The meal was eaten in relative silence in the wake of Darius' departure. Each person wrestled with what they had seen of the strange man and what his eerie appearance might mean. Then one by one, they each retired to their blankets with Devenshire taking up the first watch of the night. As the hours of the night passed with ever increasing slowness, sleep was a fleeting goal with only momentary, ephemeral grips held upon it before floating away leaving them awake and staring at a blanket of stars overhead, wondering and trying to beckon sleep back to them.

Only Brianna resisted sleep. When sleep realized that she did not pursue it, it tried to tease her with feathery strokes upon her mind, soothing her tensed muscles, loosening the rigid grip she maintained on consciousness. Just as her eyes would begin to droop and sag, she would shake her head violently and brush the fingers of sleep from her mind. The nightmares had returned and done so with a vengeance, and she knew, as surely as she knew her own name that it was waiting for her to fall asleep, so it could rush forth to haunt her again.

Brianna fought valiantly. While her mind fought back the advancing tendrils of sleep, her body betrayed her. The days ride and previous nights of little or no sleep combined to cause her body to attack from within. She realized too late that she was fighting a battle she could not hope to win. As the silken fingers of sleep stroked her mind, her body relaxed, settled into the warmth of her blankets, and coaxed her mind into inattention, so that the final soothing stroke of sleep sent her eyelids closing slowly over bloodshot green eyes. Within moments, she was fast asleep, and as sleep claimed her consciousness, her subconscious took over and summoned the nightmare to play unbridled upon the theater of her mind...

Sienna smiled the smile of the truly happy as she stood before the full-length mirror and regarded her reflection. The snow-white gown she had spent weeks sewing was finally complete and now graced her body with the exact effect she had imagined. The straps draped over her shoulders, holding the bosom of the dress high as her corset served to make her waist smaller and her bust larger. The gown tapered down from her chest to fit snugly about her small waist before smoothly following the contours of her hips to gradually flare out to just barely brush the floor with the hem.

The white silk of the gown had been expensive, and her husband had grumbled about the price. It had taken a great deal of persuasion on her part to convince him of just how badly she had wanted the material. By the third night of her 'persuasion,' she was sure she had more or less talked him into buying it for her. The next morning found her waking to find her husband already gone for the day. Upon her dresser, she had found a red rose, one from their gardens, and enough gold coins to purchase an entire bolt of the pure white silk material. With a subtle wicked smile flashing upon both her lips, and her green eyes sparkling, she had admitted to herself that there were times when being a woman had its definite advantages.

Sienna had wasted little time in summoning a carriage and going into the city to purchase the material and all the things she would need to turn the gown of her imagination into reality. She was not a seamstress, by her own admission. She knew she could have easily had any one of the many servants that worked for them sew the garment, but she had dreamed up the gown and was determined to make it herself—a task made a little more stressful given the price of the silk material and with little room for error.

While her husband was traveling abroad, taking care of one matter of their estate or another, she had set herself to the task of creating the beautiful gown in her mind and doing so before her husband returned. She pulled every gown she owned, studied the ways they were put together, and from that, she gathered what she hoped was enough knowledge to make her dress.

For days upon days she would measure, cut, and sew. Sometimes she would rip out seams repeatedly until they were to her liking. Other times, the parts of the gown would come together under her throbbing fingers as if she possessed magic. All the while, she maintained a vision within her mind of her husband returning from his journey to find her waiting to greet him in the gown she had created in her mind and then brought to life.

Often while she sewed, she thought of her husband and how perfectly happy their lives were together. Her husband was a man of considerable standing, of great wealth, and very influential. He lavished her with a love that most women merely dreamt of having. There was no part of her mind, body, or soul that doubted that her husband loved her—to the very depths of his being, he loved her. She returned that love with a depth and intensity to rival his. When his time was not being consumed with affairs of his estate or his office or his business, it was hers. It seemed the man had no time to himself. If he were not taking care of their livelihood, then his attention was entirely upon her, and her every need and want met as if it were his life's goal to fulfill them.

On the rare times that she took a break from the sewing of the gown, she would take walks through the gardens of their estate. They had planted every bush, plant, tree, and flower. No servants, no outside help at all. Just a man and his wife building something that in later years they could look upon and recall the love and toil that had gone into the creation of such beauty. Much of their happy early years had been spent digging in the soil, cutting away vines and briars, moving trees, reshaping the land surrounding their still uncompleted keep. In the skeletal shadow of their future home, they had toiled together to make something from nothing, taking a vision in their minds, and through hard work and harder love, making it a reality.

Her husband had done much the same with his cunning business sense and shrewd political knowledge. He had taken a vision in his mind, and through hard work, had made himself a very wealthy and very influential man. He was considered a king in his area, and she was proud to be his queen.

So, Sienna decided to do the same. Granted, on a much smaller scale, but the intent was the same as was the desire. She would take the image of the evening dress in her mind, and through determination, hard work, and her love for her husband, and she would make it a reality.

Only two dark blots marred the perfect light of their lives together. One was a lack of children. Her husband so desperately wanted children, sons and daughters, to pass along his wisdom, his lessons of life, and his vast empire. Sienna? She dearly loved children but for some reason found discomfort at the thought of having children of her own. She could find no logical explanation for such a feeling of dread that passed over her at the thought of having children, but no task was too great for him, and if he wanted children, she would bear him as many as she possibly could.

Yet children had not come. It was not due to a lack of will, determination, or effort. They consulted healers, watched astrologers charts, planned around her time of purification, everything anyone could possibly suggest to guarantee the successful copulation of her egg with his seed. Yet time and time again, they had failed. Sienna watched her husband accept news of each failure and watched a small part of him morn harder with each passing failure.

The other blot was an unfulfilled desire within her husband that had nothing to do with children or his wife or his life as he had built it. It was a limitation within himself that he could not overcome, and failure to overcome obstacles was something completely alien to him. The failure lay in his inability to master even the most rudimentary skills of the Mystical Arts.

It had been a dream of his since his youth. Since the time he had seen a Mage of the Mystical Arts conjure a spell in order to save a small village from a rockslide that would have easily destroyed the tiny hamlet, he had sought out Mage after Mage, had gone to retreat after retreat. In each and every case that he had thoroughly studied, he found that he simply had not been born with whatever it was that made some men capable of mastering the Arts and others incapable of the simplest of incantations. He consulted ancient scrolls, visited healers, sought out even the most latent of talented practitioners of the Arts, in the hopes of finding some way of reversing the curse the Fates had delivered upon him.

Scrolls and books of incantations were sought, found and purchased, regardless of their price and studied in earnest. Yet with each attempt to harness the power of the Arts came an even more bitter taste of defeat. He did not lack the discipline, the desire, or the will to master the Mystic Arts. He simply lacked the latent potential within his physical body to harness the very forces of the Arts and bend them to his will.

It was an obsession with Sienna's husband, and one that he carried with him always. Even now, he kept a private study in which he continued to try to force the will of nature around and grant him what his heart desired. Sienna felt that if she could give him a child, then perhaps that would take some of the sting out of the failure at not having the Mystic Arts.

As Sienna stood in front of her mirror and looked at her reflection, she smiled for this night would be a double gift of love for her husband upon his return. Not only was the gown finished and looking just as she had imagined it, it also served as a sort of wrapping for another present she would give him. Her delicate hands lowered to her flat stomach and considered the news she had for him. A life was forming within her, a child.

She regarded her reflection closely, looking for any flaw in her appearance that would take away from the magical night approaching. Her thick black hair was perfect, styled in just the fashion that he always found most appealing. Her deep-set green eyes sparkled in the light and reflected back the deep sense of peace and joy that permeated her soul.

She rearranged the white shawl around her bare shoulders and smiled at herself in the mirror. Her heart raced in anticipation of greeting her husband with the gown and the news that at least one of his unfulfilled desires was about to be granted. Her mind played over the joy that would come to his face, perhaps even tears would come to his eyes, and he would take her into his strong arms and kiss her passionately, lovingly, tenderly all at the same time. Sienna watched her cheeks flush slightly as her mind taunted her with the possibility that he would then take her into his arms, carry her up the stairs to this very room, making love to her until they were both spent and entwined in a sweat soaked embrace born of the purest of loves.

As the evening began passing into night, she assembled the staff of servants and bid them a fond night away from their duties. She wanted no one present within the walls of the keep this night save for the two of them. As the hour of his anticipated return came, she found she could not be still. She walked through the massive halls of their home, trying not to notice the ominous feeling that had descended upon this place, as if something had gone terribly wrong and was about to become much worse. Was it a woman's ability to sense when something was not right, or was it a figment of her anxious imagination at her husband's approaching return?

The hour of his return came and passed with no sign of him. She stood on one of the many balconies of the keep facing the long winding road that would bring him home. Her eyes searched the road, almost willing the sight of his carriage to come into view. Darkness began to descend and a sliver of worry crept into her mind, which only added to the crushing presence of something ominous approaching. The darkness deepened and with it, the dread and fear increased. Something was wrong. He was seldom late and never ever this late. She had double and triple checked the message she had received only two days ago. Her husband had sent word that he would be returning home on this day and had even estimated the hour of his return. Something dreadful had happened. She could feel it in the marrow of her bones. Sienna fought down the irrational panic that tried to force its way into her mind. To make matters worse, the full disk of the moon was beginning to disappear behind darker clouds. A storm was brewing, and from the faint chill in the normally warm evening air, it would be a bad one. Already in the distance, the faint flicker of lightening could be seen, and on occasion, the low steady rumble of distant thunder could be felt in the soles of her feet. Indeed, this would be a very bad storm, and she desperately despised storms.

As she paced the nearly endless rooms of the keep, which seemed to be expanding with each pass she made, she paused once before one of the many mirrors. Her face no longer beamed with pride, joy, and nervous bride-like anticipation. Fine lines of worry and trepidation marred her face, and the green of her eyes had taken on a darker hue as if reflecting the approaching storm, both inside and out. When the first blinding flash of lightning struck followed closely by the foundation-rattling clap of thunder, she found herself upon the balcony, willing her husband's coach to come into view once again. She was terrified of storms, and had been since she had was a child. Perhaps she had been hasty in giving the servants the night off. She was not prepared to weather a storm of any magnitude alone.

Just as the fear found a foothold within her mind, something caught her eye in the distance – a lamp, swinging upon something. Then another lamp came into view. The wind had already begun to blow hard. Trees swayed under the ever-increasing pressure of the wind. Wrought iron furniture began to shake and then slide, and eventually, overturned as the wind gathered within the dark soul of the approaching storm.

The lamps.

They could be the oil lamps of a carriage. She found herself holding her breath as she watched the lamps grow in size as they approached. She closed her eyes and whispered a silent prayer that this was not some figment of her desperate imagination, and that her husband, the love of her life, was returning home to hold and comfort her through the storm. To reassure her that no storm was powerful enough to damage what they shared, that no force of nature could put asunder what they had built together. After what seemed as seasons, the sound of shod horses, and the definite rattle of carriage riggings, joined the lamps. Yes! It was his carriage! He was coming home, coming home to her just when she needed him the most!

She had thought to await him in the parlor, to be lounging very lady-like albeit a touch seductively, upon one of the divans when he entered. But those plans were thrown aside as she gathered the gown about her and ran from the balcony, through the halls and to the top of the stairs. At great risk, she took the stairs two and three at a time, her heart racing faster than her feet could ever hope to manage. At this moment, all she wanted was to be in his arms, his safe, protecting, loving arms, to let him shield her from the storm and reassure her that all would be well.

As she reached the main foyer, the massive oak door swung slowly open, and even the sound of the straining hinges seemed to add to the oppressive air that dominated the entire keep. So ominous and foreboding was the feeling that came over her that she stopped as the door completed its slow swing open, and a dark figure stood in the doorway. Lightning flashed and thunder crashed behind him and the silhouette appeared to be not of her husband, but some specter of the night, some physical manifestation of the storm come to torture her with her own fear. The dark figure stood as stone in the open doorway with only its cloak fluttering in the violent whip of the wind. Its features were concealed in darkness, and for a moment, as her breath hung in her throat and her heart threatened to beat itself out of her chest, it seemed as if death itself had come calling on her doorstep.

Sienna felt her body tremble in the cold grip of fear. Cold sweat coursed down her chilled flesh and her breath refused to come except in only the tiniest amount needed to keep her alive. Her lips were suddenly dry, and her eyes were open wide as she regarded the dark shadow in her doorway. The howling wind whipped and tossed the figures dark cloak about him, yet the body beneath the cloak remained as motionless as stone under the force of the wind. With her breath coming rapid and shallow, she wet her lips, trying to summon enough air with which to speak. "My love? Is it you?" she asked, her voice sounding so tiny in contrast to the ever building rage of the storm outside.

"Yes, my sweet Sienna. It is I," the deep voice answered. It was the voice of her husband, yet it was not. There was another quality to his voice that she had never ever heard before. It was dark and sinister. He had always had a deep, mellow voice, and it had soothed her on many occasions, but this night found the new quality to his voice sending another spike of ice-cold fear into the base of her spine, and the tiny hairs on her arms and the back of her neck to stand on end.

"What... what has detained you? You are late," she managed to say, feeling a strange sensation begin to come over her. It was as if she were entering a dream without ever having fallen asleep.

"Nothing has detained me, my love. I had to delay my return so that I could arrive at night," he answered. The very sound of his voice seemed to be as a hammer upon the spike of fear in her spine, each word driving it ever deeper.

"Why?" she asked breathlessly. The disoriented feeling of things changing around her, yet nothing appearing to have changed at all, assaulted her already fear riddled senses. Panic crept into her mind, and she found herself on the verge of tears.

"So that my present for you could be given and accepted in the true setting in which it was designed," he replied as he finally stepped through the door. The large door slowly swung shut, but she could not remember seeing him actually touch it in any way. "My dear sweet Sienna. Everything has changed. The happiness we knew before is nothing compared to the happiness that awaits us. We will know seasons upon seasons of pure erotic delightful happiness." As his voice droned into her mind, into her very soul it seemed, the strange sensations only increased. There was the dark sense of something sinister very nearby. A sense of some dark danger that should be sending her screaming in terrified flight from this suddenly dark and cold place, and yet held her feet fast. There were other sensations, erotic seductive sensations, causing a new tremble to join the tremble of her fears. It was the tremble of sexual excitement and anticipation, and despite the soul wrenching fear that held her, she felt herself begin to moisten in anticipation.

"I-I do not understand. Of what are you speaking?" she managed to whisper. She had to swallow hard to keep her throat from going dry, and she found that her mouth was as dry as her throat.

"Of course, you do not understand. I did not understand at first. I was as terrified as you are now, but you will understand. All will be revealed and you will relish in our new life together. My dear Sienna," the figure slowly shook his head before continuing. "There are no words to describe what awaits you, what awaits us before the passing of this night. The joys, the delight, the raw power... all of it can be ours. Ours to hold and to share for an eternity."

Stark raving fear and raw sexual hunger tore through her. The dizzying sensations assaulted her from all sides, and she had to place a trembling hand to her temple and close her eyes to summon the will not to become lost in the violent sea of contradiction that raged at her. "You are... you are frightening me, love. Please stop it. Please come hold me. You know how I fear storms!" she whispered in a desperate plea. She felt her entire world spinning away from her in the grip of something dark and evil, and she turned to the only source of strength she had ever known. Yet as she turned to that source of strength, she could not help but feel that this was also the source of the evilness.

The figure stepped closer and closer, and as he approached, a chill unlike any she had ever known came upon her. It was a chill much like she imagined the chill of the grave would be. She raised her fear riddled green eyes, hoping to see his soft warm eyes, full of love for her. Yet the shadows that hid the details of his form from her would not yield to the flickering light of the many candles that gave off more than enough light to dispel all but the darkest shadows of the room. She could not see his face, could not see his eyes, and could make out any detail that would tell her that it was really her beloved husband and not some demon of the storm. Yet she knew, with a deep conviction she knew that the man before her was her husband. Changed, altered, no longer as he had been, but still her husband.

"Yes. I know how you fear the storm. That too will pass with this night. Very soon, you will have no reason to fear anything this realm can possibly offer you. You will know absolute power and absolute invulnerability. No longer will storms terrify you. Indeed, you will come to love storms, will revel in their violence, and find yourself standing upon the highest rise, lifting your head and screaming in defiance of the storm and the Fates and the very gods of creation. Nothing will ever harm us again. No one will dare defy us our most whimsical of wishes. This realm will be ours to take from as we please."

As his dark words whispered across her ears, into her mind, into her very essence, she found her thighs trembling in preamble to the release of her pent up passions, the knot of her release building ever tighter deep in her belly. The *fear was still present, still chilled her to the core, but the sexual sensations seemed to join and merge with the fear to bring her to ever-higher peaks of dark sexual desire and yearning. She found herself adrift in the cold dark warmth of his contradicting tones. Her jaw grew slack and her eyes were held fast to the area of the shadowy face before her where she could feel his eyes burn into her, yet she could not see them. She wanted him. As never before, she wanted him. Wanted him to take her, roughly and by force, pounding his desires into her without consideration for her physical well-being. No gentle touches, fond caresses, romantic whispers in her ears this night. No. She wanted him to take her with a violence to match the raging storm outside. Without conscious effort or thought, she slowly drew the shawl from her shoulders to let it drop to the floor behind her. Her breasts rose and fell with the rapidity of her breathing, her legs opened slightly as the trembling thighs beckoned for her release. The knot of painful pleasure continued to tighten.*

"Yes...." she whispered as her lips parted to let her tongue slide out to moisten them, as tempting a gesture as she had ever made. As the dizzying sensations claimed her mind, she gave into the darker sides of her nature, the things she kept tightly locked up within herself, not daring to allow them access to her mind, to possibly be acted upon, for a lady never did such a thing. This night, she had no desire to be a lady. As the storm continued to build, as the lightening lit up the night sky and the thunder rattled the walls of the keep, and as the rain began to pound down without mercy, she found herself wanting to be as dark and as evil as she had always heard of some women being.

The dark silhouette of her husband moved around to stand behind her, so very close, yet never touching and every inch of her body cried out for his touch. She so desperately wanted his hands upon her, roughly, violently. Kneading her flesh and molding it into any dark form that he wished.

"You have no concept of what I have been given, of what I will give you before this night ends. The raw, dark power that is more delicious than anything you have ever tasted. The sheer rawness of being able to hear the beating hearts of every soul around you, of being able to hear the very blood course through their veins with a roar to drown out the most raging of rivers. To look at someone and instantly know their deepest fears, their darkest desires!" His voice caressed her bare shoulder and a tiny gasp escaped her lips as the quivering knot of her building orgasm tightened.

"Oh gods... yes!" she whispered, wanting more, hungering for more. Her hands trailed up her body to her neck as she drug her nails across her own skin, feeling another tightening claim her. Her fingers were like eight tiny torches, searing her skin with a pleasure-filled pain that only matched the raging contradiction of sensual fear. Her moans rattled from her throat as he spoke again, each word snaking about her body to stroke the wet heat of her.

"To sweep forth to embrace them, to draw from them their fear, their desire, their very essence. It burns more than any liquor as it courses down your throat, coating your stomach with a fire that no sexual encounter can match. The fire spreads throughout your body, bringing you more pleasure than you feel you can ever possibly handle, leaving you spent yet so much

TOM SECHRIST | 281

stronger than before."

A shuddering gasp burst from her lips as her desire raged hotter than she ever remembered experiencing. Her legs trembled, and she feared they would not support her weight much longer. Her fingers trailed down her throat and to the upper slopes of her breasts. Never before had she touched herself like this, and the mysterious pleasure it brought her only fueled the fires of her release. Her hands molded themselves around her breasts, and she found she ached for his hands to replace hers.

"Are you ready, my sweet Sienna? Are you ready to leave this pale form of life behind for one that is more brilliant than any sunset could ever possibly show? Say the word, my love, and I will bring you up with me, to this new height of existence, to this new awareness that no other mortal can ever know in a million lifetimes."

As the knot of her release threatened to suddenly release and claim her in a wave of pleasure as pure as any she had ever known, she drew in a shuddering breath and closed her eyes, surrendering all to him and to the erotic darkness he had returned with. "Yes. Yes. Yes!" she whispered. "Please... take me... take me now!"

His hands took her gently by the bare shoulders and his lips lowered to her neck, kissing, his tongue darting out to lick the salty sweat from her skin. His teeth pinched together on her skin. It was when she felt the two definite points of his teeth grazing her neck that something changed. Something shifted. His hands. They had always been so warm. Even on the coldest of days, his hands had radiated warmth. Now they were cold as if the flesh were dead. His breath was equally chilling on her skin, and there was a foul stench to it as though something within his mouth were rotting away.

Fear! The fear that had dominated her only... how long ago? The fear that had slid alongside the sensuality and joined with it now tore itself free and raced up her spine to drive a blunt shaft of clarity into her perceptions.

No!!

This was wrong!!

This was evil! She knew she was in danger, deadly danger. As the two points began to press hard into the flesh of her neck her eyes flew open wide, and she twisted violently out of his grip to stagger back away from him. Her eyes, filling with tears, searched the dark form before her but the shadows that covered him would not reveal anything to her.

"Who are you!!" she screamed out at him as she struggled to make sense of what was happening. The sensations did not fade but only increased their pressure on her, disorienting her, trying to call back the dark sensuality to fog her mind and lull her into accepting whatever sinister deed this specter of her husband intended.

"You know who I am, Sienna. I am your husband. Only better than before." His words called out to her, trying to sooth her into his grip again. The warm heat evaporated quickly to be replaced by the terror chill that had held her before.

"No! You are not! My husband would not behave so. Would not say such blasphemous things!" she screamed out.

The figure shook his head again, almost sadly. "There is so much you cannot understand at this moment, things that I cannot conjure the words to make you understand. I have loved you since the moment I first beheld you. I would do nothing to harm you, to hurt you in any way. Search your heart, Sienna. You know this to be true." his words... his tone... so much like that of her husband, and yet so different than she had ever heard them. She was dizzy, shaking terribly as fear continued to scream at her, warning her, demanding that she flee from this place, which no longer held the warmth of home to her. It was with a soul rending thought that she realized that at the moment this dark figure and walked through the door, that the warm glow of home had left this place and had left it forever. She clamped her hands to her ears and squeezed her eyes tightly shut.

"Silence! No more of your lies! No more of your evilness! Leave me be! Just leave me be!" she screamed as she found she could no longer remain within these suddenly evil walls. With pure terror claiming her, she turned and ran, not remembering if she opened the door or not. She dashed out into the full violence of the storm, but for the first time in her life, she did not fear the storm. She had found something she feared far more than any storm... her husband, and what he had become. The wind whipped at her, tore at her gown. The rain sliced into her skin, feeling as if each drop were a tiny dagger that rent her skin. The lightning flashed and blinded her, the roar of thunder deafened her, and fear drove her on into the storm. She didn't know where she ran and didn't care. Just so long as she put distance between her and the demon behind her. She rounded a hedge and ran headlong into him. The impact tossed her back, and she was barely able to maintain her footing in the thickening mud. She gasped in shock at seeing him suddenly standing before her as if he had suddenly appeared there.

"Fear not, Sienna. Fear is something else that will vanish upon your awakening into this new life. You need not ever fear anything ever again." The storm wailed and moaned with such volume that she was unsure if she actually heard his words with her ears, or if by some dark magic, he was placing his words into her mind. Again, a massive bolt of lightning tore the night sky, driving the darkness back for a moment. Yet as she blinked in the flash and rain running into her eyes, the shadow across his face never lifted, was untouched by the searing light of the lightening.

"Return to the fires of hell that spawned you!! Give my husband back to me!" she screamed out and began backing away as he began advancing on her.

"I will never know the touch of death. I will never be forced to look at myself in a mirror and watch the decay of old age claim my youth. I will be forever as I am now. Take what I am offering you, sweet Sienna, and you will know all these things as well."

"NO!!!" she screamed as she turned and ran, her legs pounding against the harsh wind and sharp rain. She paused long enough to kick her feet out of her shoes, giving herself even more of a chance to out run the demon. Twice more she rounded a turn to find his menacing presence before her, and twice more he spoke to her in those dark tones, the sensations of his words tearing at her resolve until the only thing she had to cling to for survival was the fear. She ran and ran and ran, not caring what direction just so long as it was away from the sinister silhouette that claimed to be her husband. She didn't know how long she ran, and it didn't matter, until she slid to a sudden halt and found herself perched on the edge of a cliff that overlooked the ocean below. The drop was dizzying, and with the darkness and raging storm, she could not make out the sea below, only a yawning blackness that seemed to reach out for her. Her eyes searched frantically for some means of escape, some hidden path that would allow her to continue her flight, but there was nothing beyond the edge of the cliff but dark angry air.

"You see?" his dark voice sounded and she spun to find him standing there, blocking the only path of escape. "How futile your lives have been. All your lives are spent running from the inevitable. Time, as it applies to mortals, is very patient. It bides its time and it waits, letting you run and run and run, thinking you can escape the ultimate end of time... death. Yet just when you think you have outdistanced it, out ran it... you find yourself perched upon a precipice with no escape, nowhere to run to anymore, and time picks that moment to stroll up and hand you the very thing you had been running from... death."

The dark figure chuckled an evil sound as it spread its hands wide. "Very much as this night has been. You have fled from me and from the great gift that I have for you. Now you have no other place to run and have no choice but to accept what I have to offer you. I know you are terrified my love. I can remember the bitter cold taste of such terror, but I will never know it again and soon... neither shall you."

With those words, the figure began to slowly walk toward her. She stepped back, seeking some means with which to fight back, to down this demon, and flee, but fear held her reason tight and would not allow her access to it. Again, he stepped forward, and she stepped back, the heel of her bare, mud caked foot dislodging the loose rocky soil at the very lip of the cliff. There would be no further steps back. There would be no escape for her. She was doomed to become whatever dark demonic thing had claimed her husband. A fierce gust of wind pressed her back, and she was hard pressed to keep her balance upon the very lip of the cliff.

"Do not be foolish, my love. Accept my gift, and let us live an eternity together. Please, step away from the edge, take my hand, and accept me as I am now as you have always accepted me." As her terror-widened eyes watched him approach her, she could feel the dark cold blackness below stretching out to her. Suddenly, the dark form stopped advancing toward her. It stood rock still near her, but did not advance any further.

"Sienna, my love, my life. Listen to me." She blinked away the stinging droplets of rain as she studied him and considered his words. Gone were the dizzying sensations, the dark sinister tones that had inundated his voice before. The voice that now screamed out at her over the rage of the storm was truly that of her husband. The rich tones of his voice as she remembered it swam around her, and she dared to let herself feel the first tiny releases of fear that had held her. "I have been hasty, I have brought all of this upon you too suddenly, and I am deeply sorry. I have discovered what I have always wanted. I have found a way to master not only the Mystic Arts but also all forms of magical working. I have become intoxicated with my newfound abilities, and I fear I have not been behaving as myself since the discovery. Please. Forgive me."

"Is this another trick?" she stammered out, wanting desperately to believe him, and yet not able to ignore the screaming of her instincts to beware.

"No. No tricks. I have become overwhelmed by my new abilities, and I only sought to impress you with them. I did not know a storm would come and arouse your fears, and my timing was in poor taste. Come, let us go back inside, and I will tell you all you wish to know." Her husband's voice called out to her, and a tiny measure of calm eased itself into her. Something still called to her to be weary, to be alert for as much as he sounded as he always had, there was still something not totally whole about him.

"Please. No more tricks this night!" she gasped as the tears flooded her eyes, and the sobs began to rack her body. "Please, if you love me, do not frighten me anymore," she pleaded.

"I swear upon my life, no more tricks!" he said as he extended his hand to her slowly. "Take my hand, and let me take you home." As the sobs continued to shake her body, she slowly extended her hand to take his, a sense of relief that her life would be returned to her as it had been before this terrible storm came upon her. Then her fingers touched his, and she knew, in that one instant, life as she knew it was forever out of her reach now. Her fingers did not encounter the warmth of her husband's hand, but the death-chilled flesh of the demon that had taken his place, his form. As cold as his flesh was, it caused her to jerk her hand back as though she had just touched fire. So violent had been her reaction that she was now pitched backwards, off balance. Out of instinct, she moved her foot back to brace against the ground to prevent her fall. Her foot encountered empty air and she realized that she had finally found the one form of escape left to her.

"SIENNA!!" his voice cried out as she toppled backwards. Her breath hung in her throat and her heart seemed to seize in her chest in that one eternal moment between remaining on the cliff and plummeting into the yawning darkness below. Cold, death-like fingertips grazed her arm, and a sudden bolt of lightning finally displaced the shadow over his face. The color of his eyes had changed, and the warm brown tones had been replaced with an ice blue that looked so very evil. The pallor of his skin bore the touch of death, and she knew her husband was forever lost to her. Then she was falling, and she screamed.

A scream that sounded out forever... a scream and the image of her husband's face continued to the conclusion of all else...

Brianna bolted upright out of her blankets, the sheen of cold sweat plastering her hair to her forehead causing her clothes to cling to her body in a cold damp shroud. Her eyes flew open wide, as did her mouth, and in that split second upon waking, standing there in front of her was a dark silhouette... the same silhouette that had been in her dream of the woman named Sienna.

And just as Sienna had, Brianna screamed a blood-curdling scream born out of sheer terror.

CHAPTER TWENTY-

EIGHT

Brianna scrambled backwards from her blankets and the dark shadow that was suddenly no longer standing before her. Her wide, panicked filled eyes searched for the shadow, the specter that had followed her from her dream into reality to haunt her while she was awake. Still, as her insane eyes searched, she continued to scream.

A pair of strong hands gripped her shoulders and began pulling her to her feet. A deep voice sounded in her ear, but she could not recognize it. "Brianna? What is wrong?" the voice asked, but as she could not recognize the voice, nor could she recognize the words. Her panic frozen mind only perceived that the dark shadow had now come up behind her and was trying to take her. Instinct took control for she lacked the mental capacity to think reasonably. Quickly slapping her palms together and lacing her fingers together, she screamed out and swung her double fists around, catching the shadow in the mid section. With a grunt of surprised pain and a hiss of suddenly expelled air, the large figure released her shoulders as she gained her footing. Without waiting for the shadow to regain itself, she spun and took the head of the shadow in her hands and drove the head downwards while bringing her right knee up with all the strength her trembling limbs could muster. With her own natural strength embellished with the adrenaline rush of fear, her attack flipped the shadow backwards to land upon its back.

"Brianna!! What in the hell are you doing?" another strange voice called out in a dialect she could not understand. Another shadow demon come to take her? She dropped into a defensive posture, her wild eyes searching for the dark specter that had followed her from the nightmare. Another pair of hands gripped her shoulders from behind, attempting to still her struggles. Again, her animal instincts took over, and her hands flashed up to grip one of the wrists that tried to hold her. With another growling scream of fear and rage, she suddenly dropped to one knee while hauling the surprisingly lightweight of the second shadow demon over her head. The figure sailed briefly through the air to land hard upon its back with a dull thud.

As he landed hard upon his back, Darkseed blinked back the sparkles that suddenly filled his vision and wondered where in the realm Brianna had come upon such strength and agility, and what in the realm had claimed her sanity. He had been awake when her screams had pierced the still of the night. He had risen to see what was the matter when he saw Zandorth pick Brianna up from her backwards scramble. Suddenly, Brianna had lashed out with a devastating double-handed punch that had doubled the massive warrior and followed the attack up with a jerking knee lift, which had toppled Zandorth to his back as though he were nothing but a thin wisp of parchment.

Slowly, he rolled to his stomach and looked up to see Shantira approaching Brianna from the side. Pausing a moment to look into Brianna's face, he knew that whatever personality and intellect Brianna possessed was not with her now. Her eyes were terrified, wide with fear, and her complexion was as pale as death. Her body trembled, and she looked very much like a wild animal that had suddenly been cornered. As Shantira approached, he tried to call out to her, to warn her to keep her distance, but the impact with the ground had knocked the breath out of him, and his voice would not respond. All he could do was watch helplessly as Shantira tried to sooth Brianna's fear, and failed.

Shantira watched as Darkseed sailed through the air and landed hard upon his back, stunned. Beyond him was Zandorth, slowly rolling to his stomach in an attempt to get up, but his movements were slow and sluggish. Twin trails of blood poured from his nose, and his eyes were heavily glazed over. The overriding concern for Brianna's safety flared into brilliance again as she perceived of some unknown danger to Brianna. "Brianna? Be still, Brianna, it is all right. None will harm you. I swear it," Shantira called out to her in as soothing a tone as she could muster.

Brianna spun on her, and the look in her eyes stopped Shantira in her tracks. There was no trace of the warm personality of her friend in those wild green eyes. Never in her life had she seen a fear like the one that claimed Brianna at this moment. Shantira had never feared Brianna, had never had any reason to, but at this moment, looking into the wildest set of human eyes she had ever seen, Shantira feared Brianna more than any wild beast in the realm. Despite her fear, Shantira's concern demanded that she do something, anything to protect Brianna from harm, regardless of the consequences. "Brianna? Be still, dear. It is I, Shantira. I will not harm you, I only wish to help you," she said softly, soothingly. As if to drive her point home, she extended her hand, palm up, and stepped toward her. Not until Brianna moved with blinding speed did Shantira realize how very wrong she had been.

With a blur of movement, Brianna took Shantira's wrist in a grip that threatened to shatter the bone. With a vicious snarl upon her full red lips, Brianna jerked Shantira toward her. As Shantira staggered forward under the full weight of Brianna's newfound strength, Brianna jerked her knee upwards and caught her full in the stomach. Shantira cried out in pained surprise as she felt the air suddenly surge up through her to burst from her lips. Pain flared out from her stomach to engulf her, and she sank to her knees, arms wrapped around her stomach and her chest heaving, trying to suck in enough air to stay conscious. Suddenly, something smashed into the base of her neck sending a white-hot lance of pain racing down her spine and up her neck to explode into a brilliant light show of multi-colored pain within her mind. The force of the blow sent her crashing, face first, into the ground, and the kaleidoscope of pain within her brain robbed her of her senses, leaving her stunned and helpless beneath a woman she had called her friend, and at this moment feared she might take her life. Only the sound of Devenshire's voice gave the semi-conscious Shantira reason to hope she might actually live another night.

"Brianna! Calm yourself! You are not thinking clearly!"

Brianna spun on Devenshire with the same ferocity that she had done with Shantira. Devenshire halted his approach and studied the face of his friend and lover. Nowhere within the depths of her eyes did he see any hint or spark of recognition. He was as much an enemy to her as the others before him had been. He didn't know what had taken her sanity from her, but he did know that to attempt to restrain her physically would be met with the same defeat as the others had suffered. "Brianna! Calm yourself! We are your friends. We mean you no harm. Do you understand?"

Brianna stood before him, breathing heavily with her wild eyes darting all over, searching for something while keeping him in her line of sight. Devenshire kept his arms wide from his body and his hands open in a display to show he was unarmed and not a threat. Soothing tones were not reaching her, perhaps she would respond to harsher tones. "Brianna, listen to me—calm down! We are not going to hurt you, but you must relax!"

For a moment, the wild eyes studied him, narrowed in wild suspicion as they considered him. Could her hesitation be due to some small recognition? Could some part of Brianna's mind remain intact and that small part recognize him? He could not be sure, but he took the chance that perhaps she did at least find something familiar about him. Keeping his arms open wide at his sides, he stepped slowly forward. "I will not harm you. Trust me," he said in as normal a tone as he could. The green eyes opened slightly wider, and Devenshire halted his advance. He continued to speak to her, to try to make her understand that he truly meant her no harm. When her eyes narrowed again, he risked another step forward.

Suddenly, she screamed out and lunged for him, her hands curled into claws and racing toward his throat with surprising speed. Devenshire barely had time to raise his own hands to grip her wrists as she collided with him, carrying them both backwards to the ground. Devenshire tensed every muscle in his body, as he prepared for his hard impact with the ground as he struggled to keep Brianna's fingers from encircling his throat. As the jarring impact came, his strength faltered for a moment, and it was all she needed to grip him by the throat and instantly begin squeezing. Devenshire tried to tense the muscles of his neck, to hold off her grip, but her strength was born of madness and stark raving fear. No amount of strength he could muster would counter hers at this moment. Almost instantly, he could feel his airway cut off, could feel the intense pressure upon his throat and wondered which Brianna would do first—strangle him or break his neck. Despite the knowledge that he could not physically restrain her, he found himself pulling at her wrists with all his might. His arms trembled violently as his muscles contracted, pulling outward and then downward on her wrists in a futile attempt to break her iron grip. Blinking back the pressure building up behind his eyes, he looked up to see Brianna's face, contorted by the fear and the madness, set in a grim determination to squeeze the very life from him. He struggled, strained to either break her grip upon his throat or shift his body out from under hers to gain some sort of leverage to use against her before the lack of air caused him to pass out. Moving her was like trying to move stone. As the edges of his vision became ringed with black, and tiny sparkles of light erupted inside the ever-growing dark circle, he knew he was running out of time. There were few options left to him and none of them he wished to use on her, but his time was growing short, and if he did not act soon, he would die by her hand. Releasing his right hand from her wrist, he curled the slowly numbing fingers into a fist and drew it back as far as he could. He had never in his life struck a woman, but given the circumstances, he reasoned that there was always a first time for everything.

Before he could release the punch, he felt her grip begin to loosen. A tiny breath of air snaked into his nearly depleted lungs, and he sucked it in hungrily. The iron grip of her hands loosened further, and the airway opened more, allowing more air in which he gratefully accepted. Then her hands released his throat and Devenshire wasted no time in drawing in all the air his passageway would accommodate. As he closed his eyes to let his vision clear, he could feel her weight rise up off him. He rolled to his side and simply allowed himself to lie there, breathing again, which was as welcomed a sensation as he had experienced in a while. His mind considered that the madness had passed, and Brianna had come to herself, realizing what she was doing and had released him. He fully expected to hear her nearly frantic voice asking him if she were all right and spilling out her most sincere of apologies. What he was not expecting was the sound of her angry snarls and screams of protest.

With curiosity, he opened his eyes and raised himself up on one elbow to see Brianna hovering just above the ground, her entire body, save for her neck and head, bathed in a blue shimmering light. Blinking back the fuzz of near suffocation, he shifted his gaze beyond Brianna to see Darkseed standing where he had fallen. His head was lowered and his hands were outstretched, moving deftly through the tides of his powers, manipulating them to hold her. His eyes were locked fast to Brianna's struggling form suspended within the power of his spell. She writhed within the containment of the spell, screaming and snarling, fighting for all she had to free herself from the blue light. Devenshire climbed slowly to his feet and regarded her. She was like a wild beast, caught in a snare. Not understanding that she could not free herself, but willing to expend every last ounce of her strength in the attempt.

Stant, Petera, and Kendra suddenly ran up from where they had bedded down for the night. They had their bows out and arrows nocked. Their confused expressions took in the scene and looked from one person to another, waiting for an explanation. Zandorth made a downward motion with his hands, telling them to be still for the moment. Slowly they lowered their bows, but kept the arrows nocked, just in case.

"Do not just stand there, Daimion! Do something! I will not be able to hold her like this forever!" Darkseed's voice called out. The strain of his tones told him that it was indeed taking great concentration to keep enough power flowing into the spell to hold her.

Devenshire stepped up to Brianna and waited until the flashing eyes locked to him with as pure a hatred and fear as he had ever seen. Once he was sure that he held her attention, he spoke to her.

"Brianna! Listen to me! Calm yourself! Can you understand me?"

Her reply came as she snarled and tried to strike out at him with her feet and hands. With a sigh and shake of his head, he realized words would not reach her. He glanced at Darkseed, then to Shantira who was just coming to a sitting position, and then to Zandorth who was regaining his feet, wiping at the blood from his shattered nose. He looked back at Brianna.

"Forgive me, Brianna. This is necessary," and he slapped her, open palmed, across the face. It was not a gentle slap, but one that rocked her head to the opposite side from impact. Almost instantly, she ceased struggling and her head drooped for a moment. Then she slowly raised her head and blinked several times. Devenshire watched as the Brianna that he knew slowly slid back into position within her eyes. She slowly opened her mouth and began working her jaw from side to side, in a test to see if the appendage still functioned. She blinked several more times, and her breathing began to calm from the near frantic pace of a only seconds ago.

"Brianna? Can you hear me?" Devenshire asked tentatively.

She moaned and began looking around quickly, as if suddenly realizing that she was not where she thought she should be. For a split second, he got the distinct impression that she was looking for someone. Her wide eyes took in all that she could see, and when she could not find what she sought, she visibly relaxed.

"Daimion?" she asked, her voice still sounding with a touch of fear as her eyes looked to him.

"It is alright. You are safe." he replied calmly.

"The storm... the cliff... the shadow..." she stammered as she slowly looked around her again. Devenshire studied her closely, seeing how she seemed to not totally recognize her surroundings, as if she had found herself suddenly transported here from some other place.

"You must have had a terrible nightmare," Devenshire observed. He had seen that same bewildered expression on others who had experienced very powerful nightmares, the type of nightmare that at the moment of waking seemed more real than the waking world.

"Nightmare?" she asked slowly as her eyes returned to him, and he watched as she finished the transition from wild fearful creature to calm intellectual woman. She nodded slowly. "The nightmare... yes. The nightmare has returned," she muttered as she slowly closed her eyes and seemed to wilt under some great weight upon her. "It always does," she finished in a whisper.

"Are you alright?" Devenshire asked her.

After a few moments, she nodded wearily. "It was a nightmare. A very real nightmare," she responded sadly, almost hopelessly. Devenshire did not know why, but he felt as if what had claimed her in her slumber went far beyond a simple nightmare. There was despair within her and was as if she were facing something that was not new to her, but unwelcome just the same. He thought to question her about it, but decided that now was not the time. She was still addled from the nightmare and ensuing insanity of the fear it had spawned within her waking mind.

Devenshire looked to Darkseed and nodded once. Slowly, she lowered to the ground until her feet were firmly planted, and the blue glow began to fade. Devenshire prepared himself to catch her should her legs betray her without the aid of Darkseed's containment spell. To her credit, as the last hue of blue faded from around her, she slumped, but did not fall. Zandorth, Shantira, and Darkseed approached slowly, various looks of concern gracing their features.

"Are you alright?" Devenshire asked again.

Brianna again worked her jaw as her hand reached up to rub the place Devenshire's palm had struck. Slowly she nodded. "Except for my jaw. Who struck me?" she asked slowly.

"I did. I fear it was necessary to break you from the fear that held you. You attacked us and nearly strangled me before Darkseed could contain you. My apologies," Devenshire replied.

"Yes, but did you have to slap me so hard? I think you broke my jaw," she asked, continuing to work it. She tried to make her tone reproachfully humorous, as she normally would have, but the strain of what she had just endured made the effect less than it would have been.

"You were not yourself. I was not sure how much strength to use to jar your senses. I speculated that one very hard slap was better than several of lesser intensity," Devenshire replied with just the tiniest flicker of humor in his voice.

Brianna blinked slowly once before raising them to his face. "And I am supposed to congratulate you for such cunning speculation?" she asked with more of her old familiar tones, and Devenshire smiled and shrugged.

"Are you sure you are alright, Brianna?" Shantira asked as she stepped up beside her and took her by the arm. Before she focused her attention on Brianna, she had shot Devenshire a stern look that puzzled him. Then Brianna's concerns about her sudden shift in behavior returned to his mind, and he wondered if this was a manifestation of what had alarmed Brianna.

"Yes. I will be fine. Just shaken and very weak at the moment," she replied as she gave Shantira one of her warm smiles. "I hope I did not hurt you too badly. Please accept my apologies. I was not myself."

Shantira smiled warmly and gently stroked the side of Brianna's face. "Think no more of it. I will survive. All that matters is that you are safe."

A flicker of concern flashed in Brianna's eyes as she returned Shantira's smile and raised her hand to move Shantira's from her face. She turned slowly to regard Darkseed and Zandorth. A look of true shame and quilt passed across her features, especially when she beheld what she had done to Zandorth. "Please forgive me. I would never deliberately harm any of you."

Devenshire watched her closely and smiled as he saw yet another aspect of Brianna that he admired. While most people would have slumped their shoulders and lowered their gaze while uttering such an apology and admission of guilt and shame, Brianna's shoulders remained back, her head high and her eyes looking at each of them in turn. While she felt genuine shame at what she had done, she would not show defeat, would not let her quilt cower her down. As she had said to Shantira those many nights ago in the tavern, face defeat with the same zeal that you accept victory.

Darkseed smiled and shrugged. "Tis of no matter. You simply scored a fortuitous strike. I was off guard and ill prepared for your maneuver." it was the closest thing to admitting that Brianna had taken him, and taken him without a doubt, that Darkseed would make.

Brianna giggled and nodded at Darkseed's attempt to save face and accept her apology without actually doing so.

"Do not apologize for being victorious," Zandorth said in his usual stern tones as he continued to wipe blood from his nose. "There is no shame in defeating an opponent. I feel no loss of honor at having been bested. It was my own underestimation of your state that allowed you to fell me." Zandorth reached up and pinched the swelling bridge of his nose between the thumb and forefinger of his right hand. With a sharp sideways motion, he snapped the septum back into place. Everyone winced at the sound and marveled at how the warrior gave no outward indication that he had just snapped his broken nose back into place. He blinked several times and sniffed once.

Brianna finally turned to Devenshire and fixed him with as sweet an expression as he had ever seen upon her face. "To you I owe the greatest of apologies," she said softly as she walked slowly up to him and wrapped her arms about his neck. "I could have killed you, and I am deeply sorry. Do you forgive me?"

Devenshire smiled and looked into her eyes. "Of course I do. You were not yourself. I do regret having to strike you. I hope you can understand."

She smiled sweetly again and tilted her head back to look fully into his face. "I can understand, and I can forgive you for it, after one tiny detail is taken care of."

Devenshire arched one eyebrow as he regarded her upturned face. "And that detail is?"

Brianna smiled seductively as she unwrapped her arms from his neck and took a small step back. With blurring speed, her right palm snaked out and slapped him across the face. His head jerked hard to the side from the blow. "Do not ever slap me like that again! Next time? Use a bucket of water."

Devenshire blinked a couple of times to clear the sparkles from his vision as he turned his eyes to her. There was only a slight trace of genuine anger in her manner. It was simply and purely a Brianna maneuver, and one that would defy explanation. As he regarded her, she smiled a wide, sweet and innocent smile, and quickly batted her eyelashes at him before turning and walking away. Shantira and Kendra quickly raised their hands to their mouths to suppress the giggle that tried to rise at the look of pure shock that had come to his face. Darkseed was not so kind as he snorted out a laugh of genuine delight as he shook his head and turned to walk away. Zandorth had turned back at the sound of the slap and nodded once in approval before a smile snaked across his hard features and he turned back to continue walking away. Peter and Stant chuckled as they continued to watch the scene unfold.

Devenshire felt his cheeks flush with embarrassment but only smiled as he raised his hand to rub the stinging flesh of his cheek. A thousand witty retorts sprang to mind, and he settled on one, possibly not the best of them, but the one that would convey to her that he understood and accepted what she had done.

"Bitch!" he called out.

Brianna paused and turned to regard him. In an eerie copy of his own expression, she arched one eyebrow and smiled. "You would not have me any other way."

Devenshire laughed a genuine laugh of humor and merriment as he shook his head and turned to go back to his duties of first watch. As strange and unique as their relationship was, so had been her apology and his acceptance of it.

CHAPTER TWENTY-NINE

Deep into the night, Devenshire stood watch over his sleeping and trying to sleep companions. His mind turned over the events of Brianna's obvious nightmare and ensuing madness. While it all fit neatly into the confines of a normal, albeit very real, nightmare something within him had never liked accepting neatly fitting solutions. Something at the back of his mind nagged at him, called to him to study the situation further before writing it off as what it appeared to be. Yet for all of his consternation over the event, Devenshire could find no explanation for his internal unwillingness to accept the simple fact that Brianna had a nightmare, and it had scared her to the point of madness.

"Still worrying yourself over Brianna's nightmare?" Darkseed's voice said from the shadows behind Devenshire.

"Yes." Devenshire replied simply. He had sensed Darkseed's approach.

Darkseed stepped from the shadows to stand next to Devenshire, and for a moment, both men were silent as they each contemplated their own thoughts.

"I, as well," Darkseed finally admitted.

"The madness of fright lasted entirely too long," Devenshire observed as he continued to study their moonlight flooded surroundings.

"I noticed that, as well. There was something else involved. I briefly touched upon it when I held her in the spell of confinement," Darkseed replied.

That was it! That was what was keeping him from simply accepting the occurrence for what it had appeared to be. All during the exchange with Brianna, up to the point he had slapped her, his special sense had been tingling all along his spine, but he had been too preoccupied with Brianna to pay it much heed at the time.

Devenshire never took his gaze from the depths of the night as he answered. "Magic."

Darkseed nodded. "Another force was touching Brianna's mind. Not necessarily controlling her actions. More like holding the panic to her, preventing it from lifting, as it should have naturally."

"Xavier?" Devenshire offered.

Darkseed shook his head, his expression showing his level of concentration on the subject. "Not likely. The kolondra of the spell on

Brianna was not like the one I sensed in the storm."

Each practitioner of the arts had their own unique way of manipulating the mystic energies of the realm. It was very much like a mystic fingerprint, and each one was as unique as the being casting the spell. This unique method served as a way of identifying who the caster of any given spell was. It was called a kolondra.

"Did you recognize the kolondra?"

Darkseed thought a moment before shaking his head. "No. It was one I have never encountered before. It was very carefully masked, at any rate. Whoever was manipulating the Arts was skilled enough to mask their work. When I cast the binding spell, I only brushed against the trace of magic already at work within Brianna. As soon as I touched it, it vanished without a trace."

Devenshire nodded. He had expected as much. The memories of the essence he had sensed in the woods many nights before returned. Someone was following them, watching them, someone who knew the intricate workings of the Arts and how to mask themselves in their usage of them. Almost instantly, the mental image of the strange man known as Darius sprang to mind. There was something about that one, something unholy, sinister, and dangerous.

When the silence between them seemed to stretch on beyond tolerance, Darkseed clapped Devenshire on the shoulder. "Go get some sleep, Daimion. I will take watch."

Despite the confusion and troubling thoughts within his mind, Devenshire had to admit that he was in dire need of sleep. He had gotten very little rest since Shantira's village had been destroyed. He doubted he would sleep, but the act of resting would be preferable to no rest at all. With a stifled yawn, he nodded. "Wake me if you need me," he said as he turned and began making his way toward his own blankets.

Once he had stretched his frame out upon his blanket, Devenshire continued to stare up into the thick blanket of stars and ponder the many thoughts running through his mind. They were drawing ever closer to Xavier. As twisted as Xavier was, Devenshire was not about to make the mistake of assuming him to be ignorant. One did not rise to the levels of power and control that Xavier had by being foolish and careless.

With another yawn, Devenshire propped his head upon his left arm, which he had tucked up behind him to serve as a pillow. What other steps would Xavier take to attempt to stop them? Would they be prepared to face them when they came? A thousand other thoughts sought his attention, and he tried valiantly to give each one the attention they deserved, but there were too many, and soon he found his mind a raging battleground with thoughts colliding and attempting to annihilate each other, too many thoughts, too many questions, and no answers. As he tried to force order to his exhausted mind, the soft tendrils of sleep eased around his mind and body, trying to coax him into relaxation and eventual sleep. His mind would have none of it however. There were plans still to be made, strategies to be formulated, and contingency plans devised. Such things could not be done in the abyss of slumber.

You need sleep, Daimion. A thought called out in his mind. His eyes began to droop, and a distinct fog began to settle about his mind. He tried to determine if the thought had been his own or someone else's. There was something familiar in the soft mental touch upon his mind, but the thickening fog of sleep was making it impossible to sort out what was familiar about it. His eyes burned from being open too long, and each blink took more and more effort to return his eyes to a fully opened state. During one exceptionally long blink, it felt as if cool fingertips were softly stroking his forehead. At their touch, the fog at the edges of his mind thickened and rolled slowly inward, calming the raging thoughts it encountered. A sense of peace and serenity prevailed within the depths of the fog and despite his desire to remain awake, to formulate the exact course of action he should follow, the sense of peace appealed to him.

As he struggled against the ever-tightening bonds of sleep, a melodious hum whispered slowly into being within his mind. It was a soothing sound, and the voice that made it came from some deep part of his memory that he could not, at the moment, recall. The cool soft fingers continued to stroke his forehead as the strains of the hum stroked his mind, slowly allowing the peaceful fog to inch its way toward the center of his mind. The raging battle of his colliding thoughts diminished to a few intense arguments until those, too, were lulled into silence by the ever-increasing fog. Soon he found he could not recall exactly what it was that he so desperately wished to remain awake for. Given that he saw no reason to fight the warm tender embrace of sleep any longer, Devenshire fell asleep with a long, heavy sigh. It was a deep sleep that he had not had in many days.

As Devenshire sighed into sleep, and his body visibly relaxed and surrendered to the demands of sleep, a dark form, crouched at his head, lifted her hand from his forehead. Her eyes regarded Devenshire's sleeping features for several moments before a slight smile touched her pale lips as she rose to move silently away.

~*~

Dawn came slowly. The pitch of night slowly lightened in subtle colors from black to gray and into the lighter pastels of day. Birds began their daily chirping, nocturnal animals settled in for sleep while the day creatures began to stir. Only the wise of the animals known as humans were awake to witness one of the simplest and most breathtaking of natural events. Lordalise was one such animal. With his heavy cloak wrapped about him to ward off the slight chill of the morning air, he stood away from the sleeping forms of his party to silently enjoy this one event that filled him with peace and softened some of his harsher edges of his existence. No doubt, many of the cursed demons he pursued were now safely locked within their tombs, preparing for their day of death before night fell once again to call them forth to lay waste to another innocent soul. It gave him some sense of ease to know that these damnable creatures known as vampires could not enjoy a scene of such beauty, and therefore, could not mar its perfection with their foul glance.

In his mind, he could almost see the vampire known as Devenshire holing up in some dark damp cave somewhere ahead of them, hiding from the sun in fear for his hellish being. So it should be. Another demon, somewhere in the realm, was doing the same at this moment, the one who had taken his sister and had set him upon his life's course. He did not even know that one's name, but it made little difference. Lordalise didn't need a name and the ghoul would not need a name where it was going. Someday, the Fates would bring them across one another's path again, and this time, Lordalise would have his revenge.

As these darker thoughts continued, they were lessened in intensity with the rising sun. As if the intensity of the memories were tied to the color of the night sky as it lightened, so did they. Other thoughts came to his mind that delighted him beyond description at the days to come. He had finally confronted Captain Armand about his strange behavior, and the captain had shared with him the reasons behind his behavior. The brilliant Captain Armand had a new plan for capturing Devenshire and his minions, and it was simplicity in itself. Once the plan was executed, neither Devenshire nor his companions would know what had struck them until it was too late. Much, much too late.

He found he could almost not contain his eagerness to set Armand's plan into motion. Vengeance would swoop down upon Devenshire and his followers, and it would do so with swift finality. The comforting weight of his fire powder weapon at the back of his belt reassured him of that. Armand had sworn Lordalise to secrecy about the plan. With a vampire's hellish abilities, the fewer people who knew of the plan, the better.

~*~

Dawn found Devenshire and the others saddling their mounts, preparing to move out. Darkseed checked the riggings of his mount a final time before stepping back toward the fire to warm himself from the morning chill.

As he stepped up to the fire, a yawn eased its way from his lips, and he found himself stretching to ease the kinks from his back. It had been many seasons since he had slept upon the ground as often as he found himself doing now.

"Good morning, Darkseed," Brianna's voice chimed pleasantly as she stepped up to the fire from getting her mount ready.

"Top of the morning, M'Lady," he replied with a smile. "I trust you are suffering no ill effects from the nightmare?"

Brianna's eyes sought the tongues of flame and Darkseed could see the dark thoughts encase her mind. From the darkness of the flesh beneath her eyes, and the reddish tint to the whites of her eyes, she had not slept since awakening from the nightmare. Darkseed tilted his head slightly as he studied her profile. This nightmare was not a new one to her. Her expression carried the haunted look of one who had been forced to endure some hellish torture on a regular basis and had simply accepted that there was little they could do to prevent the torture or ease the pain it caused.

"No. I am fine," Brianna finally answered with a slight shake of her head before breaking her gaze from the fire. The pleasant smile she normally carried returned to her lips, and her eyes turned to seek out his, flaring with mischief. "I trust you are suffering no ill effects from the aftermath of my nightmare."

Darkseed chuckled softly. The more he got to know of her, the more he could understand Devenshire's attraction to her. She was not like any other woman he had ever encountered. She had a wonderful sense of humor and a quick wit.

"No. A touch bruised, but not seriously injured," he replied.

"That is fortunate. I still do not understand why the madness of fright took me so last night. I have never done that before," Brianna commented. Darkseed's eyes narrowed slightly as he not only listened to her words, but heard her tone of voice, as well. There was no lie in her words or her tone. But there was something there that preoccupied her mind, and she simply was not speaking of it.

"It has been a long and tense journey. Perhaps those two factors played a part in slightly unhinging your mind under the heavy weight of such a nightmare," Darkseed offered.

"Perhaps," Brianna said with a slow nod, but Darkseed knew she did not believe it, not for a moment.

"Good morning," Devenshire's deep voice said as he stepped up to the fire and began rubbing his chilled hands over the heat.

"Daimion," Darkseed acknowledged with a nod of his head.

"Good morning, Daim," Brianna said with a radiant smile.

Devenshire smiled warmly and briefly locked eyes with Brianna.

"Good morning, Bri," he said in a warm tone.

"You finally slept," Brianna observed, still watching Devenshire's features. Darkseed looked again and saw that some of the haggard edge was gone from his face. The dark circles that had only grown deeper with each passing day of the journey were all but gone. There was freshness about him that only deep sound sleep could produce.

Devenshire nodded slowly. "It would seem so. I cannot recall when I have slept so soundly."

"It was about time," Brianna said as she finally took her gaze from his face and set about pouring herself a tin of hot coffee.

Devenshire made a non-committal sound as he, too, looked back into the glowing embers of the fire, waiting for her to finish, so that he could get a cup, as well. Darkseed secretly looked at both of their faces and saw absolutely no trace of the deep emotions that had been there a moment ago. It was as if they had shared that one tender moment and having shared it, put it away in whatever tight vault each of them held deep within them.

Peaceful silence reigned over the chilled gray dawn around the campfire as each member of the party finally found their way to the warmth. Each arrival was greeted with the customary tiding of good morning and returned before silence returned.

When enough of the night had been eased back for the trail to be seen fairly easily, Devenshire broke the peace of the morning.

"We should begin riding. The trail will only grow more treacherous form this point until we leave the mountain range."

Each person nodded their acknowledgement of his statement, and each set of eyes reflected the dread they felt at another day of bunched nerves at the treacherous trail that lie ahead. With hardly a word, the fire was extinguished, and the party quickly found their mounts and climbed into their saddles.

With Zandorth and Stant leading the way, the group got underway. The dark ominous thoughts of Xavier and the Stones of Andarus having been temporarily put away in favor of the day of anxious riding that lie ahead.

~*~

In a deep and very dark cave, Darius began preparations for his day of death. With hardly a conscious thought, he summoned his rapidly fading powers and cast a protection spell over the entrance of the cave. Should any be foolish enough to try to enter the cave during the daylight hours, a very painful death would quickly descend upon them. While it was unlikely that any would venture into the cave, many seasons of existence had taught Darius to never assume anything. Again, he cursed the dawn. It robbed him of his strength, his powers, and his arrogant freedom. While night ruled, so did he, ruled with an authority and absolute power that none could touch. Yet with the first glowing tendrils of sunlight, his strength and power would soon begin to fail him, and he would be forced to scurry for dark cover, as would some nocturnal rodent. The one thing his many seasons of being had not taught him to accept was his own limitations in regards to the day.

As he stretched his tall form out upon the darkest corner of the cave, and the strange numbing sensation of his death sleep began pulling at him, he reflected that the past night had been very profitable, and the first seeds of his plans had been planted. The fruit that would soon be borne upon his plans would be so very sweet. Brianna had the nightmare, just as he had sensed she did. It was the same nightmare playing over and over again within her life span. Little did she know, but it was far more than just a nightmare. In fact, it had very little to do with anything even remotely resembling a typical nightmare. What Brianna mistook for a nightmare was actually her past essence trying to awaken in her current form. It was calling out to her, begging her to recall it and to embrace it as a part of herself, to remember what she had been and what she could be again. Yet, as with every form she had inhabited since that fateful night so very long ago, Brianna resisted. Her current identity was clinging tightly to its control of her, and it would not allow her to realize what was within her.

Darius smiled as he recalled standing over her sleeping form, tapping into her mind and freeing her nightmare to run rampant through her mind, seeming more real than it ever had before. When she awoke with a start, she had briefly seen his shadowed form standing over her and the resulting terror had momentarily loosed her sanity. With a bit of assistance from him, the insanity clung tightly to her mind and drove her to a frantic state of self-preservation. The brief skirmish with the others had been very educational. While he had watched from a distance, he saw much of what he had hoped to see.

The Warrior, Zandorth, had been taken completely by surprise. When he had stooped to pick Brianna up, he had not expected her to suddenly lash out at him, and her attack had stunned him completely. This told Darius that Zandorth relied heavily on the things he knew, familiar things. Thus, a weapon had been handed to Darius with which to use on the Warrior. His comfort of familiarity was his weakness. The massive Warrior could be attacked from a side that he would never expect an attack.

Darkseed had been a surprise, as well. The Adept had tried to physically restrain Brianna, and when that had failed, he had resorted to using his powers. This could mean that while Darkseed resisted relying upon his powers, he did not totally discount them. The powers were there, he knew they were there and he drew a great comfort and confidence in that. Darkseed relied upon his physical powers to get him through the day-to-day struggles of his mortal existence, but his powers made a comforting support to that reliance. Conclusion? When faced with a situation that his physical powers could not handle, Darkseed could be counted on to resort to using his powers. It spoke of a lack of faith in his physical being. Where there was a lack of faith, there was an opening and a weapon.

Shantira had been no surprise at all. Partially due to him knowing everything there was to know about the woman, and partially because of his presence within her mind. He had sensed the concern in not only Brianna, but also the others as well, toward Shantira's sudden protectiveness toward Brianna. He made a mental note to lessen his presence within her. Suspicions had already been aroused, and he could do without those at this critical juncture of his plans.

The smile slowly faded from his pale lips as the last subject of his study came to mind. Devenshire. Damn him to the fires of hell! Darkseed may very well be the rogue of the group but Devenshire had his moments of unpredictability that made Darkseed seem quite easy to read. Darius had known Devenshire would use some form of his limited mystic abilities to try to reason with Brianna, to use some minor spell to snap her out of her madness. Yet he had tried to talk to her, tried to reach out to her and did nothing when Brianna attacked and nearly strangled him. When Darkseed had restrained her, Darius had fully expected Devenshire to use some form of magic to probe her thoughts yet he had slapped her. Physically slapped her and with enough force that he had felt the sting upon his own flesh through the link he had been maintaining with Brianna. So surprised were both he and Brianna at this that Darius could not have maintained the link had he wished to. The action was absolutely the last thing he had expected Devenshire to do. With all the latent power within him, with all the possible mystical energies he could have used, he had struck her physically. With his upper lip peeling back in a snarl, he silently cursed Devenshire again.

His anger toward Devenshire was also fueled because of what he had sensed in Brianna's thoughts concerning Devenshire. She cared for him. She cared for him deeply. Not love, at least not as she chose to define love, but she cared, and that irritated Darius to no end. Strong emotional ties were very hard to overcome, even for one such as he. If the emotional tie Brianna felt for Devenshire were strong enough, then his plans were already in jeopardy. In all the forms Brianna had maintained through the seasons, none of them had been emotionally tied to another, at least not as strongly as Brianna was tied to Devenshire. This would more than complicate things, and it irritated Darius to near madness.

The other unknown in this dangerous equation was Devenshire's own feelings for Brianna. Did he care for her as she did for him? Was such caring possible for one who maintained such a stringent grip on his emotions? Indeed, Devenshire managed his emotions with an iron will that matched his own. If the feelings were two-way, then careful restructuring of his plans were called for. If not, then perhaps there was a way that he could diminish Brianna's feelings for Devenshire.

Of course, there was the more simple approach. Remove Devenshire as a consideration. Accidents happen. There were many perils in the realm that could strike a man down in the blink of an eye. If Devenshire were dead, then Brianna's feelings of deep caring would, after a reasonable time of mourning, be vacant. While Darius did not deny a certain sense of pleasure in ending Devenshire's life, the greater danger at hand made that option unusable, at least for the near future. As badly as it galled him, Darius had to be honest enough with himself to admit that he needed Devenshire alive.

Many options began rolling through his mind, and he gave each one careful consideration before either discarding them or filing them away for possible use at a later time. The death-sleep was claiming him, and as his eyes fluttered slowly closed, his mind continued to ponder the possibilities. The one thought that refused the dark mystic pull of his death sleep was that this time he would have her.

He swore it.

CHAPTER THIRTY

Four days later, dawn had found Devenshire and the others near the morning fire, hot coffee in hand and Devenshire's maps spread out on the ground. While the trail to this point since leaving the clearing where Xavier's storm had struck had been treacherous, it was nothing compared to what lie ahead.

Darkseed puffed on an early morning cigar as he studied the maps intently. "Had we stayed on the same path we had been following, we would have exited the mountain range here," he pointed at a place on the map, "at the Mantis Pass. Assuming the damage to our trail from the storm is as bad as it appeared to be, Armand will follow the same path."

Zandorth nodded. "If we push through this area here," he drew a line with his finger ahead of where a small pebble marked their current location, "we will come out here. It will cut nearly two days off our original path and put Armand much further behind us."

Stant studied the map as intently as the others, and his grim features preceded the shake of his head. "But your path will take us through the Gryphon Expanse." he shifted his gaze from the map to Zandorth's profile. "This is the time of mating for the Gryphons. Do you truly wish to intrude upon male Gryphons in the hunt for a mate?"

Each person looked up at Stant before exchanging concerned glances with each other. Gryphons were dangerous enough as they were, to say nothing of being in the vicinity of a female in season with a male anywhere nearby.

Petera chimed in. "To say nothing of the terrain. This path is within the most remote area of the Kil'tafore range. The most seasoned, well-trained mount would have difficulty navigating this area. Some of our horses are not accustomed to mountainous terrain. One misstep in the wrong place and it is a very long way down."

"We have little choice," Devenshire commented as he used a dagger to trace lines on the map. "If we circumvent the Gryphon's range, it will require moving in a southeastern direction for many miles before we can shift our course back to the north. That will put us exiting the range here," he tapped a point on the map. "If Xavier is following the path I suspect he is, he will be coming around the range here at Malden's Pass. Our exit will be here," he tapped the map a considerable distance from where Xavier's exit was. "We will lose nearly five days on Xavier if we circumvent the Gryphon's range."

Shantira's brow furrowed as she studied the map. "Any other course will either put us closer to Captain Armand or further away from Xavier."

"Allow me toss in one more bit of bad news," Stant injected. "This is also the time of the season when the weather can shift suddenly, and more times than not, violently. The upward drafts of warm air from the valleys to the south meet the cooling air coming over the top of Mt. Kil'tafore from the north. The meeting is never a peaceful one."

Brianna took a sip from her coffee tin and inserted her own bit of bad news to the discussion as her eyes also scanned the map. "And providing we survive that, we will be exiting the mountain range almost directly in the heart of the savage lands surrounding the Coledecci," Brianna added tapping their exit point on the map.

"Well this just keeps getting better and better," Darkseed injected as he continued to study the map, searching for a course that simply did not exist.

"We have little choice. We must keep following this path. To return to the original path would deliver us to Captain Armand, and to go around the Gryphon Expanse will put us well behind Xavier with many extra miles to make up," Devenshire concluded. It was the conclusion the others had come to in their minds, but none wanted to verbalize.

"I have spent a great deal of time in these mountains, and the path we have set for ourselves will be treacherous at best," Stant said as he swept his gaze around the group. "The undergrowth will be thick and will make the ground impossible to see at times. The trees are numerous, as well. The terrain is very rocky and uneven. One misstep could break a horse's leg or its riders' neck."

"So our choices are to risk Gryphon attacks, violent storms, uneven terrain that could cripple us or worse, or risk capture by the Royal Guard, or lose ground on Xavier and give him more time to execute his plans for the Stones of Andarus?" Kendra asked her expression and tone clearly indicating she didn't particularly care for any of the choices.

"I do not see where we have a choice," Zandorth replied resting his hand on his bent knee, and then propping his chin on the back of his hand, his gray eyes continuing to study the map.

"I agree," Devenshire added, his gaze also studying the map intently.

Brianna rubbed her aching eyes and tried to concentrate on the map and ensuing discussion about their path, but the events with the nightmare and her ensuing insanity made it impossible for her to risk sleeping, so she was not completely focused. "I completely disagree with this path, but I have no better suggestions to offer as an alternative."

Devenshire sipped his coffee and took a moment to study the group over the rim of his cup. They were tired, very much so. Each of them had borne the ravages of this quest virtually from the beginning. The eradication of Shantira's village, the nightmarish night in Lirpa, the hard pounding miles since leaving the city, the massive storm Xavier unleashed upon them, and the ever-present pressure of Armand pursuing them was taking its toll. The effects were most clearly evident on Brianna's features. She looked haggard, worn, and some of the spark in her eyes was beginning to dim. He was not aware of the nightmare, which obviously had been plaguing her for seasons. He decided that once the opportunity presented itself, he would ask her about it, perhaps even try to sort out what it meant.

Zandorth seemed to be holding up the best of the group. Adversity was nothing new to him, and as a Warrior of the Ancient Class, he was trained to handle situations like this, probably much worse than this. Darkseed was holding up well, also. His ability to distance his emotions from the situation was helping to keep the pressures of the journey from wearing on him as heavily. Shantira was doing remarkably well considering she'd had to endure the most of anyone in the group. The destruction of her village still weighed heavily on her heart, and the grief of losing nearly everyone she had ever known was gnawing at her soul like a predator chewing on a bone from its latest kill. The nightmarish break-neck race through Lirpa, and the ensuing miles of fleeing and pursuing were wearing on her, as well. The youthful spark was gone from her eyes, and she looked even more haggard and worn than Brianna. Her odd behavior toward Brianna also concerned him. He wasn't sure if the source of this behavior was due to the loss of her village or something else. It was a problem he would have to investigate as soon as the opportunity presented itself.

The elves were fresh to the quest and had not yet endured the challenges the others had, but that did not mean that they, too, would not soon be worn down by the constant pressure of pursuit and being pursued.

He lowered the coffee tin and looked down at the map again, this time looking for something other than the best path to follow to evade Armand and catch Xavier. It only took a moment to find what he was looking for.

Korpera.

Perfect.

"We will follow this path until we exit the mountain range. Then we will divert slightly to the east to this point," he said pointing to an area of the map.

"That will take us northeast. Xavier is heading due north! Zandorth protested.

"True, but only a little bit, and the loss will be minimal," Devenshire replied.

Darkseed's brow furrowed in confusion. "Why that way, Daimion?"

Devenshire looked up at Darkseed and gave him a tight, mischievous smile. "Korpera."

Darkseed's confused expression shifted into a radiant smile of acknowledgment accompanied by a slow nod of approval. "Excellent."

"Who or what is Korpera?" Brianna asked, shifting her confused gaze between Devenshire and Darkseed.

"A city on the edges of the savage lands. It is the last outpost of civilization between here and the northern edge of the Coledecci," Darkseed answered.

"Why would we go there? We have ample supplies," Stant said. "This will take us off course to catch up to Xavier."

"There is no reason to go to Korpera," Zandorth added.

"I can think of one very good reason to go," Devenshire replied sweeping his gaze around the travel weary group. With a tight smile he added, "Revelry."

"What?" Shantira asked, not sure if she truly understood what he meant.

"We have been pushing hard since leaving Lirpa. We have been pursued while pursing Xavier. We have endured attacks, storms, and a nerve-wrenching trail. We are all growing tired and trail worn. We need a night of revelry, of escape, of having a few hours of not worrying about what comes up from behind us and what has become of the madman we pursue. In short, we need a diversion," Devenshire said.

"It is a mistake!" Zandorth injected. "We will lose precious time, time Xavier can use to unleash his hellish plans!"

Devenshire could see the agreement with the warrior's statement flicker through everyone's eyes, but he could also see the relief a night of merriment offered, as well—except in Zandorth's eyes of course. "Very true. However, if we do not take a moment for ourselves, to revel in what it is to truly live, then we will lose sight of what we strive to protect. If we forget what it is we are fighting for, then what is the point?" His gaze swept the entire group. "We have trials and horrors to come that will make our night in Lirpa seem like child's play. I am speaking of one night, just one, that we can relax and enjoy ourselves, to evade the phantoms that have haunted us since the destruction of Shantira's village." He looked back down at the map, which showed the massive expanse of the Coledecci. It was an irregular oval shape, which was very narrow at one end. He took up his dagger and tapped the map with the point. "Here is Korpera. He then traced an invisible line with the tip of his dagger through the narrowest part of the Coledecci. "We would take our night of revelry in Korpera and set out early the next morning heading directly after Xavier. Following that course would take us directly through the sparsest area of the Coledecci." He moved the dagger to the area of the Kil'tafore range where they would exit. "This is where we will exit the mountain range." He then drew a line directly north, which took their path through a denser section of the Coledecci. "If we proceed directly due north, we would be forced to pass through the Coledecci in a much more dangerous area." He withdrew the dagger from the map and let it hang from his fingers as he swept the group with another penetrating gaze. "So my diverting to Korpera for one night, we earn two rewards: a night of revelry and having to cut through the cursed forest range in a safer area to make up the difference." Devenshire shrugged as he pursed his lips. "It seems to me that what we would gain far outweighs what we would lose."

Each person took a moment to consider his words, and then exchanged silent glances with one another. Only Zandorth's features remained rigid and unreadable. He clearly did not agree with the diversion or the reasons behind it. But then, Devenshire reflected with a mental smile, he wouldn't.

"I know what we fight for. I cannot lose sight of that! I do not need a night of drunken revelry to remind me what is at stake!" the warrior grumbled.

"That may very well be true for you, Zandorth. However, the rest of us are not warriors of the Ancient Class nor have we had your training. The rest of us need a source of release, a way to relieve ourselves of this pressure we have been under since this quest began," Darkseed answered.

Zandorth shook his massive head. "It is foolish! It will cost us time and distance on both Xavier and Armand!"

Brianna smiled tiredly. "I, for one, am willing to risk it. Daimion is right, what good will we be in fighting Xavier if we are too worn from the trail? While we all know what we are fighting against and fighting for, a reminder of what we would lose should Xavier succeed is well worth the risk."

"I agree," Shantira added. "I have lost everything that ever tied me to this realm." Her eyes grew distant as she stared into the flames of the campfire. Devenshire could see the reflection of the flames in her eyes and knew the flames in her mind were not of the fire before her. "The only thing that gives my life meaning now is the pursuit of Xavier and stopping him from destroying anyone else's home...

anyone else's life." Her voice trailed off slightly as tears began to gather in her eyes. She quickly blinked them back and raised her weary gaze to the others. "No one wants Xavier worse than I do! I will not rest until my blade pierces his brutal heart, and I watch the light of life leave his hellish gaze! But I agree with Daimion. I need this night of revelry, a night of being carefree, a night to remind myself of what is to come after we stop Xavier, or what will be lost should we fail."

Petera and Kendra nodded in agreement before looking to Stant. He was the eldest of their group, and he would have final say in their position. Stant shifted his gaze to Zandorth, and it was clear in his bearing that he agreed with the warrior's assessment. He switched his gaze to the hollow, haunted look in Shantira's eyes, and his brow furrowed slightly as he saw the deep, empty pain that cloaked the young woman's soul. His eyes drifted down to the map and remained there for several moments as he contemplated the situation.

"Stant?" Kendra asked expectantly.

Stant's gaze remained locked to the map but it wasn't truly looking at the map. "Zandorth is right. This is pure folly. We will be giving up tactical advantages by diverting to Korpera." He sighed heavily as he looked up at the slowly brightening sky. "I do not think we have a great deal of hope in stopping Xavier in what he plans. We may very well be the first to bear witness to whatever hell he unleashes upon this realm, but I also recognize that someone has to try, regardless of how hopeless it appears to be." He shifted his gaze to Zandorth. "Before any battle, regardless of how assured a warrior is of victory or how utterly hopeless the battle appears to be, every soldier needs one last night of revelry, of being free, and reminding himself what it is to truly be alive. Every warrior has to be able to face his fate as a man, a man who lived his life on his terms and not those dictated by others." Stant and Zandorth locked eyes and a silent understanding passed between them. "I say we go to Korpera."

All eyes turned to Zandorth as he continued to stare at Stant. The warrior then shifted his hard gaze to each person around the map coming to rest finally on Devenshire. His mouth drew into a tight line as he continued to consider everything that had been said and weighing it against what he knew should happen. "It is foolish! It is a waste of time, a commodity, and I need not remind you that we are in short supply of," he said as he moved his gaze to Stant again, nodding once, "yet, if we are to fail, then we should die on our terms, not those of a madman!" He looked back at Devenshire again. He was about to concede to Devenshire, and that galled him but in that way that was hard to define within the confines of his relationship to Devenshire. With a look of disgust, he shrugged. "Go on! Have your night of drunken revelry!"

Devenshire smiled only slightly as he nodded. "I am sure you will not be enjoying a tankard of ale either, Zandorth."

Zandorth's features never shifted as he continued to stare at Devenshire. "Going to Korpera is foolish. Not enjoying a healthy tankard of ale while there would be madness."

An air of released tension suddenly seemed to float up from the group. Tired smiles mixed with subdued excitement as they each realized that they would have at least one more night of freedom before rushing headlong into whatever Xavier was planning.

"Hail to the camp!" came a distant shout. Everyone quickly rose to their feet, hands drifting toward swords or bows. Devenshire peered into the shadows of the trees, reaching out with his powers to see who was out there.

"Arness." he said as a matter of fact.

"What?" Kendra asked with growing excitement.

"It is Arness," Darkseed replied as he stepped up beside Devenshire.

"Come!" Devenshire shouted into the gloom.

Slowly, a silhouette took form, which then gave way to Arness walking into the small clearing, leading his horse by the reins. The elf looked tired and worn. His face and clothes were dirty from many days upon the trail. He paused several feet away, his clouded expression hesitantly looking at Devenshire. "Permission to enter the camp," he said, following the proper etiquette for coming upon a camp he was not part of.

"That depends upon your intentions," Devenshire replied, holding his hard gaze on Arness.

"I wish to join your quest. I have had a great deal of time to consider what has been said, and what is to come," he replied. His face took on a look of shame and regret as his eyes left Devenshire's to look at the ground. "I regret my words and actions upon learning of what you go to face. I was not prepared for it. I wish to offer an apology, and my services in what is to come."

"Are you certain?" Devenshire asked. "You are right to give sway to what is to come, but you must be certain in your heart and your soul. I have no desire to engage in whatever is to come and not be certain of those with me. I can understand and forgive your actions, but only once. If you are not wholly with us, then leave us now and be done." Devenshire replied.

"I have had many days to consider all that has been said and what is to come. If I am to die in whatever Xavier plans for these stones of yours, then I wish to die facing him instead of cowering in fear as a coward." Arness raised his eyes to lock in a determined stare with Devenshire. "I am a man, and I will fight like one... and if it is within the hands of the Fates... die like one!"

Devenshire's face remained unreadable as he studied Arness for several moments. Kendra's excitement was barely contained as she shifted her wide eyes from Devenshire to Arness and back again. "Please, Daimion? I know he can be an impulsive ass at times, but he is truly a noble man."

Devenshire looked at her for a moment before shifting his gaze back to Arness. "And he is a kinsman."

Kendra nodded. "Aye. He is a kinsman."

Finally, Devenshire nodded once. "Then join us."

Kendra squealed in excitement as she dashed across the clearing to leap into Arness's arms. Stant and Petera also moved forward to greet their kinsman. The reunion was joyous, and Devenshire allowed them their moment.

"Are you sure?" Darkseed whispered from his side.

Devenshire slowly shook his head. "No. We will allow him to join us, but we will keep an eye on him."

Zandorth stepped up on the other side of Devenshire. "If you do not trust him, why allow him to join us?"

Devenshire continued to study Arness as Brianna and Shantira moved forward to welcome him, as well. "Arness is a random element at best. What better way to keep track of such random elements than to have them under your watchful gaze?"

"Such a course is risky," Zandorth observed.

"Agreed, but for the time being it is better to observe him," Devenshire replied.

"And if he proves to be less than what he presents to us?" Zandorth asked.

Devenshire turned his head to look at Zandorth, a tight smile playing at the corners of his mouth. "Then he is all yours."

Zandorth grunted. "That is the smartest thing I have heard you say since this madness began."

CHAPTER THIRTY ONE

The ride dragged anxiously through each day, each step a welcome gain on the goal of making it successfully through the most treacherous part of their journey so far. Yet each step was anticipated with a gut wrenching twist of nerves. The path wound through the outer rims of the Mt. Kil'tafore range and through the fringes of a Gryphon breeding ground. Everyone had been warned to remain as quiet as possible. While it was likely the Gryphons were further into the mountain range, there was always the possibility of a stray Gryphon flying by. One shrill call from a Gryphon would bring the entire flock down upon them.

Zandorth took the lead with Stant right behind him. They were the two members of the team with the most experience riding through treacherous terrain. Kendra followed Stant with Petera behind her. Shantira rode next with Brianna behind her. Arness rode behind Brianna with Devenshire bringing up the rear. Arness had volunteered to ride in the last position, but Devenshire had insisted on riding last.

At times, the days ride would take them across paths barely as wide as the horse's hooves, while on another day, the trail was somewhat flat and relatively level. There were several times when it looked as though the less disciplined animals would bolt from the tricky footing. Yet each member of the team exhibited excellent control over their nervous mounts and held them to the trail. On several occasions Zandorth would alter their course due to some obstacle or path he felt was simply too hard to navigate. Deviating from the path would carry them further into the Gryphons' territory, but it could not be helped. Each deviation would only heighten the tension of the group as the perilous path was left behind, and then greeted by the distant screams of Gryphons. Occasionally, they could hear the strong, steady wing beats of the creatures as they hunted for either food or a mate. So far, though, they had not seen the beasts, which meant they had avoided them.

As each very long day dragged on, it seemed as though they would never reach the exit of this perilous path. Each day, the sun's progress across the sky seemed to take far longer than it should have. Nerves were drawn as tight as bow strings, breaths were extremely shallow, and muscles were bunched until they were as hard as rocks. The only bright point of their journey was the breathtaking vista laid out before them. All of the Mt. Kil'tafore range, along with the very distant flat lands below, formed a view that was awe inspiring, at the very least.

Just past midday on the fifth day, there was a change in the air that each person felt. They began glancing away from the trail to look up at rolling gray storm clouds forming overhead. There was a subtle change in the fragrance of the air, the feel of it even. Rain was coming. They could smell it in the air and could feel it in the cooling temperature. The travelers watched helplessly as the storm began to form, feeding off the conflicting hot and cold air masses. To the mountain rise to their right, they could see the wispy strings of heavy rain as the storm began unleashing its fury on the higher elevations. They watched as the rain began to sweep down the mountain, heading directly for them. With growing dread, cloak hoods were drawn up over heads and each person braced themselves as the first flash of lightening peeled through gray clouds followed by a rumble of distant thunder. A quick check of the surrounding terrain revealed no shelter, so with heavy sighs of resignation, they forged ahead as the first heavy droplet of cold rain hit. Within moments, they were caught in a heavy deluge of chilled rainwater. Lightning flashed overhead and rumbling thunder rattled both the ears and nerves of the soaked travelers. The one positive note from the rain was that Gryphons didn't like to get wet and would seek shelter from the storm.

The rain lasted for the bulk of the afternoon soaking them to their cores. Teeth were clenched against their urge to chatter in the cold. Fingers took on a bluish tint as they shivered from the frigid onslaught of cold, wind driven rain. Eyes squinted against the assault, trying to shield themselves from the rain but not wanting to lose sight of the treacherous trail ahead. Their progress slowed considerably as their view of the trail was diminished by the twisting twirling curtain of rain. It made the difficult path even more worrisome to the animals, especially those not accustomed to riding through rugged mountainous terrain. Still another danger from the prolonged rain was the possibility of mudslides or eroding edges of narrow ledges that they were sometimes forced to ride across. They had no choice but to push on.

The fact that the Gryphons, as well as most other predators, would not be out during the rainstorm was of very little comfort. It was getting late into the afternoon, and if the rain continued, they would be forced to endure the chill of night while being drenched in the relentless storm. If the rain ceased before nightfall, then the predators would be out in force, searching for food, forcing them to battle a bone rattling chill and a nerve-racking fear. In either case, they knew they would have to make camp for the night without a fire to either cook or dry out by. Unlike the flatlands far below, predators in the higher mountain ranges were not deterred by fire. A fire would all but ring the dinner bell for any number of bolder predators including Gryphons. Regardless of what the evening held, it promised to be a very long, cold, and wet night being spent in the higher elevations of the mountain range where the nights were considerably colder.

The rain finally abated by late afternoon, and the clouds began to break up. After hours of relentless rain, the sun breaking free from the clouds was a welcomed sight, even if it were low in the sky. Each rider was soaked to their core, and the chill from the advancing darkness would only serve to make them more miserable than they already were. Even as the last drops of rain splashed down, the distant cries of hungry Gryphons began echoing off the mountain walls and cliffs. Nerves that had slowly began to unwind in the absence of the predatory creatures once again bunched at the sounds of their piercing shrieks.

Zandorth motioned that the path ahead was wider and could be navigated more easily. That was a welcomed indication. It meant that while they would still need to be aware on the trail ahead, the worst of it was behind them. The drop-offs didn't appear as sharp, the ground seemed a little more level, and the horses didn't seem as anxious. It began to appear that they would actually pass through this trial unscathed.

Then a horse screamed.

Every breath hung in its throat as the scream echoed off the nearest rock faces. The echo seemed particularly loud in the silence they had surrounded themselves in since early this morning. It wasn't clear which horse screamed, but it was very clear in the silence that followed the scream that it had gotten the nearest Gryphon's attention.

Zandorth and Stant instantly held up their fists, indicating that everyone should stop and remain absolutely still. Worried eyes shifted skyward, searching the darkening sky for any sign of where the Gryphons would come from. It wasn't a matter of if they would come but rather which direction they would come from. After what seemed like an eternity, there came the distinct sound of beating wings... many of them. Hands reached silently for sword hilts or bow grips. Ears strained for any indication of where the creatures were. While they could hear their wing beats, they knew that once the Gryphons landed, they would be extraordinarily silent. They were treacherous hunters in the air and exceedingly stealthy predators on the ground. They were very clever and astute predators, and it would not be an easy thing to avoid them.

Just ahead, the trail took a dip and crossed underneath a massive rock shelf that jutted out from the side of the mountain. It was large enough to accommodate all of them and their mounts. Even as Zandorth motioned for the ledge, they had begun moving toward it. It wasn't much, but it was at least a possibility to avoid the hunters.

Gryphons had the head, forelegs, and wings of an eagle, and the body of a lion. They ranged anywhere from four to six and a half feet tall at the shoulders with females being slightly smaller. They were between seven to ten feet in length, from beak to flank with the tail adding up to another two feet. They normally weighed about three hundred to seven hundred pounds with very little body fat.

Gryphons had a very flexible spine and an extremely streamline form. The back legs were muscular and ended in feline-like paws, ranging from one to one and a half feet in width and equipped with very sharp black retractable claws that normally measured six inches in length. The tail was flexible and prehensile, used like a rudder when running or flying. On the ground, they could run at speeds up to thirty miles per hour and speeds of up to a hundred and ten miles per hour in flight. When flying, they normally maintained an average speed of twenty-five to thirty miles per hour using wind currents to keep them adrift.

From the base of the beak to the highest point of the back, just behind the shoulders is where the dense feathers ended, and the fur began. Usually glistening and smooth, the feathers were completely waterproof. Gryphons would spend two or more hours a day grooming their feathers in order to keep them neat and to maintain their ability to repel water. The Gryphon's eagle-like wings sprouted from the tops of the muscular shoulders and boasted a twenty to twenty-five foot wingspan. The Gryphon's head was very much like that of an eagle's with a sharp, razor edged sickle beak, usually one to two feet in length from the nostrils to tip. The forelegs were very muscular and shaped like a lions' legs but were covered with feathers. The front legs ended in talons with four inch razor sharp claws. The talons were capable of crushing small rocks.

Gryphons' lion part was always the golden color of a lion but their feathered parts were varied with different shades of brown, grey, white or a mixture of colors. The colorations of Gryphons was very much like the strips of a tiger. The pattern of stripes on a tiger were as individual as a fingerprint was for humans. So was it with the color patterns on a Gryphon.

Gryphon's were extraordinary hunters. They had extremely good eyesight, capable of seeing a mouse on the gound from a height of one hundred feet in the air with the ability to swivel their heads like an owl, one hundred eighty degrees in a circle. Despite the fact thaty they didn't have external ears, they boasted exceptional hearing, normally being able to hear something as faint as a mouse underground from considerable distances.

Gryphons were extremely adaptable, dealing with extreme weather changes easily so long as there was food. Outside the nesting season, they tended to work in flocks. During the mating season, however, the males became more territorial and less tolerant of anything except a female. Once a Gryphon found a mate, they would mate for life, never leaving one another's side unless it was to hunt for food while the other remained with any young still within the nest. If one Gryphon in a pair died, its partner would not live for much longer. Some speculated that the surviving Gryphon would die from lonliness or a broken heart.

Devenshire, being in the rear position, just barely guided his Friesian under the overhang before the first Gryphon flew overhead, its eagle eyes scanning the ground below for any indication of where the horse scream had originated. From under the ledge, they watched the Gryphon bank in a slow right hand turn and fly back the direction it had come. Suddenly, another Gryphon swooped into view from the left followed quickly by two more gliding in from the right. Each bated breath grew even shallower as the hunting party continued to circle overhead. The Gryphons were sure the screaming horse was nearby, and they were not about to give up the prospect of a meal the size of a horse. No one moved. No one dared to even breathe while the beasts circled overhead. Each time the muscles of a horse bunched a rider tensed, fearful that the animal would do something to betray their position. After what seemed like perpetuity, the sounds of beating wings slowly retreated into the distance. The Gryphons had moved on. For many moments after the last sound of beating wings faded, the travelers simply sat rock still, letting the creatures get far away before any of them moved. Finally, tense glances began to relax and small smiles swept across lips as the riders exchanged relieved expressions.

"That was close!" Arness said as he looked behind him at Devenshire who answered his whisper with a frown and a sharp shake of his head. Each person snapped their heads around at Arness with anxious expressions. While they could not hear the Gryphons, the Gryphons had very acute hearing and could still very well be within earshot.

"What?" Arness asked, unsure of why so many heated glares were being directed at him.

Suddenly, a Gryphon head appeared over the edge of the rock shelf, staring at them with dark eyes upside down. Just as each rider stared back at the massive eagle head, the beak opened and a sharp, shrill cry blasted into the tiny space they occupied and nearly deafened them.

"Damn!" Devenshire swore. "Move!" he shouted as he drew his sword. While they were far enough under the shelf that the Gryphon could not reach them with its beak, it was a death trap nonetheless. He mentally saluted the beasts on their cleverness. One of them had stayed behind while the others had flown away, tricking their potential prey into giving away their position. Pulling back on the reins and using knee commands, he urged the Friesian backwards and out of their failed hiding place. They would need fighting room now.

As soon as he was clear of the ledge, he spun the horse around and kicked deep into the flanks forcing the horse into a full gallop. Hopefully the Gryphon would come after him and give the others a chance to escape from the hiding place turned certain tomb. The other Gryphons, having heard the first one's cry, would be turning around to return and probably bringing more for this potential feast. He glanced back over his shoulder to see the Gryphon staring after him. It slowly squatted down, bunching its powerful legs underneath it before leaping high into the air, its massive wings unfolding and catching the wind and then lifting the large animal into the air with swift and powerful strokes.

Zandorth and Stant urged their mounts forward to get clear of the ledge and then swung their mounts to the right and up onto more level ground, giving them more room to fight. Kendra, Shantira, Darkseed, and Brianna exited their now useless hiding place and joined Zandorth and Stant. In the growing shadows of the fading day, they could see the Gryphon in pursuit of Devenshire. His black attire and black horse made it difficult to track them, but they were definitely gaining a good start on their flight from the Gryphon.

"Daimion!" Brianna shouted and she had concern clear in her eyes as well as her voice.

"I would not be overly concerned for Daimion..." Darkseed said with his voice thick with dread. She swung her eyes around to see his features crouched in concern and looking skyward. Following his gaze, she saw what had made him so concerned. Just as her eyes focused on the dark silhouette soaring through the sky, she heard the ominous, bone chilling scream of the returning Gryphons. The other three beasts sailed over the mountaintop and slowly circled the area the group occupied. It was almost a lazy circle, but they all knew this was to be short lived. The hunters were locating their prey, locking them in their sights. They would very quickly go into a deadly dive, front legs extended with talons and claws open and ready.

Zandorth hefted the comforting weight of his broadsword as he gathered his reins and studied the circling predators. "Spread out! Give yourselves room to fight! Keep moving and keep clear of their talons!" He didn't wait to see if they followed his instructions as he savagely jerked his mount's head around and kicked it hard in the flanks.

Devenshire tightened his knees to the shoulders of the Fresian and steered the mount into a tight break neck turn around a large boulder. Gritting his teeth, he fought to remain in the saddle as the horse executed the tight turn, nearly throwing him from the saddle with the centrifigal force. The Gryphon screamed in protest as it raced past the boulder, unable to manuver the tight turn, and was forced into an awkward series of body twists and wing flaps as it tried to keep from crashing into an outcropping of rock beyond the boulder. As soon as Devenshire came out of the tight turn, he dug his heels in and leaned low over the animal's neck, driving his mount at full gallop toward the others. Just as he was about to twist his head around to see what had become of the Gryphon, he saw something that made his blood run cold.

Shantira was racing toward him, her mount running full on, and behind her was a Gryphon swooping down on her retreating form. The animal's wings were spread wide, the feathers fluffed to catch the maximum amount of air while its forelegs were already outstrecthed with talons wide open. It's head was tucked low, its eyes locked on the horse and rider. If something didn't happen immediately, there would be nothing to stop it from snatching up both Shantira and her mount, and then with a few powerful beats of its massive wings soar off into the sky with it's two course meal...

Petera twisted his body in the saddle and used the stirrups as leverage as he dove off the back of his horse just as the Gryphon swooped past. He hit the ground on the back of his shoulder and used the momentum to roll him back to his feet, his left hand already nocking the arrow he had pulled from his quiver. With the expert execution born of many repetitions of the act, he quickly pulled the bowstring back, spinning in the direction the Gryphon had gone. Just as he locked his vision on his target, he saw Stant take a hard swipe from a front claw, knocking him several feet into the air off the back of his mount. Fighting down the concern for his kinsman, Petera lined up his shot and released the arrow. He watched as the Gryphon suddenly lurched sideways from the impact of the arrow and heard it scream out in pain as it pumped its wings to gain altitude. Petera bolted into a dead run toward the shadowed heap where Stant had landed...

Zandorth fended off the swooping claw of a Gryphon before quickly twisting at the waist and stabbing upwards with his massive broadsword at the quickly passing underbelly of the creature. A warm splash of liquid along his arm and upper torso told him he had wounded the animal. Wiping his forearm across his eyes to clear the blood, he watched as the wounded Gryphon frantically beat its wings to gain altitude, but couldn't. He lost sight of it as he plummeted down the ledge they had just been riding along. He snapped back forward to see what had become of the others as well as the remaining predators. The growing darkness was making it hard to see, and he knew the Gryphons would not be plagued with such a limitation. He wanted to dismount in order to make himself a harder target, but that would leave his mount vulnerable to attack, and Gryphons had a definite taste for horsemeat. Given the option of eating a human or a horse, a Gryphon would inevitably choose the horse. The human would simply be an appetizer. His mount, sensing the danger it was in, became nervous and more difficult to handle. It whinnied in protest of being forced to remain still in the presence of animals that clearly wanted to eat it. Zandorth kept hard pressure on the reins as well as with his knees to keep the animal under control. He saw one of the Gryphons bank to the right and disappear behind a grove of pines. He shifted his gaze downward to see Petera running toward Stant's prone form. He considered wheeling his mount around and racing to help the elder elf, but a scream from behind him forced him to spin around in time to see another Gryphon diving toward Brianna as she raced her mount toward what appeared to be a cave higher up the mountainside...

"Get down!" Devenshire shouted at Shantira as he raised his sword. Shantira's wide gaze briefly met his, and she nodded quickly. She pulled her left foot free of the stirrup and deftly lowered her body to the side of her mount, using her leg muscles and a firm grip on the pommel of her saddle to keep her in place. Just as she settled into this new position, the Gryphon screamed as its front feet snapped closed on the air her body had occupied only a breath before. Devenshire raced past Shantira at that moment and swung out with all his strength to sink his blade deep into the Gryphon's right ankle.

With an even shriller scream, the beast jerked its wounded leg up quickly, jerking the blade out of Devenshire's hand. Almost simultaneously, the Gryphon's right rear leg snaked out in a swipe at him as it passed. Devenshire's eyes widened as he watched the extended claws race toward him. Without hesitation, and moving purely from instinct, he kicked his feet free of the stirrups and threw himself backwards. The claws raced past his face with mere inches to spare. He may have missed the claws, but the momentum of throwing himself backwards caused him to roll off the back of his mount. He hit the ground hard and then bounced and rolled across the rocky terrain...

Darkseed brought his feet up into the saddle, and then he leapt up onto the ledge they had previously hidden under. Free from its rider and sensing the danger it was in, his mount wasted no time in bolting for the cover of a nearby grove of trees. Being on the rock shelf would give him a better vantage point to see what was happening even if it limited his mobility in evading the swift attack of a Gryphon. Taking a quick visual survey of the situation, he saw Devenshire on the ground. He was moving, but they were sluggish, and he knew his friend was dazed. Actually, from this distance, and with the poor lighting, he couldn't tell if Devenshire might be injured. A flicker of movement brought his attention around to see Shantira pivot herself back up into the saddle and bring the mount to a staggering stop. She looked back over her shoulder and saw Devenshire trying to climb back to his feet. She jerked the reins, forcing her mount to turn and yelled as she dug her heels in, sending the horse into a dead run toward Devenshire.

Swinging his gaze around, he saw Brianna racing up the hill toward what appeared to be a cave. He could feel the powerful beat of wings in the air, and he looked up to see the Gryphon swooping down on Brianna's position. He set his jaw and quickly called on his powers. With a sweeping motion, he thrust his right hand out, unleashing a bright blue beam of light from the palm of his hand. The beam struck the Gryphon in the side, knocking it to the right and then slamming it hard into the ground. Darkseed shifted his gaze around to see Petera running toward a shadowy heap that looked like a man. A slight flicker of movement caught his eye, and he saw Zandorth spin his mount around and race toward Petera and the form.

The Gryphon he had knocked out of the air lay in a massive heap near the path Brianna was riding toward, but he knew his spell had not killed the animal. There hadn't been enough time to put that kind of power into it. It was very much alive, but stunned and possibly injured, which made it even more dangerous than when it was simply hungry.

"Brianna!" he called out, but he doubted she heard him at this distance and with all the commotion from the other Gryphons. To his horror, he saw the head of one he'd downed suddenly lift and look directly at Brianna and her racing mount. With a sharp chill running down his spine, he quickly brought his hands up and tried to summon his powers to strike out again. As the tingle of power raced through his body, he focused his attention on the Gryphon as it brought its claw up to strike out at Brianna. He slapped his hands together and then thrust both hands, palms up, toward the creature. Twin tendrils of bright blue mystical power lanced out from his palms and then entwined with each other to shoot across the distance between himself and the Gryphon…

Through her peripherals, she saw the massive shadow of the Gryphon slam into the ground up ahead of her and to her right.

Brianna had spotted the cave and thought it would make an excellent hiding place. She knew one of the Gryphons was bearing down on her, but she dared not look. She had seen a flash of blue light from behind her just before the Gryphon crashed hard into the ground. Then she saw the downed animal raise its head and strike out at her with its front talon complete with long sharp claws. She knew she was far too close to evade the strike. With her eyes wide, she dove to her left off the mount. She braced herself for the impact with the ground as she heard the wet tearing sound of the Gryphon's claws sinking deep into the side of her mount followed immediately by the horrifying scream of the wounded horse.

She hit the ground hard and rolled with the momentum of the fall. She came up on her knees and watched in horror as the Gryphon lifted her dying mount off the ground. It screamed in fear and agony as its legs pawed at the empty air, searching for some form of purchase to evade the inevitable. The Gryphon brought the struggling horse up and struggled to bring its numbed legs under it to regain its footing. The struggles of the dying horse tore at its already mutilated flesh, causing its body to slip in the tight grip of the talons. In instinctual response, the Gryphon's head snaked out and severed the horse's head with a harsh snap of its powerful beak. The horse's head hit the ground with a wet, sickening thump as the body went rigid, quivered briefly, and then went limp in death.

As the Gryphon was nearly back on its feet, a massive bolt of blue light snaked through the air to strike the animal on the side of the head. The Gryphon shuddered under the power of the blue light for a moment before tearing its beak open to let lose a horrific scream of pain. The blue light faded and the Gryphon instantly collapsed into a heap, its talon still clutching the headless body of Brianna's mount.

Brianna shifted her gaze to the direction the blue beam had come from to see Darkseed standing atop the ledge, his hands still thrust out toward the Gryphon. His intense gaze left the Gryphon and shifted to her. She smiled and nodded at him. She expected a return gesture and was puzzled to see his eyes grow wide in terror. In the thickening darkness, she realized that he was not looking at her, but rather behind her. She spun around in time to see a Gryphon explode from a tree line off to her left, propelled on its powerful legs, its wings folded neatly against its sides. Its head jerked around in a very bird-like fashion as its eyes took in the scene before it. Its intense gaze seemed to lock onto the prone, unmoving form of the Gryphon with her horse skewered on its talons. Then the tiny membranes that passed for eyelids flickered over the eyes before they came to rest on her. It cocked its head to one side as it studied her for a second then its beak parted to unleash a shrill cry that threatened to deafen her. As it completely emerged from the tree line, she could see the feathered end of an arrow protruding from its side just behind where the wings came out. She swallowed hard. The creature was wounded and angry. She would be little more than a quick snap of its beak.

"Damn!" she softly swore as the Gryphon gathered itself to leap at her...

Devenshire struggled to his feet, shaking his head in a valiant effort to clear the cobwebs from his sparkling vision. He tried to get his bearings and found it increasingly difficult. The impact with the ground had left him dazed and unsure of his surroundings. With gritted teeth and internally cursed himself for his weakness. He forced his eyes open and looked up only to see Darkseed down the Gryphon with Brianna's horse impaled on its talons. Just beyond the downed Gryphon was Brianna on her knees. Another Gryphon emerged from the tree line and looked at Brianna.

"Daimion!" he heard Shantira's voice call out. He turned to see her racing toward him.

"Keep going!" he shouted as he reached up to grip the pommel of the saddle before swinging himself up onto the back of the mount behind Shantira. "Ride hard, get to Brianna!" he shouted into Shantira's ear as he wrapped his arms around her to grip the pommel of the saddle. She gave a brief nod as she urged her mount toward Brianna...

Kendra rode hard, harder than she had ever ridden before in her life. Stant had gone down hard and was not moving, and she knew she had to get to him. She could see Petera loose an arrow and then break into a dead run toward the elder elf. While Petera and Arness were like brothers, Stant was much more like a father to her. She used the loose ends of her reins to smack against the hips of her mount in an attempt to urge more speed from the animal. The Gryphons did not matter to her save for making sure Stant was not an easy meal for them. Then she heard the spine-chilling scream from above and to her left. A Gryphon. Was it locked on to her? Or had it picked out Petera and Stant for its prey. She dared not risk a look back to see which the truth was. She locked her terrified gaze on the shadowy heap that was Stant and rode for all she could muster.

Then she both heard and felt the powerful beat of large wings directly behind her...

Darkseed watched as Devenshire mounted Shantira's horse and coming to rest behind her. He saw him yell something at her, and though he could not hear him, he knew he was instructing her to ride to Brianna. He switched his gaze to Brianna to see the wounded Gryphon squat in preparation of a pounce. He quickly brought his hands up and began forming another power lance like the one he had unleashed on the first Gryphon. As the tingle of pent up power spread through him, he heard the unmistakable cry of another Gryphon. He snapped his eyes upwards and what he saw made his blood run cold. A Gryphon with a sword imbedded in one of its front ankles was swooping down on him at a high rate of speed. With a chilling realization, he knew the animal was moving far too fast for him to redirect his spell to say nothing of unleashing it.

"Oh bloody hell..." he whispered as his vision became filled with the view of a large talon descending upon him. There was only time for one act. It was a hopeless act, but it was an act nonetheless...

Devenshire felt something ripple through him, a sense of dread, a sense of foreboding that had nothing to do with the perilous position Brianna was now in. While Shantira raced her mount toward Brianna, Devenshire tightened his grip on the pommel, ready to leap out to carry Brianna out of the path of the attacking Gryphon. There was something else wrong, something else that vied for his attention, crying out to him to beware. He swiveled his head to his left just in time to see the Gryphon's talon snap closed on empty air... air that had just a heartbeat ago been occupied by his closest friend... his friend who had thrown himself backwards to avoid the certain death of being caught in the Gryphon's talon. With cold horror, Devenshire watched as the act that had saved Darkseed from the Gryphon's talon now launched him backwards into the wide empty void of the space beyond the ledge they had all ridden along. As if in slow motion, Darkseed's body sailed out into the massive void, almost as though he had taken flight. Then, without preamble, his body suddenly disappeared below the edge of the outcropping.

"Raven!!" he cried out as loudly as he could as if his sheer will would catch him and bring him back to the safety of hard ground.

They had spent the past several days riding that ridge and Devenshire knew that there was nothing beyond the ledge but open air...

...all the way to the base of the Mt. Kil'tafore mountain range...

...and the afterlife beyond that.

EPILOGUE

Caleb quickly finished the last line the old man had recited to him. He quickly dipped the quill into the ink well and poised his trembling hand above the page, ready to record the next utterances of his benefactor. As the silence grew in length, he felt dread spread through him. It was as the day before. The silence meant that they had reached the end of this days story telling. He refused to believe it. He raised his gaze to the old man who was gazing into the fire, his smoldering pipe clutched loosely in his right hand.

"No…" Caleb whispered.

"What?" the old man asked, never moving his gaze from the fire.

"You are stopping the tale for the day?" Caleb asked.

"Yes," the old man answered as he hoisted the pipe to his lips to finish off the last of the evening smoke.

"I think I have learned my lesson about patience you referred to yesterday. We should continue the tale," Caleb said in as soothing a tone as he could muster. He was eager for more of the story but equally eager not to enrage his cranky host.

The old man sadly shook his head, still looking deep into the flames. "For you, it is a story, a tale to amuse and entertain, and possibly educate. For me, it is history. A very painful reminder of things I had not recalled for a very long time and wish I did not have to recall at all."

Caleb paused. He had not even considered this before. For him, the Devenshire Chronicles were indeed a heroic tale of a time long gone. An educational tool he could use to restore order to his life and remind the world of what had come before. Yet, for the old man, it was indeed history, a recollection of events that, at some point, had to hold very painful memories for him.

The old man slowly swiveled his head to gaze at Caleb. "Have you indeed learned the lesson of patience as you have claimed?"

Caleb snapped out of his thoughts and nodded eagerly. "Yes." Perhaps the story would continue after all.

"You babbling idiot!" the old man scoffed as he pulled on the pipe stem. "You have learned nothing! It is as if your mind were missing! You have learned nothing of patience! Had you, you would not have insulted me with the dribble you just uttered!"

Caleb winced as he realized that not only did he not trick the old man into continuing Devenshire's story, he had succeeded in insulting him. With a heavy sigh, he laid the quill down and folded his aching hands in his lap. "My apologies, sir. I only sought the continuation of the tale."

"And you shall have it," the old man said roughly. "But on my terms, not yours! Do you understand?"

"Yes, sir," Caleb replied softly.

"Now, go to the kitchen and prepare an evening meal. I hunger!" the old man grumbled as he returned his attention to the fire.

Caleb reread the last passage from the old man's story again, feeling great angst at not knowing how the battle with the Gryphons turned out. "Could you at least tell me what became of Darkseed?"

The old man sighed in exasperation. "Why do I not simply move ahead to the end of the tale and tell you how all of this ends? Would you like that?"

Actually, Caleb reflected, he would. He also knew that such an answer would only serve to enrage the old man and could quite possibly result in him not finishing the tale. With a slow shake of his head Caleb replied, "No, sir. Not at all."

"Then I suggest you prepare the evening meal, and do so quickly!" the old man shot back. "I tend to become disagreeable when I am hungry!"

Caleb looked up at the man's profile and felt his eyes widen in shock and disbelief. He wasn't sure he could stand it if the old man were any more disagreeable.

Following very irritated directions, Caleb moved out of the main chamber of the cave and into the chilled confines of the nearly frozen kitchen. The old man had insisted on Caleb having another tin of the bitter tea before beginning the evening meal, and he was glad for as he stirred a fire within the frozen stove, he found the tea instrumental in helping him complete the task. It was an arduous task to take frozen meat and vegetables and turn them into a piping hot meal. While Caleb marveled at how the old man had managed to engineer a working cooking stove within the frozen rock of the cave, he had to also acknowledge how hard it was to turn a rock hard frozen piece of meat into a hot and appetizing meal.

After hours of preparation, he was finally able to bring the old man a plate. On the simple tin disk was a thick steak with onions, broccoli, and carrots on the side. He waited as the old man cut a piece of the steak free from the rest of the meat and popped it into his mouth. It amazed Caleb that he waited anxiously for the old man's appraisal of the meal. The old, cantankerous bastard was lucky he was eating a hot meal, let alone a steak dinner.

"Of all of the pieces of beef I have eaten in my life," the old man said after swallowing his first bite, "this is definitely one of them."

Caleb's brow furrowed. "What exactly does that mean?"

The old man fixed him with an annoyed glare, which Caleb quickly accepted as the only answer he was going to get as far as the quality of the food. With a heavy sigh, he retreated to the poorly lit, freezing kitchen to retrieve his meal. He moved back into the warmth of the main living chambers and gingerly moved the drying pages of today's' story telling aside to make room for his meal. Since he had not had breakfast nor lunch, his stomach was growling at him in earnest. He sat down upon his furs and quickly cut out a large hunk of beef before shoveling it into his mouth. As he chewed, he realized that while it was not the worst beef he had ever eaten, it was far from the best, and he understood the old man's reaction. Yet he was starving, so he was not about to let standards get in the way of the first meal he had eaten in days. He cut another large hunk of meat and scooped up a healthy compliment of carrots before shoveling the massive load of food into his mouth. He closed his eyes as he chewed, savoring the flavors and the very act of eating.

He wondered to himself how the old man kept such an abundant frozen store of a variety of meats. There was no game this far into the Wastelands, and the frail old man surely could not make the journey to the lower lands, to say nothing of hunting for, killing, dressing, and processing anything larger than a rabbit. Then there was the mystery of the abundance of vegetables in the old man's kitchen, onions, carrots, beets, turnips, and a host of other vegetables. There was no way that the Wastelands could support or sustain a garden of any kind and yet he could not argue that there were indeed vegetables here. It was just another in the many mysteries surrounding the old man that demanded answers. Caleb promised himself that once he had Devenshire's story perhaps he would seek answers to these questions.

Suddenly, there came a clank of metal directly in front of him. Jumping in a start, he looked up to find that the old man was standing next to him, having sat a tin on the table in front of him. He was startled to say the least. He had not heard the old man rise from the chair or move toward him with the shuffling steps. It was as if his ancient benefactor had simply and suddenly appeared at his side, setting the tin down on the table.

"A little wine to enjoy with our meal," the old man said in oddly soft tones before moving back toward his chair. The hairs on the back of Caleb's neck stood on end as he stared down into the tin of wine. While he might have been so engrossed in his meal to not hear the old man walk up next to him, he was sure he would have noticed the man moving to fill a tin with wine.

"How..." Caleb whispered as his gaze shifted between the old man and the tin of wine.

"You have a question?" the old man asked as he carefully eased his frail frame down into the chair.

"How were you able to retrieve a tin, fill it with wine, and present it to me without me hearing you?"

The old man fixed Caleb with a gaze that was half-reproachful and half something else, as though the old man were enjoying a private joke. "So you will now reject my gesture simply because you are too dim-witted to realize what I was doing?"

Caleb, as he was rapidly growing accustomed, felt like a child who had just been reprimanded for being too curious. "No, sir. Not at all. I deeply thank you."

Silence then ruled as the meal was eaten in peaceful solitude. Caleb attacked his plate of food with the ferocity of a predator taking down its first kill in days. As the last bite vanished within his jaws, he leaned slightly back and closed his eyes, enjoying the flavor of the meal as well as the feeling of being full. The slight tingle from the wine did not hurt his enjoyment of the meal either.

Caleb swallowed the last bite of vegetables and washed it down with the last swallow of wine from his tin. It was a glorious feeing to have a full belly after weeks of barely having enough to keep him going. He looked over at the old man to find his plate empty, as well. Odd, he reflected. He did not remember hearing the old man eat, but he apparently had eaten since his plate was empty.

"I am retiring," the old man said as he rose from the chair and began ambling toward the doorway leading deeper into the cave. "Make sure you tend to the fire and the wood box before going to sleep."

"Yes, sir," Caleb answered. As the old man reached the doorway, Caleb could not stop himself. "Sir?"

"What?" the old man snapped in reply, placing a frail hand on the doorway to steady himself without looking back at him.

"Did Darkseed die?"

The old man chuckled and shook his head in deep amusement before withdrawing his hand and shuffling through the doorway to vanish into the darkness beyond.

AND NOW, FOR A SNEAK PEEK OF

BOOK THREE

The Devenshire Chronicles

THE AMULET OF TALMARA

Coming 2014

Tom
Sechrist

THE DEVENSHIRE CHRONICLES SERIES CONTINUES WITH "THE AMULET OF TALMARA"

Xavier rose from his bed, slipping his nude form into one of his finest silk robes and began descending the stone steps of the platform upon which his massive four-poster bed sat. As he descended, he gave considerable thought to the woman who lies naked, crying, and bound to the bed, her sobs of pain, humiliation, and fear all but lost to his perceptions.

The heady scent of incense wafted through the room, and he inhaled deeply, savoring the deep-seated sense of relaxation and contentment that always came after he partook of one of his beauties from his stables. This one had been a new one, and he was still in the initial stages of 'training' her.

As he crossed the stone floor of his bedchambers toward another elevated platform, a slight frown touched his features. He had not taken as much pleasure and enjoyment from this embrace as he usually did, especially with a new one, and that puzzled him. There had been something missing with this one, some sense of a vital component to his pleasure that had eluded him. Never before had he come away from his bedding of one of these beauties with a sense of... something lacking?

As he ascended the steps of the second platform, he turned this over in his mind, pondering exactly what it was that had been so different in this encounter. Puzzles such as this never failed to irritate him, and he found he could not rest until he had pinned down the answer. He eased himself down into the massive high backed chair at the top of the platform that sat before a pedestal. Upon the pedestal, cushioned on a large velvet pillow, sat the Stones of Andarus. Yet even they only vaguely registered on his mind as he considered what had been so nearly disappointing in the taking of the woman behind him.

Xavier began a deep, nearly meditative, train of thought on the situation. The woman had been taken only a few days ago. The name of the village she had been taken from was lost to his memory, but it mattered little anyway. Xavier had seen her during one of his meditations, enhanced by a newly discovered herb...

With the aid of this newly discovered herb, Xavier found he could

336 | TOM SECHRIST

mentally roam higher planes of thought with greater ease and with greater potential for discoveries. During one such journey through the lofty heights of free thought, Xavier had found his mind's eye tuned to a small village nearby. In this village, he had seen many women, some beautiful, some not. But one woman had caught his mind's eye and held it upon her. While the woman played with a small child outside of a modest hut, Xavier had watched her, had felt the stirrings of lust within him, and knew he must have her, must add her to his stable of pleasure slaves in the catacombs below his retreat.

The woman had been young and beautiful, and he had spent hours watching her from his herb enhanced higher state of awareness. He had watched her go about her daily chores of caring for the child, maintaining the dwelling of her husband, and working the meager crops they grew to sustain them. At night, he would watch the husband take her to his bed and would watch with growing desire the way she would surrender herself completely to him. She poured her very essence into pleasing her husband and no task, spoken of or hinted at, was beyond her if it brought him pleasure. The heated nights of their passion had left Xavier's desire raging, and more than one of the women below had taken the brunt of his enraged arousal from the village woman.

When he could bear not having the woman any longer, he had personally led the raid that took her from the village. The husband had bravely fought to protect his mate, more bravely and with a ferocity that had surprised even Xavier. In his rage to defend what he felt was his, he had managed to kill five Followers.

Yet in the end, he lay broken and bleeding upon the floor of his dwelling. As he lay dying, the woman was at his side, weeping and still trying to find some way to bring him comfort. They spoke of their undying love for one another and other such silly matters of emotion that never ceased to irritate Xavier.

With a scowl, he had crossed to the couple and without preamble, stomped down on the man's throat, crushing the air passages and snapping his neck as though it were a twig.

The woman had screamed in horror and more tears flooded her beautiful eyes. Another scream sounded nearby, and Xavier turned to see the small child huddled in the corner, trembling with a fear only a child could feel. A dark smile had crossed Xavier's face as he regarded the child, and the woman did not miss the way he looked at her child.

She had tried to go to the child, but two Followers restrained her as Xavier crossed to the corner the child huddled in and knelt down. Her screams and pleas for him to leave the child be were ignored as his dark eyes bore into the terrified eyes of the child.

"You are scared?" Xavier had asked the small boy.

The child was capable of only nodding through the tears as his entire body shook with fear. Xavier studied the toddling child's face, the healthy chubbiness of the cheeks, the dimples, and smooth new skin of youth. The light blue of the eyes beneath the curly mane of blonde locks. But more than the outward appearance was the pure innocence in the eyes of the child.

Without his bidding, and without warning, memories surfaced within Xavier's mind as he considered the child. Memories of his own youth, of his own beginnings in this realm. Nearly forgotten memories of his mother and father and the happiness they had shared together. His eyes narrowed dangerously as these unwanted memories filtered up through his mind, and he could not stop them.

His mother had been beautiful beyond compare, and his father as bold and gallant as any he had known at the time. The love they shared was so deep, so plentiful, that none could look upon them and not feel touched by it. There were days of joyous play, endless laughter, and of feeling as loved as any child ever could have with the way his mother would cuddle him when he was frightened. Her soft voice always made the demons of his fear evaporate with the loving touch of her hand holding his as they strolled through the days of his youth, the soft press of her lips that would make any pain instantly disappear, the way she loved him and made him feel as if there were no other child anywhere more loved than he was.

The nearly endless hours spent with his father, learning the things that boys are expected to know, and the play with his father was always the most enjoyable. They would wrestle and it never ceased to amaze and delight the small Xavier how he could best his giant father. Eternal days of lounging on a creek bank with the deep resonance of his father's voice telling him stories or explaining one of the never-ending series of questions a small boy has. Each question was given careful consideration and answered in detail.

Those had been the days when happiness had been all he had known. Life was but one continuous moment of joy. When his mother and father thought him to be occupied with another discovery that small boys seemed to find every moment of every day in the most mundane of things, they would steal a moment for themselves and kiss or hug or simply hold one another's hand, thinking their son too preoccupied to notice. But he had noticed, and the sight of their love for one another was his strongest sense of security.

Then came the day that Xavier learned he was to become a brother. His mother was to have another child, and the joy that came upon their already happiness-engorged lives made their hearts swell. New questions had to be asked, and his father was only too happy to answer them. The days on their favorite creek bank were now spent exploring the great depths of what it meant to be a big brother and what exactly such a great title encompassed. Young Xavier soon learned, with his small mind having no other way to define it, to be a big brother was to be a back up father to the new baby. His father was the head of their family and absolute ruler of their little kingdom. Now that another child was soon to be a part of their family, Xavier learned that he was to be the Prince, the heir to the throne of the happiest, most fulfilling kingdom in the land.

Suddenly, Xavier lashed out at these thoughts, shattered them into fragments, and then crushed the fragments under the heel of his mental boot. Anger tore through him as the memories tried to call to a part of him that no longer existed. An angry scowl darkened his features as the beautiful portrait of his youth was torn and torn again, the canvas being rent over and over again.

His dark eyes suddenly bore into the woman's child before him. The innocence within the child, the happiness he had seen the three of them share that so closely resembled a happiness that he had not known for many seasons, and knowing he would never ever feel again, fanned the flames of his rage. How dare they! The happiness and contentment of his youth had been savagely ripped from him, and who were these people to think they could experience something that was now forever out of Xavier's reach? The memories had been unwelcome, unwanted, and this child had been the reason they had surfaced.

With a snarling twist of his upper lip, Xavier had reached out and taken the child by the throat, which brought another series of screams from the mother. The child would have cried out too, had Xavier not been squeezing his throat with such force. Xavier rose, bringing the small child with him, supported only by the hand curled around his throat.

"Who do you think you are?!" Xavier had snarled at the child, his own body trembling with the rage to match the trembling of the child's body in fear.

"How dare you!!" he had growled as he turned, holding the child before him by the throat. His glare burned into the pleading eyes of the woman trying to break free of her captors to run to her child.

"You think you have a right to my happiness?! You think you can just walk through this life and take what I was stripped of?! NO!!" he had shouted as he suddenly twisted his wrist hard to the side. The snap of bone was as loud as any crash of thunder could ever be. The tiny body in his grip went rigid for a moment, convulsed once, and then went limp.

For uncounted moments, Xavier had stared into the wide eyes of the child, watched the spark of life fade until only the initial expression of shock was all that remained. With the fading of the light of life in the light blue eyes, another wave of darkness swept over him, again taking the memories to the deepest, darkest recess of his mind and far from his consideration. The pain and longing that the memories had brought faded with the life of the child, and as before, Xavier was as he had been.

He then dropped the lifeless body to the floor and swept from the dwelling, issuing a curt order for his Followers to bring the woman who was now a sobbing heap of grief. In one moment, he had taken from her all that she held dear, and soon he would make another of his slaves. As he had mounted his horse that night, he found that the remorse he knew he should have felt for his actions had been less pronounced as they were with each new dark act he committed.

Xavier's mind returned to the present, and he considered the woman behind him, and why his taking of her had been so much less pleasing than it should have been. It had not been the result of any guilt feelings on his part for killing her husband and child. He had done far worse to some of his other women. No, his mind had been on something else. His full attention had not been on the woman. The question was what had preoccupied his mind. Then the answer came. His mind had been on someone else while he had been taking the woman. That someone else had been the woman traveling with Devenshire known as Brianna.

All during his taking of the woman, his mind had been thinking of Brianna and how sorely he had wished for it to be her underneath him, wished for it to be her body he touched, her thighs he slipped between, her cries that rang out in his ears.

That was it. His mind had been so preoccupied with the black haired beauty that his encounter with the woman now on his bed had been so much less fulfilling. Brianna's image floated up in his mind, and he found his mind conjuring the wide and varied ways he would have taken her had she been the one bound naked to his bed.

With each time his mind considered Brianna, he knew he would have to have her, to take her and break her, and make her his slave of pleasure and do so very soon for he found it more and more difficult to not think of her. The image of her, as he had seen her in the Orb of Vision, returned to haunt him as it had nearly every day since he had first seen it.

The sparkle in her green eyes, the thick luster of her black hair, the way her breasts moved with each breath she took. The way her hips rounded seductively into her long supple legs. The very air of self-assuredness and subtle seductive charm that oozed from her without a conscious thought. Xavier felt himself becoming aroused again, both inside and out. Not in a very long time had he encountered one who preyed upon his thoughts with such intensity as Brianna did. He would have her. He would take her... and take her and take her... until she begged for him to take her again. She would bend, and eventually break to his will—he swore it.

His eyes beheld the Stones of Andarus, and his thoughts turned to why he could not tap into them. For days now, he had sat here and studied the Stones. He had gone back over the ancient scrolls and legends surrounding them. There was a vital key missing—something all the others had missed when they had attempted to gain access to the Stones, and that error had cost each and every one of them their lives. Xavier knew why they had failed, but how to counter that element eluded him and that tasted vile to him.

The reason the other Mages and Sorcerers had failed was because of a strange latent magic aura that surrounded the Stones. It could not be detected by any direct spell of Knowledge. It was akin to a hidden trap. Any mystical energies that came into contact with the aura would instantly awaken the latent spell of absorption, which would forge an unbreakable link to the source of the probing magic and begin drawing in all forms of mystical energy... including the mystical energy of life itself until nothing was left.

It was through a meditative spell that Xavier had discovered the absorption magic. Since his meditative spell surrounded the Stone, instead of touching them directly, it had allowed him to see the strange magic aura without activating it. Now the question was how to counter the assimilation spell to gain access to the Stones deeper secrets. The trouble was that any mystical energy directed at the Stones or the aura of inclusion would instantly trigger the protective spell and reduce the caster of the magic to little more than dust within moments.

So the problem now was how to negate or counter the absorption magic without directly touching it. There had to be a way, but Xavier could find no such way, and frustration returned to his thoughts as his gaze bore into the Stones as if to force them to reveal their secrets to him.

Xavier leaned forward to study the Stones closer and winced in pain as his right shoulder moved. The woman had bitten him during his taking of her. Sliding his hand underneath the silk of his robe, Xavier let his fingers gingerly trace the jagged outline of the bite. It was deep and would need tending before too much longer, but for now, he let the bite remain as a reminder of the strength of his will over the woman's will. He withdrew his hand and regarded the thin coating of his blood on his fingertips. With a leering smile, he smeared the blood across his fingertips with his thumb as his gaze returned to the Stones.

There had to be a way to get past the protective absorption spell. There had to be. Xavier refused to consider the possibility that there was no way to get past it. He had come too far to surrender now. All of his plans, all of his visions for his future, lie within those three egg shaped stones, and he would not be denied.

Xavier reached out his hand, careful to suppress any trace of his powers, and sought to gently touch the center of the three Stones as if by physically touching one of them, he could, by his very force of will, draw out the answers he sought.

The moment his fingertips touched the cool surface of the Stone something happened. There was a tremendous crash of sound and something seized his fingers, locking them tight to the surface of the Stone in a grip tighter than anything Xavier had ever encountered. Almost instantly, the room began to spin, and a purple haze seemed to emanate from the center Stone at the point where his fingers had touched it.

His breath caught in his throat, and his eyes flew open wide as a sense of intense power overcame him. His thoughts were frozen in his brain, his body became as rigid as iron as the hue of lavender light began to crackle with tiny bolts of darker purple energy, which seemed to seek out the flesh of his fingers, penetrate the skin to emerge from the other side only to twist and jolt into him again. The twisting jolting purple light slowly encompassed his fingers, then his hand, moving steadily up his wrist and up his arm.

Xavier tried to summon his powers to ward off the power seeping up his arm, into his flesh, into the very marrow of the bones of his arm, but his brain would not respond, and would not form the mental commands to summon his powers. Indeed, he could feel no trace of his powers anywhere within him. Whatever manner of power resided within the lavender light, it isolated him from his abilities.

The room began to grow dim, air became thin, and his mind reeled under a thousand perceptions that he had no idea how to understand, how to interpret. The purple glow, laced with tiny flashing bolts of darker lavender energy swirled up his left arm, permeating the flesh and bone, stabbing into his nerves, invading even the tiniest blood vessel. His body went rigid and began to tremble under the force of his own locked muscles. The light was overtaking him, taking control of him, mutating him. Was it possible? Had he somehow inadvertently activated the absorption spell? If so, he was lost. There would be no glorious conquest for him, no total all-encompassing power with which to rule this world and all the others beyond it.

Fear came. The first true fear he had felt in a very long time. It was cold and bitter, and he despised it for what it was. The light reached his shoulder, and he struggled against the intense painful grip that the light held upon his body. He struggled to free his mind, to find some way to tap into his powers, to find some way to fight back, but not even his mind would obey him. The tiny flashes of purple energy were now as deeply inside of him as they were outside of him. They permeated every single fiber of his arm, and there was no doubt as to where they were going as they pulsed and stabbed their way up his shoulder toward his neck.

So this was failure. This was what absolute defeat was like. It was even fouler to him than the fear, and he could find no way of fighting back, to force defeat from him and emerge victorious as he always had before. From his first steps upon his life's path to now, he had never known true defeat. Setbacks, momentary retreats to regroup and plan again? Yes, but never true and absolute defeat. All his seasons of intense study of the Mystic Arts, and then the alliance with the Dark Mystics to gain even more power, all had been for nothing. None of his skill and power combined could stop one egg shaped stone from wiping his existence from the realm with the ease of dusting off an old book.

The purple light reached the base of his neck, paused for a moment, and Xavier found that perhaps he could find a way to win. The advancing power was no longer moving, but simply staying at the base of his neck. Just as the thought that he could possibly win registered on his twisted consciousness, the lavender light exploded outwards in all directions at once and with amazing speed. Tiny bolts of lavender lightening lanced out to all parts of his body. His heart, lungs, stomach, intestines, all were struck and infiltrated by the bolts, and stabbing twisting pain screamed out from every contact. Yet the most painful and fear riddled attack came as the bolts lanced up the side of his neck and directly into his brain.

His eyes flew open even wider as the energies quickly overtook his mind. The whites of his eyes began to tinge, to darken, and eventually turn a purplish color, which quickly swept in to cover and hide the pupil and iris, making his eyes solid orbs of lavender. The pain was more intense than any he had ever felt or imagined. His vision left him in a swirling haze of purple, and a deafening roar sounded in his ears. He could feel the tendrils of power invade every nuance and nerve ending in his body and brain. His thoughts were entwined in the tendrils much the way a vein would latch onto a lattice and quickly grow to envelope it.

No part of him remained untouched by the power, and it quickly swept his thoughts and feelings and emotions, and even the essence of himself away. First, he was blinded, and then the roar grew in his ears until two very loud and painful pops eradicated his hearing, leaving an even more deafening silence in their wake.

Xavier tried to call out, to scream for someone, anyone to help him. But the quickly growing tendrils of power choked off his throat. He could not even draw the breath needed for such a cry of help. Panic replaced the fear as he struggled against a power he could not even begin to fathom. He was helpless, powerless before magic more ancient than any he had ever even considered. The bitter taste of defeat came again, and as the last of his perceptions faded, he realized he had an eternity to consider his failure and the ever-bitter taste of his final defeat.

Without a single thought or action, there was nothing. No light, no sound, no feeling, no sensation at all. Xavier found himself afloat in a sea of virtual nothingness. Not so much as a single emotion existed here. Was this the afterlife? Heaven? Hell? Or perhaps his essence had been drawn into the Stones by the absorption spell, and this was to be his eternal fate. At least in hell he could have felt the fires burn the flesh from his bones, could have felt the fear and remorse. Those would have been far more preferable than an eternity of this... this... nothingness.

Did he truly exist anymore? In any frame of the meaning of the word? Without feeling, without emotion, without anything to connect himself to what he had once been — did he exist now? The empty response told him no, and he could not even muster sadness at that thought. So, as with all the practitioners before him, he had failed and had become just another flickering essence within the massive void of the Stones of Andarus.

Then a sensation flickered briefly. It had been so faint and so brief that Xavier had discounted it as some lingering ghost of the life he was no longer a part of, that whatever he was now he had so desperately wanted to return to his physical body, that he had conjured the sensation.

Then it came again, a definite sensation, a feeling of pressure on what would have been the backs of his legs if he still possessed such things. The sensation grew, intensified, and became solid. Not only the pressure on what would have been his legs, but his legs themselves. Another sensation fluttered and began growing alongside the first one. A definite pressure of something pressed against his buttocks and back as if he were sitting in his chair again.

A very numb sensation came to his mind, as if he were awakening after a long and deep slumber. As this sensation registered upon his consciousness, other sensations began returning. The ache of joints he had truly believed he no longer had, the soft feel of silk against his bare body, and the throb of a headache.

Xavier felt emotions return to him as well, and he refused to give into the feeling of hope that he had somehow survived his encounter with the Stones and was simply awakening instead of having been drawn into the cold nothingness of the Stones. This could very well be some twisted sadistic trick of whatever had captured his essence, perhaps even the demented essence of the Mage, Andarus. He may have been reduced to an empty essence, but he would be damned if he would provide any further entertainment for his captor.

As more sensations and emotions returned to his awareness, sounds returned as well. The soft whisper of a candle flame, the gentle sigh of air moving about him, and even the sobs of the woman who had been bound to his bed reached his ears, and despite his determination not to react to these sensations, he could feel his spirit rise, and bring hope with it.

Slowly and painfully, he became aware of his closed eyelids, and as he cracked them open, he was nearly blinded again by the brightness of the dim candlelight. With the first stab of light into his eyes, every nerve in his body was suddenly brought back to life with a searing pain. With a hoarse moan, he curled himself into a tight ball in his chair, hugging himself against the concentrated pain that burned at him from every direction.

How long he huddled in his chair and moaned against the onslaught of pain he did not know. As bad as the pain was, he found himself welcoming it for it brought to his mind the solid reality that he had, indeed, survived his encounter with the absorption spell, and was still in his realm, still in his body, and still very much alive.

Finally, the pain began to subside. The waves of intense pain began to ease away, leaving soreness in its wake. But having faced an eternal void filled with nothing but blackness, even the soreness was welcomed. Again, he opened his eyes to find that he was still in his chambers, still in his silken robe, and still sitting before the three Stones as if nothing had ever happened.

With a tremendous and very painful effort, he raised himself back to a seated position and simply slumped there, allowing his racked body time to recover from the massive onslaught of power it had been forced to absorb. As he leaned his head back against the chair and closed his eyes again, he began considering what had happened to him, what he had triggered by simply touching the Stone.

It had not been the absorption spell—his continued existence proved that. Then what was it? What had he touched? The memories of the thousands of perceptions slamming into his mind at once returned. At the time, he had not been able to separate and study them, to discover their true meaning. But now, in the sore aftermath of the attack, he sat absolutely still and focused his slowly awakening mind on discerning what the perceptions had meant.

They were alien perceptions. Unknown symbols had been branded into his mind, and memories that were not his, ancient words of incantations that made no sense to him. Images, millions upon millions of images flooded his mind and none of them looked even vaguely familiar... except the last image. The last image was of a man, a man aged before his time and driven mad with a thirst he could not quench. The man in the image stood before an alter which held pieces of crystal, his arms held high above his head, his head thrown back in the fatal instant of releasing a spell.

Suddenly, Xavier's eyes snapped open, and his expression of

fatigued soreness was slowly replaced with dawning knowledge. Andarus. The last image had been of Andarus at the instant he had unleashed whatever spell he had used to draw in the power of creation from the Great Beyond. The image had been at the moment that Andarus ceased to exist and the stones that bore his name came into being.

Xavier's wonder filled eyes slowly lowered until they beheld the Stones. That was it! He had somehow circumvented the absorption magic and had tapped into the Stones themselves. A slow smile spread across his features as he considered his thoughts. His eyes grew wider, and his limbs began to tremble with excitement as he pondered the possibility. He had actually gotten past the absorption spell and had touched the edge of the core of the Stones. The alien perceptions... the unknown symbols and words... they had all been some sort of message. From the very essence of Andarus most likely. His heart raced, and his mind reeled under the possibility.

Xavier forced himself, with little success, to calm down. To think clearly and not let the emotionalism of the moment of discovery cloud his thinking. He forced his mind to honestly find some other explanation for what had just happened to him. With all his might, he tried to find another explanation, but could not. The only possible answer could be that he had tapped into the Stones. But how? What had he done that no other practitioner of magic before him had done? He put more concentration to stilling his racing heart and even faster racing thoughts. He could not allow himself to be carried away now, not when his first possible success was at hand. Calm and rational thought was desperately needed.

With slow and deliberate thoughts, he retraced his actions leading up to the encounter with whatever that was that had swept forth from the Stones. He had carefully closed off his powers, sealing them away inside himself as to not inadvertently activate the absorption spell, and then he had merely touched the center of the three Stones. But how could mere physical contact do such a thing? There was no way of knowing how many pairs of hands had handled the Stones in their long existence. There was no record anywhere of anything like this happening before. What had been so different about this physical contact? What?

As Xavier's mind raced to find the answer, half-fearful that the answer lie within his own mind and would fade from it before he could discover it, he raised the tips of his left fingers to his chin. The moment they made contact, he winced and growled as a hot pain raced up his arm from his fingertips. Jerking his hand down as if he had touched something hot, he scowled down at his fingertips.

There was a faint lavender glow on his fingertips. It pulsed and throbbed with a light all its own before it slowly began to fade. For a moment, Xavier feared that the purple light of power was about to claim him again, but at the sight of the fading light, and equally easing pain, he realized that what he had felt and seen were the fading resonance's of his physical contact with the Stones. A quick check of his right hand fingertips revealed no such occurrence there, and another quick visual scan revealed no other part of his body bearing any marks from the encounter, save the tips of his fingers on his left hand, the fingers that had actually touched the Stones.

As his eyes returned to his fingertips, he caught the last flickering remnants of the purple light as it faded from sight. What was left behind caused Xavier's eyes to narrow with growing suspicion? Could it be that simple? Could the great riddle of the Stones have been answered by something so obvious? At first, he refused to believe it. But the more he pondered it, the more sense it made. It was an old rule in protection riddles. The simpler the solution, the harder it would be to comprehend. As his thumb gently caressed the still tender flesh of his fingertips, his eyes drifted back to the Stones, and a slowly growing smile formed followed by a chuckle. The chuckle repeated itself, and then again, until it grew into a full laugh. Evil laughter, full of dark mirth, echoed off the stone walls of his bed chambers as he realized what he had done, and quite by accident. He looked at the bloodstain on his fingertips… he had solved the riddle of how to tap into the Stones of Andarus.

Blood…

THE DEVENSHIRE CHRONICLES CAST OF

CHARACTERS

Character Portraits by Tom Sechrist

THE HEROES

DAIMION DEVENSHIRE

(Pronounced: Day-me-on / Deven-shire)

No one knows where he came from, and no one is sure where he is going. He lives in the moment, takes from that moment all that it has to offer and then moves on to the next moment.

There is a seductive charm about him that defies explanation. There is also a sense of mystery that surrounds him. Beneath his gallant, jovial and aloof manner lays a dark memory which has spawned an almost equally dark past; both of which he spends each sunrise fleeing from, yet never seems to be able to out distance.

While he has a very fond eye for the ladies, he holds his heart deep within himself, refusing to allow even the faintest whisper of love to be considered. He neither seeks love, nor reciprocates it. Even the one woman who knows him better than any cannot even begin to scratch the surface of his iron will to keep his secrets... and his pain... to himself and himself alone.

BRIANNA STANDISH

(Pronounced: Bree-ahn-ah / Stand-ish)

Beautiful, seductive, and fiercely independent. Those are the words that best describe The Lady Brianna Standish. She is a woman who refuses to conform to the more "traditional" roles of the women of her time, much to the chagrin of medieval society.

She attracts and enjoys a great deal of male attention, but refuses to even consider the possibility of marrying. She guards her heart closely, only letting tiny fragments of it show, and even those are watched closely.

Brianna is a woman who takes great pride in her appearance, but is far from vain. She accepts her appearance as a part of who she is and neither flaunts or hides any part of herself. She is at ease with her life as she has established it and makes no qualms about her "behavior" with men that many other women find bordering on trampish. As Brianna would say:

"I am a woman. I like men. Little else needs consideration."

RAVEN DARKSEED

(Pronounced: Ray-vin / Dark-seed)

Charming, dashing, witty, and very unpredictable. Darkseed is a man who serves only one end... the attainment of the things that bring him pleasure. One never knows exactly which side of an issue Darkseed will come down on, but once he does, he will remain until the bitter end.

Darkseed was discovered at a young age to possess the latent abilities of the Mystical Arts and was quickly sent to a Retreat where his powers could be examined and to teach him how to master them. It was soon discovered that Darkseed had the potential to become an Adept of the Mystical Arts... a rarity, to say the least.

He is the closest thing there is to a best friend to Daimion Devenshire, and he is the only one who knows all of Devenshire's scars... and the demons that spawned them.

Raven Darkseed delights in testing himself, without the aid of his powers, against many situations. He maintains his powers and uses them on occasion, but for the most part, Darkseed does things the "old fashioned" way... by hand. He believes that he masters his powers, not the reverse.

SHANTIRA DUBRIS

(Pronounced: Shan-tier-ah / Due-bree)

Shantira is young, beautiful, willful, and innocent in many ways. Her entire world consists of her small village and the people within it. They encompass the entire universe to the young woman who has never been anywhere else. When that is taken from her, she finds herself adrift in a world that has suddenly become so much larger than she had ever dreamed possible.

During a raid upon her village, Shantira flees into the woods, luring the bandits after her and giving her village a chance to deploy its defenses. But she is soon cornered, and it is obvious what the bandits intend to do to the fair, young Shantira. Just as her rape, and eventual death, seems inevitable, a stranger comes to her rescue. This stranger touches the awakening woman within her, stirring the whispers of emotions into screams of desire, confusion, and... *love?*

Daimion Devenshire sweeps into her life with an explosion of action, saving her from certain death, and shaking the woman within her to the core. Shantira, who has never known love, passion, or desire, is ill prepared to deal with the raw emotions Devenshire strokes within her.

ZANDORTH KRAHL

(Pronounced: Zan-dorth / Crawl)

Zandorth Krahl is a Warrior of the Ancient Class, a vanishing sect of brave and noble warriors. These men valued honor above and beyond all else and will go to great lengths to preserve, not only their own honor, but that of their realms, as well.

Zandorth is no exception for his honor is everything to him, and to insult it, is to unleash a fury that is unbridled. Life is very black and white to Zandorth. You are either right or you are wrong, you are good or you are evil—you are his friend or you are his mortal enemy. There are no gray areas with Zandorth.

Krahl holds no truck with the Mystical Arts or anyone who practices them. To Zandorth, the physical body the Fates provided is all you need—save for a finely crafted broadsword, of course.

Despite his seemingly archaic ethics, set of beliefs, and behavior, Daimion Devenshire was once heard as claiming of Zandorth—

"If I were to travel to the depths of hell, and I could only take one comrade with me, it would be, without hesitation, Zandorth Krahl. Only Zandorth would have the gumption to walk right up to Satan, and most probably, would punch him square in the face."

STANT

(Pronounced: Stah-nt)

Stant is the eldest of three elves that join Devenshire's quest to stop Xavier and his plans for the Stones of Andarus. With his experiences and wisdom, he could very well be the leader of the elves, but he prefers not to lead, relishing in the opportunities that following provides for observing and learning.

Stant served in a combined human/elf regiment in the Goblin Wars, serving under General Trenton Standish, Brianna's father. Through many brutal, bloody, but victorious campaigns against the Goblin horde, Trenton and Stant formed the sort of friendship that only two men who pass through near death experiences together can forge.

Stant, while not the official leader of the group of elves, finds himself often serving as a father figure to the younger elves. A role he may profess to dislike but does nothing to shirk.

KENDRA

(Pronounced: Ken-drah)

Kendra is an elfin woman who has spent most of her life in the company of men, and thusly, behaves very much like a man. She is free spirited and makes no qualms about her admiration of the male form.

The lack of a lady-like presence in her upbringing causes her to make many behavioral errors that are frowned on by medieval society in regards to the proper behavior of a lady. While such mistakes will embarrass her, she makes no attempts to correct her behavior. She relishes her freedom, and her indomitable spirit demands she live her life on her terms... not societies.

Like most elves, she has a natural proclivity with a bow, and she has studied sword fighting, as well. While she can hold her own with a sword, she prefers the almost natural extension of herself in her bow.

She has a strong, albeit purely physical, attraction to Devenshire, which stokes the fires of jealousy within Shantira. While Kendra is not a cruel woman, she does take a tiny bit of delight in the anguish her pursuit of Devenshire causes Shantira.

PETERA

(Pronounced: Pet-er-ah)

Petera is the youngest of the group of elves who join Devenshire's quest to stop Xavier and his sinister plans for the Stones of Andarus. As elves measures age, he would roughly be 19 human years old. His travels with his kinsman, Stant, Kendra, and Arness, have helped him mature more quickly than most elfin adolescents. While the vast majority of elves had long ago left the human lands opting to return to their native islands across the great ocean, there are small pockets of elves who elected to stay in the human lands, learning all they could about humans, their culture, their history, and their natures.

Petera is a very inquisitive being and finds delight and learning opportunities in almost any situation. He looks at the realm with the fresh eyes of a young person who honestly believes that there is inherit good in nearly all beings.

It is a shame that the quest to stop Xavier will teach him otherwise.

THE VILLIANS

XAVIER

(Pronounced: X-aiv-e-her)

Xavier has spent his entire life studying the Mystical Arts, mastering them with a skill matched by few others. At one time, it was believed that he would become the next High Master Adept, but he began exploring the darker powers of the Dark Mystics, and he soon found even more power.

Striking an alliance with the demon sorcerers of the underworld, Xavier attacks the Retreat of Duvall, killing the High Master Adept and claiming the retreat as his own. Soon he amassed a large following of those who worshiped him, believed him to be some great deity, or those who simply liked Xavier's method of indulging himself in all the earthly pleasures this world had to offer.

Now he has the Stones of Andarus and sets almost all other pursuits to study of how to tap into the dark power within them. The Stones are said to hold a tiny fragment of the power of creation, and it is said that such power should not be released and could not be controlled if it ever were. But Xavier's impressive knowledge of the Mystical, and his alliance to the Dark Mystics, may be the combination of power needed to accomplish the impossible.

However, there may be a kink in his plans. A kink by the name of Daimion Devenshire. With his "Orb of Vision," Xavier has learned of Devenshire's plans to attempt to stop him. Normally, this would not be a concern to Xavier, but Devenshire is the one person in the realm who can still pose a threat to him.

There is something about Devenshire, known only to Xavier, that unhinges the mad Mages arrogant confidence.

DARIUS THIEBERIAN

(Pronounced: Dar-e-us / Thigh-beer-ian)

Darius Thieberian was once a man of considerable standing. He held great wealth, power, and influence. He had a beautiful wife, a magnificent home, and all the things any mortal man could want. Yet it was not enough... he wanted more.

Since childhood, he had wanted nothing more than to master the Mystical Arts, but it was found that he simply did not have the gift. The disappointment was utter and complete.

One night, he met a dark stranger who offered him a way to master the Mystical Arts as well as access to even greater power... darker power. So enthralled at the prospect of having that kind of power, Darius accepted. The dark stranger had been a vampire, and he had given Darius the Dark Gift, turning him into a vampire, as well. What Darius did not realize was that while he gained the power he had longed for, he lost everything else in the trade.

That was many, many seasons ago, and Darius is now a very powerful vampire, commanding considerable mystical abilities. Darius revels in his dark existence, savoring the terror he can inflict and enjoying the rich wine of human blood.

The only tiny whisper of humanity within him is sparked when he happens across The Lady Brianna. In her, he sees the essence of someone else, an essence that has haunted him through the many seasons since his conversion. He must have her, not as a source of nourishment, but a way to return to his un-dead heart the one human emotion he has never forgotten... love.

But there are other matters at hand. He learns of Xavier's plans for the Stones of Andarus and knows that he must stop the mad man. Yet, as arrogant as Darius is, he realizes that even his hell-spawned powers are not enough—he will need help. It is a realization that sickens him to his dark core.

LORDAL/

LORDALISE

(Pronounced: Lor-dahl / Lor-dahl-iss)

Lordal is a very prosperous bandit king.

Lordalise is a member of the Order of Hunters, a group dedicated to the eradication of vampires from the realm.

They are one in the same.

Lordalise was once a very influential man, commanding great respect in every circle of society he moved in. When his younger sister was killed by a vampire, he joined the Order of Hunters and dedicated every fiber of his being to eradicating vampires as a whole, and the one who killed his sister in particular.

A mistake led to his being expelled from the Order of Hunters, and his drive to survive soon landed him in a group of bandits. His natural leadership skills very quickly propelled him into the upper echelons of the group of bandits. After a time, he was eventually appointed as the "king" of the bandits.

When a small group of his men attack Devenshire and company and meet with a dominating defeat, Lordal sets off in pursuit of them, intent on exacting his revenge. In the course of his pursuit of

Devenshire, he comes to believe that Devenshire is a vampire, and once again, assumes the mantel of Hunter, even though he no longer has the right to do so.

CAUGHT IN THE MIDDLE

CAPTAIN GREGORY ARMAND

(Pronounced: Greg-ory / Ar-mond)

Gregory Armand is a man of honor. He believes strongly in the need to maintain some form of law and order in the realm, and he has spent his entire life working towards that goal. He served as a sheriff in several small towns in the early years of his career, working his way up to Constable before enlisting in His Majesties Royal Guard. Through hard work and dedication, he ascended to the rank of captain and was given his own detachment.

Now he is in pursuit of Devenshire and company, believing that Devenshire is a vampire and those traveling with him are his mindless minions. His sense of honor tells him that he must stop at nothing to eliminate Devenshire. It is that same sense of honor that prevents him from realizing that he has become nothing more than a pawn in someone else's game of vengeance.

THE
QUESTION
MARKS

RACHELLE TAMBREY

(Pronounced: Raw-shell / Tam-bray)

She possesses a beauty that is ageless, a youth of spirit that defies the passage of time, and endures a pain that marches the passage of time with her, torturing her with each step.

Rachelle Tambrey gazes out at the world with eyes that seem to dance with a light all their own and a wisdom that goes far beyond her apparent age. This is because she is older than her apparent age... much older.

She has long since abandoned any hopes of finding true happiness in her existence. Love, happiness, and contentment are all but alien to her now.

But all of her perceptions of her life as it was, is, and could be, completely changed when she encounters Daimion Devenshire. There is something about him that defies explanation. He is different, not like the countless other mortal men she has encountered in her long life. There is something within him that speaks to her of someone who shares a deep hidden pain, of someone who shares her own unique view of the world and life in general.

However, she knows that she can never give in to that tiny spark of emotion that he strikes in her, and she had all but forgotten. With sadness, she knows that what she could find with him she must turn away from... for her sake as much as his.

BACKELLAR MOON

(Pronounced: Back-eller / Moon)

Backellar Moon is a man who very much believes that the world is his oyster.

He makes his living from "relieving" others of the burden of their coins. It's an arduous task but one he executes with the fervor to rival most priests.

Backellar Moon is nothing if not an opportunist. When Devenshire and company tear through Lirpa, Moon sees an opportunity to increase his wealth. He sets out after the "criminals" from Lirpa to see where they go and what potential for exercising his considerable skillset would present.

While Moon prefers the more subtle method of stealth in executing his craft, but it is not to say that he isn't without skill in the arts of combat. Like any wild animal, he can become very dangerous when cornered.

His pursuit of wealth, and of Devenshire and his friends, will lead him into challenges he had never dreamt possible... and will challenge him in ways he would have never thought possible.

NAIOP

(Pronounced: Nie-op)

Naiop is a very mysterious man with even more mysterious abilities.

He travels the realm, seeking out those who suffer from intense grief and pain…

And then he relieves them of that grief and pain.

None who he relieves of their pain and grief are ever seen again.

ARNESS

(Pronounced: Arn-ess)

Arness is the fourth member of the group of elves who were to join Devenshire on his quest to stop Xavier. However, when he discovers just what is at stake, he decides it is a suicide mission, and Devenshire is insane for undertaking it. He tries to draw his kinsman away from the quest, but unlike him, they decide to stay with the quest.

He harbors deeply rooted romantic feelings for Kendra, and when she shows a definite interest in Devenshire, his jealousy drives him further into the search for vengeance.

EPILOGUE
&
PROLOGUE

CALEB

(Pronounced: Kay-lib)

Caleb is a young man who finds himself at odds with just about every facet of his world, his time. He yearns to live in a time when things were simpler, more open, and honest.

He hears tales of a man named Devenshire who lived many years ago. The tales are replete with the many great deeds Devenshire was supposed to have accomplished in his time. It is in these tales that Caleb finds the essence of what has been missing from his own life. With vague clues, and insubstantial leads, Caleb leads a party of six in search of the legend of Devenshire.

His quest nearly ends with his death in the massive frozen tundra of the Wastelands. Just as it appears that the tale of Devenshire is simply lost in the incredible passage of time, Caleb finds a very old, very fragile, and very cranky link to the past and to…

The Devenshire Chronicles.

THE OLD MAN

You may call him sir.

FROM THE AUTHOR

I can't tell you how many times I wrote and re-wrote the "From the Author" section for Book One, "The Stones of Andarus." I had originally written it sometime in the early 2000s, and as circumstances in my life changed, so did parts of the "From the Author" section. The point being, I had 13 years to perfect it.

Now, with the release of "The Stones of Andarus" and the completion of "Predator & Prey," I find myself needing a new "From the Author" section, and I find the task a little daunting. It's a simple thing really — very small in the over all process of writing a novel. However, it serves to show me just how far my career has come since 1998. I am now in a position that I need a new "From the Author" section. For me... that's pretty impressive and pretty gratifying given that the first one was written 12 or so years ago.

The journey from the release of "The Stones of Andarus" to the end of writing "Predator & Prey" has been, in a word, difficult. It seems that anything associated with Devenshire and his story is destined to be a trial to complete. In some ways, it reminds me of Caleb, the wayward traveler appearing in the prologue and epilogue of each book. He has lost everything in his search for the story of Devenshire. While my plight in writing his story isn't quite so dramatic, it has been a difficult journey, to say the least. I thought that once "The Stones of Andarus" was complete, the rest of the series would be a cakewalk... not so much.

"Predator & Prey" presented its own challenges in completing. For starters, I suffered from the worst case of writer's block I have ever had, and many times over that year, it looked like "Predator & Prey" would never get finished. A trip to visit my in-laws in Wyoming proved to be the key. In that beautiful remote place, my mind was finally able to shake off the block and churn out some of the best work I've produced in a year.

Another issue that appeared was my own impatience. Lately, I have been plagued with a feeling that is best described as a "ticking clock" in my mind. I have a crushing feeling that time is slipping away from me and that I have to get Devenshire's story (as well as other stories) out very quickly. I have this regret for all the years I wasted between Devenshire's birth to the official release of the first book. I know this must be some aspect to approaching middle age, but it can be daunting nonetheless. I have learned to keep this crushing sense of the passing of time at bay, but it did flare up to dominance within me for most of the year I spent working on "Predator & Prey." Without realizing it, this sense of escaping time turned the joy I have for writing into an arduous task that I just *had* to complete quickly. In other words, it turned my passion into my job, and in that, my writing was no longer enjoyable. The trip to Wyoming showed me the grand scale of life and nature, while softening the impact of that ticking clock. I still feel the press of time upon me, but it doesn't drive me any longer, and the joy for writing has returned.

There were other issues that reared up to get in my way during the year of writing this novel. Some would be of no interest to anyone reading this, and others are too personal and won't be shared in this forum. Suffice it to say, it's been a journey this past year, and while a large part of it has been arduous, the overall trip is one I wouldn't have missed for the world.

As with "The Stones of Andarus," there are so many people to thank and acknowledge for their contributions to "Predator & Prey." There is no way I can individually thank everyone, but there are a few people who have earned and deserve to be recognized.

My beautiful wife Renee Sechrist. She is, without a doubt, the driving force in every aspect of my life. She is the person who put me back on the path of telling Devenshire's story. She is the person who supports me when my craft fails me and reassures me that it is a passing thing. She also tells me to stop being so hard on myself and let it flow naturally. She has done remarkable work on my websites. The first site was fantastic. She decided it was in need of a re-vamp, and she worked endlessly on it, teaching herself code and processes, developing graphics and slaving away to make the website absolutely stunning.

She is my rock... my anchor... the sun in the center of my universe. I am a strong person, and I have overcome many obstacles and adversities in my life, but there are times that I wonder how I ever got this far before meeting Renee. She is my one-woman cheerleader, my sounding board, even my emotional scratching post at times. She never ceases to amaze me, inspire me, and, most importantly, love me. I am, indeed, the luckiest man in the world. She has embraced my story and my characters as her own... with the possible exception of Brianna. She never has really liked Brianna.

My kids. When I say my kids, I mean all of them—birth children as well as stepchildren. I chose not to differentiate between the two. They are amazing people who have dealt with their fair share of adversity. Some self-inflicted, some not. They have made their choices and mistakes and missteps, but they keep moving forward. Perhaps not as quickly or in the same manner Renee and I might have chosen, but that's not our call to make. Just as Renee and I had to, they have to find their own way in this world. All we can do, as parents, is try to educate them, give them advice, cringe at their mistakes but keep our mouths shut, and ultimately, love them for the individual people they are and not the idealized carbon copies of us we'd like them to be.

To my wonderful, and extraordinarily talented editor, Rogena Mitchell-Jones. Where to start with how this wonderful woman has helped me? Rogena took on the arduous task of re-editing "The Stones of Andarus" as well as editing "Predator & Prey" — back to back. She never ceases to amaze me with how she can firmly yet gently point out what is really great about my stories and what could use a little work. Authors can be a bit... sensitive... when it comes to their "babies." The slightest criticism can put us into a literal fetal position in the middle of the floor because these aren't just our books... they are our children. They contain parts of our hearts and souls. Rogena has mastered the technique of telling me what needs to be fixed without sending me into a dark corner to brood. She is a rare jewel, and we, myself as well as Daimion, are both blessed to have her on our side.

Thank you Rogena! You are the best!!

As always, and ultimately, to you, my faithful reader. While I would have written this story regardless of whether or not it ever was published, your participation in this adventure makes the journey so much more enriching, and I can't begin to thank you enough for being a part of it. I hope you enjoy this tale as much as I enjoyed bringing it to life. While it has been arduous at times, frustrating at times, and downright impossible at times... I wouldn't have missed it for anything.

As before, from Daimion, Brianna, Shantira, Raven, Zandorth, Stant, Kendra, Petera, and me... Thank you!

Until we meet again, safe journeys and be well!

www.ingramcontent.com/pod-product-compliance
Lightning Source LLC
Chambersburg PA
CBHW060813030726
47503CB00002B/474